John Calvin Stockbridge,  Brown University Library

# The Anthony Memorial

A catalogue of the Harris collection of American poetry with bibliography and

bibliographical notes by John C. Stockbridge

John Calvin Stockbridge,  Brown University Library

**The Anthony Memorial**
*A catalogue of the Harris collection of American poetry with bibliography and bibliographical notes by John C. Stockbridge*

ISBN/EAN: 9783337404741

Printed in Europe, USA, Canada, Australia, Japan

Cover: Foto ©Andreas Hilbeck / pixelio.de

More available books at **www.hansebooks.com**

# CATALOGUE

OF THE

# Harris Collection of American Poetry

WITH

## BIOGRAPHICAL AND BIBLIOGRAPHICAL NOTES

BY

JOHN C. STOCKBRIDGE.

PROVIDENCE
1886.

# INTRODUCTION.

The clause in the will of Senator Anthony which refers to his gift of "The Harris Collection of American Poetry" to the Library of Brown University, reads as follows:

"I give to the Library of Brown University the collection of American poetry which I have recently bought of the estate of my late cousin, Caleb F. Harris, and which, I am told, is the best collection extant. I request that it be kept together, and that over the alcove in which it is placed, there be an inscription in Latin by Professor Lincoln: *"The Harris Collection of American Poetry; commenced by Albert G. Greene, continued by Caleb Fiske Harris and Henry B. Anthony. By the latter presented to this Library."*

As soon as the necessary arrangements were made, the collection was removed, shortly after the death of Mr. Anthony, to the Library Building of the University and placed in a cheerful room, fitted for its reception, where, doubtless, it will remain as long as the building stands. In accordance with the wishes of the generous donor, the following Latin inscription, prepared by Prof. John Larkin Lincoln, LL.D., and printed in plain black capitals, occupies a conspicuous position on the southeastern wall of "The Harris Collection Room:"

POESIS AMERICANA HARRISIANA
QVAM AB ALBERTO GORTON GREENE INCOHATAM
ET A CALEB FISKE HARRIS MAXIME AVCTAM
VNICE A SE PERFECTAM
HVIC BIBLIOTHECAE TESTAMENTO LEGAVIT
HENRICVS BOWEN ANTHONY

This inscription contains, in brief, a history of this altogether unique and remarkable collection of American Poetry, and, at this point, it may not be necessary to give its details. These will appear as we present the sketches of the lives of the three individuals who were especially concerned in the formation, enlargement and enriching of the collection. The sketches are as follows:

### ALBERT GORTON GREENE.

Albert Gorton Greene was born in Providence, R. I., February 10, 1802, and was a son of John H. and Elizabeth (Beverly) Greene. Samuel Gorton, who is represented in the middle name of Mr. Greene, was one of the most remarkable characters in the annals of early Rhode Island history, and the story of his experiences with the authorities of the " Bay State " has the charm and the fascination of a romance. The ancestors of Mr. Greene were among the first settlers of Warwick, and held a high rank among the citizens of the little State which they so honorably represented in many departments of civil and social life. He was fitted for college in the University Grammar School, Providence, and was so far advanced in his preparatory studies as to be qualified to enter the Sophomore class of Brown University in 1817, from which institution he graduated in 1820. He studied law with the distinguished Hon. John Whipple, and was admitted to the Rhode Island bar in 1823, and commenced the practice of his profession in Providence. After a few years of faithful devotion to the duties of his vocation, he was elected, on the organization of the city government under its new charter in 1832, clerk of the City Council, and clerk of the Municipal Court, holding the two offices for some twenty-five years; at the end of which period he was chosen Judge of the Municipal Court, and occupied this position for not far from nine years, 1858–67. The state of his health was such that in 1867 he resigned his office.

Although occupied for so many years with the onerous and exacting duties of the responsible positions he occupied and so acceptably filled, he was always "a man of letters,"—a lover of good books, and deeply interested in everything connected with the educational interests of the State of which he was a native, and of the city which was his adopted home. The original school bill of Rhode Island was drafted by his skillful hand. For fourteen years he was the honored President of the Rhode Island Historical Society. In the founding of the Providence Athenæum he took an active and conspicuous part. He early began to lay the foundation of a collection of American poetry which was acknowledged to be without a rival, in the variety of the authors represented, and in the value of the books collected. In " the still air of delightful studies " he found a happy relief from the too often vexatious cares and annoyances of his professional life, and his library was the choice place to which he was never weary of resorting, that he might enjoy the companionship of the select spirits who, at his bidding, were so ready to be the friends of his quiet but not lonely hours.

Judge Greene was himself a poet, and would have gained deserved distinction had he given himself more than he did to the work of original composition. It is hardly necessary to say that he was the author of one of the quaintest and most popular ballads of the day. Who has not read, and smiled as he read,—

> "Old Grimes is dead ; that good old man
> We never shall see more :
> He used to wear a long, black coat,
> All button'd down before"—

a ballad which, in our college days, we used to sing so lustily to the good old tune of "Auld Lang Syne." But as "John Gilpin" gives us only one side, and that side a very partial one, of the real character of Cowper, so "Old Grimes" is to be looked upon as a pleasant *jeu d'esprit* of one whose thoughts usually ran in channels quite different from what we might suppose, if we judged him solely by his famous ballad. How tender and beautiful is his " Adelheid " :

"Why droop the sorrowing trees,
　　Swayed by the autumn breeze,
　　　　Heavy with rain?
　　　　　　Drearily, wearily,
　　　　　　Move as in pain?
　　　　Weeping and sighing,
　　　　They ever seem crying,
'Adelheid! Adelheid!' evening and morn:
'Adelheid! Adelheid! where has she gone?'

"With their arms bending there,
　　In the cold winter air,
　　　　Icy and chill,
　　　　　Trembling and glistening,
　　　　　Watching and listening,
　　　　　Awaiting her still,
　　　With the snow round their feet,
　　　Still they the name repeat—
'Adelheid! Adelheid! here is her home;
'Adelheid! Adelheid! when will she come?'

"With the warm breath of spring
　　　Now the foliage is stirr'd;
　　On the pathway below them
　　　A footstep is heard.
　　Now bent gently o'er her,
　　　How joyous the greeting
　　Now waving before her
　　　Each sound seems repeating—
'Adelheid! Adelheid! welcome again.'
　　Their branches upspringing,
　　The breeze through them ringing,
　　The birds through them singing,
　　　Unite in the strain—
'Adelheid! Adelheid! welcome again!'"

Perhaps, however, the poem on which, were he living, he would
prefer to stake his reputation, and which, we are assured, those nearest
to him most affectionately recall, was the one written soon after the

death of the Rev. Dr. William E. Channing. The occasion for which this ode was prepared was a commemorative service which was held in the First Congregational Church in Providence, R. I., October 12, 1842, to do honor to the lately deceased Boston clergyman. The discourse was preached by the pastor of the church, Rev. Dr. E. B. Hall, whose gifted wife wrote the hymn that was sung on the occasion. The ode by Judge Greene is here given in full:

> "Not for him, but for us, should our tears be shed;
> Mourn, mourn for the living, but not for the dead;
> Let the dirge be unsung, and awaken the psalm:
> No cypress for him who lies crowned with the palm;
>> Who has gone to his rest
>> When his labor was done,
>> From the world he has blest
>> To the heaven he has won.
>
> "Though the light of his life to our vision is o'er,
> The light of his spirit will burn evermore;
> For truth in the world, like the sun in the skies,
> Fades only to brighten, and sets but to rise.
>> It moves ever onward,
>> Though dimmed is its ray;
>> And still on the earth
>> It is day,—ever day.
>
> "How calmly he uttered his beautiful thought;
> How meekly he bore all the honors it brought;
> How bravely he spoke to oppression and wrong;
> In that calmness, that meekness, that courage, how strong!
>> Though with tears for his parting
>> Our eyes may be dim,
>> For ourselves they are falling,
>> Not for him,—not for him.
>
> "We bless thee, O God, that the spirit is free,
> Which was true to itself, unto man and to thee;
> Thou hast called it from trial, released it from pain,
> But its life and its teachings will ever remain.

> The good and the true
> Never die,—never die :
> Though gone, they are here,
> Ever nigh — ever nigh."

Soon after resigning his position as Judge of the Municipal Court, in 1867, Mr. Greene removed to the home of his daughter, the wife of the Rev. Samuel White Duncan, D.D., in Cleveland, Ohio, where he died January 4, 1868. For a delightful tribute to the memory of Judge Greene from the pen of George William Curtis, see *Harper's Magazine*, vol. xxxvi., pp. 529, 530.

## CALEB FISKE HARRIS.

Caleb Fiske Harris was born in Warwick, R. I., March 9, 1818. He was the son of Stephen Harris, M.D., and Eliza (Greene), a daughter of Capt. James Greene, who was a descendant of John Greene, an associate of Roger Williams, and one of the original purchasers of Shawomet, now called Old Warwick. The sister of Mrs. Eliza Greene Harris was Mary Kinnicut Greene, the mother of Senator Anthony. The early Rhode Island ancestor of the subject of this sketch was Thomas Harris, a brother of the William Harris, with reference to whom Gov. Arnold says : " He filled a large space in the early history of the colony as an active, determined man, resolute in mind and vigorous in body, delighting in conflict, bold in his views on the political dogmas of his time, fearless in his mode of expressing them, striking always forcibly and often rashly for what he believed to be the right, and denouncing with the energy of a concentrated intellect all men or measures that did not conform to his ideas of truth and justice. No man, unless it be Roger Williams, has left a deeper mark upon the record of his State." Thomas Harris was born in England, and came to this country and settled in Salem, Mass., removing, about the year 1636-7, to Providence. As his name does not appear among the thirteen original proprietors of Providence, among whom was his brother William. he must have arrived at the new settlement after they had laid the foundation of the town in 1636. Caleb Harris, the great-grandfather of Caleb Fiske Harris, was a man of acknowledged ability, and for a time was a judge of one of the courts of Providence. Dr. Stephen Harris was educated in part at Brown University, the death of his father preventing him from completing the prescribed course of study. He pursued his medical studies at Dartmouth College and with Dr. Fiske, of Scituate, and settled at the place now called Quidnick. The wife of Dr. Harris, as has been intimated, was Eliza Greene, to whom he was married December 3, 1809. Subsequently he removed to Centreville, R. I., and engaged in manufacturing, besides discharging the duties of his profession. His business partners were Resolved Waterman and Dr. Sylvester Knight. The former, who died July 8, 1886, would have reached the great age of one hundred years had he lived to December 10, 1887. Mrs. Harris, the mother of Caleb F., died March 23, 1820, when her son was a little more than two years of age, and his father, the Doctor, died October 10, 1858, aged 72. As was said of him: "He was a remarkable man in some respects. He was bold in larger affairs as he was cautious in minutiæ. His promise was slowly given, but the fulfillment of it, however difficult, was so faithful as to be proverbial. He was practical, but progressive; cautious, but self-confident; resolute, but never infatuated. He was a lover of money, but he loved truth and integrity as aids to character, as well as money. The excitements of business stimulated all the energies of his body and mind, withdrawing the latter from a profession in which he must have been distinguished, and taxing the former, which was naturally feeble, with incessant occupation. The objects of his ambition were commercial, and he fully reached them. He was beloved in private and respected in public."

The subject of this sketch pursued his preparatory studies at the Academy in Kingston, R. I., and entered Brown University in 1834. The class of which he was a member stands high among the classes of the University for the number and the character of the men who have achieved success and honorable distinction in the callings of life to which they have devoted themselves. Mr. Harris did not complete the full course of college study. From his father he inherited a love for business, the stir and excitement of which were, in his early manhood, more congenial with his tastes than were the quiet pursuits of a literary life. After leaving the University he went to New York and engaged in the commission business, the firm being Franklin & Harris, afterwards Franklin, Harris & Mott, and finally C. F. Harris. In 1856 he removed to Providence and continued to be interested in business, and so remained till the war. Gradually he closed up his affairs and retired on a generous fortune, occupying a spacious and well-appointed mansion on Waterman street, not far from the University.

At precisely what time in the life of Mr. Harris was developed that remarkable love for books which became so absorbing a passion with him, the writer of this sketch is unable to state. It is not unlikely it was a thing of gradual growth, gaining in strength, as do all human passions, by what it fed upon. Like Judge Greene, he took a deep interest in the collection of the works of American poets, and in all matters pertaining to early American history. Old and rare books he sought after, and the collectors in this country and abroad found him one of their warmest friends. His pressing orders for their literary treasures were cheerfully responded to ; and, perhaps, all the more so since no exorbitant value which they might place upon a coveted volume was any bar to its purchase if he set his mind on having it. At one time, while travelling in France, his niece being his companion (a lady who spoke the language with ease, which he did not do, although he read French without difficulty), he found himself in Lyons, in the bookstore of an old Jew. A beautiful "missal" was shown him, which proved so attractive that he made up his mind that he must have it. In reply to the question of his niece as to its price, so large a sum was named by its owner that Mr. Harris, accustomed although he was to pay what others would regard as extravagant prices for books, hesitated, and finally left the store, the precious volume unpurchased.

Some hours after he told his niece to prepare herself for a second interview with the Israelite, for he was bound to have that volume, cost what it might. Back to the shop they retraced their steps. The bargain was made. The full price charged was paid, and the prize was his. In various ways Mr. Harris had thus collected a valuable library which, as has been said, was especially rich in American poetry and plays. Soon after the decease of Judge Greene, January 3, 1868, one thousand volumes of his library, none of them duplicates of his own books, were purchased by Mr. Harris. So rapidly did this special department of American poetry grow, that in 1874 it numbered 4,129 separate works, including various editions, and up to the time of the death of its owner, the increase was not less than one thousand volumes. In 1874, Mr. Harris printed a volume of goodly size, entitled "*Index to American Poetry and Plays in the Collection of C. Fiske Harris.*" This volume was sent to his personal friends and others, lovers of good books, and elicited some correspondence to which it may not be out of place to allude a little in detail.

The following was written by Mr. Bryant:

"New York, March 12, 1875.

"Dear Sir:—Your work, Index to American Poetry and Plays, has amazed me by showing me what multitudes of persons on our side of the Atlantic have wasted their time in writing verses in our language.

"I do not know that I can offer any suggestions of any value for the improvement of your work. It seems to me very full, and must have cost you much labor. You have, of course, consulted Allibone's Dictionary of Authors, in which is a good deal of information concerning editions.

"As to my publications, you have omitted one or more. There was one edition published in London of my poems—Andrews, the publisher, I think in 1832—a duodecimo volume, and I am pretty sure that I have in the country a small edition published in Liverpool. But my books are mostly in the country, on Long Island. When I get there, if I can think of it, I will write you to help you complete your list so far as my poems are concerned, but I may not remember to do it.

"Yours respectfully,

"W. C. BRYANT."

As the editions referred to do not seem to be in "The Harris Collection," without doubt Mr. Bryant did "not remember to do it."

J. Munsell, the distinguished printer and publisher of Albany, N. Y., writes under date of February 24, 1875 : "I have the pleasure to acknowledge the receipt of your extensive Catalogue of American Poetry and Plays.  I thank you for your courtesy, and observing that you do not have a little privately printed translation of *Laus Patriae Celestis*, by O. A. Morse, I enclose a copy to add a mite to your collection."  Mr. M. alludes also to one or two other works, not in the "Collection," to which he directs the attention of Mr. Harris, and closes his note by again thanking him for his kindness.

Samuel G. Drake writes under date, Boston, February 26, 1875 : "I have just received your very beautifully printed 'Index to American Poetry and Plays.'  I had reason to believe you possessed a very large collection of works in that department of American literature, but was not prepared to find you had such an immense body of poetry.  Topsy said, when she heard a large amount of money was paid on some occasion, 'she didn't believe it, 'cos ther wasn't so much money in the whole world.  Now, really, I didn't think there was so much poetry by Americans in the whole world.  Accept my thanks for your kindness in allowing me to place in my collection a copy of your exceedingly valuable volume."

The Hon. William L. Appleton writes from Boston, February 26, 1875 : "I have your bibliography of American Poetry, for which accept my thanks."  He then gives him the names of the authors of certain books to the titles of which an interrogation mark had been prefixed, indicating that Mr. Harris did not know who they were, and closes by saying : "I will some day send you a list as complete as possible of all in my library which does not appear in your Index."

Lemuel L. Boardman, Esq., sends the following from Augusta, Me., under date of March 25, 1875 : "Accept my thanks for a copy of your 'Index to American Poetry,' the receipt of which is gratefully acknowledged. You have a wonderful collection, and I trust you may be able at some day to print a full catalogue as you propose."

Dr. Samuel A. Green writes from Boston, February 26, 1875: "I write to thank you for the copy of the 'Index,' which reached me yesterday. *It will be to me a very useful book, and I shall prize it very highly.* The class poem No. 730 was by James Russell Lowell." Dr. Green goes on to inform Mr. Harris with regard to the authorship of other volumes whose titles are in the "Index."

John Ward Dean writes from the Society House of the New England Historic Genealogical Society, 18 Somerset street, Boston, February 27, 1875: "I thank you heartily for the beautiful and well arranged volume which you have had the kindness to present me with. To collect such a vast collection of American poetry must have cost you a great amount of labor, and it shows you are an indefatigable worker. I hope the tastefully arranged index to your collection may help you to add to its riches, and assist in procuring biographical information about the writers of this poetry for your proposed Catalogue."

Charles Deane, Esq., writes from the Massachusetts Historical Society Rooms, March 1, 1875, thanking Mr. Harris very warmly for a copy of his "Index."

George H. Moore, of the Lenox Library, New York, September 6, 1875, writes: "I am afraid that in the multitude of my pressing duties, I have omitted to express to you my grateful sense of obligation for your polite attention in sending me a copy of your very interesting and valuable ' Index to American Poetry and Plays.' I can only say now, as I thank you very sincerely, that I shall be only glad to contribute in any way in my power to promote your design."

J. Hammond Trumbull writes from Hartford, March 2, 1875: "I am very much obliged to you for the copy you are so kind as to send to me of your valuable and elegant ' Index to American Poetry and Plays.' Having received it only within the last hour, I have not yet had time for more than a glance." Mr. T. proceeds to give information about certain anonymous writers, and makes this interesting statement with regard to the author of "Federalism Triumphant," which he says was written "by Leonard Chester (graduate of Yale, 1769—d. 1803), as I know by an autograph letter of his in my possession. The authorship was carefully concealed, and until now has, I think, been unknown except to myself in this generation."

S. Austin Allibone writes from Philadelphia, April 12, 1875: "Please accept my thanks for the copy of your Index to American Poetry which you were so kind as to send me."

It would be easy to add to the foregoing, other letters in which the writers return their thanks to Mr. Harris for sending to them copies of his "Index." They furnish sufficient evidence of the great interest taken by the most distinguished bibliophiles in the country in the work to which, with so much enthusiasm, Mr. Harris devoted some of the best years of his life. This interest would have been greatly increased could they have known what he could tell them about the more than one thousand volumes he added to his collection after the publication of the "Index." Some of the rarest treasures of the collection came into his possession after 1874, and are now classified, and notes on very many of them published in this Catalogue.

It remains only to say that the zeal of Mr. Harris in the gratification of his passion for books in the department which he had made a specialty knew no abatement down to the close of his life. His death was sudden, and was caused by drowning, as the result of the upsetting of a boat in which only himself and Mrs. Harris were sailing on Moosehead Lake, in the State of Maine, the sad event occurring October 2, 1881, both of the parties sharing a common fate.

### HENRY BOWEN ANTHONY.

Henry Bowen Anthony, a lineal descendant of John Anthony, of Hempstead, England, who came to Boston in 1634, and to Rhode Island in 1640, was born in Coventry, R. I., in the county of Providence, April 1, 1815. His parents were exemplary members of the Society of Friends, for which religious community he always cherished, through life, a sincere respect and esteem, his own thoughts on sacred subjects being, in a good degree, in harmony with the Quaker faith in which he was reared. Having pursued his preparatory studies chiefly in a private school in Providence, he entered Brown University in 1829, and was graduated in the class of 1833. For a few years after leaving college he was associated with his brother in manufacturing business, a part of each year being spent in Savannah, Ga. The vocation, however, did not accord with his tastes which had been developed and matured in his college career, and he decided to turn his attention to journalism. At the early age of twenty-three, in the year 1838, he became the editor of the *Providence Journal*, devoting to it the best energies of a cultured intellect, and bringing to the performance of the onerous duties which devolved on him, a determination to meet the demands of readers representing all classes in the community, and to furnish for their daily perusal, a paper that should not only awaken their interest, but command their sincere respect and their hearty support.

The time when Mr. Anthony entered upon his work as a journalist was one of the most important and exciting periods in Rhode Island history, and the position of the editor of the leading paper of the State was one of great delicacy and great difficulty. The events connected with what is known as the "Dorr Rebellion" are too familiar to need to be recited in a sketch necessarily so limited as this. In the language of Prof. William Gammell, who, in more ways than one, has rendered such ample justice to the rare abilities and the marked accomplishments of his college friend, Mr.

Anthony "was obliged daily to discuss the fundamental principles of American government, which were then far less settled than they are at present, and to set forth and urge upon public attention the only mode in which the constitution of a State can be changed without peril to all social interests and rights. During the whole of this excited period, the *Journal* wielded a commanding influence. Its editorial columns were marked by signal ability and judgment, and the services which it rendered to the cause of constitutional government were gratefully acknowledged by the people of the State as reflecting the highest credit on its youthful editor and manager. It was by him that its position among the journals of New England was secured, that its principles and purposes were defined, and its reputation established. He did for it a work similar to that which we connect with the names of Hale, of Bryant, of Greeley and of Raymond, for the great journals which they severally created and conducted. Whatever advantage or distinction it then acquired was due to his versatile genius and to his rare ability as a writer for the press."

The citizens of Rhode Island, recognizing the skill and wisdom with which the youthful journalist had carried on the discussions which were so influential in the vindication and maintenance of the great principles of "law and order," called him to the highest position to which their suffrages could elect him, and, in 1849, he was chosen Governor of the Commonwealth, an honor which was repeated in 1850. He would have been continued in office but for his positive declinature of the position. Meanwhile, he gave unremitting attention to his editorial duties, not ceasing to be a journalist because he sat in the chair of Governor. There is good reason to believe that, without regret, he laid aside his gubernatorial cares that he might devote his whole time to the pursuits of his chosen profession, and, if possible, bring the paper, which was the choice of his affections, nearer his ideal of what such a periodical should be.

To the congenial pursuits of his profession Mr. Anthony gave himself with singular earnestness, and with but occasional intermissions for the next six or seven years of his life. The close of the term of senatoria service in Congress of the Hon. Philip Allen on the fourth of March, 1859, made it necessary to elect a Senator to represent the State of Rhode Island at the Capitol in Washington. The Whigs—the political party with which Mr. Anthony had been so long identified—being in the ascendant in both branches of the General Assembly, he was elected to what he always regarded as one of the most important and honorable positions a citizen of the United States can fill. He took his seat in Congress on the fifth of December, 1859. This was the second Congress of the administration of President Buchanan, one of the darkest and dreariest periods in American history. Although among the youngest members of the august body to which he had been elected, being only forty-four years of age, few of the associates of Mr. Anthony were better acquainted with the serious problems which were constantly coming before Congress for discussion and for solution. For years, at the head of an important journal, he had had occasion to consider these matters, and had given earnest and profound thought to the grave topics which engaged the attention of the best think-ers in all parts of the country. He loved the Union. Gladly would he have saved it from the horrors of bitter civil strife. But when it became clear that the questions at issue must be submitted to the stern arbitra-ment of the sword, he accepted the alternative, and through all the sorrow-ful years of the civil war, he faithfully stood by the constituted authorities and bore his part in maintaining what he believed to be a righteous cause.

We cannot, in our brief sketch, present anything like a detailed account of Mr. Anthony's career in Congress. We allude only to one or two impor-tant positions which he filled. As was most fitting, considering what were his antecedents, he was placed, soon after taking his seat, on the Joint Com-mittee on Public Printing, and at the beginning of Mr. Lincoln's adminis-tration was made Chairman of the Committee. With a brief interval in 1880–81, he held this position during his whole term of office in Con-gress. Early in his congressional career he was placed also on the Com-mittee on Naval Affairs, serving from 1863 to the time of his death. He was elected President *pro tempore* of the Senate in 1869, and again in 1871.

3

But for circumstances beyond his control, he would have been chosen more than once again, near the close of his life, to the same high post of honor. When the Forty-eighth Congress met in December, 1883, his associates in office honored themselves, as well as one who had secured the respect and affection of men of all parties, by again calling him to preside over their deliberations. His knowledge of the precariousness of his health and the conviction that he was physically incapacitated from performing the duties of the President of the Senate, compelled him to decline the service to which, with such hearty good will, he had been called. It is a touching circumstance which may well be referred to as illustrating the strong and tender hold which he, now "the Father of the Senate," had upon that distinguished body, that, at the opening of Congress at the time just referred to, the organization of the body was postponed until he was able to take his seat, from which he had been debarred by ill health, and when he advanced to take the customary oath on entering upon the fifth term of his Senatorial life, "the entire Senate arose and remained standing during its administration."

His term of service in Congress was longer than that of any other member who had been connected with the body, with the exception of Mr. Benton, who, for thirty years, represented the State of Missouri. The senatorial life of Mr. Anthony began, as has already been stated, December 5, 1859, and was terminated by his death September 2, 1884. Reckoning from the time when, by election, he became a Senator from Rhode Island, that is, from March 4, 1859, his term of service lacked but a day or two of being twenty-five and a half years.

This sketch would be incomplete without a reference to Mr. Anthony's connection with "The Harris Collection of American Poetry," and to his personal love for poetry, of which he has given evidence in the valuable additions he made to the collection, and in the productions of his own pen.

In a drawer of one of the cases of "The Harris Collection" containing some of its rarest and costliest treasures, there has been placed for safe keeping, under lock and key, along with other valuable books, an octavo volume of twelve pages only of printed matter, and some twenty-five blank pages, to give a reasonable thickness to the book. The external dress of the volume is a rich and most attractive looking binding, in the highest style of the binder's art, the sight of which would bring joy to the bibliophile's heart. On opening this beautiful volume, two titles meet the eye of the reader. These titles are separated by an explanatory note which covers nearly a page. The first title is as follows: " The Fancy Ball. A Poem. Providence: Sidney S. Rider. 1875." A single line is on the reverse side of the leaf and reads: "A PRIVATE REPRINT OF ONE HUNDRED COPIES." The note referred to is as follows:

"These verses were written in 1837, and were intended to describe an entertainment given at the residence of Mr. Barnsley, one of the merchant princes of Savannah, a gentleman well remembered by the older citizens, for his courtesy, his high character and his elegant hospitality. Of those who participated in the gay and brilliant scene, the greater number must have passed away; for the date is divided from us by more than the space of a generation, and the writer cannot, in looking over his rhymes, recall the names of half of those whose charms inspired them.

"A few months since he visited the beautiful city of Savannah, which had so greatly enlarged and improved since he saw it, and he found in its new life and bustle a few grave matrons and elderly men who had danced at the 'Fancy Ball.' His pride of authorship was unduly aroused when two of them quoted more than he could from his boyish lines, which were preserved only in their memory, for there appeared to be no copy extant. From the only one within his reach he has reprinted a hundred copies, mainly that he may send them to friends who so kindly remembered him, and as a memorial of a delightful visit and of most hospitable kindness.

"No corrections have been made from the original edition, although the errors of style and composition will be evident to the most careless reader. To alter the verses would be, in some sort, to endorse at mature age an effusion whose apology is that it was written by a very inexperienced pen immediately after the occasion which it commemorates, while the music was still ringing in the writer's ears, and the dazzle of the brilliant scene had hardly passed from before his eyes; and with the certainty that it would meet only the kindly criticism which gives its full approval in advance.

"HENRY B. ANTHONY.

"PROVIDENCE, June, 1875."

The second title, the original one, reads thus: "The Fancy Ball. A Sketch. Printed for Private Circulation. Pulaski House, Savannah, March 31, 1838."

Our space allows us to present only the introductory and closing lines of the poem:

> "As floats the fancies of a gorgeous dream
> That vanished with the morning's earliest beam;
> As haunts the ear some half-remembered strain
> It once hath heard, and seems to hear again;
> As flowers whose beauty and whose bloom hath fled,
> Each bright leaf withered and each green one dead,
> A grateful, an undying fragrance bear,
> To tell what blushing beauty once was there;—
> So turns my memory to that brilliant sight
> When wit and beauty held their festal night;
> When thronged hall its glittering groups displayed
> Of Nature's loveliness, by art arrayed;
> Of graceful forms that mocked the sculptor's art,
> And eyes whose glances reached the coldest heart,
> Of all that beauty loves or taste admires,
> Of all that valor warms or genius fires."

The writer then goes on to give a "pen-picture" of the charming tableaux which passed before his eye. What gives added interest to the volume, which is in "The Harris Collection," is the circumstance that a Savannah lady, who was present on the occasion, sent, in response to a request of Mr. Anthony, the names of all the characters he describes in his poem, and these names are inserted in the margins of its pages. After describing with graceful pen the brilliant scenes of the festive evening, a pensive mood comes over the writer's mind, and he thus brings his poetic production to a close:

> "Alas! alas! this week-day, work-day life!
> That all that's brighest, all that's noblest, best,
> All that consoles us for its weary strife,
> And all that gives to time it's little zest,
> Should be, at most, but *fancy's* transient beam,
> Fade in a *tableau*, vanish in a dream!"

The only other poems of Mr. Anthony's that were put into book form were three in number. They were published with the following titles: "The Dorriad, the Hero of Two Flights," the first of the three; "The Attack on the Arsenal," the second, and "The Chepachet Campaign," the third. It is hardly necessary to say that these "squibs," as Mr. Anthony calls them, allude to incidents which occurred in what is known in Rhode Island history as "The Dorr Rebellion," in 1842.

Senator Anthony died at his residence, Benevolent street, Providence, R. I., at fifteen minutes before two o'clock on Tuesday afternoon, September 2, 1884, at the age of sixty-nine years, five months and one day. His funeral was honored by the presence of President Arthur and a large number of United States Senators, and other gentlemen from Washington, with many distinguished friends of the deceased, who were present to give testimony to their sincere respect and affection for the departed.

In bringing this Introduction to a close, the compiler of the Catalogue of "The Harris Collection of American Poetry" desires to place on record his grateful appreciation of the kindly interest which has been expressed by so many persons in the work which has engaged his attention for so many months. These expressions have come to him not only from almost every section of his own country, but from England as well, whose poets and lovers of poetry will be gratified to note what share America has had in enriching a most important department of our common English literature. The hope is cherished that both at home and abroad there may be a laudable curiosity which the pages of this goodly-sized volume will gratify, to know, with a good degree of definiteness, what are the contents of a library so remarkable and so altogether unique as has, by the munificence of the late Senator Anthony, found a permanent home in the beautiful Library Building of Brown University.

One sad thought is awakened in the mind of the compiler as he brings his pleasant task to an end; and that is, that the friend who more than all others encouraged him to undertake this work, and has been ever ready to cheer him in its prosecution, shares not with him the joy of its completion. The pleasant hours passed with that friend in the common enjoyment of the priceless treasures of the John Carter Brown Library, and in delightful talks about rare and costly books, will ever keep green and fresh in his memory the name and the virtues of one who took so high a rank among our most distinguished American Bibliographers, the HON. JOHN RUSSELL BARTLETT.

J. C. STOCKBRIDGE.

BROWN UNIVERSITY LIBRARY,
Room of the Harris Collection of American Poetry,
June 30, 1886.

# CATALOGUE.

Abadie (P.)  The Fireman, etc.  16°, pp. 130.  New York, 1852.

Abandoned, The.  (Anon.)  A Sketch of Life as it may be found in New England.  12°, pp. 32.  Boston, 1848.

Abbey (H.)

Henry Abbey, originally named Henry La Mont Abbey, was born at Rondout, N. Y., July 11, 1842. His grandmother, Lucy Knox, was a lineal descendant of the great Scotch Reformer, John Knox. Having obtained a good academical education, after a brief experience as assistant editor of a weekly paper published in his native town, he went to New York. For a time he edited *The Orange Spectator*, and in 1864 returned to Rondout and was appointed Teller in a bank in that place, devoting his spare hours to writing for several periodicals, and to the preparation of a number of volumes for the press. He has published up to this date (1880) seven books. His residence is Kingston, N. Y.

— Ballads of Good Deeds and other Verses.  Sq. 16°, pp. 169.  New York, 1872.

— May Dreams.  12°, pp. 143.  New York, 1862.

— Poems.  12°, pp. 149.  New York, 1879.

— Ralph, and other Poems.  Sq. 16°, pp. 64.  Rondout, N. Y., 1866.

— Stories in Verse.  16°, pp. 128.  New York, 1869.

In this volume there is an autograph letter of Mr. Abbey, written to Richard Grant White, to whom the poem is dedicated.

Abbot, (Anne W.)  Autumn Leaves.  Original pieces in Prose and Verse.  12°, pp. 200.  Cambridge, 1853.

Abbott (E.)  The Baby's Things : A Story in Verse for Christmas Eve.  12°, pp. 53.  New York, 1871.

Academic Recreation : By the Columbian Peitho-Logian Society of Columbia College.  Vol I.  16°, pp. 288.  New York, 1815.

Acaico, (I.)  Idilios Griegos de Bion de Esmirna, etc.  8°, pp. 31.  Guanajuato, 1868.

ACROSTICS FROM ACROSS THE ATLANTIC, and other poems, humorous and
sentimental. By a Gothamite. (Anon.) Sq. 16°, pp. vi, 63.
London, 1869.

ACTION, THE PLEASURES OF. (Anon.) 18°, pp. 32. Philadelphia, 1846.

ADA. A Tale. (By Janvier, *pseud.* Woodward?) 12°, pp. 75. Philadelphia, 1852.

> The supposed author is Joseph Janvier Woodward, M. D., born in Philadelphia, 1833,
> took his degree at the University of Pennsylvania, 1853, and was the author of several
> medical works which have been commended.

ADAMS, (C. S.) A Poem on the Use of Tobacco. 12°, pp. 24. Boston,
1838.

— An Address (Temperance) in verse, at Harwich, Mass., July 4,
1835. 12°, pp. 8. Barnstable, 1835.

ADAMS, (G. L.) Moral and Religious Musings. 18°, pp. vi, 108.
Schenectady, 1835.

ADAMS, (W. W.) The Book of Job in Poetry ; or A Song in the Night.
Lg. 8°, pp. iv, 380. New York, 1864.

ADAMS, (J.)

> John Adams, only son of Hon. John Adams, of Nova Scotia, was born in 1704, grad-
> uated at Harvard in 1721, and subsequently was settled as an assistant, contrary to the
> wishes of Rev. Nathaniel Clapp, pastor of the First Congregational Church in Newport, R.
> I. After a while Mr. Clapp refused to permit Mr. Adams to preach, himself conducting
> the services of the church both parts of the day. As a consequence nearly one-half of the
> church and congregation withdrew. A new church was formed, of which Mr. Adams was
> ordained pastor April 11, 1828, remaining not far from two years. He removed to Cam-
> bridge, where he devoted himself to literary pursuits. He had a well deserved reputation
> as an eloquent preacher and an accomplished linguist, being, as described by his uncle,
> Matthew Adams, " master of nine languages," and was " familiar with the best writings
> in ancient and modern literature." He died in 1740, at the early age of thirty-six. It is said
> that the Fellows of Harvard College were his pall-bearers, and the most distinguished
> persons of the State were mourners at his funeral. Five years after his death his poems
> were collected and published with the following title :

— Poems on Several Occasions, Original and Translated, by the late
Reverend and Learned John Adams, M. A. *Hoc placuit semel,
hoc decies repetita placebit.* Hor. de Art. Poet. Printed for D.
Gookin, in Marlborough street, over against the Old South Meeting House, 1745.

> The volume is an 18°, of 176 pages.

ADAMS, (J. J.) The Charter Oak, etc. 12°, pp. ix, 60. New York,
1830.

— Same. 1839.

**Adams, (J. Q.)**

John Quincy Adams was born in Braintree, Mass., July 11, 1767, and was the sixth President of the United States. He died in the Capitol at Washington, February 21, 1848.

— Dermot MacMorrogh, or The Conquest of Ireland. 16°, pp. xv, 108. Columbus, 1834.

— Poems of Religion and Society. 16°, pp. iv, 116. Auburn, N. Y., 1859.

**Adams, (J. T.)** Poems. 12°, pp. 47. No place, no date.

**Adams, (Mrs. J. F.)** Poems and Essays. 8°, pp. 124. Lawrence. No date.

**Adams, (R. C.)** History of the United States in Rhyme. Sq. 16°, pp. 72. Boston, 1884.

**Address, An, to a Provincial Bashaw.** (By a Son of Liberty.) Sq. 12°, pp. 8. Printed in the Tyrannic Administration of St. Francisco. (Probably Sir Francis Bernard.) No place. 1769.

Bernard was an English lawyer. From 1758 to 1760 he was Governor of New Jersey, and then was appointed Governor of Massachusetts. By bringing troops to Boston he awakened the hostility of the citizens, and made himself obnoxious by his attempts to enforce the acts which were bitterly opposed by the people, and finally led to the war of the Revolution. In 1760 he was recalled to England, and died in 1779.

**Addresses, Rejected; or, The New Theatrum Poetarum.** From the 19th London Edition. 3d American Edition. 12°, pp. 159. Boston, 1841.

**Addresses, The Rejected.** New Park Theatre, N. Y. 18°, pp. 182. New York, 1821.

**Ad Interim and Ad Outerim; or, Confidential Disclosures of State Secrets.** 2d Edition. 8°, pp. 30. Washington, 1868.

**Adler, (G. J.)**

George J. Adler was born at Leipsic, Germany, in 1821, came to the United States in 1833, graduated at the New York University in 1844, and was professor in that institution, 1846–54. He composed Latin and German School Manuals, and an excellent German and English Dictionary. His death took place in the city of New York, August 24, 1868.

— Iphigenia in Tauris. Translated from the German of Goethe. 12°, pp. 155. New York, 1856.

**Advent Poem.** (Anon.) (Written in pencil, White.) 12°, pp. 16. No place, no date.

4

Æsop in Rhyme. (By Marmaduke Park, *pseud.?*) 12°, pp. 288. Philadelphia and New York, 1855.

Affairs in North America. Title-page wanting.

This poem has reference to the state of the country in the early stages of the Revolutionary war.

Africa. (Anon.) 2d Edition. 12°, pp. 20. Andover, 1826.

The name of the author was, without doubt, Ann Evans. See reference to the poems in Memoirs of W. L. Garrison, Vol. 1.

Age of Error, The; or, A Poetical Essay on the Course of Human Action. By a Philadelphian. (Anon.) O curas hominum! O quantum est in rebus inane! Per. Sat. II. 8°, pp. 16. Philadelphia, 1797.

No clue is given to the name of the author. "Nineteen and youthful enthusiasm," he says, "are the only confessions I can make to the critic, whose breast may swell with indignation at the faults of the poem."

The general argument of the poem is this, viz.: "Our structure of happiness is alone built on the moral tendency of our actions; and virtue is the only basis which can support it."

Agg, (J.)

John Agg was an English poet and novelist, whose productions were issued from the London press, 1808–13. He came to the United States not far from the year 1816. A large part of the Preface to the volume, whose title is here given, is taken up with "Some Observations respecting the Causes of the Increasing Emigration from England to America." The author is enthusiastic in his praises of his adopted home. "Striking, indeed, is the contrast" between England and America. "The glory of Britain," he exclaims, "has passed its meridian, and shapes a declining course; the sun of Columbia majestically rises above the political horizon, and distant nations mark its increasing splendor with envy and apprehension. May its beams shine to the remotest shores of the world; and may ages beyond the calculation of fancy find cause to rejoice in its radiance!"

— The Ocean Harp: A Poem; In Two Cantos: with some smaller pieces, and a monody on the death of John Tyng Dorsey, M. D. 24°, pp. xxviii, 182. Philadelphia, 1819.

Aiken, (G. L.) Uncle Tom's Cabin Dramatized. 12°, pp. 60. New York. No date.

Ainslie, (H.)

Hew Ainslie was born April 5, 1792, in Ayrshire, Scotland, on the estate of Sir Hugh Dalrymple Hamilton, his father, George Ainslie, being employed by the Knight for several years. He was well educated, and, for a time, was the amanuensis of the celebrated Dugald Stewart, of whose last work he made a copy for publication. He came to the United States in 1822, and purchased a small farm in Hoosick, Rensselaer County, N. Y. Influenced by the attractions held out by Robert Owen, he removed, in 1825, to New Har-

AINSLIE, (H.) — *Continued*.

mony to try the experiment of communism, but being disappointed he took up his residence as a brewer, first at Shippingport, Ky., then at Louisville, and then at New Albany. He seems not to have been very fortunate in his business affairs. For a time he resided in Jersey City, and died in Louisville March 12, 1878.

— Scottish Songs, Ballads and Poems. 12°, vii, 216. New York, 1855.

AKERMAN, (LUCY E.) Nothing but Leaves. 8°, pp. 73. Providence, 1875.

AKERS, (ELIZ.) (Florence Perry.)

Mrs. Elizabeth (Chase Akers) Allen was born in Strong, Me., in 1832, spent her early life in Farmington, Me., and devoted herself to literary pursuits. She married, in 1866, Mr. E. M. Allen, and subsequently took up her residence in Greenville, N. J., removing to that place in 1872.

— Poems. 18°, pp. 251. Boston, 1866. Blue and Gold Series.

ALBUM, THE. (F. & R. Lockwood, Publishers.) 16°, pp. x, 154. New York, 1824.

ALCOTT, (A. B.)

Amos Bronson Alcott was born at Wolcott, Conn., November 29, 1799. He was a representative of " The Transcendental School," and contributed many articles to the famous periodical, " The Dial." He is called " The Ideal Philosopher of Concord."

— Sonnets and Canzonets. 16°, pp. iv, 149. Boston, 1882.

ALDERMAN ROONY AT THE CABLE BANQUET. Lg. 8°, pp. 113. New York, 1866.

— Same. At the Great Exhibition. Another Epic. (By Himself, Anon.) 12°, pp. 22. New York, 1867.

ALDRICH, (T. B.)

Thomas Bailey Aldrich was born at Portsmouth, N. H., in 1836. For a time he was assistant editor of the *New York Home Journal*. Among American poets he takes high rank, and his periodical articles are received with great favor.

— Flower and Thorn. Later Poems. 12°, pp. ix, 149. Boston, 1877.
— Same. 4th Edition. 16°, pp. 150. Boston, 1882.
— Mercedes and Later Lyrics. 12°, pp. 111. Boston, 1884.
— Pampinea, etc. 12°, pp. vi, 72. New York, 1861.
— Poems. 18°, pp. 161. New York and London, 1863. Blue and Gold Series.
— Same. 18°, pp. 240. Boston, 1865. Blue and Gold Series.
— The Ballad of Babie Bell, etc. 12°, pp. vi, 117. New York, 1859.
— The Bells ; A Collection of Chimes. 12°, pp. 144. New York, 1855.

ALDRICH, (T. B.)— *Continued.*

— Same. The Course of True Love never did Run Smooth. 12°, pp. xii, 41. New York, 1858.

ALE, IN PROSE AND VERSE. (Gray and Savage.) 4°, pp. 97. New York, 1866.

ALESSANDRO, (P. D') Monte Auburno. 16°, pp. 22. Stati Uniti di America. 1835.

ALEXANDER, (J. H.)

John Henry Alexander was born at Annapolis, Md., in 1812. He was the author of many scientific papers published in England, France, Germany and the United States. He died at Baltimore, March 2 1867.

— Catena Dominica. 12°, pp. v, 177. Philadelphia, 1855.

— Same. Introïts, or Ante-Communion Psalms, etc. 18°, pp. viii, 186. Philadelphia, 1844.

ALEXANDER, (W.) Poetical Works. 8°, pp. xiv, 263. Philadelphia, 1847.

ALGER, (H.) Nothing to Do. An Accompaniment to "Nothing to Wear." Illustrated by the Author. 12°, pp. 57. New York, 1857.

ALGER, (W. R.)

William Rounseville Alger was born at Freetown, Mass., December 11, 1823, graduated at the Harvard Theological School in 1847, and became a Unitarian minister. He is the author of several well-known works.

— The Poetry of the East. 12°, pp. viii, 280. Boston, 1856.

— The Poetry of the Orient. 12°, pp. vii, 337. Boston, 1865.

ALGERINE SLAVES. (Anon.) 12°, pp. 173. Newburyport, 1798.

The work bears the signature "Juvenis," and is preceded by a Journal of John Foss. The title-pages are independent, but the pagination is continuous.

ALLAN, (P. J.)

Peter John Allan was born at York, England, June 6, 1825, and was the third son of Dr. Colin Allan, a surgeon in the army, who was stationed at Halifax. In 1836, Dr. A. removed to Fredericton, N. S., where he spent the remaining years of his life. The subject of this sketch studied law, but did not devote himself to the practice of his profession, preferring "the thorny path of literature." The personal appearance of Mr. Allan is described as having been unusually prepossessing. "In stature he stood six feet three inches, at the least; his features classical, sufficiently regular, manly and intelligent; his dark eye sparkled with wit and good humour, and when he wore his beard and moustache, he might have sat as a Cavalier to Vandyk." His life was a brief one. He had sent the manuscript of a poem which he had written to England for publication, but before it was printed he had passed away, at the early age of twenty-three.

ALLAN, (P. J.) — *Continued.*

Mr. A., in justification of his devotion to literary pursuits, says : " My lot having been cast on the wrong side of the Atlantic, in a colony where the Muse cannot find a resting-place for the sole of her foot — in its very little Capital, whose politics would be mere private scandal to a European ear, and whose society is strangely limited — can it be a matter of surprise that I should have sought relaxation from more severe studies in the amiable foible of verse-making? "

— Poetical Remains. 12°, pp. xxiv, 171. London, 1853.

ALLEN, (B.) (*pseud.* Osander.)

Rev. Benjamin Allen, an Episcopal clergyman, was born at Hudson, N. Y., and was rector of St. Paul's Church, Philadelphia, 1821–29. He died on board ship, on his return from a tour abroad.

— Poems. 12°, pp. 180. Hudson, 1811.
— The Death of Abdallah. 24°, pp. vi, 192. New York, 1814.

ALLEN, (B., JR.) The Phœnix ; or The Battle of Valparaiso. 16°, pp. viii, 37. New York, 1814.

This volume is dedicated to Col. Henry Rutgers. Ten pages are devoted to the official letter of Capt. D. Porter, dated " Essex Junior, July 3, 1814, at sea," in which he gives an account of his movements from the time he left the Delaware, October 27, 1812, to the date of the destruction of the Essex, of which he was the Commander.

— Urania, or the True Use of Poesy. 24°, pp. 192. New York, 1814.

ALLEN, (CHARLOTTE.) Poems. 16°, pp. vi, 143. Boston, 1841.
— Same. Second Edition. Boston, 1843.

ALLEN, (ELEANOR.) The Siege of Agrigentum. 16°, pp. 79. Boston, 1841.

ALLEN, (J.) A Poem on the Existence of God. An Ode on Creation. To which are added several Hymns, and an Eulogy on Gen. George Washington. 16°, pp. 36. Haverhill, 1803.

ALLEN, (ELIZABETH.) The Silent Harp, or Fugitive Poems. 12°. Burlington, 1832.

ALLEN, (ESTHER C.) Washington. 18°, pp. 15. Brooklyn, 1861.

ALLEN, (MRS. H. B.) A Poetical Geognosy. 12°, pp. 34. Boston, 1841.

ALLEN, (J.)

James Allen was born in Boston, July 24, 1739. In his youth he devoted but little attention to study, contrary to the earnest wish of his father, a merchant of considerable wealth in Boston. He was three years in Harvard College, spending his time in an aimless, unprofitable way, and then he renounced the pursuits of learning. His chief employment was writing essays and verses upon political themes. The subject of the poem, whose

ALLEN, (J.) — *Continued.*

title is given below, was " The Boston Massacre," and it was written at the request of Dr. Joseph Warren, and the town authorities voted to publish it. The political principles of the writer being regarded as unsound, the authorities declined to print it. Some of his friends, however, took it upon themselves to publish it.

— The Poem, voted to be published with the late Oration, etc.   4°, pp. 30.   1772.

ALLEN, (MRS., of Maryland.)   Pastorals, Elegies, etc.   16°, pp. 163. Abington, Md., 1806.

ALLEN, (P.)

Paul Allen was born at Providence, R. I., in 1775, and graduated at Brown University in 1793. As an associate with Pierpont and John Neal, he was a contributor to several periodicals. For a time he was editor of the *Federal Republican* of Baltimore, etc· " Noah " originally consisted of twenty-five cantos. Under the revision of Mr. Neal it was reduced to five cantos. Mr. A. died in 1826.

— Noah.   18°, pp. xi, 103.   Baltimore, 1821.
— Occasional Poems.   12°, pp. vi, 141.   Salem, 1801.

ALLEN (W.)

William Allen, D. D., was born at Pittsfield, Mass., January 2, 1784, graduated at Harvard College 1802, was President of Bowdoin College 1820–39, and is best known in the literary world as the author of " American Biographical and Historical Dictionary." He died July 16, 1868.

— Poem at the Berkshire Jubilee, August 22 and 23, 1844.   Bound with Sermon of Dr. Hopkins and Oration by J. A. Spencer, Esq. Large 8°, pp. 244.   Albany, 1845.   Several other Poems are found in the volume.

— Wunnissoo, or the Vale of Hoosatunnuk.   A Poem, with notes.   12°, pp. 237.   Boston, 1856.

ALLFUDGE'S INSTRUCTIONS TO THE NEW YORK POLICE IN VERSE.   (By an Up-town Democrat.   Anon.)   3d Edition.   12°, pp. 35.   New York, 1859.

ALLIN, (ABBY).   Home Ballads :   A Book for New Englanders.   In Three Parts.   12°, pp. 238.   Boston, 1851.

Miss Allin, by marriage, became Mrs. D. S. Curtiss.

ALLSTON, (J. B.)   Sumter.   8°, pp. 11.   Charleston, 1874.

ALLSTON, (W.)

Washington Allston was born in Georgetown, S. C., November 5, 1779, and graduated at Harvard in 1800. He devoted his life to art, spent many years abroad, where he painted those master-pieces which have given him a world-wide reputation. He died at Cambridge, Mass., July 9, 1843.

Allston, (W.)— *Continued.*

— Lectures on Art, and Poems.   Edited by R. H. Dana, Jr.   12°, pp. xi, 380.   New York, 1850.

— The Sylphs of the Seasons, etc.   12°, pp. vii, 168.   Boston, 1813.

Almendares, La Profecia del.   Fragmento de un Canto.   1850.   12°, pp. 19.   Nueva York, 1860.

Almy, (Annie W.)   Early Poems.   18°, pp. 56.   Boston, 1866.

Alsop, (R.)

Richard Alsop was born at Middletown, Conn., in January, 1761.   He pursued a partial course of study at Yale College, but did not graduate.   For a number of years he devoted himself to literary pursuits, and became a proficient in the modern languages of Europe. "The Charms of Fancy," and another poem, "The Conquest of Scandinavia," were written, but no part of the first was published during his life, and only portions of the second. He was associated with other poets in the production of several works, *e. g.*, "The Echo" and "The Political Green-House."   His death occurred at Flatbush, Long Island, in August, 1815.

— Charms of Fancy.   Lg. 12°, pp. xii, 214.   New York, 1856.

— The Enchanted Lake.   8°, pp. vii, 67.   New York, 1806.

Ambler, (A. I.)   Jessie Reed, etc.   16°, pp. 108.   Philadelphia, 1867.

Amenquade, (L'.)   Poëme.   8°, pp. 22.   Philadelphia, 1780.

Amelia.

Mrs. Amelia B. (Coppuck) Welby was born at St. Michaels, Md., in 1821.   In 1838 married Mr. George B. Welby, of Louisville, Ky., where she subsequently lived.   Her death took place at Lexington, Ky., May 2, 1852.

— Gems of Poetry, with Biographical Sketch of Amelia B. Coppuck. With Selections from American and British Poets.   2d Edition. Sm. 16°, pp. 224.   Philadelphia, 1851.

Amer, One Week At.   (Anon.)   12°, pp. viii, 119.   Boston, 1858.

America: A Dramatic Poem.   12°, pp. 110.   New York, 1863.

America Cup, The.   A Nautical Poem, descriptive of the five international races between the yacht Livonia, representing the twelve yacht clubs of the Royal Yacht Squadron of England, and the yachts Columbia and Sappho of the New York Yacht Club, for the possession of the Challenge Cup, won by the Yacht America in in the year 1851.   8°, pp. 118.   New York, 1874.

America Discovered.   A Poem.   In 12 Books.   By an American. (Anon.)   12°, pp. iv, 283.   New York, 1850.

AMERICAN IN ALGIERS, THE.  12°, pp. 33.  New York, 1797.

AMERICAN LIBERTY.  (Anon.)  12°, pp. 12.  New York, 1775.

AMERICAN MAGAZINE, THE, AND MONTHLY CHRONICLE FOR THE BRITISH
COLONIES.  Vol. I.  Containing from October, 1757, to October,
1758, Prose and Poetry.  By a Society of Gentleman.  8°, pp.
656.  Philadelphia.

AMERICAN POEMS.  Original and Selected.  Edited by Elisha Smith.
Vol. 1.  8°, pp. 304.  Litchfield, 1793.
Only volume published.

AMERICAN SKETCHES.  Farmers' Fireside.  12°, pp. 12.  Concord, N.
H., 1822.

AMERICANS IN PARIS.  A Comedy.  (Anon.)  12°, pp. 32.  New York,
no date.

AMERICAN UNIVERSAL MAGAZINE, THE.  Prose and Poetry.  Vols. II,
III.  12°, pp. 338, 464.  Philadelphia, 1797.

AMES, (N.)  (Alguno Señor, *nom de plume.*)
Nathan Ames graduated at Harvard in 1848.  He was the author of "The Bard of
Lind," being ten parodies of Longfellow and others purporting to be expressly written
for the "Greeting to America of Jenny Lind."  Mr. A. died in 1865.

— Pirates Glen and Dungeon Rock.  16°, pp. viii, 64.  Boston, 1853.

AMORY, (T. C.)  William Blackstone, Boston's First Inhabitant.  2d
Edition.  12°, pp. 38.  Boston, 1877.

ANDRÉ, (J.)
John André, an Adjutant-General in the British army in the war of the Revolution,
was born of Swiss parentage in London, in 1751, received his first commission as an army
officer in 1771, and came to America in 1774 as a lieutenant in the Royal Fusiliers.  The
story of his connection with the treachery of Benedict Arnold, and his execution as a spy
October 2, 1780, are familiar to all readers of American history.  In 1821 his remains were
disinterred and removed to Westminster Abbey.

— The Cow Chase.  8°, pp. 69.  Albany, 1866.
This satirical poem by Major André has been regarded with special interest from the
circumstance of its being among the last of the writings of this talented but indiscreet
young officer.  It is founded upon an unsuccessful attempt of a party, under General
Wayne, to capture a block-house upon the Hudson, in New Jersey, and but a short distance from New York, July 2, 1780.

AMOURS DIVINE ; OR LOVE-SCENES IN THE ORIENT.  (Anon.)  12°, pp.
69.  New York, 1871.

ANDROS, (RH. S. S.)  Chocorua, etc.  8°, pp. vi, 88.  Fall River, 1838.

ANGEL IN THE HOUSE, ETC. (Anon.) 16°, pp. x, 201. Boston, 1856.

ANGEL, THE GUARDIAN, ETC. (Anon.) Sq. 18°, pp. 64. Philadelphia, 1864.

ANIMAL MAGNETISM. A Farce. (Anon.) 18°, pp. 31. Philadelphia, 1828.

ANIMALS, KINDNESS TO. Select Poems. 16°, pp. 108. New York, 1846.

ANKSTELL, (J.) An Epistle from Yarico to Inkle. (The author's name written by some one in ink.) By the Rev. John Ankstell, A. B., together with their characters as related in *The Spectator*.

> Quod genus hoc dominum? quaeve hunc tam
> Permittit patria?

Marblehead: Printed for the Sons and Daughters of Columbia, MDCCXCII. (Written) By Isaac Story, a member of H. College.

For the story of Yarico and Inkle, see *The Spectator*, Vol. I, No. 2.

ANNIVERSARY ODE. Columbian Reading Society, 1806. 12°, pp. 7. No place, no date.

ANNIVERSARY ODE. Union Book Society of Washington, 1808. (Anon.) No place, no date.

ANSWER: A CONCISE TO THE QUESTION, WHO AND WHAT ARE THE SHAKERS? (Anon.) 24°, pp. 8. Union Village, 1825.

ANTHOLOGY, THE MONTHLY, AND BOSTON REVIEW. Prose and Poetry. 10 Vols. From the Library of N. L. Frothingham. Lg. 8°. Vol. I, pp. 672. Vol. II, pp. 678. Vol. III, pp. 672. Vol. IV, pp. 686. Vol. V. pp. 688. Vol. VI, pp. 435. Vol. VII, pp. 430. Vol. VIII, pp. 432. Vol. IX, pp. 430. Vol. X, pp. 432.

ANTHON, (C. E.) Translation of Baron Münch-Bellinghausen's "The Son of the Wilderness." 12°, pp. ix, 166. New York, 1848.

Allibone refers to Charles E. Anthon as author of Pilgrimage to Treves, in 1844. 12°, New York.

ANTHONY, (H. B.) For Sketch, see Introduction. Dorriad, or the Hero of Two Flights. 12°, pp. 12. Boston, 1842.

— Dorriad and The Great Slocum Dinner. With Introductory Remarks and Annotations. 12°, pp. 55. Providence, 1870.

ANTHONY, (H. B.) — *Continued.*

— Fancy Ball.   12°, p. 12.   Providence, 1875.

> Two copies of this poem are in the "Harris Collection." In one, are pencil notes by the author. In the other are a letter and notes in pencil by Mrs. Margaret M. Welman, of Savannah. For a fuller account of the poem, see sketch of Mr. Anthony in the Introduction.

ANTIGONIAN AND BOSTONIAN BEAUTIES, THE.   A Poem, by *W. S.*, A. B.   8°, Boston, [1754.]

> Who *W. S.* was is doubtful. One authority says William Smith, the first Provost of the University of Pennsylvania. On the title-page of the volume some one has written Charles Chauncy. The following is written on a fly-leaf in pencil: "William Shirley, Governor of Massachusetts, published 'Electra,' a tragedy, and 'Birth of Hercules.'" A Masque, 1705. (See Allen's Biographical Dictionary, 3d Edition.)

ARCHIBALD, (A. K.)   Poems.   16°, pp. iv, 200.   Boston, 1848.

ARCTIC QUEEN.   (Anon.)   12°, pp. 62.   No place, no date.

AREY, (MRS. H. E. G.)

> Hannah Ellen Grannis was born in Cavendish, Vt., April 14, 1810. She began her career as a contributor to the *Daily Herald* of Cleveland, Ohio. For several years previous to 1848, she was an accomplished teacher in her adopted home. She married Oliver Arey in that year. For several years she had the editorial charge of periodicals in Buffalo and New York. "The Youths' Casket" and the "Home Monthly" were edited by her.

— Household Songs and other Poems.   12°, pp. xii, 254.   New York, 1855.

ARISTOCRACY.   (Anon.)   8°, pp. vii, 16.   Philadelphia, 1795.

ARISTOCRAT AND TRADES UNION ADVOCATE.   (Anon.)   18° pp. xix, 35.   Boston, 1834.

ARMSTRONG, (P.)   A Theatric Elegy on the death of George F. Cooke, Esq.   18°, pp. 8.   New York, 1812.

ARNELL, (D. R.)   Fruit of Western Life, or Blanche, and other Poems.   12°, pp. 215.   New York, 1847.

ARNOLD, (A. B.)

> Anthony Brown Arnold was born in Providence, R. I., May 14, 1791. His Pilgrim ancestors were among the early settlers of Plymouth. The opportunities for obtaining an education by Mr. A. were limited. Early in life he engaged in secular pursuits, and was an active business man for more than sixty years, retiring at the age of sixty-eight. He was well known in his native city as one who took a deep practical interest in all religious and philanthropic movements. For a long time he wrote a poem every week for his class in the Sunday-school. These were published with the title below. Mr. Arnold died in 1885.

— Weekly Offerings to a Sabbath School, and other Poems.   8°, pp. 222.   Providence, 1875.

Arnold, (G.)

George Arnold was born in the city of New York, June 24, 1834, and removed with his parents, when he was three years of age, to Alton, Ill., where he resided for twelve years. In 1849 he came East with his parents, who took up their residence at Strawberry Farms, N. J. A few years after, he began, in New York, his career as a worker in the fine arts, and obtained a wide reputation as an art critic. After a time he laid aside the brush and devoted himself especially to literary pursuits, writing largely for magazines, periodicals, etc. He died at Strawberry Farms, November 9, 1865. An edition of his works, edited by William Winter, and published by Fields, Osgood & Co., Boston, has the following title:

— George Arnold's Poems. Complete Edition, including: I. Drift, and other Poems. II. Poems, Grave and Gay. 12°, pp. 384. Boston, 1871.

Arnold, (Mrs. Harriet S.) Birthday Gift. 24°, pp. 428. Dedham, Mass. Several poems in the volume.

Art of Love. Translated from the French. (Anon.) 18°, pp. viii, 144. Philadelphia, 1839.

Art, The, of Domestick Happiness, etc. (Anon.) 24°, pp. 316. Pittsburgh, 1817.

Artman, (W.,) and Hall, (L. V.) Beauties and Achievements of the Blind. Prose and Poetry. 12°, pp. 387. Auburn, N. Y., 1859.

Archer, (J. G.) Voices from the Hearth. 12°, pp. 168. Montreal, 1863.

Ashe, (S. M.) Le Gran Quivera; or, Rome Unmasked. 12°, pp. viii, 148. New York, 1852.

— Monterey Conquered. A Fragment from La Gran Quivera; or, Rome Unmasked. 12°, pp. 148. New York, 1852.

Aspect of the Times, The, etc. By a native of Newark. (Anon.) 18°, pp. vi, 73. Newark, 1831.

Ass on Parnassus, etc. (By Jeremiah Quiz. Anon.) 18°, pp. 108. Philadelphia, 1815.

Association, The, etc., of the Delegates of the Colonies, at the Grand Congress, held at Philadelphia, September 1, 1774; versified and adapted to music. Calculated for Grave and Gay Dispositions; with a Short Introduction. By Bob. Jingle, Esq., Poet Laureate to Congress. [Philadelphia.] Printed in the year MDCCLXXIV.

Published by the Tories to ridicule the proceedings of Congress.

Astrop, (R. F.) Original Poems, etc. 16°, pp. 132. Philadelphia, 1835.

Atkinson, (Mary E.) On the Mountains. 18°, pp. 16. Philadelphia, 1874.

Attempt (An) to Vindicate the American Character, being principally a reply to the intemperate animadversions of Thomas Moore, Esq. (Anon.) 8°, pp. vi, 43. Philadelphia, 1806.

> The general scope of the "Attempt" may be learned from the following:
>
> "The hired libeller may have a claim upon our pity or contempt, but the wanton and groundless asperities of Mr. Moore must wound our feelings and arouse our indignation. That he was not influenced by any hopes of court favor, I freely admit; but who can with patience contemplate such palpable inconsistencies as constitute his character — a heart endued with refined sensibility, yet liable to be utterly lost in the misconceptions of the understanding; a mind gifted with brilliant talents, yet often without the power of ordinary perception, and in many respects an irrecoverable slave to prejudice."

Atlantic Souvenir for 1830. 16°, pp. vi, 326. Philadelphia, 1830.

Atlee, (E. A., M. D.) Essays at Poetry, or a Collection of Fugitive Pieces; with the Life of Eugenius Laude Watts. 12°, pp. vii, 152. Philadelphia, 1828.

Auld, (J. B.) The First Good and the First Fair. 8°, pp. 16. New York, 1835.

Aunt Carrie's Rhymes for Children. (Anon.) 12°, pp. 90. Boston and Cambridge, 1855.

Austin, (A. W.) The Woman and the Queen. A Ballad, etc. 12°, pp. viii, 98. Cambridge, 1875.

Austin, (J. J.) The Golden Age to Come. A Sacred Drama. 12°, pp. 124. Boston, 1854.

Autodicus, (*pseud.*) The Critique of the Vision of Rubetta. A Dramatic Sketch. 8°, pp. 32. Philadelphia, 1838.

Avery, (D.) A Poetical Address on Temperance. 12°, pp. 47. Pawtucket, 1855.

Avery, (Mrs. R. J.) Wood Notes Wild. 16°, pp. iv, 202. Nashville, 1843.

Ayres, (J. A.) The Legends of Montauk. With an Historical Index. 8°, pp. 127. New York, 1849.

> The Legends and the Index are full of information for all who desire to acquaint themselves with the history of Neapeague, the Indian name of the section of which they treat.

BABCOCK, (D. H.)  Scenes of the Past.  18°, pp. 72.  Boston, 1844.

BABCOCK, (J. M. L.)  The Spirit of Peace.  A Poem delivered before
the Mechanics Library Association, Boston, February 22, 1851.
16°, pp. 15.  Boston, 1851.

BABCOCK, (J. S.)

James Stanton Babcock was born in South Coventry, Conn., November 7, 1815, graduated at Yale in 1840, taught in Tuscaloosa, Ala., two and a half years, returned to his
northern home, having formed a plan for extended study, which he was prevented from
carrying out by a sickness which terminated fatally April 13, 1847.  As a linguist, Mr. Babcock's attainments were remarkable, and, had he lived, he would have attained a high
rank among the scholars of his country.

— Visions and Voices.  12°, pp. vi, 240.  Hartford, 1849.

BACON, (E.)  Aegri Somnia : Recreations of a Sick Room.  12°, pp.
xii, 107.  New York, 1843.

The writer says : "The following articles, as their title purports, literally the ' Recreations of a sick room,' long protracted, and the creations of much weakness and infirmity
have appeared, as they were written, in a daily and weekly newspaper under somewhat
unfavorable circumstances as to form and correctness."

— Vacant Hours.  12°, pp. 61.  Utica, 1845.

BACON, (W. T.)

William Thompson Bacon was born at Woodbury, Conn., August 24, 1814, graduated
at Yale in 1837, and in 1842 was settled as a Congregational minister in Trumbull, Conn.,
"As a poet," Everest says "his lighter poems possess much simplicity and grace.  He
has a fine perception of natural beauty, and his graver productions are pervaded by a
current of deeply reflective moral and religious sentiment."

— Poems.  12°, pp. 134.  Boston, 1839.
— Poems.  Lg. 8°, pp. 214.  New Haven, 1839.
— Same.  3d Edition.  16°, pp. xvii, 214.  Boston, 1840.

This edition of Mr. Bacon's poems has, in the Introduction, an essay on the proper
office of the poet.

— Same.  Poems.  12°, pp. x, 275.  Cambridge, 1848.

BAGS, (J. D.)  The Fugitive : An Epic Poem in one canto.  By P. Virgilius Maro.  Translated by John Dryden Bags.  With Notes and
Explanations.  12°, pp. vii, 44.

This poem professes to have been "communicated" from the spirit of Virgil, and is a
satire on the events connected with the rendition of the fugitive slave, Anthony Burns.

BAILEY, (E.)

Ebenezer Bailey was born in Newbury, Mass., and graduated at Yale in 1817.  "The
Triumphs of Liberty" was a prize ode, recited at the Boston Theatre in 1825.  Kettell

BAILEY, (E.) — *Continued.*

> says: "It is a chaste and spirited production, superior to anything of the kind which our national anniversaries have called forth." Mr. B. was, for several years, Principal of a Ladies' High School in Boston. He died in 1839.

— Triumphs of Liberty.  8°, pp. 8.  Boston, 1825.

BAILEY, (P. J.)  The Angel World, etc.  16°, pp. 114.  Boston, 1850.

BAILEY, (URANIA LOCKE.)

> Urania Locke Stoughton was born at Gill, Franklin county, Mass., November 30, 1820, married B. D. Bailey, of Providence, R. I., June 10, 1847. She wrote much for magazines, etc. Several of her shorter poems have acquired a wide reputation. Among these is one beginning, "The Master has come over Jordan," which was set to music at the request of Rev. Dr. Goodell, of Constantinople, and has been introduced into tune books in this and other countries. Mrs. B. died March 25, 1882.

— Star-Flowers.  12°, pp. 152.  New York, 1882.

BAKER, (D. P.)  Choice Selections from Wah-ha-hah.  A Tale of Indian Life.  16°, pp. 24.  Jackson, Mich., 1859.

BAKER, (G. A., JR.)  Point-Lace and Diamonds.  Sq. 16°, pp. 153.  New York, 1875.

BAKER, (G. M.)  Amateur Dramas for Parlor Theatricals, etc.  16°, pp. iv, 254.  Boston, 1867.

— Our Twelve Months' Cruise.  A Valedictory delivered before the Mercantile Library Association, Members' Course, May, 1866.  4°, pp. 16.  Boston, 1866.

> This is one of fifty copies printed for private disposition, and is an elegant little quarto of sixteen pages.

— Valedictory Poem.  Delivered before the "Members' Course" of the Mercantile Library Association, Wednesday, April 15, 1865.  Sm. 4°, pp. 12.  Boston, 1865.

BAKER, (S.)  Election to Eternal Life, etc.  12°, pp. 24.  Millbury, Mass., 1833.

BALDWIN, (J. D.)

> John Dennison Baldwin was born at North Stonington, Conn., September 28, 1809. He pursued his studies in part at Yale, but did not graduate. The college in 1839 conferred on him the honorary degree of A. M. He read law and divinity, and in 1834 became a Congregationalist minister. Subsequently he was a journalist in Hartford, Boston and Worcester. He was a member of Congress from Massachusetts from 1864 to 1870. His death occurred at Worcester, July 7, 1883.

— The Story of Raymond Hill and other Poems.  12°, pp. vi, 124.  Boston, 1847.

BALDWYN, (AUGUSTA.) Poems. 16°, pp. vi, 163. Montreal, 1859.

BALL, (B. W.) Elfin Land: and other Poems. 16°, pp. viii, 150. Boston, 1851.

BALL, THE FANCY. (Anon.) Said to be W. L. Learned, Esq. 8°, pp. 28. Albany, 1846.

BALL, THE OFFICERS', ETC. (Anon.) 12°, pp. 12. Ballstown, no date; probably 1765.

BALL, THE SNOBLACK; OR, PILL GARLIC AND HIS FRIENDS. (By "The Spectator.") 8°, pp. 72. New York, 1865.

BALLAD, THE BRIDAL. ("Quilp," *pseud.*) pp. 78. Norfolk, 1846.

> Cushing, in his "Dictionary of Literary Disguises," gives "Quilp, Jr.," William H. Halstead. Little Pieces: Verse and Prose. Norfolk, Va., 1868.

BALLADS. A small Bound Volume. 8°. No place, no date.

— The Book of. Edited by Gaultier, and Illustrated by Doyle, Leech and Crowquill. Sm. 12°, pp. 256. Edinburgh and London, 1857.

— Christian. (Anon.) 12°, pp. 138. New York, 1840.

— The Illustrated Book of, etc. Edited by R. W. Griswold. 4°, pp. 164. Philadelphia, 1844. An elegant copy.

BALLOU, (M. M.)

> Maturin M. Ballou was born in Boston in 1822, and was editor and proprietor of "Ballou's Pictorial" and "The Flag of our Union." He has published "History of Cuba," etc.

— Miralda, or The Justice of Tacon. A Drama. 12°, pp. 29. Boston, 1858.

BANAGAN, (I.) Avenia: A Tragical Poem on the Oppression of the Human Species, etc. 18°, pp. x, 358. Philadelphia, 1805.

BANCROFT, (G.)

> George Bancroft was born in Worcester, Mass., October 3, 1800, graduated at Harvard College in 1817, studied in Germany, and took the degree of Ph. D. at Göttingen in 1820, returned to the United States in 1822, and has devoted the most of his life to literary pursuits, especially to the writing of "The History of the United States." At this date (1886) he resides in Washington.

— Poems. 12°, pp. 77. Cambridge, 1823.

> This copy of Mr. Bancroft's early poems in the "Harris Collection" is in perfect condition, the once soiled leaves having been cleansed, so far as was possible, and the margin of the dedication leaf, which was removed in some way, replaced. The volume is bound

BANCROFT, (G.) — *Continued.*

in half red morocco, the upper edges of the paper gilded, and the leaves untrimmed. The first poem, "Expectation," portrays the feelings of the tourist as he leaves his home for foreign travel, and is dated Paris, June, 1821. Then follow six poems descriptive of scenes and experiences in Switzerland in September and October, 1821. Next in order are twelve poems written in Italy in 1822. The volume concludes with " Pictures of Rome," written at Worcester, Mass., July, 1823.

Duycklnck says: " A thin volume of his poems witnesses to his poetical enthusiasm for the arts and nature, as he traversed the ruins of Italy and the sublime scenery of Switzerland."

BANKS IN DANGER, OR NEW YORK IN AN UPROAR FROM A GREENWICH RACE. 18°, pp. 13. New York, 1811.

Banks was the name of a favorite horse belonging to " a gentleman from famed Bordeaux," residing in Greenwich, N. Y. The poem is somewhat after the style of " John Gilpin."

BANNER, THE STAR SPANGLED. Darley's Illustrations. 4°, pp. 4. New York, 1861.

BANNISTER, (N. H.) Putnam, the Iron Son of '76. 12°, pp. 30. Boston, no date.

BANQUET, THE RUSSIAN. A Drama. (By Hector Snapdragon, *pseud.*) 16°, pp. 12. Boston, about 1813.

BARBER, (J. W.) Bunyan's Pilgrim's Progress. Exhibited in a Metamorphosis, etc. 18°, pp. 15. Hartford, 1821.

BARD, THE AMERICAN. No. 1. Ossian's Poem of " Colna-Dona," Heredia's " The Land of the Aztecs," and a Translation from a Genoese Improvisatore, " The Priests of California." 12°, pp. 16. New York, 1860.

BARELS, (ANNA.) OP HET ZALIC AFSTERVEN, etc. Sq. 8°, pp. 5. Steenwyk, no date.

This is a Dutch poem, at one time the property of Müller, of Amsterdam, the volume having been in his " Librairie Ancienne."

BARKER, (J. N.)

James Nelson Barker, an American dramatic writer, was born in Philadelphia in 1784, and died in 1858.

— How to Try a Lover. 16°, pp. 67. New York, 1817.

— Marmion. A Drama. 18°, pp. vii, 79. New York, 1816.

— Superstition. A Tragedy. 12°, pp. 68. Philadelphia, no date.

— Tears and Smiles. A Comedy. 18°, pp. 85. Philadelphia, 1808.

— The Indian Princess. 18°, pp. 74. Philadelphia, 1808.

BARHYDT, (D. P.) Life. 18°, pp. 89. New York. 1851.

BARLOW, (J.)

> James, not Joel, Barlow was the author of the poem, the title of which is given below. A note written with ink on page fourth says: "This is a rather shameful satire on poor Packenham, who had in some way affronted the poet and conceited author, Mr. Barlow, a sort of English Grammar School-master." It professes to have been written by Thomas Moore, whose name appears on the title-page as its author. There is, however, every reason to believe that the real writer was Barlow.

— The Peacock, the Baboon, and the Moneyspinners: a newly discovered Poem by Thomas Moore, Esq. 18°, pp. 18. Mexico, 1841.

BARLOW, (J.)

> Joel Barlow, LL. D., was born at Reading, Fairfield county, Conn., in 1755, studied at Dartmouth College for a part of the course, and graduated at Yale College in 1778. He served for a time as Chaplain in the American army in the war of the Revolution. While occupying this position he wrote "The Vision of Columbia," which was the basis of his great national epic, "The Columbiad." After the war he studied law, and in 1785 was admitted to the bar. In 1788 he went to Europe, and was a deeply interested observer of the events connected with the French Revolution. In 1792 he published "The Conspiracy of Kings," suggested by the coalition of the European Sovereigns against Republican France. While residing in Chamberry, France, in the winter of 1793-94, he wrote his popular poem, "Hasty Pudding." In 1795 he was appointed Consul to Algiers. In 1797 he returned to Paris, where he embarked in commercial speculations, and became wealthy. He continued his residence in Paris until 1805, when he returned to the United States and took up his residence in Washington, where he built an elegant mansion, to which he gave the name of "Kalorama." In 1808 he published his "Columbiad." In 1811 he was appointed Minister to France, where, in the discharge of his official duties, he died at Zarnowitch, near Cracow, December 22, 1812.

— An Elegy on the late Hon. Titus Homer, Esq. 8°. pp. 15. Hartford, 1780.

— Poem spoken at Yale Commencement, September 12, 1781. 12°, pp. 16. Hartford, no date.

— Hasty Pudding. 8°, pp. 14. Stockbridge, Mass., 1797.

> Other editions in the "Collection" are New Haven, 1796; Salem, 1799; New York, 12°, no date; Brooklyn, 1833; New York, 1847, and New York, 1856.

— Reply to H. Gregoire. (Not a poem.) 8°, pp. 14. Washington, 1809.

— The Columbiad. 8°, pp. xiv, 426. London, 1809.

— Same. 2 vols. 12°, pp. 258, 218. Philadelphia, 1809.

— Same. In one vol. 8°, pp. xv, 448. Washington, 1825.

— The Conspiracy of Kings. 4°, pp. 20, London, 1792.

— Same. 4°, pp. 20. London, 1792.

— Same. 8°, pp. 30. Newburyport, Mass., 1794.

— The Vision of Columbus. 8°, pp. xx, 244. Hartford, 1787.

C

BARLOW, (J.) — *Continued.*
— The Vision of Columbus. 2d Edition. 12°, pp. 258. Hartford, 1787.
— Same. 8°. Paris, 1793.
— Same. 5th Edition. 8°. London, 1794.
— Same. 18°. Baltimore, 1814.
— Same. 18°. Baltimore, 1816.
— Same. 16°. Centreville, Ind., 1824.

BARLOW, (W. S.) The Voice of Prayer. 8°, pp. 30. New York, 1871.

BARNES, (CHARLOTTE M. S.) Plays, Prose and Poetry. 16°, pp. 489. Philadelphia, 1848.

BARN YARD RHYMES : Showing what opinions the Turkey, the Cock, the Goose and the Duck entertain of Allopathia, Homopathia, Electro-Galvanism and the Animalcule Doctrines. 8°, pp. 80. New York, 1838.

BARNES, (W.) Poems in the Dorset Dialect. 16°, pp. viii, 207. Boston, 1864.

BARNETT, (M.) Yankee Peddler ; or, Old Times in Virginia. A Farce. 12°, pp. 16. New York, no date.

BARNITZ, (A. T. S.)
Albert Trovillo Siders Barnitz was born in Bedford county, Pa., March 10, 1833, and when an infant removed to Crawford county, Ohio. He studied law in Cleveland, and was a teacher of elocution in that city.

— The Mystic Delvings. 12°, pp. 288. Cincinnati, 1857.

BARRETT, (J. D.) Concord : A Poem delivered before the Lyceum, Concord, Mass., January 22, 1851. 12°, pp. 32. Boston, 1851.

BARRETT, (P.) Flowers by the Way-Side. A Book for Children and Youth. 16°, pp. xi, 144. Richmond, 1856.

BARRETT, (S. A.) Maintonomah, etc. 12°. New York, 1849.

BARRY, (G.) Poems on Several Occasions. 18°, pp. 101. Baltimore, 1807.
The author, Garrett Barry, Esq., says in the advertisement in this volume: "Many of the following poems were written before the author attained his sixteenth year."

BARRY, (S.) The Dutchman's Ghost ; or, All Right. A Farce. 12°, pp. 16. New York, no date.

— The Persecuted Dutchman ; or, The Original John Schmidt. A Farce. 12°, pp. 15. New York, no date.

BARTLETT, (E.)

Elisha Bartlett was born in Smithfield, R I., in 1805, and was graduated from the
Medical Department in Brown University in 1826, and practiced in Lowell, Mass.  He was
a professor in the following institutions:  Dartmouth College, 1839; Transylvania University, Ky., 1841; University of Maryland, 1844; a second time at Transylvania, 1846; Louisville, 1849; University of New York, 1850, and in the New York College of Physicians and
Surgeons in 1851, to his death, July 19, 1855.

— Simple Settings, in Verse, for Six Portraits and Pictures.   From
    Mr. Dickens' Gallery.   16°, pp. 80.   Boston, 1855.

BARTLETT, (J.)

Joseph Bartlett, born in 1763, graduated at Harvard in 1782, published an edition of
his poems in 1823, dedicated to John Quincy Adams, in which may be found " Aphorisms
on Men, Manners, Principles and Things."  He died in 1827.

— A Poem, etc.   8°, pp. 20.   Delivered in Boston, July 3, 1823.
    Boston, 1823.                                                       •
— Aphorisms on Men, Manners, Principles and Things, etc.   12°, pp.
    x, 148.   Boston, 1823.

BARTLETT, (S. R.)   Concord Fight.   12°, pp. 33.   Boston, 1860.

BARTLEY, (J. A.)

James Avis Bartley, of Orange county, Va., dedicates this volume to his father.  He
addresses a Prefatory Letter to the public, in which he says: " These poems were written
with pleasure; if they be read with pleasure, I shall be requited amply."  In a somewhat
bellicose spirit he remarks in this letter: " If critics censure me unjustly or intemper-
ately, I will fight them."

— Lays of Ancient Virginia, etc.   12°, pp. 203.   Richmond, 1855.

BARTON, (A.)   The Disappointment; or, The Force of Credulity.   16°,
    pp. iv, 95.   Philadelphia, 1796.

BARTRUM, (J. P.)   The Psalms newly Paraphrased.   18°, pp. 196.
    Boston, 1833.

BARRYMORE, (W.)   The Snow Storm; or, Lowina of Tobolshow.   A
    Melo-Dramatick Romance.   16°, pp. 36.   Baltimore, 1833.

BATCHELDER, (E.)

Eugene Batchelder was born in New Ipswich, N. H., and graduated at the Harvard
Law School in 1845.  He resided in Cambridge, Mass., and died in Dover, N. H.

— A Romance of the Fashionable World.   16°, pp. 180.   Boston,
    1857.
— Border Adventures; or, The Romantic Incidents of a New England
    Town, etc.   12°, pp. 48.   Boston, 1851.
— Brother Jonathan's Welcome to Kossuth.   8°, pp. 27.   Boston, 1852.

BATCHELDER, (S., JR.)  Poetry of the Bells.  A Collection of Poems by
Mrs. Hemans, A. C. Coxe, J. R. Lowell, Charles Lamb, H. W.
Longfellow, O. W. Holmes, A. Tennyson, etc.  12°, pp. 72.  Bos-
ton, 1858.

BATEMAN, (MRS. SIDNEY F.)  Self: An Original Comedy.  12°, pp. 46.
New York, 1856.

BATES, (D.)

David Bates was born at Indian Hill, Hamilton county, Ohio, March 0, 1809.  His early
youth was spent on a farm.  He then engaged in mercantile pursuits, and finally took up
his residence in Philadelphia, becoming a member of a business firm in that city.  " He
wrote for most of the prominent magazines and periodicals, and enjoyed the confidence
and appreciation of men of letters."  He died January 25, 1870.

— Poetical Works.  Edited by his son, Stockton Bates.  16°, pp. xii,
276.  Philadelphia, 1870.

— The Eolian.  12°, pp. xi, 210.  Philadelphia. 1849.

BATES, (S.)  Dream Life, etc.  16°, pp. 120.  Philadelphia, 1872.

— Party and its Experiments.  Read before the Harrison Democrats of
East Boston, September 8, 1840.  12°, pp. 24.  Boston, 1840.

BATTERSHALL, (W. W.)  Yale Valedictory Poem, June 22, 1864.  8°,
pp. 16.  New Haven, 1864.

BATTERSON, (H. G., D. D.)  Christmas Carols.  18°, pp. 72.  Philadelphia, 1877.

BATTLE OF AUGHRIM; OR, THE FALL OF MONSIEUR ST. RUTH.  (Anon.)
16°, pp. 47.  Boston, 1848.

BATTLES OF JOSHUA, THE.  (Anon.)  12°, pp. 12.  Philadelphia, 1843.

BAXTER, (LYDIA.)  Gems by the Wayside; or, Religious and Domestic
Poems.  12°, pp. xii, 283.  New York, 1855.

BAXTER, (W.)  Poems.  12°, pp. iv, 244.  Cambridge, 1852.

BAY PSALM BOOK.  The Whole Booke of Psalmes, Faithfully Translated
into English Metre.  Whereunto is prefixed a discourse declaring
not only the lawfullness, but also the necessity of the heavenly Ordi-
nance of Singing Scripture Psalmes in the Churches of God.

BAY PSALM BOOK — *Continued.*

## Coll. III.

*Let the Word of God dwell plenteously in you, in all wisdome, teaching and exhorting one another in Psalms, Himnes and Spirituall Songs, singing to the Lord with grace in your hearts.*

## Iames V.

*If any be afflicted, let him pray. And if any be merry, let him sing psalms.*

## Imprinted 1640.

The above is the original title of the Bay Psalm Book. The title of the reprint is as follows: A Literal Reprint of the Bay Psalm Book, being the earliest New England Version of the Psalms, and the First Book Printed in America. Fifty copies for subscribers. 8°, not paged. Cambridge: Printed for Charles B. Richardson, New York, 1862.

This reprint, of which there are two copies in "The Harris Collection," was made at the Riverside Press, Cambridge, under the supervision of Dr. Nathaniel B. Shurtleff, and is an exact copy, in the minutest particular, of the original printed in 1640. One copy was printed on parchment; five on India paper; fifteen on thick paper (of which the Public Library of Boston has one), and fifty on common paper. Of the two copies in "The Harris Collection," one is on thick paper, and the other on common paper.

The Bay Psalm Book, being the first book published in the United States, has, for bibliophiles, a peculiar interest. It was the joint production of the Rev. Richard Mather, of Dorchester, the Rev. Thomas Weld, and the Rev. John Eliot, "persons eminently qualified for the task, as being familiar with the Hebrew and Greek languages." "If the verses are not always so smooth and elegant as some may desire or expect," say the translators, "let them consider that God's Altar needs not our pollishings; for wee have respected rather a plaine translation, than to smooth our verses with the sweetness of any paraphrase; and we have attended conscience rather than elegance, fidelity rather than poetry, in translating the hebrew words into english language."

Prof. Moses Coit Tyler, in his History of American Literature, Vol. I, p. 276, says: "The verses, indeed, seem to have been hammered out on an anvil, by blows from a blacksmith's sledge. Everywhere in the book is manifest the agony it cost the writer, to find two words that would rhyme more or less; and so often as this arduous feat is achieved, the poetic athlete appears to pause awhile from sheer exhaustion, panting heavily for breath."

The following is a specimen taken from the 29th Psalm:

"The mighty voyce of Iehovah  
upon the water is  
the God of glory thundereth  
God on great waters is,  
Iehovah's voyce is powerfull  
Gods voyce is glorious  

Gods voyce breaks Cedars: yea God breaks  
Cedars of Lebanus  
He makes them like a calfe to skip  
*the mountaine* Lebanon,  
and like to a young Vnicorne  
*the hill* of Syrion."

The Hon. John R. Bartlett says: "The original edition of the Bay Psalm Book was the first book printed in the British American Colonies. It is of excessive rarity. But

**BAY PSALM BOOK.** — *Continued.*

nine copies only are known to be extant, distributed as follows: 1. Harvard University, Cambridge, Mass. (imperfect). 2 and 3. The Boston Public Library. 4. Mrs. George Livermore, Cambridge, Mass. 5. John Carter Brown Library, Providence, R. I. 6. The American Antiquarian Society, Worcester, Mass. (imperfect). 7. Cornelius Vanderbilt, New York. 8. The Bodleian Library, Oxford. 9. The Lenox Library, New York. So that there are really but seven perfect copies of the book."

The John Carter Brown copy belonged originally to the Rev. Richard Mather, one of its authors (whose well known autograph it contains in many places), declaring it to be " His Booke." It subsequently came into the hands of the Rev. Thomas Prince, the friend and disciple of Cotton Mather, Richard's grandson. By Prince it was made a part of his famous New England Library, as it appears by his book-plate, on the reverse of the title-page. From the Prince Library it passed by way of exchange into the hands of Dr. Shurtleff, by whose heirs it was sold at auction in Boston, October 12, 1876, and purchased by the late C. Fiske Harris, of Providence, for $1.025. Upon the decease of Mr. Harris, in October, 1881, his fine library was dispersed, and the Bay Psalm Book purchased by its present owner. A copy was purchased by Cornelius Vanderbilt, at the "Brinley sale," for $1,200. (See Tyler's Hist. Am. Lit., vol. 1, pp. 274–77.)

**BEACH, (L.)** Jonathan Postfree; or, The Honest Yankee. A Musical Farce. 18°, pp. 38. New York, 1809.

**BEACH, (S. B.)**

"The hint for the fable of the following poem," says the author, " was furnished by the numerous ruins which yet remain visible in the interior of North America, and particularly in the vicinity of the Ohio and the Mississippi; ruins which demonstrate that, long anterior to the first voyage of Columbus, the section of country which I have designated was inhabited by a nation more civilized than the wandering tribes in whose possession it was found by the English and French." The poem is founded on the supposition that in the ninth century a Norwegian Chief colonized a section of country near the junction of the Ohio and the Mississippi rivers.

— Escalala: An American Tale. 12°, pp. vi, 109. Utica, 1824.

**BEASLEY, (F. W.)**

Frederic Williamson Beasley, D. D., was born in 1807 at Albany, N. Y., graduated at the University of Pennsylvania in 1827, was ordained a Protestant Episcopal minister, and settled in Eddington, Pa. Under the signature of Caspar Almore he wrote " Papers from Overlook House." He died in Philadelphia county in 1878.

— Henry Venola, the Duellist. 12°, pp. viii, 64. Philadelphia, 1841.

**BEAUTIFUL WORLD, THE.** A Magazine, etc. Vol. IV. No 2. 8°, pp. 24. Boston, 1874.

**BEECHER.** Ye Tilt on; or, Ye Muddle of Ye Mutual Friends. A Burlesque in Verse. 12°, pp. 24. New York, no date.

**BEERS, (ETHEL LYNN.)** All Quiet Along the Potomac, etc. 12°, pp. 352. Philadelphia, 1879.

BEHOLD THE MOTHER, ETC. (By a Clergyman of Maryland. Anon.)
2d Edition. 24°, pp. 91. Baltimore, 1864.

BELDAZZLE'S BACHELOR "STUDIES." (Anon.) Sq. 16°, pp. 71. New
York, 1874.

BELISLE, (D. W.) The Parterre. A Collection of Flowers culled by
the Wayside. 18°, pp. 128. Philadelphia, 1849.

BELKNAP, (J., D. D.)
Jeremy Belknap was born in Boston, June 4, 1744, graduated at Harvard in 1762, was
pastor of a Congregational church in Dover, N. H., 1767-77, and in Boston till his death in
1797.

— Polyanthos. 5 vols. 16°, pp. 287, 283, 285, 288, 285. Boston,
1806.
— Sacred Poetry. 18°, pp. 262. Boston, 1804.
— Same. 5th Edition. Boston, 1808.
— Same. Boston, 1808.
— Same. Boston, 1817.
— Same. Boston, 1820.

BELL, (MRS. EMMA M.) Poems. 16°, pp. viii, 197. Philadelphia,
1872.

BELL, (ROSALIE.) Lilies and Violets; or, Thoughts in Prose and Verse
on the True Graces of Maidenhood. 12°, pp. vii, 442. New
York, Boston and Cincinnati, 1855.

BELL, SCHILLER'S SONG OF. Translated by W. H. Furness, and other
German Poems by F. H. Hedge. With sixteen illustrations.
12°, no paging. Philadelphia, 1851.

BENEDICT, (A.) Poem. Yale College, July 1, 1821. 8°, pp. 15. New
Haven, 1821.

BENEDICT, (D.)
David Benedict was born at Norwalk, Conn., October 10, 1779, graduated at Brown
University in 1806, and for many years was a minister in the Baptist denomination, and
was known as "The Baptist Historian." At the advanced age of 95 he published a "History of the Donatists." He died in 1874.

— Poem. 8°, pp. 19. Boston, 1807.

BENEDICT, (F. L.)
Mrs. Ann S. Stephens wrote the preface to this volume. She says that when she was
co-editor of "Peterson's Ladies' National Magazine," she became the recipient of several

BENEDICT, F. L.—*Continued.*

poems and stories sent anonymously. The author was discovered to be a lad not over sixteen years of age residing in the Wyoming Valley. It was ascertained that subsequently he went abroad. On his return he gathered up his poems, written, many of them, in the Old World, and they are published in this volume.

— The Shadow Worshiper, etc. 12°, pp. viii, 197. New York, 1857.

BENJAMIN, (P.)

Park Benjamin was born at Demarara, in British Guiana, came to the United States in early life, studied for a time at Harvard, graduated at Washington, now Trinity, College, Hartford, in 1829; studied law, but preferred the profession of letters; was a journalist in New York; was associated for a time with C. F. Hoffmann, then with Horace Greeley in the editorship of *The New Yorker*, and wrote much for various periodicals. He died in 1864.

— Infatuation. Delivered before the Boston Mercantile Association, October 9, 1844. 8°, pp. 31. Boston, 1844.

BENJAMIN, (S. G . W.)

Samuel Green Wheeler Benjamin was born in Greece in 1840. He became early distinguished as an artist. He wrote, in addition to the works whose titles are here given, "The Atlantic Islands," "Contemporary Art in Europe," "Art in America," etc. In 1884 he received an appointment as United States Minister to Persia.

— Constantipole. The Isle of Pearls, etc. 16°, pp. 96. Boston, 1860.

— Ode on the Death of Abraham Lincoln. 12°, pp. 15. Boston, 1865 .

BENNETT, (E.) The Brigand. 16°, pp. 36. New York, 1842.

BENNETT, (EMILY F. B.) Poems. 8°, pp. 262. New York, 1865.
— Songs of the Rivers. 12°, pp. 262. New York, 1865.

BENNISON, (MRS. D. M.) Poems. 18°, pp. iv, 144. Boston, 1847.

BENSON, (M.) Love and Money; or, The Fair Caledonian. A Farce in Two Acts. 18°, pp. 18. New York, 1813.

BENSON, (C.) Anacreontics. Sq. 12°, pp. 75. New York, 1872.

BENSON, (E.) Sketch of Gaspara Stampa, with selections from her Sonnets. Translated by George Fleming. 16°, pp. 84. Boston, 1881.

Gaspara Stampa, called "The Sappho of Venice," was an Italian poetess born at Padua about 1524. She wrote under the assumed name of Anasilla, from Anasso, the ancient name of the Piave. A victim of unrequited love she died, as is supposed, by her own hands, at Venice in 1554.

BERGH, (H.) "Married Off." (A Newport Sketch. With Comic Illustrations.) 12°, pp. 54. New York, 1862.

Bernard, (B.) The Balance of Comfort. 12°, pp. 32. London, no date.

Bernard, (W. B.) Plays. 16°, viz. : His Last Legs, pp. 41. The Passing Cloud, pp. 59. The Irish Attorney, pp. 38. The Nervous Man, pp. 45. The Evil Genius, pp. 48. The Middy Ashore, pp. 21. The Mummy, pp. 24. Platonic Attachments, pp. 24. St. Mary's Eve, pp. 39. New York, Boston and London, no date.

Berry, (Mrs. Stephen.) The Snow Flakes. 16°, pp. 23. Portland, 1868.

Best, (L.) The Planet; A Song of a Distant World. 16°, pp. 161. Cambridge, 1869.

Bethune, (G. W.)

George W. Bethune, D. D., was born in the city of New York in 1805, graduated at Dickinson College in 1822, and at the Princeton Theological Seminary in 1825, and was the minister of churches in Rhinebeck, N. Y., Utica, N. Y., Philadelphia and Brooklyn. He died in Florence, Italy, April 28, 1862. " Dr. B. was distinguished for his fine taste, his varied culture, and his love of nature."

— Lays of Love and Faith. Lg. 8°, pp. 184. Philadelphia, 1847.

Bettner, (G., M. D.) Harmoniae Cælestes ; or, Christian Melodies. 12°, pp. viii, 147. New York, 1833.

A presentation copy to Mrs. Sigourney.

Better Sort, The ; or, The Girl of Spirit. A Farce. 8°, pp. iv, 80. Boston, 1789.

Beveridge, (J.)

John Beveridge was born in Scotland, and, for a time, was a schoolmaster in Edinburgh. He removed to New England in 1752, where he resided five years. In 1758 he was appointed Professor of Languages in the College and Academy of Philadelphia.

— Epistolae Familiares et alia Quaedam Miscellanea. Familiar Epistles, and other Miscellaneous Pieces. Wrote originally in Latin Verse. To which are added several Translations into English Verse, by different hands, etc. 12°, pp. xi, 88. Philadelphia, 1765. A rare copy, elegantly bound.

Biddle, (H. P.)

Horace P. Biddle was born in Fairfield county, Ohio, about the year 1818, received a good education, and was admitted to the bar in April, 1839. He settled in Logansport, Ind., in October of the same year, which became his permanent residence. He contributed

7

BIDDLE, (H. P.) — *Continued.*

to several periodicals articles in prose and poetry. A second edition of his "A Few Poems" was highly commended by Washington Irving. For six years, 1846–52, he was Presiding Judge of the Eighth Judicial Circuit Court, Ohio, and was chosen to fill other offices of trust and honor. His residence is still in Logansport.

— A Few Poems.  12°, pp. 240.  Cincinnati, 1858.
— Same.  16°, pp. xvi, 341.  New York, 1868.

BIDDLE, (N.)

Nicholas Biddle was born in Philadelphia in 1786, graduated at Princeton College in 1801, and, from 1823 to 1839, was President of the United States Bank. His literary taste was of a most marked character for excellence. "His works," as Allibone remarks, "evince great vigor of mind, and classical taste of no ordinary character." He died in 1844.

— Ode to Bogle.  4°, pp. 8.  Philadelphia.  Privately printed.

BIGELOW, (A.)  The Sabbath.  12°, pp. vi, 56.  Worcester, 1842.

BIGELOW, (J., M. D.)

Jacob Bigelow was born at Sudbury, Mass., in 1787, graduated at Harvard in 1806, received the degree of M. D. from the Pennsylvania Medical School in 1810, for many years was physician to the Massachusetts General Hospital, was Rumford Professor of Materia Medica, etc., in Harvard. As the author of several medical and botanical works, Dr. B. acquired great reputation. He had much to do in the founding of Mt. Auburn Cemetery, and displayed much taste in laying out the grounds, designing the gateway, etc. He was also the author of several poems, some of them of a humorous character. His death occurred January 10, 1879, at the great age of 92 years.

— Eolopesis.  American Rejected Addresses.  12°, pp. 240.  New York, 1855.
— Phi Beta Kappa Poem, Harvard, August 29, 1811.  8°, pp. 15.  Boston, 1811.
— Same.  Salem, 1811.

BIGELOW, (MRS. MARION A.)  The Northern Harp, etc.  16°, pp. 400.  New York, 1853.

BIGLOW, (W.)

William Biglow was born in Natick, Mass., in 1773, graduated at Harvard in 1794, and subsequently became Principal of the Boston Latin School, which, for several years, he conducted with distinguished success. Among his pupils Edward Everett held a high rank. Several text-books were prepared by him for the use of his own scholars. He wrote much for the periodical press; also histories of the towns of Natick and Sherburne. His death occurred in 1844.

— Poem on Intemperance.  12°, pp. 12.  Cambridge, 1834.
— The Re-Recommencement.  8°, pp. 8.  Salem, 1812.

Biglow, (W.) — *Continued.*

— Sawney, Redivivus et Restauratus ; or, Miscellaneous Verses.   18°,
pp. 36.   Boston, 1816.

> Several of the poems were written when the author was in Harvard College.

Bigney, (M. F.)   The Forest Pilgrims, etc.   12°, pp. xii, 258.   New
Orleans and New York, 1867.

Bird, (M. B.)   The Victorious.   A Small Poem on the Assassination of
President Lincoln.   16°, pp. xvii, 57.   Kingston, Jamaica, 1866.

Bird of Birds ; or, A Musical Medley.   (Anon.)   18°, pp. 141.
New York, 1818.

Bishop, (J.)   A Poem on the Maine Law.   18°, pp. 15.   Pawtucket,
1853.

Bishop, (L.)   Teuchsa Grondie.   A Legendary Poem.   8°, pp. 446.
Albany, 1870.

Bishop, (Mrs. Harriet E.)   Minnesota.   Then and Now.   16°, pp. 97.
St. Paul, 1869.

Bishop, (P. P.)   Liberty's Ordeal.   16°, pp. 128.   New York, 1864.

> Mr. Bishop dedicates his poem to Hon. Jesse P. Bishop.   He says: "I have written
> this poem because of my belief that, in times like these, an American citizen should bring
> all his faculties to the support of his government."

Bissell, (C.)   Phi Beta Kappa Poem at Yale, July 24, 1861.   16°, pp.
18.   New Haven, 1861.

— The Panic, as seen from Parnassus, etc.   12°, pp. 286.   New York,
1860.

Blackamore in the Wood ; or, A Lamentable Ballad on the Tragical End of a Gallant Lord and Virtuous Lady, etc.
(Anon.)   16°, pp. 12.   New Haven, 1802.

Blackwell, (R.)   Original Acrostics on some of the States and Presi-
dents of the United States, etc.   8°, pp. 48.   Richmond, Va.,
1871.

— Original Acrostics on some of the Southern States, etc.   12°, pp. 169.
Baltimore, 1873.

Bladensburg Races, The.   Reprinted.   4°, pp. 16.   (75 copies.   No.
73.)   Written shortly after the capture of Washington City,
August 24, 1814.   No place, 1816.

BLADENSBURG RACES, THE. — *Continued.*
— Same. 32°, pp. 12. No place, 1816.

"The whole production," says Horatio King, "reveals an undercurrent of disrespect and bitterness, especially towards Madison, which leads us to the supposition that the verses were written soon after the battle. They were printed in 1816, but the author of them, so far as I am aware, is unknown." (For an interesting article on "The Battle of Bladensburg," see Magazine of American History, Vol. xliv, pp. 436–457.)

BLAIR, (F. O.) Poem delivered at Wilbraham, Mass., 1844. 12°, pp. 13. Boston, 1844.

BLAKE, (EMMA M.) Reliquæ. Privately printed for Daniel Blake. Sq. 16°, pp. viii, 140. Charleston, 1854.

BLAKE, (MISS LOUISA.) Poems. 12°, pp. 138. Boston, 1832.

BLAKE, NANCY, (*pseud.?*) Letters to a Western Cousin. 8°, pp. 36. New York, 1864.

BLAKE, SARAH; OR, THE LITTLE WAITRESS. (Anon.) 18°, pp. 8. No place, no date.

BLAKELY, (A.) The Sabbath. A Sermon in Poetry. 12°, pp. 24. Rochester, 1859.

BLAUVELT, (—.) Fashion's Analysis; or, The Winter in Town. A Satirical Poem. By Sir Anthony Avalanche. With Notes, Illustrations, etc. By Gregory Glacier, Gent. Part I. 16°, pp. 84. New York, 1807.

BLEECKER, (ANN ELIZA,) AND FAUGERRES, (MARGARETTA V.)

Mrs. Bleecker was the daughter of Brandt Schyler, of New York, born in 1752, married in 1769 John J. Bleecker, of New Rochelle, N. Y., and died in 1783. This volume is rare. W. L. Stone sought in vain to find it.

— Works. Prose and Poetry. 16°, pp. 375. New York, 1793.

BLISS, (H.) The Genius of Federalism. 12°, pp. 24. Pittsfield, 1813.

BLOCKHEADS, THE; OR, THE AFFRIGHTED OFFICERS. A Farce. (Anon.) 12°, pp. 19. Boston, 1776.
— 16°, pp. v, 43. New York. 1782.

BLOOD, (B.) The Colonnades. Lg. 8°, pp. 113. Author's Private Edition. Amsterdam, N. Y., 1868.

BLOUNT, (ANNIE R.) Poems. 12°, pp. vi, 276, Augusta, Ga., 1860.

BLUNT, (MRS. ELLEN K.) Bread to My Children. 12°, pp. 124. Philadelphia, 1856.

BOGART, (E.)

Elizabeth Bogart, daughter of Rev. David S. Bogart, was born in the city of New York. Under the instructions of her father she became an accomplished scholar. At an early age she began to write for the periodicals of the day, chiefly for the *New York Mirror*, under the signature of " Estelle." One of her short pieces of four stanzas, " He Came Too Late," has been especially admired.

— Driftings from the Stream of Life. A Collection of Fugitive Pieces. 12°, pp. 309. New York, 1866.

BOIES, (LAURA ANN.) Rural Rhymes. 8°, pp. 189. Saratoga, 1860.

BOKER, (G. H.)

George H. Boker was born in Philadelphia, October 6, 1823, graduated at Princeton in 1842, studied law, but did not practice, his tastes inclining him to literary pursuits. In 1871 he was appointed minister to Constantinople, and in 1874 to St. Petersburg. At the end of five years he returned to his native city.

— Anne Boleyn. A Tragedy. 12°, pp. viii, 225. Philadelphia, 1850.
— Calaynos. A Tragedy. 18°, pp. 64. London, no date. [1849]
— Hymn for the 87th Anniversary of American Independence. 8°, pp. 2. No place, no date.
— Plays and Poems. 2 vols., 16°. pp. 424, 450. Boston, 1856.
— Poems of the War. 12°, pp. vi, 201. Boston, 1864.
— The Podesta's Daughter, etc. 16°, pp. vi, 156. Philadelphia, 1852.

The same in manuscript presented by the author for the benefit of the " Central Sanitary Fair." 4°, pp. 28. Philadelphia, May 4, 1864.

BOKUM, (H.) Translations in Poetry and Prose, from German. 16°, pp. v, 146. Boston, 1836.

BOLLES, (J. R.) Solitude and Society, with other Poems. 2d Edition. 12°, pp. 118. New London, 1847.

BONAPARTE: WITH THE STORM AT SEA, ETC. (Anon.) 8°, pp. iv, 92. New York, 1820.

BOOK OF SONNETS, A. By a Virginian. (Anon.) 16°, pp. 31. Lynchburg, Va., 1867.

BOOK, THE FIRST OF. American Chronicles of the Times. 12°, not paged. Boston, 1775.

BOOTH, (J. B.)

Junius Brutus Booth was born in London in 1796, and was a popular tragedian. In 1821 he visited the United States, where he performed with great applause, being especially successful in the character of Richard III. He died on his return to the east from California in 1852.

Booth, (J. B.) — *Continued.*
— Ugolino.  18°, pp. 36.  Philadelphia, no date.
— Same.  12°, pp. 27.  Boston, no date.

Booth, (Mrs. M. H. C.)  Wayside Blossoms.  18°, pp. 106, vii.
 Philadelphia, 1865.

Borthwick, (J. W.)  The Harp of Canaan.  8°, pp. 269.  Montreal,
 1866.

Boston City: Measured by the Author of the "Phillipiad."  8°,
 pp. 60.  Boston, 1849.

Bosworth, (B.)  Signs of Apostacy.  18°, pp. 4.  No title-page.

Botsford, (E.)  Sambo and Toney.  16°, pp. 46.  Georgetown, S. C.,
 1808.

Botsford, (Mrs.)  Viola; or, The Heiress of St. Valverde.  18°, pp.
 96.  Louisville, Ky., 1820.

Botta, (V.)

 Vincenzo Botta was born at Cavalier Maggiore, in Piedmont, Italy, November 11, 1818.
 For several years he was a professor in the royal and national colleges in Turin, and in
 1849 became a member of the Sardinian Parliament.  Subsequently he came to the United
 States, and for several years has been professor of Italian in the University of New York.

— Dante as Philosopher, Patriot and Poet, etc.  8°, pp. x, 413.  New
 York, 1865.

Boucicault, (D.) and Seymour, (C.)  Wanted—A Widow.  A Farce.
 12°, pp. 16.  New York, no date.

Boulton, (T.)  The Voyage.  12°, pp. vi, 54.  Boston, 1773.

Bourne, (W. O.)  Poems of Hope and Action.  8°, pp. viii, 143.
 New York, 1850.
— The Republic.  School Edition.  12°, pp. 8.  New York, 1861.
 This poem was suggested by reading a line in the *London Times*, "The great republic
 is no more."

Bowen, (H. W.)  Verses.  12°, pp. 128.  Boston, 1884.

Bower of Spring, The, etc.  (Anon.)  16°, pp. x, 107.  Philadelphia,
 1817.

Bowles, (W. L.)  The Missionary.  18°, pp. 144.  Philadelphia, 1815.

Boyd, (W.) Woman. A Poem delivered at a Public Exhibition, Harvard, April 19, 1796. 12°, pp. 15. Boston, 1796.

Boyesen, (H. H.) Idyls of Norway, etc. Sq. 16°, pp. vii, 185. New York, 1882.

Boyle, (Esmeralda.) Thistle-Down. 12°, pp. viii, 159. Philadelphia, 1871.

Brackenridge, (H. H.)

Hugh Henry Brackenridge was born in Scotland in 1748, graduated at Princeton 1771, studied law and settled at Pittsburg, Pa., about 1782, and in 1799 was appointed Judge of the Supreme Court of the State. He died in 1816.

— Battle of Bunker Hill. A Dramatic Piece of Five Acts, in Heroic Measure. 12°, pp. 49. Philadelphia, 1776.

Bound in red morocco, and a perfect copy.

— Gazette Publications. 12°, pp. 348. Carlisle, 1806.

Brackett, (E. E.)

Edwin E. Brackett was born in Vassalborough, Me,, October 1, 1810. He is an artist by profession, and has obtained a wide reputation by his portrait-busts.

— Twilight Hours; or, Leisure Moments of an Artist. 16°, pp. iv, 95. Boston, 1845.

Brackett, (J. W.) The Ghost of Law; or, Anarchy and Despotism. Dartmouth Phi Beta Kappa, August 23, 1803. Sq. 12°, pp. 24. Hanover, 1803.

Bradbury, (W. B.) Oriola. Hymn and Tune Book, 30th Edition, ob. 24°, pp. 272. Cincinnati, etc., 1862.

Bradford, (J. S.) Autumn Winds, etc. 12°, pp. 115. New York, 1809.

Bradley, (W. H.)

William H. Bradley was a native of Rhode Island. He received from Brown University in 1824 the degree of M. D. He died in 1825.

— Giuseppino. 18°, pp. 68. Philadelphia, 1822.

Bradstreet, (Mrs. Anne.)

Anne, daughter of Gov. Thomas Dudley, was born in Northampton, England, in 1612, and at the early age of sixteen — 1628 — married Simon Bradstreet. Soon after marriage she left her home, with her husband, in company with certain wealthy Puritans, among whom were Gov. Winthrop, Sir Richard Saltonstall, her father, Thomas Dudley, and William Codington, reaching New England June 22, 1630. That year her husband was chosen

**BRADSTREET, (MRS. ANNE.) — *Continued.***

"Assistant," and was annually re-chosen for forty-eight years. Upon the overthrow of the infamous Andros, he was elected Governor of the "Bay State," having reached the great age of ninety years. After several removals, the Bradstreets, in 1644, settled near Andover, Mass., on what is still known as the Bradstreet farm, where they resided during the twenty-six remaining years of the life of the subject of this sketch, she dying in 1672, at the age of sixty. "The most of her poems," says Professor Tyler, "were produced between 1630 and 1642, that is, before she was thirty years old; and during these years she had neither leisure, nor elegant surroundings, nor freedom from anxious thoughts, nor even abounding health. Somehow, during her busy life-time, she contrived to put upon record compositions numerous enough to fill a royal octavo volume of four hundred pages,—compositions which entice and reward our reading of them two hundred years after she lived." (See Tyler's Hist. of Amer. Lit., vol. I, pp. 277-292.)

— The Tenth Muse Lately Sprung up in AMERICA ; or, Severall Poems compiled with great variety of VVit and Learning, full of delight, Wherein especially is contained a compleat discourse and description of The Four Elements, Constitutions, Ages of Man, Seasons of the Year. Together with an Exact Epitomie of the Four Monarchies, viz. : The Assyrian, Persian, Grecian, Roman. Also a Dialogue between Old England and New, concerning the late troubles. With divers other pleasant and serious Poems. By a Gentlewoman in those parts. Printed at London for Stephen Bowtell, at the signe of the Book in Popes Head Alley, 1650.

This London Edition, 16°, pp. 207, 1650, is believed to have been the First Edition of Mrs. Bradstreet's Poems. Griswold, and Allibone in the earlier editions of his "Dictionary of Authors," speak of an edition published in 1640, of which the London Edition was a reprint, but we find no proof that such an edition was published. Allibone has corrected the error in the later editions of his Dictionary. The copy in the Harris Collection is in perfect order and elegantly bound. It cost $125.

— Same. 2d Edition. Boston, 1678.
— Same. 3d Edition. Boston, 1758.
— Same. Edited by J. H. Ellis (entered by A. E. Cutter). 4°, pp. lxxvi, 434. Charlestown, 1867.

No. 76 of an edition of two hundred and fifty.

**BRAINARD, (J. G. C.)**

John G. C. Brainard was born at New London, Conn., October 21, 1796, graduated at Yale College in 1815, was admitted to the bar in 1819, in 1822 became editor of the *Connecticut Mirror*, and continued in this position till 1827. He died of consumption September 26, 1828.

— Occasional Pieces of Poetry. 12°, pp. 111. New York, 1825.
— Poems, with a Memoir. 16°, pp. lxiv, 191. Hartford, 1842.

Branagan, (T.)

Thomas Branagan was born in Dublin, Ireland, December 28, 1774. He exhibited a roving disposition from his early youth, and became a sailor. After visiting many foreign ports, he settled for a time on an estate in Antigua, W. I., where he became an overseer on two or three plantations in succession, remaining upwards of two years, and being occupied in various ways for two more years. The condition of the slaves awakened his sympathy, and led him to decide that he would never again become an overseer on a West India plantation. At the age of not far from thirty he came to the United States. He warmly espoused the anti-slavery cause, and with pen and voice did everything in his power to overthrow the system.

— Avenia; or, A Tragical Poem on the Oppression of the Human Species and Infringement on the Rights of Man. In six books. With Notes, Explanatory and Miscellaneous. Written in Imitation of Homer's Iliad. 12°, pp. 358. Philadelphia, 1805.

The design of this poem is to depict the horrors of the slave trade and of the system of domestic slavery. This volume has been put into elegant binding, with gilt-edged leaves, thoroughly cleaned, and its title-page made perfect, a piece torn from the bottom having been replaced.

— The Excellency of the Female Character, etc. 16°, pp. xii, 308. New York, 1807.

— The Excellency of Virtue, etc. 16°, pp. iv, 228. Philadelphia, 1808.

— The Penitential Tyrant; or, Slave-Trader Reformed: A Pathetic Poem, in Four Cantos. Second Edition, enlarged. 18°, pp. vii, 290. New York, 1807.

Branch, (W., Jr.) Life. A Poem in Three Books. 12°, pp. xii, 218. Richmond, 1819.

Brannan, (W. P.)

William Penn Brannan was born at Cincinnati, March 22, 1825, and spent his youth on his father's farm. He became a successful portrait and landscape painter, and was also a poetical contributor to several leading literary journals. His humorous sketches in prose were very widely circulated through the newspapers. For some time he practiced his art in Chicago. He died in 1865.

— Vagaries of Vandyke Brown. An Autobiography in Verse. 16°, pp. 230. Cincinnati, 1865.

Brashears, (N.) Poems on Miscellaneous Subjects. 12°, pp. 112. Washington, 1826.

— Same. 2d Edition. 1830.

— The Satirist, etc. 12°, pp. 59. Washington, 1832.

Breck, (C.) The Fox Chase. A Comedy. 18°, pp. 64. New York, 1808.

— The Trust. A Comedy. 18°, pp. 82. New York, 1808.

8

BRECK, (J.) West Point; or, A Tale of Treason. An Historical Drama. 16°, pp. 21. Baltimore, 1840.

BRECKENBRIDGE, (J.) The Crusades, etc. 8°, pp. 327. Kingston, 1846.

BREWER, (W. A.) Recreations of a Merchant; or, The Christian Sketch Book. 16°, pp. vii, 192. Boston, 1836.

BREWERTON, (G. D.) Ida Lewis, the Heroine of Lime Rock. 16°, pp. 66. Newport, R. I., 1869.

BREWSTER, (L. D.) Poem before the Senior Class, Yale College, June 13, 1855. 8°, pp. 16. New Haven, 1855.

BREWSTER, (MARTHA.) Poems on Divers Subjects. 16°, pp. 35. New London and Boston, 1757.

BRIDE, THE, OF FORT EDWARD. Founded on an Incident of the Revolution. 16°, pp. viii, 194. New York, 1839.
   The author is supposed to have been Miss Delia Bacon.

BRIDE, THE, OF THE ICONOCLAST. A Poem. Suggestions toward the Mechanical Art of Verse. (Anon.) 12°, pp. 131. Boston, 1854.

BRIDGES, (SALLIE.) Marble Isle, Legends of the Round Table, etc. 16°, pp. 272. Philadelphia, 1864.

BRIGGS, (CAROLINE A.) Utterance; or, Private Voices to the Public Heart. A Collection of Home Poems. 12°, pp. 255. Boston, 1852.

BRIGHT, (M. H.) Dies Iræ. 8°, pp. 9. New York, privately printed. 25 copies. 1866.
   " Mr. M. H. Bright sends us a new version of the famous old monkish song, the 'Dies Iræ,' his aim being, he says, to render it literally, while he conforms at the same time to the trochaic measure of the original Latin."—*From the Round Table*, Oct. 27, 1866.

BRINE, (MARY D.) Madge, the Violet Girl, etc. 4°, pp. 114. New York, 1881.

BRITAIN, (N.) AND SHERWOOD, (L. H.) The School Song and Hymn Book. 16°, pp. 386. New York, 1855.

BRITTAN, (T. S.) Scripture Patriots. 18°, pp. 131. New York, 1834.

Broad Hint, A. (Anon.) 8°. No place. Date in pencil, 1829.

> Not published. The whole title is " A Broad Hint to No Body; if it suits Any Body, it will not disappoint Every Body." The following is written in pencil on the title page : " Refers to Rev. —— Parkinson's *crim. con.* case."

Broadcloth, (Doctor.) The United States Political Looking Glass, Hydrometer and Thermometer. 12°, pp. 48. Albany, 1824.

Broadside for the Times. (Anon.) 12°, pp. 24. New York, 1861.

Brooke, (H.) Gustavus Vasa, etc. 16°, pp. 83. Philadelphia, 1778.

Brooke, (W.) Julia. 12°, pp. 100. Boston, 1855.

Brooks, (C. T.)

> Charles T. Brooks was born in Salem, Mass., in 1813, and graduated at Harvard College in 1832. His acquaintance with Dr. Follen led to his introduction to the writings of the most eminent German authors, and he distinguished himself as a translator of their works. Having studied theology at the Divinity School at Cambridge, he was settled as a Unitarian minister in Newport, R. I., where he commenced his labors in January, 1837, his ordination taking place the following June, at which time Dr. W. E. Channing preached the sermon. His only pastorate was at Newport, where he died June 14, 1883.

— Aquidneck : A Poem pronounced on the Hundredth Anniversary of the Incorporation of the Redwood Library, Newport, R. I., August xxiv, MDCCCXLVII. With other Commemorative Pieces. 12°, pp. iv, 69. Providence, 1848.

— Faust. Translated with Notes. 16°, pp. 234. Boston, 1856.

— Same. 2d Edition. Boston, 1857.

— German Lyrics. 12°, pp. viii, 237. Boston, 1853. •

— Master Pigmy and the Spark that went a Sparking. From the German of H. Hoffman. Illustrated. 8°, pp. 16. Philadelphia, no date.

— Roman Rhymes. 12°, pp. 46. Cambridge, 1869.

— Schiller's Homage of the Arts. 16°, pp. viii, 151. Boston, 1847.

— The Jobsiad. A Grotesco-Comico-Heroic Poem, from the German of Dr. Carl Arnold Kortüm. 16°, pp. xviii, 181. Philadelphia, 1863.

— The Layman's Breviary ; or, Meditations for Every Day in the Year. From the German of Leopold Schefer. Sq. 16°, pp. iv, 452. Boston, 1867.

— The World-Priest. Translated from the German of Leopold Schefer. Sq. 16°, pp. xv, 393. Boston, 1873.

BROOKS, (C. T.) — *Continued.*
— The Wisdom of the Brahmin.  A Didactic Poem.  Translated from
    the German of F. Büchert.  Books I—VI.  Sq. 18°, pp. ix, 252.
    Boston, 1882.
— William Tell.  A Drama.  From Schiller.  · 12°, pp. 120.  Provi-
    dence, 1838.

BROOKS, (CONSTANTINA E.)  Ballads and Translations.  12°, pp. 144.
    New York, 1866.

BROOKS, (J. G.)

James Gordon Brooks was born at Claverack, N. Y., in 1801, and graduated at Union
College in 1819.  In 1828 he married Miss Mary E. Aiken.  In connection with Mrs. Brooks,
he published in 1829 a volume entitled "The Rivals of Este."  He died in 1841.

— Phi Beta Kappa.  Yale, September 12, 1826.  8°, pp. 28.  New
    York, 1826.

BROOKS, (MRS. M.)

Maria Gowan, called by Southey "Maria del Occidente," was born at Medford, Mass.,
about the year 1795, and at an early age married Mr. Brooks, a merchant of Boston, who
died a few years after their marriage.  Southey speaks of Mrs. B. as "the most impassioned and magnetic of all poetesses."  She died at Matanzas in 1845.

— Judith, Esther, and other Poems.  24°, pp. 112.  Boston, 1820.
— Zóphiël; or, The Bride of Seven.  2d American, from the 1st Lon-
    don Edition.  18°, pp. 255.  Boston, 1834.

BROOKS, (N. C.)

Nathan Covington Brooks was born in Cecil county, Md., in 1809.  He became President of the Baltimore Female College in 1848.  His series of Greek and Latin classes has
enjoyed a well-deserved reputation, as has also his "History of the Mexican War."

— Scriptural Anthology.  18°, pp. 180.  Philadelphia, 1837.
— The History of the Church.  Read before the Diagnothian Society of
    Marshall College, July 5, 1841.  12°, pp. 60.  Baltimore, 1841.
— The Literary Amaranth; or, Prose and Poetry.  12°, pp. 264.
    Philadelphia and Baltimore, 1840.

BROOKS, (SARAH W.)  Blanche; or, The Legend of the Angel Tower.
    12°, pp. 43.  New York, 1861.
— The Legend of St. Christopher, etc.  12°, pp. v, 172.  Providence,
    1859.
— Even-Songs, etc.  Sq. 16°, pp. 103.  Boston, 1868.

BROTHER JONATHAN'S EPISTLE TO HIS RELATIVES. 12°, pp. 25. Boston, 1852.

BROUGHAM, (J.)

John Brougham was born in Dublin, May 9, 1814, and came to the United States not far from the year 1842. He was the author of more than one hundred dramatic pieces. A full sketch of his life may be found in Volume I. of his plays, published in New York, 1856. He died June 7, 1880.

— Columbus et Filibustero!! A Comedy. 12°, pp. 24. New York, no date.

— Dred. 12°, pp. 43. New York, no date.

— Franklin. An Historical Drama. 12°, pp. 27. New York, no date.

— Life in New York. A Comic Drama. 12°, pp. 26. New York, no date.

— Metamora; or, The Last of the Pollywogs. A Burlesque. 12°, pp. 18. Boston, no date.

— Neptune's Defeat; or, The Seizure of the Lear. 12°, pp. 24. New York, no date.

— Po-ca-hon-tas; or, The Gentile Slave. 12°, pp. 32. New York, no date.

— Take Care of Little Children. A Farce. 12°, pp. 14. New York, no date.

— Temptation; or, The Irish Emigrant. A Comic Drama. 12°, pp. 22. New York, no date.

— The Great Tragic Revival. 12°, pp. 10. New York, no date.

— The Irish Yankee; or, The Birthday of Freedom. 12°, pp. 28. New York, no date.

— The Miller of New Jersey; or, The Prison Walk. 12°, pp. 28. New York, no date.

— The Musard Ball; or, Love at the Academy. 12°, pp. 12. New York, no date.

— The Red Mask; or, The Wolf of Bohemia. A Melo-Drama. 12°, pp. 26. New York, no date.

— AND GOODRICH, (F. B.) The Dark Hour Before Dawn. A Play. 12°, pp. 44. New York, no date.

BROWN, (D. P.)

David Paul Brown was born in Philadelphia in 1795, was admitted to the bar at the age of 21, began in early life to contribute to periodical literature, and reached great dis-

Brown, (D. P.) — *Continued.*

tinction as a lawyer. "The Forum, or Forty Years' Full Practice at the Philadelphia Bar," 2 volumes, 8°, is pronounced by Allibone "excellent." Mr. Brown died July 11, 1872.

— Sertorius and Prophet of St. Paul. 8°, pp. 87, pp. 50. Philadelphia, 1830.

Brown, (E.) The Trial of Cain, the first Murderer, in Poetry. By rule of Court ; In which a Predestinarian, a Universalian, and an Armenian argue as Attornies at the Bar ; the two former as the Prisoner's Counsel, the latter as Attorney General. "Prove all things, hold fast that which is good."—*Paul.* 18°, pp. 32. Boston, 1827.

— Same. 24°, pp. 62. New York, 1834.

Brown, (J. N.)

John Newton Brown, D. D., a distinguished minister of the Baptist denomination, was born at New London in June, 1803, graduated from Hamilton, now Madison, University, in 1823, was ordained in Buffalo in 1825, and through life was engaged in ministerial and literary work. He compiled "Encyclopædia of Religious Knowledge," in its day a valuable work. He died in Germantown, Pa., May 14, 1808.

— Emily, etc. 16°, pp. viii, 276. Concord, N. H., 1840.
— The Apocalypse. A Poem delivered at Waterville, Me., August 2, 1836. 16°, pp. 20. Augusta, Me., 1836.

Brown, (J. S.) The Bouquet, etc. 16°, pp. 124. Lancaster, 1858.

Brown, (J. W.)

John W. Brown was born at Schenectady in 1814, and became an Episcopal minister. He died in 1849.

— Geraldine ; or, The Guardian Angel, etc. 16°, pp. 73. New York, 1846.
— Michael Agonistes ; or, The Contests of the Spirits. 12°, pp. 94. New York, 1843.
— The Christian Offering and Churchman's Annual. 12°, pp. 204. New York, 1839.
— The Christmas Bells. 12°, pp. 221. New York, 1842.

Brown, (L.)

The author, Leonard Brown, was born in 1838. He says that "the greater part of his 'Poems of the Prairies' were written before the war, and while the author was quite young. A blacksmith's apprentice in his youth, he had few advantages of early instruction from books."

BROWN, L. — (*Continued.*)

— Poem. Delivered in Kalamazoo, Mich., June 21, 1854. 8°, pp. 12. New York, 1854.

— Poems of the Prairies. New Edition. 16°, pp. x, 186. Des Moines, 1868.

BROWN, (S.)

> Solyman Brown, M. D., was born at Litchfield, Conn., November 17, 1790, graduated at Yale College in 1814, and for several years preached as a licensed Congregational minister, and was also a teacher. In 1812 he removed to New York and became a Swedenborgian preacher, and was, moreover, an instructor in the classics. Subsequently he became a dentist, and for two years was one of the editors of " The American Journal and Library of Dental Science."

— An Essay on American Poetry, etc. 12°, pp. 191. New Haven, 1818.

— Dental Hygeia. A Poem on the Health and Preservation of the Teeth. 12°, pp. 54. New York, 1838.

— Dentologia. 8°, pp. 46. New York, 1840.

— Llewellen's Dog. 12°, pp. 12. New York, 1840.

BROWN, THE HISTORY OF. (Anon.) 18°, pp. 24. Philadelphia, 1849.

BROWN UNIVERSITY. Centennial Celebration, September 6, 1864.

> In the volume are the Centennial Ode by Right Rev. George Burgess, D. D., Bishop of the Diocese of Maine, and the Poem of Hon. Charles Thurber at the dinner.

BROWN, (W. W.) Bread, if You Please, etc. 8°, pp. 12. Cleveland, no date.

BROWNE, (FRANCES E.) Poems. 16°, pp. iv, 155. Cambridge, 1846.
— Same. Boston, 1848.

BROWNE, (W. C.) Harp, The Wesleyan. 3d Edition. 18°, pp. 213. Boston, 1841.

BROWNELL, (H. H.)

> Henry Howard Brownell was born at East Hartford in 1820, graduated at Trinity College in 1841, studied law, devoted himself to literary pursuits, in the civil war was a volunteer, and became the Secretary of Admiral Farragut. He died in Hartford in 1872.

— Ephemeron. 12°, pp. viii, 58. New York, 1855.

— Lyrics of a Day ; or, Newspaper Poetry. By a Volunteer in the United States Service. 12°, pp. 160. New York, 1874.

— War-Lyrics, etc. 12°, pp. 243. Boston, 1866.

BRYAN, (D.)

> This poetical "appeal" was made in behalf of R. S. Coffin, "the Boston Bard," who was wasting away with consumption. The author, Daniel Bryan, was born in Virginia, and, for a time, was a Senator in the Legislature of that State. Subsequently he was Postmaster at Georgetown, D. C.

— The Appeal for Suffering Genius.  Lg. 8°, pp. xiii, 80.  Washington, 1826.

— The Day of Gratitude.  Poems occasioned by the visit of La Fayette to the United States.  8°, pp. 104.  Philadelphia, 1826.

— The Mountain Muse, comprising Adventures of Daniel Boone.  16°, pp. 252.  Harrisonburg, Va., 1813.

BRYANT, (J. D., M. D.)  Redemption.  A Poem.  16°, pp. 366.  Philadelphia, 1859.

BRYANT, (J. H.)

> John Howard Bryant, a brother of William C., was born at Cummington, Mass., July 22, 1807.  In 1831 he removed to Princeton, Ill., and has, through life, devoted himself to agricultural pursuits.

— Poems.  12°, pp. 93.  1855.

BRYANT, (W. C.)

> William Cullen Bryant was born at Cummington, Mass., November 3, 1794, and began to publish his poetical productions at the age of ten.  In 1808, at the age of thirteen, his "Embargo," a political satire, was published.  He entered Williams College in 1810, but did not complete the full course of study.  In 1815 he was admitted to the bar. "Thanatopsis" was published in 1816.  He removed to New York in 1825, and in 1826 became editor of *The Evening Post.*  This position he held through life.  He made several trips to the old world, and during his absence contributed many articles in the form of letters, etc., to his paper.  His place for all coming time among the best American poets is assured.  After a life of great literary activity he died June 12, 1878.

— Poems.  12°, pp. viii, 240.  Boston, 1832.

— Same.  12°, pp. viii, 240.  New York, 1832.

— Same.  Edited by Washington Irving.  12°, pp. xii, 235.  London, 1832.

— Same.  4th Edition, pp. viii, 274.  New York, 1836.

— Same.  6th Edition, pp. xii, 276.  "      "   1840.

— Poems.  Illustrations by E. Leutzè, engraved by American artists.  8°, pp. 378.  Philadelphia, 1847.

— The Fountain, etc.  12°, pp. 100.  New York and London, 1842.

— Same.  Complete in one volume. - 12°, pp. 378.  Philadelphia, 1848.

— Same.  1852.

— Same.  2 vols.  16°, pp. x, 296 ; 286.  New York, 1855.

BRYANT, (W. C.) — *Continued.*
— The Fountain, etc.  18°, pp. 264.  New York, 1856.
— Same.  Illustrated with 71 engravings by the Brothers Dalziel.  Sm. 4°, pp. 344.  New York, 1858.
— Same.  18°, pp. 264.  New York, 1864.  Blue and Gold Series.
— Selections from the American Poets.  18°, pp. xii, 316.  New York, 1840.
— Same.  18°, pp. xvi, 256.  New York, 1844.
— The White Footed Deer, etc.  16°, pp. 24.  New York, 1844.
— Fable for Critics.  12°, pp. iii, 78.  New York, 1848.
— Same.  2d Edition.  12°, pp. v, 80.  New York, 1848.
— The Forest Hymn.  Illustrated.  Sm. 8°, pp. 32.  New York, 1860.
— Thirty Poems.  12°, pp. 222.  New York and London, 1864.
— The Iliad of Homer.  15th Edition.  12°, 2 vols., pp. xviii, 332; 335.  Boston, 1870.
— The Odyssey of Homer.  9th Edition.  12°, 2 vols., pp. vi, 272; 256.  Boston, 1871.
— Introduction to "A Library of American Poets."  4°, pp. xxxi, 789.  New York, 1871.

BUBBLES. YE BOOK OF.  A Contribution in Aid of the New York Sanitary Fair.  pp. 68.  New York, 1868.

BUCK, (J. S.)  Milwaukee's Early Days.  8°, pp. 16.  Milwaukee, 1874.

BUDS AND BLOSSOMS, MOUNTAIN.  (Anon.)  12°, pp. 204.  Petersburg, 1825.

BUFFINTON.  (G. E. C.)  A Game of Chess, etc.  Comedy.  16°, pp. 48.  Providence, 1875.

BULFINCH, (S. G., D. D.)
Stephen Greenleaf Bulfinch was born at Boston, June 18, 1809, and graduated at Columbia College, Washington, D. C., in 1826.  His father, Charles B., (1763–1844) was one of the principal architects of the Capitol at Washington.  Stephen G. studied theology at the Cambridge Divinity School, and was ordained as a Unitarian minister.  He was the author of several volumes of poetry.  His death occurred at Cambridge, Mass., October 12, 1870.

— Lays of the Gospel.  12°, pp. 194.  Boston, 1845.
— Poems.  16°, pp. vi, 108.  Charleston, 1834.
— The Harp and the Cross.  A Collection of Religious Poetry.  12°, pp. xi, 348.  Boston, 1857.

BULLOCK, (CYNTHIA.)

Cynthia Bullock was born at Lyons, Wayne county, N. Y., March 7, 1821. She was one of eighteen blind children collected in 1833 by Dr. Alerby, in New York, for the purpose of experimenting on the capacities of the blind. By the death of her father her family was left destitute. She became a teacher in the literary and musical department of the New York Institute for the Blind.

— A Bunch of Pansies. 12°, pp. x, 143. New York, 1852.
— Washington, etc. 12°, pp. 108. New York, 1847.

BULLS AND BEARS, THE; OR, WALL STREET SQUIB, No. 1. 16°, pp. 19. New York, 1854.

BULLS, TWO, THE STORY OF. 12°, not paged. New York, 1856.

BUNCE, (O. B.)

Oliver Bell Bunce has written under the signatures of *B*, *Bachelor Bluff*, and *Censor*. He has devoted himself to journalism, and is the editor of "Appleton's Journal."

— Love in '76. An Incident in the Revolution. 12°, pp. 22. New York, no date.

BUNGAY, (G. W.) Acrostics, etc. 24°, pp. 128. New York, 1837.

BUNKER HILL. A Commemorative Poem. 8°.

Neither the name of the author, nor the date of publication, is given. A newspaper clipping pasted on the last leaf says: "We have received from a friend a copy of a play published soon after the memorable battle of Bunker Hill, and intended to commemorate that event. It was written by a Lieutenant-Colonel in the Continental army, and is dedicated to 'Richard Stockton, Esquire, member of the honorable the Continental Congress for the State of New Jersey.' The *dramatis personæ* are the officers engaged on both sides, and the play, which is in blank verse, partakes strongly of the character of the patriotic poetry of that day." In the dedication, the author says the poem "was at first drawn up for an exercise in oratory, to a number of young gentlemen in a Southern Academy, but being now published, may serve the same purpose in other American Academies."

BUNNER, (H. C.) Airs from Arcady and Elsewhere. 16°, pp. 109. New York, 1884.

This volume, published in the attractive style in which Charles Scribner's Sons send out their productions, is dedicated to Brander Matthews.

BUONAPARTE, EPISTLE TO. (By a Lady. Anon.) 12°, pp. 11. Philadelphia, 1814.

BURGESS, (G., D. D.)

George Burgess was born at Providence. R. I., October 31, 1809, graduated at Brown University in 1826, was tutor in the University 1820–30, studied in Germany, was Rector of Christ Church, Hartford, 1834–47, was consecrated Bishop (Protestant Episcopal) of the Diocese of Maine, October 31, 1847, and became, at the same time, Rector of Christ's Church, Gardiner, Me. He died at sea, April 23, 1866. For list of his published writings, see Allibone, p. 287.

BURGESS, (G., D. D.) — *Continued.*

— Poems. 12°, pp. viii, 276. Hartford, 1868.

— The Book of Psalms. Translated into English Verse. 12°, pp. xi, 276. New York, 1840.

— The Martyrdoms of St. Peter and St. Paul. 12°, pp. 48. Providence, 1834.

— The Strife of Brothers. 8°, pp. 47. New York, 1844.

BURGOO ZAC, (a *pseud.*) The Quiet Romance of William Whack. 8°, not paged. Cincinnati, 1871.

BURGOYNE, GENERAL, LAMENTATIONS OF. 18°, pp. 8. No place, no date.

BURK, (J.) Bethlem Gabor, Lord of Transylvania, etc. An Historical Drama. 16°, pp. 49. Petersburg, 1807.

— Female Patriotism; or, The Death of Joan D'Arc. 12°, pp. 40. New York, 1798.

— Bunker Hill; or, The Death of General Warren. 16°, pp. 39. Baltimore, 1808.

— Same. 16°, pp. 44. New York, 1817.
> An elegant copy, bound in red morocco.

BURK, (J. D.) The Death of General Montgomery. 12°, pp. 68. Norwich and Providence, 1777.

BURKE, (C.) Rip Van Winkle. 12°, pp. 27. New York, no date.

BURKE, (J.) Chivalry Slavery. Lg. 8°, pp. 183. New York, 1866.

— Stanzas to Queen Victoria, etc. Lg. 8°, pp. 208. New York, 1866.

— (Sennoia Rubek, *pseud.*) The Burden of the South. Poems on Slavery. 8°, pp. 96. New York, 1864.
> Bound in this volume is R. H. Stoddard's "Abraham Lincoln." pp. 11. New York, 1865.

BURLEIGH, (G. S.)
> George Shepard Burleigh, a younger brother of W. H. Burleigh, was born at Plainfield, Conn., March 26, 1821. Everest says: "He very early developed the poetical faculty, being remarkable when a mere child for the facility with which he composed verses, and for the euphony that characterized these juvenile efforts." His present residence (1886) is Little Compton, R. I. He is the author of one of the Odes sung at the celebration of the 250th anniversary of the settlement of Providence, R. I., June 23, 1886.

— Elegiac Poem on the Death of Nathaniel Rogers. 18°, pp. 32. Hartford, 1846.

— The Maniac, etc. 12°, pp. vi, 240. Philadelphia, 1849.

— Signal Fires. 12°, pp. viii, 162. New York, 1856.

BURLEIGH, (W. H.)

William Henry Burleigh, a lineal descendant on his mother's side of William Bradford, so long the governor of Plymouth Colony, was born at Woodstock, Conn., February
2, 1812. In 1837 he removed to Pittsburgh, where he published the *Christian Witness*, and
subsequently the *Temperance Banner*. Returning east in 1843, he took up his residence in
Hartford, and had charge of the organ of the Connecticut Anti-Slavery Society, then published under the name of the *Christian Freeman*, and afterwards of the *Charter Oak*.
This position he occupied for some six years, removing to Syracuse, N. Y., in 1849, where
he spent five years, devoting himself to the interests of the New York State Temperance
Society. For a year or two his residence was in Albany. In 1855 he was appointed Harbor Master of New York, and subsequently one of the Board of Port Wardens, which office
he held till within a year of his death. Into all the great reforms of the day he entered
with abiding and unflagging interest, promoting these with voice and pen up to the full
measure of his ability. He died at Brooklyn, N. Y., March 18, 1871.

— Our Country: Its Dangers and its Destiny.  12°, pp. vi, 43.  Alle-
ghany, Pa.

— Poems.  With a Sketch of his Life, by Celia Burleigh.  12°, pp.
xi, 306.  New York, 1871.

— Poems.  12°, pp. viii, 248.  Philadelphia, 1841.

— The Rum Fiend, etc.  12°, pp. 44.  New York, 1871.

BURNET, (J. R.)  Tales of the Deaf and Dumb.  With Miscellaneous
Poems.  16°, pp. 230.  Newark, N. J., 1835.

BURNETT, (J. G.)  Blanche of Brandywine.  A Play.  12°, pp. 40.
New York, [1858.]

BURNS' CENTENNIAL CELEBRATION.  Songs Written for.  8°, pp. 8.
Chicago, 1859.

BURNS, ROBERT.  Report of Centennial Celebration, January 25, 1859.
Several Original Poems in the Report.  8°, pp. 47.  Boston, 1859.

BURROUGHS, (C., D. D.)

Charles Burroughs was born at Boston, December 27, 1787, graduated with the Latin
Valedictory at Harvard in 1806, received Deacon's orders in the Episcopal Church at the
hands of Bishop White at Philadelphia, December 10, 1809, was ordained Priest at Portsmouth by Bishop Griswold, May 20, 1812, and became Rector of St. Paul's Church in that
place, retaining this position for the long period of forty-five years, resigning his office in
1857. Columbia College, in 1833, conferred on him the degree of Doctor of Divinity. He
was an accomplished scholar, an able, instructive preacher, and interested in all affairs
which concerned the intellectual, moral and religious improvement of his own parish and
the community in which, for so many years, he was a prominent citizen. He died March
6, 1868. Dr. B. was one of the founders of the General Theological Library in Boston.

— The Poetry of Religion, etc.  16°, pp. 101.  Boston, 1851.

BURROWES, (G., D. D.)  Octorara.  A Poem, and Occasional Pieces.
Sq. 12°, pp. 108.  Philadelphia, 1856.

Burt, (A.)  Journeyman Weaving.  16°, pp. 24.  New York, 1831.

"The following verses," says the author, "are founded on the supposition of some attempts having been made by the Journeymen Cotton Weavers here to arrest the further reduction of their wages, and are supposed to be the substance of the several speeches likely to be delivered at the various meetings held on the subject."

— The Coronation ; or, Hypocrisy Exposed.  Also, Sullivan's Island, with Notes.  12°, pp. xi, 77.  Charleston, 1822.

— Poems : Chiefly Satirical.  12°, pp. 150.  New York, 1833.

Burtt, (J.)

The only information we can gather of John Burtt is that he was born in Scotland, near the home of Burns, whose " gifted numbers," he says, "he learned at an early age to lisp, and his young heart beat responsive to the hope of becoming, at some future period, a rival to his fame.  But," he adds, " the bitter winter of adversity destroyed the flattering illusion, and the discipline of experience has chastened his vanity, and convinced him of his weakness."  When he came to America, and the date of his death, we do not know.

— Horæ Poeticæ ; or, The Transient Murmurs of a Solitary Lyre.  16°, pp. xi, 183.  Bridgeton, N. J., 1819.

Business Lyrics.  By the best poets, (dead and alive.)  Compiled by E. J. C.  (Anon.)  16°, pp. 36.  Providence, 1881.

Buster, Phil. E. (pseud?)  The World's Peace Jubilee, etc.  16°, pp. 26.

Bustle, The.  (Anon.)  12°, pp. 82.  Boston, 1845.

Buswell, (H. F.)  Dedication Poem.  Memorial Hall, Lancaster, Mass., June 17, 1868.  8°, pp. 6.  Boston, 1868.

Butler, (C. M.)

An eminent clergyman of the Protestant Episcopal Church, born at Troy, N. Y., 1810.

— Themes for the Poet.  8°, pp. 23.  Hartford, 1852.

Butler, (Mrs. F. K.)

Frances Ann Kemble was born at London in 1811, and belonged to a family many members of which were distinguished actors.  She made her first appearance on the stage in the character of Juliet, October 5, 1829.  While on a visit to this country, in 1834, she married Mr. Pierce Butler, of Philadelphia, from whom she was divorced in 1849.  She acquired great celebrity in England and America by her Shakespeare readings.  For full notice of her works, see Allibone, pp. 1014-16.

— Poems.  18°, pp. 144.  London, 1844.
— Same.  16°, pp. 152.  Philadelphia, 1844.
— The Star of Seville.  12°, pp. 130.  New York, 1837.

BUTLER, (J. H.)

> Joseph H. Butler was born at Bristol, England, in 1807, and came to the United States in 1833, and took up his residence in Troy, N. Y. The Rev. A. Potter, D. D., who wrote the preface to this volume, says that Mr. B. was "a mechanic without property." At fourteen he could not read a word. He had, however, a poetic vein which in after years he cultivated, and published his poems under the following title:

— Wild Flowers of Poesy. A Collection of Poems. 16°, pp. 108. Troy, N. Y., 1843.

BUTLER, (W. A.)

> William Allen Butler was born at Albany. N. Y., in 1825, graduated at the New York University, 1843, and settled in New York as a lawyer.

— Barnum's Parnassus, etc. 16°, pp. 52. New York, 1850.

— Nothing to Wear. Illustrated by Hoppin. 12°, pp. 68. New York, 1857.

— Two Millions. 16°, pp. 93. New York, 1858.

BUTTERWORTH, (H.) An Historical Address and Poem delivered at the Centennial Celebration of the incorporation of the town of Barrington, R. I., June 17, 1870, with an Historical Appendix. The address was by T. W. Bicknell, and the poem by Hezekiah Butterworth. 8°, pp. 192. Providence, 1870.

BUTTON, (SUSAN S.) Poems. 12°, pp. xii, 336. Litchfield, Ohio, 1858.

BYER, (M.) Selling Out Ye Pope. A Satire. 12°, pp. 64. New York. 1873.

BYLES, (M.)

> Mather Byles, a descendant, on his mother's side, from John Cotton and Richard Mather, was born at Boston, March 26, 1706; graduated at Harvard in 1725, was ordained as pastor of the Hollis Street Church, Boston, December 20, 1733, his relation with his parish being pleasant until the Revolutionary war, when he became obnoxious on account of his outspoken Tory sentiments. His connection with the church was dissolved in 1776. His death occurred July 5, 1788. Dr. Byles was distinguished for his wit, some specimens of which may be found in Sprague's "Annals of the Am. Pulpit," vol. i, pp. 377–82. (For a discriminating critique on Dr. Byles, see Prof. Tyler's Hist. Am. Lit. vol. i, pp. 192–98.)

POEM on the Death of George I. and Accession of George II. 16°, pp. 5. No place, no date.

POEM presented to His Excellency William Burnet, Esq., on his arrival at Boston, July 19, 1728. 12°, p. 6. No place, no date.

BYLLESBY, (L.) Patent Right Oppression Exposed; or, Knavery Detected, etc. By Patrick N. I. Elisha, Esq., Poet Laureate, (*pseud.*) 12°, pp. xi, 189. Philadelphia, 1814.

> On fly-leaf in pencil: "For an account of the poem, see MSS. in copy in 'List of Historical Society, Penn.'"

CADY, (C. M.)  Libretto of Spring Holiday.  8°, pp. 15.  New York, 1856.

CALAMITY AT LAWRENCE, MASS., JANUARY 10, 1860.  By an Eye-witness.  12°, pp. 20.  Boston, 1860.

> Descriptive of the frightful disaster connected with the fall of the " Pemberton Mills," when, under circumstances of aggravated horror, many lives were lost.

CALDCLEAUGH, (W. G.)  Branch, The, etc.  12°, pp. 96.  Philadelphia, 1862.

CALDWELL, (C.)

> A learned physician of Philadelphia, born in 1772, and died in 1853.

— Elegaic Poem on the Death of Washington.  12°, pp. 12.  Philadelphia, 1800.

CALDWELL, (H. H.)  Oliatta, etc.  12°, pp. 200.  New York, 1855.
— Same.  12°, pp. 134.  Boston, 1858.

CALDWELL, (W. W.)

> William W. Caldwell was born at Newburyport, Mass., in 1823, and graduated at Bowdoin College in 1843.  His poetical translations are from the German.

— Poems, Original and Translated.  12°, pp. xii, 276.  Boston, 1857.

CALENDAR FOR BIRTHDAYS.  (Anon.)  12°, pp. 77.  Baltimore, 1866.

CALIFORNIA BROADSIDES.  (Anon.)  No place, no date.

CALL, A SOLEMN.  (By a Citizen of Newburyport.)  12°, pp. 11.  Newburyport, no date.

CALLAO, THE RUIN OF, IN 1746.  An Opera.  24°, pp. 30.  Lima, 1847.

CALLEN, (J.)  Three Cantos of a Poem.  1. The Fate of Poets.  2. The Apocalyptic Vision.  3. The Progress of Art.  8°, pp. 24.  Philadelphia, 1835.

CALVERT, (G. H.)

> George Henry Calvert was born at Baltimore, January 2, 1803, and was a great-grandson of Sir George Calvert, the first Lord Baltimore.  On his mother's side he was a lineal descendant of the painter Rubens.  He graduated at Harvard in 1823, and, for a time, studied at Göttingen.  Returning to Baltimore, he was, for several years, editor of the *Baltimore American*.  In 1843 he removed to Newport, R. I., making that city his permanent residence.  His fellow-citizens elected him Mayor in 1853, which position he filled most acceptably.  His present residence (1886) is Newport, R. I.  The *Literary World*, as quoted by Allibone, says: " Mr. Calvert is a scholar of refined tastes and susceptibilities, educated in the school of Goethe, who looks upon the world at home and abroad in the light not merely of genial and ingenious reflection, but with an eye of philosophical, practical improvement."

— Anyta, etc.  12°, pp. vii, 170.  Boston, 1866.

Calvert, (G. H.)—*Continued.*
— Arnold and André.  12°, pp. 95.  Boston. 1864.
— Cabiro.  Cantos I and II.  12°, pp. 36.  Baltimore, 1840.
— Same.  Cantos III and IV.  12°, pp. 87.  Boston, 1864.
— Comedies.  12°, pp. 125.  Boston, 1856.
— Count Julian.  12°, pp. 69.  Baltimore, 1840.
— Don Carlos.  A Dramatic Poem.  Translated from Schiller.  12°, pp. 203.  Baltimore, 1834.
— Ellen.  12°, pp. 48.  New York, 1869.
— Same.  12°, pp. 57.  New York, 1869.
— Mirabeau.  An Historical Drama.  Lg. 16°, pp. 103.  Boston, 1883.
— Poems.  12°, pp. 125.  Boston, 1847.
— Sibyl.  Sq. 18°, pp. 55.  Boston, 1883.
— Threescore, etc.  12°, pp. 90.  Boston, 1883.

Camille ; or, The Fate of a Coquette.  (Anon.)  12°, pp. 42.  New York, no date.
— Same.  12°, pp. 64.  New York, no date.

Campbell, (E. R.)  The Heroine of Scutari, etc.  12°, pp. 334.  New York, 1857.

Campbell, (J. W.)
John W. Campbell was born near Miller's Iron Works, Augusta county, Va., February 23, 1782, removed to Bourbon county, Ky., in 1791, was in large measure self-educated, admitted to the bar in Ohio in 1808, rose rapidly in his profession, elected Democratic Representative to Congress in the fall of 1816, and was in Congress ten years, at the end of which period he removed to Brown county, Ohio, where he settled on a farm.  In 1829 he was appointed District Judge of the United States for the State of Ohio, and in 1831 removed to Columbus, which was his home until his death, September 4, 1833.  A volume of his works, compiled by his widow, was published at Columbus, Ohio, in 1838.  In this volume (pp. 170–80) are nine short poems, the production of his pen.

Canadian Ballads.  (Anon.)  12°, pp. viii, 124.  No place, no date.

Canary Bird, The.  (Anon.)  18°, pp. 72.  Philadelphia, 1830.

Canfield, (Mrs. A. S.)  Alida ; or, Miscellaneous Sketches of Incidents during the late American War, *i. e.,* of 1812.  With Poems.  12°, pp. xi, 241.  New York, 1841.

Canning, (J. D.)  Poems.  18°, pp. viii, 205.  Greenfield, Mass., 1838.
Josiah D. Canning, of Gill, Mass., wrote under the signature of the *Peasant Bard.*

— Thanksgiving Eve.  18°, pp. 48.  Greenfield, 1838.

CANNON, (C. J.)

Born in 1800; died in 1860.

— Dramas.  12°, pp. 335.  New York, 1857.
— The Oath of Office.  A Tragedy.  12°, pp. 91.  New York, 1854.
— The Poet's Guest.  12°, pp. 72.  New York, 1841.

CAREY, (ALICE.)

Alice Carey was born at "Clovernook," near Cincinnati, in April 1820, began to publish her rythmic compositions at the age of eighteen in the Cincinnati press.  In 1850 she
removed, with her sister Phœbe, to New York, which became her permanent residence.
Her poetry takes high rank among the productions of American poets, and has received
warm commendations from Griswold, Prof. Hart, Whitaker and Bryant.  She died in
1871.

— A Lover's Diary.  With Illustrations.  Sq. 16°, pp. ix, 240.  Bos-
     ton, 1868.
— Ballads, Lyrics and Hymns.  16°, pp. 333.  New York, 1866.
— Lyra, and other Poems.  12°, pp. 178.  New York, 1852.
— Poems.  16°, pp. ix, 399.  Boston, 1855.

CAREY, (M.)

Matthew Carey was born in Dublin, Ireland, in 1760.  In 1783 he came to the United
States, where he resided until his death in 1839.  (See Duyckinck, vol. i, pp. 640–41.
Allibone, vol. i, p. 340.)

— The Columbian Muse.  Selections.  12°, pp. 224.  New York, 1794.
— The Plagi-Scurriliad.  8°, pp. xi, 27.  Philadelphia, 1786.

The Plagi-Scurriliad is called a "Hudibrastic Poem," and is dedicated to Col. Eleazer
Oswald, who had made what he conceived to be a scurrilous attack on him as a journalist.  The following is the "Approbation":

"In the Court of their Majesties, Detraction, Scurrility and Dullness:

     "Present—their Majesties in Council:

"Having duly examined the Hudibrastic poem, styled the Plagi-Scurriliad, written by
Matthew Carey, and dedicated to our right-trusty, well-beloved and long-adopted son,
Colonel Eleazer Oswald, proprietor of our chosen paper, the *Independent Gazetteer*,— we
do hereby declare our most hearty approbation thereof,—and our strongest hopes, that
all our friends in the upper regions will be thereby more fully enabled to conform to our
precepts, agreeably to the example of our son.

"Given at our Court in Pandemonium the third day of the Ides of March, in the year
of our reign five thousand seven hundred and eighty-nine.

          "Signed,

                              " WHISPER,
                              " DIRT-DAUB,   } Sec^ys."
                              " BLOCK-HEAD,

— The Porcupiniad.  A Hudibrastic Poem.  In Four Cantos.  Canto
     I.  12°, pp. vii, 52.  Philadelphia, 1799.

10

Carey, (Phœbe.)

Phœbe Carey, a sister of Alice, was born at "Clovernook" in 1828. She removed to New-York in 1850, and the fortunes of the sisters were substantially one and the same. She died in 1871.

— Poems and Parodies. 12°, pp. 200. Boston, 1854.
— Poems of Faith, Hope and Love. 12°, pp. v, 249. New York, 1868.

Carleton, (G. W.) Our Artist in Cuba. Fifty drawings in wood. Leaves from the Sketch-Book of a Traveller during the winter of 1864–5. 16°, pp. 50. New York, 1865.

Carleton, (W.) Farm Ballads. Illustrated. Lg. 8°, pp. 108. New York, 1873.

Carman, (A. F.) The "Fast" Age. 8°, pp. (with Oration by A. H. Green) 42. Troy, 1854.

Carpenter, (W. H.), and Arthur (T. S.), Editors. The Baltimore Book. 12°, pp. 296. Baltimore, 1838.

Carter, (B. M.) Miscellaneous Poems. 12°, pp. 95. Philadelphia, 1820.

Carter, (N. H.)

Nathaniel H. Carter was born at Concord, N. H., September 17, 1787, and graduated at Dartmouth College in 1811. Among his classmates were Rev. Dr. William Cogswell, Hon. Amos Kendall, Hon. Joel Parker and Hon. Ether Shepley. After teaching for a time, he removed to New York, and in 1810 became the editor of *The Statesman*, the organ of the party which supported De Witt Clinton. He visited Europe in 1825, and published in 1827 two volumes, comprising his Journal of his Tour. He died at Marseilles in January, 1830.

— Pains of Imagination. A Phi Beta Kappa Poem. Dartmouth College, August 19, 1824. 8°, pp. v, 31. New York, 1824.

The author says: "The Poem was intended as a counterpart of 'The Pleasures of Imagination,' by Akenside, although it was written without a single recurrence to the pages of that work, or, indeed, to any other, with the exception of a passage in Virgil, for the purpose of ascertaining the correctness of a classical allusion."

Cartland, (M.) An Epistolary Lament. Supposed to have been written by a surviving Hunker soon after the New Hampshire election. 12°, pp. 24. Concord, N. H., 1855.

Carver, (W.) Select Pieces in Prose and Verse. 12°, pp. 36. New York, 1834.

Carter, (Sarah C.) Lexicon of Ladies' Names, with their Floral Emblems. 18°, pp. 208. Boston, 1853.

CARY, (A. B.)  Florence Nightingale; or, The Angel of Charity.  8°, pp. 32.  Brooklyn, 1857.

CASE, (W.)  Title written, not printed.  Poems Occasioned by Several Circumstances.  12°, pp. iv, 20.  New Haven, 1778.

> Judge Greene says: "I think this copy is the original edition, wanting the title-page and two leaves at the end, and not the edition of which I have copied the title-page."

— Revolutionary Memorials.  With an Appendix.  Edited by Rev. Stephen Dodd.  12°, pp. 69.  New York, 1852.

CASSELS, (S. J.)  Providence, etc.  12°, pp. 356.  Macon, Ga., 1838.

CATHLEY, (C.)  The Ship Union and her Pilot.  8°, pp. 16.  New York, 1852.

CATO'S MORAL DISTICHES.  Englished in Couplets.  Lg. 12°, pp. 28.  Philadelphia.  Printed and sold by B. Franklin, 1735.

> The name of the author is unknown.  Scaliger's opinion is that he was an unconverted Gentile, who lived about the time of Commodus or Severus; that is, the beginning of the third century.

CAUGHEY, (A. H.)  Home, etc.  12°, pp. 82.  New York, 1862.

CHACE, (L. B.)  The Young Man About Town.  A Comedy.  8°, pp. 40.  New York, 1854.

CHAIR, THE OLD.  (Anon.)  12°, pp. 12.  Boston, 1849.

CHALLEN, (J.)

> Rev. James Challen was born at Hackensack, N. J., and was a publisher in Philadelphia.  The scene of this poem is laid in the Island of Mackinaw.

— Igdrasil; or, The Tree of Existence.  12°, pp. 170.  Philadelphia, 1859.
— Island of the Giant Fairies.  12°, pp. 23.  Philadelphia, 1868.

CHANDLER, (ELIZABETH MARGARET.)

> She was born at Centre, Del., near Wilmington, in 1807.  Early in life she removed to Philadelphia, where she remained till 1830, when she took up her residence near the village of Tecumseh, Mich., where she died in November, 1834.

— Poetical Works.  12°, pp. 180.  Philadelphia, 1836.
— Same.  12°, pp. 120.  Philadelphia, 1845.

CHANDLER, (MARIA F.)  The Spirit Harp.  12°, pp. viii, 112.  Springfield, Mass., 1851.

CHANNING, (W. E.)

> William Ellery Channing, nephew of Rev. Dr. Channing, was born June 10, 1818, and is the author of several tales of deserved celebrity.

— Near Home.  18°, pp. 52.  Boston, 1858.
— Poems.  12°, pp. 151.  Boston, 1843.
— The Woodman, etc.  12°, pp. 92.  Boston, 1849.

CHAPIN, (P.)  Evangelic Poetry.  12°, pp. iv, 207.  Concord, 1794.

CHAPLET, THE.  A Collection of Poems by (E. H. C.), edited by Rev. Henry D. Moore.  12°, pp. x, 120.  Philadelphia, 1846.

> E. H. C. is the *pseud.* of Rev. Nathan Davis. The letters, E. H. C. M., stand for "Editor of Hebrew Christian Magazine."

CHAPLET, THE MOURNERS'.  (Anon.)  24°, pp. 128.  Boston, 1844.

CHAPMAN, (E. H.)  The Parsonage.  24°, pp. 153.  Cleveland, 1849.

CHAPMAN, (G. W.)  A Tribute to Kane, etc.  12°, pp. 161.  New York, 1860.

CHARD, (T. S.)  The Waking.  Sq. 18°, pp. 25.  Chicago, 1869.

"CHARLESTON."  A Poem.  Answered by a Charleston Lady.  12°, pp. 12.  No place, 1848.

CHARLESTON BOOK.  Prose and Verse.  (Anon.)  12°, pp. viii, 404.  Charleston, 1845.

CHARLTON, (R. M. AND T. J., M. D.)

> Judge Robert M. Charlton was a resident of Savannah, Ga. He died in 1854. "His compositions," says Allibone, "have been greatly admired."

— Poems.  12°, pp. 174.  Boston, 1839.

CHASE, (ELIZABETH.)  Miscellaneous Selections,  12°, pp. 228.  No place, 1821.

CHASE, (L. B.)  The Spirit of '76.  12°, pp. 59.  New York, 1855.

CHASE, (MARY M.)  Writings.  Prose and Poetry.  12°, pp. xlvi, 336.  Boston, 1855.

CHATTERTON, (A.)  Buds of Beauty, etc.  18°, pp. x, 106.  Baltimore, 1787.

> An elegantly bound copy.

CHESTER, (J. L.)  Greenwood Cemetery, etc.  12°, pp. 132.  New York, 1843.

CHEEVER, (E.)

Ezekiel Cheever was born at London, January 25, 1615, and came to America in 1637. For twelve years he taught in New Haven, of which Colony he was one of the original founders. In 1661 he removed to Charlestown, Mass. For thirty-eight years he was a teacher in the Boston Latin School, and the memory of "Master" Cheever is held in grateful recollection to this day. He died August 21, 1708.

— Selections from his MS. Poems. 8°, pp. 3. Boston, 1828.

CHEEVER, (G. B.)

George Barrett Cheever was born at Hallowell, Me., April 17, 1807, and was a graduate of Bowdoin College in 1825, Longfellow and Hawthorne being classmates. He settled in Salem, Mass., as a Congregational minister in 1833, and made himself famous by his publication of his famous "Deacon Giles's Distillery," for which a certain distiller prosecuted him, and he was condemned to prison for thirty days. He removed to New York in 1839, and was pastor of the Church of the Puritans, 1846–67. (See Allibone for list of his writings.)

— The American Common-Place Book. 12°, pp. 405. Philadelphia, 1839.
— Same. 1841.
— The Poets of America. 12°, pp. 405. Hartford, 1852.

ΧΗΝΩΠΙΑ; OR, THE CLASSICAL MOTHER GOOSE. Sq. 18°, pp. 28. Cambridge. Printed (not published) 1871.

CHEVELEY, LADY; OR, THE WOMAN OF HONOUR. (Anon.) 16°, pp. 47. Philadelphia, 1839.

CHEVES, (E. W. F.) Sketches in Prose and Verse. 12°, pp. xv, 264. Baltimore, 1849.

CHILD'S FIRST CATECHISM. (Anon.) 18°, pp. 17. Providence, 1840.

CHILDREN IN THE WOOD. (Anon.) A Musical Piece in Two Acts. 12°, pp. 30. Boston, no date.

— (Anon.) 18°, pp. 57. New York, 1795.

CHIMASIA: A Reply to Longfellow's Theologian. (By Orthos, *pseud.*) 12°, pp. 96. Philadelphia, 1864.

CHISEL, (C.) Lamentation of Free Masonry. 12°, pp. 22. Norwich, 1829.

CHITTENDEN, (A. J.) Candidating Fair, The. A Student's Dream of Trial Preaching. (Anon.) 12°, pp. 48. Andover, Mass., 1873.

CHIVERS, (T. H.) Conrad and Eudora; or, The Death of Alonzo. A Tragedy. 16°, pp. 144. Philadelphia, 1834.

CHIVERS, (T. H.)—*Continued.*

— Eonchs of Ruby.  12°, pp. 168.  New York, 1851.

— Nacoochee; or, The Beautiful Star, etc.  12°, pp. 143.  New York, 1837.

— Virginalia; or, Songs of my Summer Nights,  12°, pp. 132.  Philadelphia, 1853.

CHRISTIAN YEAR, THE.  For Children.  (Anon.)  12°, pp. 144.  New York, 1850.

CHRISTIE, (W.)  Select Psalms, etc.  8°, pp. viii, 58.  Philadelphia, 1821.

CHURCH, (B.)

Benjamin Church, M. D., was born at Newport, R. I., in 1734, graduated at Harvard in 1754, studied medicine in London, and settled in Boston.  Being an outspoken Tory, he was prosecuted and banished.  He died in 1776.

— A Poem on Governor Jonathan Law, of Connecticut.  Sq. 8°.  No place, 1751.

— The Choice.  12°, pp. 15.  Boston, 1757.

— Same.  12°, pp. 16.  Worcester, 1802.

— The Christian.  A Poem in Four Books.  16°, pp. 111.  Philadelphia, 1783.

CHURCH, (E.)  The Dangerous Vice. . . . . A Fragment.  8°, pp. 16.  Columbia, 1789.

CHURCH KNAVIAD; OR, HORACE IN WEST HAVEN.  (Anon.)  18°, pp. 91.  New Haven, 1864.

CIST, (L. J.)

Lewis J. Cist was born at Harmony, Pa., November 20, 1818, and removed to Cincinnati when a child, residing in that city till 1850, when he took up his residence in St. Louis and became Assistant Cashier in a leading bank.  He distinguished himself as among the most devoted and successful collectors of chirographic curiosities in the United States.

— Trifles in Verse.  12°, pp. 184.  Cincinnati, 1845.

CITY PEOPLE, OUR.  By One of 'Em.  (Anon.)  12°, pp. 27.  Washington, 1874.

CIVIL WAR.  A Poem Written in the Year 1775.  (Anon.)  4°, pp. 35.  No place, no date.

The author's own copy, interleaved with additions and corrections.

CLACK, (MRS. LOUISE.)  General Lee and Santa Claus.  Large 12°, pp. 26.  New York, 1867.

CLAPP, (S. C.)

Samuel Capen Clapp was born April 1, 1810, and, at the age of fifteen, was put apprentice to learn the printing business. For both vocal and instrumental music he had a decided taste, as well as for poetry. His poems were designed chiefly to be the accompaniment of favorite tunes. He died October 28, 1831.

— Poetic Selections. 12°, pp. 12. Boston, 1832.

CLAPP, (W. W., JR.) La Fiammina. Founded upon a French Play, by Maria Uchard. 12°, pp. 35. Boston, no date.

— My Husband's Mirror. A Domestic Comedietta. 12°, pp. 14. Boston, no date.

CLARK, (ANNIE E.) Poems. 18°, pp. 146. Philadelphia, 1866.

CLARK, (L.) Kendridge Hall, etc. 12°, pp. 113. Washington, 1859.

CLARK, (R. E.) The First Book of Paradise Lost, in Rhyme. 12°, pp. 32. Lynchburg, 1867.

CLARK, (S. T.) Josephine, etc. 12°, pp. 239. Boston, 1856.

CLARK, (W. A.) The Learned World. 8°, pp. xvii, 270. Boston, 1864.

CLARKE, (G. W.) The Dreams of Pindus. 18°, pp. 115. Philadelphia, 1829.

— The Wreath of the West. 18°, pp. 115. Philadelphia, 1828.

CLARKE, (J.) The Boss Devil of America. Sq. 18°, pp. 109. Boston, 1878.

CLARKE, (MRS. M. B.)

Mary Bayard Devereux was born in Raleigh, N. C., married W. J. Clarke, and resided for some time at San Antonio de Bexar, West Texas, but subsequently returned to her native State.

— Wood Notes, or Carolina Carols. A Collection of North Carolina Poetry, compiled by Tenella (*pseud.*), in two vols. 12°, pp. 237; 237. Raleigh, 1854.

— Mosses from a Rolling Stone. 18°, pp. 168. Raleigh, N. C., 1866.

CLARKE, (McD.)

McDonald Clarke, known as "The Mad Poet," was born at New London, Conn., June 18, 1798, and removed to New York not far from the year 1819. He died March 5, 1842. It is said that "it was his hobby to fall in love with, and celebrate in his rhymes, the belles of the city. This was sometimes annoying, however well meant on the part of the poet."

— A Farce; or, The Belles of Broadway. 8°. Part I, pp. 24. Part III, pp. 24. New York, 1829.

CLARKE, (McD..) — *Continued.*
— Afara III.  12°, pp. 20.  New York, 1829.
— Death in Disguise.  A Temperance Poem.  18°, pp. 36.  Boston,
     1833.
— Poems.  12°, pp. 288.  New York, 1836.
— Sketches.  18°, pp. 128.  New York, 1826.
— The Elixir of Moonshine, etc.  16°, pp. 150.  Gotham, 5822.
— The Gossip.  No. one.  18°, pp. 223.  New York, 1823.

CLARKE, (MRS. M. J.)  The Child's First Catechism.  2d Edition.  18°,
     pp. 18.  Providence, 1864.

CLARK, (W. G.)
     Willis Gaylord Clark was born in Otisco, N. Y., in 1810.  As editor and proprietor of
     the *Philadelphia Gazette* he secured a wide and justly deserved reputation.  He furnished
     a number of articles for the "New York Knickerbocker Magazine," which subsequently
     were introduced into "Ollapodiana."  He died in 1841.

— Poems in "Literary Remains."  8°.  New York, 1844.
— Poetical Writings.  First Complete Edition.  24°, pp. 156.  New
     York, 1847.
— Second Complete Edition.
— The Past and Present.  12°, pp. xii, 23.  Boston, 1834.
— The Spirit of Life.  A poem before the Franklin Society, Brown
     University, September 3, 1833.  12°, pp. x, 71.  Philadelphia,
     1833.

CLARKE, (T.)  Sir Copp.  A Poem for the Times.  12°, pp. viii, 122.
     Chicago, 1865.

CLARKSON, (H. M.)  Evelyn; A Romance of "The War Between the
     States," etc.  12°, pp. 69.  Charleston, S. C., 1871.

CLARKSON, (L.)  Rag Fair, with Illustrations by the Author.  4°, not
     paged.  Philadelphia, 1879.

CLASON, (I. S.)
     Isaac S. Clason was born at New York in 1796, and died in 1830.  (Difference of
     authority where he was born.  Allibone says, *1796;* Lippincott, *1789.*  Take your choice.)
     He wrote 17th and 18th Cantos, a continuation of Byron's Don Juan.

— Horace in New York.  Part I.  12°, pp. 47.  New York, 1826.

CLASS POEM, HARVARD, 1857.  (Anon.)  8°, pp. 30.  New York, 1857.

CLEAVELAND, (MRS. E. H. J.)  No Sects in Heaven, etc.  Sq. 16°, pp.
     95.  New York, 1869.

CLEMMER, (MARY.)  Poems of Life and Nature.  12°, pp. 279.  Boston, 1883.

CLIFFORD, (F.)  The Present Age.  12°, pp. 28.  New York, 1851.

CLIFFTON, (W.)

> William Cliffton was born at Philadelphia in 1772, his father being a wealthy mechanic in the Society of Friends.  About the time of his majority he renounced the Quaker dress, and turned his attention to music and drawing.  He was a warm friend of the Administration, and vindicated it in several satires, the longest of which is "The Group."  He died in 1799.

— The Group ; or, An Elegant Representation.  A Farce.  18°, pp. 16.  Philadelphia, 1795.

— Same.  Illustrated.  Sm. 4°, pp. 35.

— Poems.  18°, pp. xviii, 119.  New York, 1800.

— Tit for Tat.  8°, pp. 25.  Philadelphia, 1796(?).

COAQUANOCK.  A Song of Many Summers, in Four Cantos.  Sq. 12°, pp. 60.  Published by "The Germantown Social Publication Co."  Philadelphia, 1878.

COATES, (E. R.), AND ROGERS, (ANN L.)  Offering.  Lg. 8°, pp. 59.  Philadelphia, no date.

COBB, (C. F.)  The Vision of Judgment Revived.  8°, pp. 20.  Washington, 1870.

> Mr. Cobb has written under the signature of " Bloc."

COBB, (MARY L.)  Poetical Dramas for Home and School.  12°, pp. 189.  Boston, 1873.

COCHRANE, (C. B.)  Mimosa, etc.  12°, pp, 112.  New York, 1869.

COCKINGS, (G.)

> George Cockings, in his Preface to " War: An Heroic Poem," says: " I was born in Devonshire, in the west of England; lived great part of my time in Dartmouth, in Devon; from thence came to Newfoundland, where I have lived several years, between the intervals of going out and home; and from thence came now to Boston; thus far concerning myself."
>
> In the " Biographia Dramatica," vol. i, part 1, p. 132, is the following: "Cockings, George, had, in early life, a small place under Government, at Boston, in America.  In the latter part of his life he was in England, and, on the resignation of Mr. Shepley, obtained the place of Register of the Society of Arts, Manufactures and Commerce in the Adelphi, which he held for thirty years, and died the 6th of February, 1802.  He was the author of a poem entitled ' The American War,' and, at one time, read Milton, etc., by way of a lecture to his friends.  Beside the above mentioned poem, he wrote several other wretched performances, and among the rest one play called ' The Conquest of Canada; or, The Siege of Quebec.  An Historical Tragedy.  8°, 1766.'  The signature over which Cockings wrote in this country was ' Camillo Querno, Poet Laureate to Congress.' "

11

Cockings, (G.) — *Continued.*

— Arts, Manufactures and Commerce.  8°, pp. iv, 36.  London, 1772.

> Bound in the same volume, "Benevolence and Gratitude." 6°, pp. ii, 44. London, 1772.

— War: An Heroic Poem.  From the Taking of Minorca by the French, etc.  12°, pp. xvi, 190.  Boston, 1762.

> Bound up with this volume is the author's "Britannia's Call to her Brave Troops and Hardy Tars." pp. 46.
>
> This copy of Cocking's "War" was the property of Silvanus Hopkins, Esq., Furnace Hope, Scituate R. I.  Mr. Bartlett says that "this poem was popular in its day, and passed through four editions. There were earlier editions, or portions of the poem, on 'War,' published without date."  In addition to the works of Cockings referred to, it may be mentioned that he was also author of "*Stentorian Eloquence and Medical Infallibility,*" a satire in verse on itinerant preachers, published in 1771; and of "Benevolence and Gratitude," a poem, published in 1773.

— Same.  4°, pp. 28.  London and Portsmouth, N. H., 1792.

Codman, (H.)  The Roman Martyrs.  A Tragedy in Three Acts.  Lg. 12°, pp. 83.  Providence, 1879.

Cody, (I.)  Tragedy.  Founded on the History of Joseph and his Brethren.  12°, pp. 63.  Schenectady, 1808.

Coe, (R.)

> Richard Coe was born at Philadelphia, of Quaker parents, February 13, 1821.  "His pieces," says Griswold, "are marked by refinement of feeling, and have frequently a quaintness reminding us of some of the older religious poets."

— Poems.  8°, pp. 117.  Philadelphia, 1850.
— The Old Farm Gate.  16°, pp. 159.  Philadelphia, 1852.

Coffeen, (J. F.)  The Fate of Genius, etc.  12°, pp. 72.  Cincinnati, 1835.

Coffenbery, (A.)  The Forest Rangers.  A Poet Tale of the Western Wilderness of 1794.  12°, pp. iv, 220.  Columbus, 1842.

Coffin, (A., Jr.)  Death of General Montgomery.  18°, pp. 71.  New York, 1814.

Coffin, (N. W.)  America.  An Ode, etc.  16°, pp. viii, 124.  Boston, 1843.

Coffin, (R. S.)

> Robert Stevenson Coffin was born at Brunswick, Me., 1797(?).  For some time he worked at his trade as a printer, in Newburyport, Mass.  During the war of 1812 he was a sailor, and was captured and held as a prisoner on board a British frigate.  After the war he continued to work at his trade in Boston, New York and Philadelphia.  He died at Rowley, Mass., in 1857.  He was self-styled "The Boston Bard."

Coffin, (R. S.)— *Continued.*

— Life of the Boston Bard, written by himself. 12°, pp. 303. Mt. Pleasant, N. Y., 1825.

— Miscellaneous Poems. 18°, pp. vi, 156. Philadelphia, 1818.

— Oriental Harp. 8°, pp. 252. Providence, 1826.

— Poems by the Boston Bard. 24°, pp. 64. New York, 1823.

— The Eleventh Hour ; or, Confessions of a Consumptive. 12°, pp. 36. Boston, 1827.

— The Printer, etc. 12°, pp. iv, 84. Boston, 1819.

Cole, (J.) The American War. An Ode. 12°, pp. 66. No place, date written in pencil, 1779.

An imperfect copy. Six pages of the Preface and the Appendix wanting.

Cole, (S. W.) The Muse. 18°, pp. vi, 216. Cornish, Me., 1827.

Coles, (A.) Dies Iræ, in Thirteen Original Versions. 18°, pp. 65. New York, 1859.

— Same. 2d Edition. 8°, pp. xxxiv, 65. 1860.

Colesworthy, (D. C.)

Daniel C. Colesworthy was born at Portland, Me., July 14, 1810, was a practical printer, and an editor and poet.

— The Year. 12°, pp. 114. .Boston, 1873.

Colgan, (W. J.) Poems. 12°, pp. 112. New York, 1844.

Collectanea. Compiled by S. C. Stevens. Sm. 24°, pp. 144. Haverhill, N. H., 1823.

Collection of Verses. Applied to November 1, 1765, etc., including a prediction that the S——p A——t shall not take place in North America. Also a Poetical Dream concerning Stamped Papers. 8°, pp. 24. New Haven, no date.

College Musings ; or, Twigs from Parnassus. (Anon.) 18°, pp. x, 110. Tuscaloosa, Ala., 1833.

Collegiad, The. (Anon.) 12°, pp. 14. London, 1837.

Collins, (J.) The Rumseller's Last Dream. Sq. 18°, pp. 7. No place, no date.

COLMAN, (B., D. D.)

Benjamin Colman was born at Boston in 1673, graduated at Harvard College in 1693, and was the first minister of the Brattle Street Church, Boston. He died in 1747.

— Elegy on his Death. (O. E. Anon.) 16°, pp. 8. Boston, no date.

— Poem on the Death of Rev. Samuel Willard. Bound with Rev. Mr. Pemberton's Sermon. 18°, pp. 14. Boston, 1707.

Elegantly bound.

COLMAN, (J. F.) The Island Bride, etc. 12°, pp. 164. Boston, 1846.

COLMAN, (Miss.) Wild Flowers. 24°, pp. 126. Boston, 1846.

COLT, (Mrs. THEODORA D. W.) Stray Fancies. 8°, pp. 219. Boston, 1872.

COLTON, (G. H.)

George H. Colton was born at Westford, Otsego county, N. Y., October 29, 1818, graduated at Yale in 1840, became editor and proprietor in 1844 of "The American Review, a Whig Journal," etc., and occupied this position till his death, December 1, 1847. His poem, "Tecumseh," was written when he was but twenty-three years of age, and is highly commended in Griswold's "Poets and Poetry of America," p. 541, edition 1860.

— Tecumseh; or, The West Thirty Years Since. 12°, pp. vii, 312. New York, 1842.

COLUMBIA, GENIUS OF. A MS. (Anon.) 4°. No place, no date.

COLUMBIAN LYRE, THE. Specimens of Transatlantic Poetry. 18°, pp. 300. Glasgow, 1828.

COMPANION, THE POET'S, AND RHYMING DICTIONARY. (Anon.) 12°, pp. 70. New York, 1849.

COMFIELD, (MRS. AMELIA S.) Alida; or, Miscellaneous Sketches, etc. 12°, pp. 240. New York, 1849.

CONANT, (S. S.) The Circassian Boy. Translated through the German, from the Russian of Michail Lermontoff. Sq. 18°, pp. 87. Boston, 1875.

CONCISE ANSWER to the question, Who and What are the Shakers? 18°, pp. 16. Stockbridge, Mass., 1826.

CONDOTTIERI, THE. Two Poems. (Anon.) 12°, pp. vii, 59 and 20. A Satire. Philadelphia, 1821.

The first of these two poems relates the adventures of the Condottieri, bands of lawless and independent soldiery, who, early in the seventeenth century, became the terror

CONDOTTIERI, THE.— (*Continued.*)

and the scourge of Italy. It is dedicated to Robert Walsh, Esq. The second poem, dedicated to Alexander S. Coxe, Esq., is a satirical portrait of the follies of Philadelphia Society.

COXE, (S. W.) The Proud Ladye, etc. 18°, pp. 144. New York, 1840.

CONFERENCE ON SOCIETY AND MANNERS IN MASSACHUSETTS. (Anon.) 18°, pp.     Boston, 1820.

CONFERENCE, THE ; OR, SKETCHES OF WESLEYAN METHODISM. (Anon.) 12°, pp. 92. Bridgeton, N. J., 1823.

CONGDON, (CAROLINE M.) The Guardian Angel, etc. 12°, pp. 250. Auburn, 1857.

CONGDON, (C. T.)

A well-known American writer, connected for many years with the *New York Tribune*. He was born at New Bedford, Mass., and pursued his studies for a time in Brown University.

— Flowers Plucked by a Traveller on the Journey of Life. 12°, pp. 71. Boston, 1840.

CONGRESS. The Dogs, in three Chantlets. An autograph MS. neatly written. 8°, not paged. No place. Written not far from 1778.

"A dirty poem, much in the style of Dean Swift, intended to ridicule the Americans when they first revolted."

CONKEY, (MRS. M.) Cottage Musings ; or, Select Pieces in Prose and Verse. 12°, pp. 184. New York, 1835.

— Same. 12°, pp. x, 184. New York, 1835.

CONNOLLY, (C. C.) Tones on the Harp. 12°, pp. 199. Washington, 1861.

CONRAD, (R. T.)

Robert T. Conrad was born in 1808 at Philadelphia, and was distinguished as an orator and a dramatic writer. He died in 1858.

— Aylmere ; or, the Bondman of Kent, etc. 12°, pp. 329. Philadelphia, 1852.

CONTINUATION, A, OF HUDIBRAS. In two Cantos. (Anon.) 16°, pp. (4) and 76. London, 1773.

In the same volume, and on paper having the same water-mark as the printed portion of it, is a manuscript continuation, believed to be in the hand-writing of the author of the first two Cantos, containing

Canto the Third. Never printed. pp. 77–108.
Canto the Fourth. [Unfinished.] pp. (11).

Convention, General, An Epistle to the. (By a Country Bard. Anon.) 12°, pp. 12. No place. October, 1847.

Conway, (H. J.)

Hiram J. Conway was born in England in 1800, and died at Philadelphia, April 12, 1860.

— Hiram Hireout. 12°, pp. 21. New York, no date.

— Our Jemimy. A Farce. 12°, pp. 25. New York, no date.

Conwell, (C. C.) The Hymns of Homer, etc. 12°, pp. 122. Philadelphia, 1830.

Cook's Dream; or, What is Poverty? (Anon.) 18°, pp. 12. Boston, 1834.

Cook, (E.) The Sot-Weed Factor; or, A Voyage to Maryland. A Satyr: In which is describ'd The Laws, Government, Courts and Constitutions of the Country, and also the Buildings, Feasts, Frolics, Entertainments and Drunken Humours of the Inhabitants of that Part of America. In Burlesque verse, by Eben Cook, Gent. London: Printed and sold by *Dr. Bragg*, at the *Raven* in *Paternoster-Row*, 1708. (Price, 6s.)

The above is the full title of the original, of which the copy in " The Harris Collection " is a reprint, forming No. II. of Shea's Early Southern Tracts, with an introduction by Brantz Mayer. The volume is a 4°, pp. vi, 20. No place, no date. Sot-Weed means the sot making or inebriating weed; a name for *tobacco* used at that time. A Sot-Weed Factor was a tobacco agent or supercargo.

Mayer says: "We may, I imagine, very reasonably suppose 'Eben Cook' to have been a London 'Gent,' rather decayed by fast living, sent abroad to see the world and be tamed by it, who very soon discovered that Lord Baltimore's Colony was not the Court of her Majesty Queen Anne, or its taverns frequented by Addison and the wits, and whose disgust became supreme when he was 'finished' on the 'Eastern Shore' by

'A pious, conscientious Rogue,'

who, taking advantage of his incapacity for trade, cheated him out of his cargo, and sent him home without a leaf of the coveted 'Sot-Weed.'" This poem is, very likely, the result of that homeward voyage. With proper allowance for breadth and burlesque, angry exaggeration and the discomforts of such a "Gentleman" as we may fancy Master Cook to have been, it is well worth preservation as history, if not photographing the manners and customs of the ruder classes in a British Province a century and a half ago. The original tract is very rare.

Cook, (H. C.) Musings and Meditations. 12°, pp. 217. Providence, 1852.

Cook, (W.) Poems. 12°. Salem, 1852.

— Same. 1859.

— Sunbeam Through Pagan Clouds. 18°, pp. 15. Salem, 1853.

COOKE, (P. P.)

Philip Pendleton Cooke was born at Martinsburg, Berkeley county, Va., October 26, 1816, graduated at Princeton, in 1835, was admitted to the bar, and married before reaching his majority. Besides his political productions, he wrote several tales for the "Southern Literary Messenger." He died January 20, 1850.

— Froissart Ballads, etc. 12°, pp. xi, 216. Philadelphia, 1847.

COOLEY, (J. E.)

Born in Massachusetts in 1802, published in 1839 "The American in Egypt."

— Extracts from Humbugiana. 12°, pp. 24. Gotham, 1847.

COOLIDGE, (G.) Anniversary Poems. 8°, pp. 16. Boston, 1844.

COOMER, (G. H.) Miscellaneous Poems. 12°, pp. viii, 168. Boston, 1851.

COOPER, (W.) Original Sacred Music. pp. 12. Boston, no date.

COPCUTT, (F.) Edith. A Play. 12°, pp. 83. New York, 1857(?).

COPELAND, (W. P.) Stanlico Africanus. Stanley's Trip from Zanzibar to Ujiji. 18°, pp. 16. No place, no date.

COPPÉE, (H., LL. D.)

Henry Coppée was born at Savannah, Ga., October 13, 1821, was for a time a student at Yale, and graduated at West Point in 1845. For several years he served in the army, was in the Mexican war, was an instructor in West Point from 1848 to 1855, resigned the latter year, was professor of English literature in the University of Pennsylvania from 1855 to 1866, president of the Lehigh University from 1866 to 1875, when he was appointed professor of History in that institution.

— A Gallery of Famous English and American Poets, with an Introductory Essay by Henry Coppée. 4°, pp. xxxii, 448. Philadelphia, 1873.

Illustrated with nearly one hundred and fifty steel engravings, executed in the finest style of the art, mostly from original designs by distinguished artists. An elegant volume, neatly bound with gilt edges.
This volume is in the special Anthony part of the collection, and is one of the finest in the entire collection in its general "make-up."

CORDORA. A Poetical Romance. (By F. S. M. Anon. S. M. Fitton [?]). 12°, pp. 86. St. Louis, 1849.

CORDOVA, (R. J. DE)

A New York banker.

— The Prince's Visit. Illustrated. 8°, pp. 34. New York, 1861.

CORNELL, (J. F. D.)  Arthur and Constance; or, The Power of Love.
12°, pp. 24.  New York, 1858.

COUCH, (W.)  Hymns.  16°, pp. 64.  Andover, N. H., 1819.

COURAGE.  The Sweepers.  A Satyr.  (By A. and B. Mechanics.)  12°,
pp. 8.  No place, 1774.

Cox, (C. C.)  Female Education.  8°, pp. 44.  Frederick, Md., 1858.

Cox, (J.)  Rewards and Punishments, etc.  12°, pp. 20.  Philadelphia,
. 1795.

Cox[E], (A. C.)
> Arthur Cleaveland Coxe, son of Rev. Dr. S. H. Cox, was born at Mendham, N. J.,
> May 10, 1818, graduated at the University of the city of New York in 1838, studied theology
> in the General Theological Seminary, New York, and was ordained Deacon in the Protest-
> ant Episcopal Church, July, 1841.  After filling the office of Rector in several churches, he
> was chosen Bishop of Western New York in 1865.  He occupies a distinguished place
> among the religious poets of the country.

— Advent.  A Mystery.  12°, pp. 132.  New York, 1837.
— Christian Ballads.  32°.  Oxford, 1848.
— A New Edition.  18°, pp. 254.  Oxford, 1853.
— Same.  5th Edition.  Philadelphia, 1855.
— Same.  15th Edition.  18°, pp. 227.  Philadelphia, no date.

COXE, (S. H., JR.)  The Progress of the Church.  Pronounced before
the Euglossian Society of Geneva College, August 1, 1843.  12°,
pp. 21.  Geneva, 1843.

COXE, (L. DE T.)  Yacht Seadrift.  Her Log.  Cruise of August, 1867.
12°, pp. 18.  No place, no date.

CRAFTS, (W.)
> William Crafts was born in Charleston, S. C., January 24, 1787, graduated at Harvard
> in 1805, and was an eminent lawyer in his native city.  For some time he was editor of
> the *Charleston Courier*.  He died at Lebanon Springs, N. Y., September 23, 1826.

— Sullivan's Island.  8°, pp. 100.  Charleston, 1820.
— The Romance of the Sea Serpent.  12°, pp. 172.  Cambridge, 1849.
> Two or three songs in this volume.

CRAIGENGELT, (A., *pseud.*)  Rhodoshake's Visit from the Moon.  8°,
pp. 63.  New York, 1832.
> Bound in the same volume are R. H. Stoddard's "Footprints," and Street's "Our
> State."

Cranch, (C. P.)

Christopher Pease Cranch was born at Alexandria, D. C., March 8, 1813, and was the son of Judge William Cranch. He graduated at Columbian College, Washington, D. C., in 1831, and studied theology at Cambridge. He became well known as a landscape painter. His poems have been warmly commended.

— Poems.   12°, pp. 116.   Philadelphia, 1844.

— Satan :   Libretto.   Sq. 18°, pp. 36.   Boston, 1874.

Crapo, (W. W.)   Poem.   Yale.   June 16, 1852.   8°, pp. 47, (with Oration by H. Sprague.)   New Haven, 1852.

Crawley, (Eliza).   Poems.   12°, pp. 192.   Charleston, 1826.

Cream of Tartar.   (Anon.)   Lg. 8°, pp. 32.   New York, 1871.

Creation, The ; or, A Morning Walk with Anna.   (Anon.)   18°, pp. 52.   Philadelphia, 1843.

Cressy, (N.)   The Battle and Monument of Bunker Hill compared with the Agonies and Triumphs of the Cross.   12°, pp. 24.   Portland, no date.

Crider, (H. M.)   Pedagogics.   12°, pp. 87.   York, Pa., 1866.

Crihfield, (A.)   The Universaliad ; or, Confession of Universalism, etc.   12°, pp. x, 192.   Cincinnati, 1849.

Crisfield, (Mrs. C. L.)   A Wayside Flower, etc,   12°, pp. 92.   Baltimore, 1875.

Crockett, Davy ; or, The Nimrod of the West.   The Only Cure for Hard Times.   (Anon.)   12°, pp. iv, 46.   New York, 1837.

Croke, (J. G.)   Lyrics of the Law.   Sq. 18°, pp. 312.   San Francisco, 1884.

Crosby, (Frances J.)   Libretto of the Flower Queen.   12°, pp. 15.   New York, 1852.

— The Blind Girl, etc.   12°, pp. 157.   New York, 1844.

— Monterey, etc.   12°, pp. 203.   New York, 1851.

Croswell, (W., D. D.)

William Croswell was born at Hudson, N. Y., November 7, 1804, and graduated at Yale in 1822. Among his classmates were Rev. Drs. Edward Beecher, H. N. Brinsmade, T. Stillman, John Todd and T. E. Vermilye, Hon. Osmyn Baker, M. C., Professors G. T. Bowen, E. H. Leffingwell and I. H. Townsend, and Harvey P. Peet, LL. D. He studied theology at the General Theological Seminary, New York, was ordained Deacon in the

CROSWELL, (W., D. D.) — *Continued.*

> Protestant Episcopal Church by Bishop Brownell, and was Rector of Christ Church, Boston, 1829–40, of St. Peter's Church, Auburn, N. Y., 1840–44, and of the Church of the Advent, Boston, 1844, to his death, November 9, 1851.

— Poems.   16°, pp. xlviii, 284.   Boston, 1867.

CROWN, (J.)

> John Crown, or Crowne, the son of an Independent minister, was born in Nova Scotia not far from the middle of the seventeenth century.  To escape from the gloomy restraints of the place of his nativity, he went to England, and for a time was a Gentleman Usher in the family of an old Independent lady.  Weary and disgusted with this situation he turned his attention to writing, and soon became a favorite at the Court of Charles II.  Court favor, however, proved precarious, and he petitioned the King to put him into a position where he could be reasonably assured of a permanent support.  Charles made it a condition of granting his request that he should write a Comedy.  "Sir Courtly Nice" was the result; but just before it was put upon the stage Charles died, and Crowne was left unprovided for.  With regard to this Comedy, Dennis, in his "Original Letters," London, 1721, says:  "Tho' I have more than twenty times read over this charming comedy, yet I have always read it, not only with delight, but rapture.  And 'tis my opinion that the greatest Comick Poet that ever lived in any age might have been proud to have been the author of it."  Crowne died about the year 1703.  He was the author of seventeen tragedies and comedies.  His dramatic works were collected and collated by W. E. Burton, in Philadelphia, in 1848, the original editions being bound in four volumes.  The following are the plays:

VOL. I.

1. Juliana; or, The Princess of Poland.  London, 1671.
2. History of Charles the Eighth of France.  London, 1692.  Or, The Invasion of Naples by the French.  London, 1672.
3. The Country Wit.  A Comedy.  London, 1675.
4. Calisto; or, The Chaste Nymph.  London, 1675.

VOL. II.

1. Andromache.  A Tragedy.  London, 1675.
2. The Destruction of Jerusalem.  In Two Parts.  London, 1677.
3. City Politiques.  A Comedy.  1683.

VOL. III.

1. The Ambitious Statesman.  London, 1679.
2. The Miseries of Civil War.  A Tragedy.  London, 1680.
3. The same.  Part II.  London, 1681.
4. Thyestes.  A Tragedy.  London, 1681.
5. Sir Courtly Nice; or, It Cannot Be.  London, 1685.

VOL. IV.

1. Darius.  A Tragedy.  London, 1688.
2. The English Frier; or, The Town Sparks.  London, 1690.
3. Regulus.  A Tragedy.  London, 1694.
4. Married Beau.  London, 1694.
5. Caligula.  A Tragedy.  London, 1698.

> Mr. Harris took much interest in collecting the works of John Crowne.  Several written pages of criticisms on his plays are preserved in the collection.  It is an interesting circumstance that the four volumes referred to reached Providence on or about the day of the death of Mr. H.

CROWN, (J.) — *Continued.*

— Dœneids; or, The Noble Labors of the Great Dean of Notre-Dame in Paris, etc. 8°, pp. 32. London, 1692.

— History of Charles the Eighth, etc. 8°, pp. 79. London, 1692.

— Dramatists of the Restoration. 4 vols. 8°, pp. xviii, 342, 396, 457, 426. Edinburgh and London, 1873.

The four volumes of the dramatic writings of Crowne make up only a part of the series.

— Henry the Sixth; or, The Murder of the Duke of Glocester. 8°, pp. 70. London, 1681.

— Sir Courtly Nice; or, It Cannot Be. A Comedy. 18°, pp. 81. London, 1731.

— The Married Beau. 8°, pp. 66. London, 1694.

— The Old English Drama. 4 vols. 8°. London, 1671–98.

— Thyestes. A Tragedy. 8°, pp. 56. London.

CRUICKSHANKS, (J., JR., *pseud.*) A Bouquet of Flowers, etc. 12°, pp. 38. New York and London, 1851.

CRUMMELL, (A.) The Man: The Hero: The Christian: Thomas Clarkson. 8°, pp. 44. New York, 1847.

CUMMING, (J. D.) Thanksgiving Eve. 12°, pp. 48. Greenfield and Mirick, 1847.

"CUPID ABROAD," ARRESTED. (Anon.) Jupiter Tonans Donnerhagel, (*pseud.*) 8°, pp. 20. Gettysburg, 1846.

CURE FOR THE SPLEEN, A; OR, AMUSEMENT FOR A WINTER'S EVENING; being the substance of a conversation on the times, over a friendly tankard and pipe, between Sharp, a country parson; Bumper, a country justice; Fillpot, an innkeeper; Graveairs, a deacon; Trim, a barber; Brim, a Quaker; Puff, a late Representative. Taken in shorthand by Roger de Coverly. 8°, pp. 32. America, 1775.

CURRIE, (E. A.) Masonry. 8°, pp. 25. Baltimore, 1851.

CURRIE, (HELEN.) Poems. 18°, pp. 150. Philadelphia, 1818.

CURTIS, (H. P.) Uncle Robert, etc. 12°, pp. 34. Boston, no date.

CURTIS, (J. W.) Poems. 12°, pp. 168. New York, 1846.

CUSHING, (E. J.) Business Lyrics, by the best Poets (dead and alive). Compiled by E. J. C. 12°. Providence, 1881.

Cushing, (E. J.) — *Continued.*

These poems by E. J. Cushing are humorous imitations of English and American poets. The following is the first verse of a poem entitled "Eighteen per Cent. By II. W. Longfellow":

> "The hour of three was well-nigh past
> When up a broker's staircase fast,
> A youth, who held in hands like ice,
> Some paper, with this strange device,
>                 Eighteen per cent."

Among the poets imitated are Southey, Goldsmith, Pope, Moore, Scott, Longfellow, Holmes and Poe.

Custis, (G. W. P.)

George Washington Parke Custis was born in Maryland in 1781, and was the adopted son of Gen. Washington. He died in 1857.

— Pocahontas.  A National Drama.  12°, pp. 47.  Philadelphia, 1830.

Cutler, (E. J.)  Liberty and Law.  18°, pp. 11.  Boston, 1862.

Cutts, (Mary.)  The Autobiography of a Clock.  12°, pp. 247.  Boston, 1852.

Cutter, (B. H.)  Eulogy on General Scott, etc.  16°, pp. 8.  No place, 1861.

— Poetical Lecture Suggested After Seeing the Model of Solomon's Temple.  18°, pp. 20.  Flushing, 1860.

— The New England Kitchen.  18°, pp. 8.  No place, 1864.

Cutter, (G. W.)

George Washington Cutter was born in Kentucky, and was captain of volunteers in the Mexican war. One of his best known poems is "The Song of Steam."

— Buena Vista, etc.  12°, pp. 168.  Cincinnati, 1848.

— Poems.  Additional and Patriotic.  8°, pp. 279.  Philadelphia, 1857.

— Poems and Fugitive Pieces.  12°, pp. 273.  Cincinnati, 1857.

Cuyahoga County, The Bench and Bar of.  (Title-page gone.)  12°, pp. 42.

Cynick, The.  By Growler Gruff, Esq., aided by a Confederacy of Lettered Dogs.  16°, pp. iv, 210.  Philadelphia, 1812.


Dabney, (R.)

Richard Dabney was born in the county of Louisa, Va., not far from 1787. The name is the same with that of the celebrated author of "The History of the Reformation," D'Aubigné. After completing his early education he was for a time an assistant teacher in a school in Richmond. Subsequently he returned to his native place, where he spent the rest of his life. It is painful to add that that he became an opium-eater and a lover of ardent spirits, dying prematurely in November, 1825.

Dabney, (R.) — *Continued.*

— Poems Original and Translated. 2d Edition. 18°, pp. iv, 172. Philadelphia, 1815.

Dade Asylum, The; or, Mental Monument to Major Dade and those who have fallen in the Florida War. (Anon.) 18°, pp. 40. Charleston, 1839.

Dadmun, (J. W.)

A well-known minister of the Methodist Episcopal Church.

— "Revival Melodies." 8°, pp. —. Boston, 1858.

Dagnall, (J. M.) Daisy Swain, the Flower of Shenandoah. A Tale of the Rebellion. Illustrated. 16°, pp. vi, 167. Brooklyn, N.Y., 1865.

Dagnall, (J. W.) The Mexican; or, Love and Land. 16°, pp. 228. New York, 1868.

Founded on the invasion of Maximilian.

Daily, (H. C.) Guide to the Great Falls of the Potomac. Sq. 18°, pp. 18. Washington, 1884.

Dailey, (W. B.) Saratoga. A Dramatic Historical Romance. 12°, pp. 96. Corning, N. Y., 1848.

Dake, (O. C.) Midland Poems. 12°, pp. 284. Lincoln, Neb., 1884.

Dakota Language, Hymns in. Edited by S. R. Riggs and J. P. Williamson. 18°, pp. 162. New York, no date.

Dale, (Azania.) Country Verses. 12°, pp. 87. Washington, 1865.

Dana, (R. H.)

Richard Henry Dana, a descendant of Anne Bradstreet, was born at Cambridge, Mass., November 15, 1787, graduated at Harvard College in 1808, was admitted to the bar in 1811, was editor of the "North American Review," 1818-19. His first published poem was "The Dying Raven," which appeared in the "New York Review," then edited by W. C. Bryant, in 1821. "The Buccaneer," his most celebrated production, appeared in 1827. He ranks very high among American poets. His death occurred February 2, 1879.

— Poem at Andover, September 29, 1829. 8°, pp. 15. Boston, 1829.

— Poems. 18°, pp. xiii, 113. Boston, 1827.

— The Buccaneer, etc. 32°, pp. xviii, 156. London, 1844.

— Same. London, 1850.

Danforth, (J.)

John Danforth was born in Roxbury, Mass., November 8, 1660, graduated at Harvard in 1677, ordained pastor of the church in Dorchester, Mass., June 28, 1682, and died May

DANFORTH, (J.) — *Continued.*

26, 1730, being the last minister of the "First Church" in Dorchester who died in office before Nathaniel Hall, D. D., who died in 1875.

In his "Annals," Blake says: "He was sᵈ to be a man of great Learning, he understood yᵉ Mathematics beyond most men of his Function. He was exceedingly Charitable, & of a very peacefull temper. He took much pains to Eternize yᵉ names of many of yᵉ good Christians of his own Flock; And yet yᵉ World is so ungratefull, that he has not a Line Written to preserve his Memory. No, not so much as upon his Tomb; he being buried in Lt. Gov. Stoughton's Tomb, that was covered with writing before."

— Kneeling to God, at Parting with Friends ; or, the Fraternal Intercessory Cry of Faith and Love. Setting Forth and Recommending the Primitive Mode of taking *Leave*, etc. Sm. 8°, pp. 63. Annexed to this discourse is a Poem to the Memory of Mrs. Anne Eliot, pp. 64–65. Also one to the Memory of Mr. John Eliot, "the Apostle to the Indians," pp. 66–72. Boston, 1697.

This little volume, purchased at the Brinley sale for $15.00, is bound in Bedford's most attractive style. It finds a place in "The Harris Collection" because of the two poems referred to. After consulting several "Collections" of American Poetry without finding any reference to these poems, we conclude that they are very rare. If we are to believe the worthy Dorchester pastor, Mrs. Eliot was a most remarkable person, justly entitled to his loftiest panegyric :

> "With all the World *America* shall Vye,
> For to produce thy Peer : Now cast thine Eye
> All round about that Spacious Room
> None shalt thou see
> Of Best Women
> Much more *Triumphant* than
> Thy self to be.

> " Haile ! Thou *Sagacious* & Advent'rous Soul !
> Haile, Amazon ! Created to Controll
> Weak Nature's Foes, & t' take her part.

> " The King of Terrours. Thou 'till the Com-
> Irrevocable came to stay thy Hand,     (mand
> Didst oft *Repel*, by thy *Choice Art :*
> By *High Decree,*
> Long didst thou stand
> An Atlas, in Heav'n's Hand
> To th' *World* to be."

In strains equally lofty does he eulogize the husband of Mistress Eliot, who died a little more than three years after the death of this, his peerless consort. Judged by our modern standards, what shall be said of the poetry of this remarkable production? We select the following extracts :

> "S Hall Eliot slip away? & not his *Sons*
> Spy & Regret it, with Athletick Groans?
> None Cry *Alarm*, when *Horse* & Chariots taken?
> None Feel, when Israel's weal's Foundation's shaken?
> Lately, stately Stone pluckt out; none 'spy it?
> Nor run to Stop the woful Breach made by it?"

DANFORTH, (J.) — *Continued.*

How impossible it is to describe the dreadful calamity which has taken place in the death of Eliot is set forth in the following terms :

> " Since Babel's Trait'rous *Tower* was Thunder-
> By Heav'ns Inraged Ire, & fell, & split  smit
> Can tell the wounds, which this *one too* alone
> Hath *more than Scarr'd the World* with; next th' Ex
> At first *from Paradise*, & th' *next Convulsion*     (pulsion
> In Grandsire *Japheth's* Time, no Storm before,
> The Universal *World* e're delug'd more."

Eliot, as scholar, translator, eloquent divine, if we take the decision of the poet, never had a peer :

> " One Testament *Seventy Intrepreters*
> Translate to *Greek, Antiquity* avers;
> *Both Testaments*, yet Eliot alone
> Converts in the Indian Tongue & Tone;
> *Abel*, tho' dead, yet speaks, in one Tongue more;
> Isay's, Apollo's Eloquence, before,
> Ne're Rode in such a *chariot :* Like Phynian     .
> (Tho' skill'd in Pulse) would scarce tell the
>                 Condition
> Of his own Gospe : Paul, with his much Learning,
> Would here be Posed :
>         For 'though to many *Regions* He did pass,
>         Yet no *West-Indian Antiquary* was"

The above must suffice as furnishing an illustration of this singular production of some 340 lines.

DANIEL, (C. T.)   William and Annie ; or, A Tale of Love and War, etc.   18°, pp. 112.   Guelph, 1864.

DANIELS, (MRS. EUNICE T.)

Miss Eunice K. True was born at Plainfield, N. H., November 14, 1806, and was married in 1830 to William H. Daniels.  She died June 16, 1841.

— Poems.   12°, pp. 184.   New York, 1843.

DANN, (A.)   Glimpses of Light and Shade.   Read before the Euglossian Society, Geneva College, August 3, 1842.   8°, Geneva, N. Y., 1842.

DANNELLY, (MRS.)   Destruction of the City of Columbia, S. C.   12°, pp. 24.   Charleston, 1866.

DANVERS, MASS., CENTENNIAL CELEBRATION, June 16, 1852.   Poem by Andrew Nichols.  pp. 37, etc.   8°, whole number pp. 208.   Boston, 1852.

D'ARCY, (U. D.)   The Black Vampyre ; A Legend of St. Domingo. 18°, pp. 72.   New York, 1819.

D'ARUSMONT (FANNY WRIGHT) ALTORF.

Born in England in 1795. About the year 1830 she made herself notorious by the pub.
lication of doctrines which, it is said, she subsequently repudiated. She died in Cincinnati in 1852.

— A Tragedy.  8°.  London, 1822.

DAUGHTERS OF EVE.  (Anon.)  12°, pp. 91.  Schenectady, 1829.

DAVID AND URIAH.  (Anon.)  12°, pp. iv, 34.  Philadelphia, 1835.

DAVID, (E.)  Offers of Christ No Gospel Preaching.  18°, pp. 20.
Philadelphia, 1770.

DAVIDSON, (L. M.)

Lucretia M. Davidson was born at Plattsburg, N. Y., September 27, 1808; began to
write poetry when she was a child, her earliest published poem having been written at
the age of eleven. She displayed remarkable precocity and intellectual brilliancy, and at
the time of her death, before she was seventeen years of age, she left no less than 278
pieces, 140 having been destroyed previous to that event. She died August 27, 1825.

— Amir Khan.  pp. 174.  New York, 1829.

— Biography and Poetical Remains, by Washington Irving.  12°, pp.
359.  Philadelphia, 1841.

— Poetical Remains.  12°, pp. 312.  Philadelphia, 1841.

— Same.  With a Biography by Miss Sedgwick.  A new Edition
revised.  12°, pp. 248.  New York, 1850.

— Poems.  Illustrated by Darley.  12°, pp. 270.  New York, 1871.

DAVIDSON, (M. M.)

Margaret M. Davidson, a sister of Lucretia, born in 1823. Her poetry attracted the
attention of Washington Irving, who wrote a memoir of her. She died in 1838, before
she was 16 years of age.

— Poetical Remains.  12°, pp. 248.  Boston, 1854.

DAVIDSON, (R.)  Geography Epitomized.  12°, pp. 60.  Morristown,
1803.

DAVIS, (MARTHA ANN.)  Poems of Laura.  18°, pp. 106.  Petersburg,
Va., 1818.

DAVIS, (R. B.)

Richard Brigham Davis was born in the city of New York, August 21, 1771, and was
educated at Columbia College. His life was devoted chiefly to literary pursuits. In manners and address he is said to have resembled Oliver Goldsmith. "His simplicity was
most remarkable in one who had been born and brought up in the midst of a crowd of his
fellow-men." He died in 1799.

— Poems.  12°, pp. xxxi, 154.  New York, 1807.

DAVALOS, (ISABEL.) The Maid of Seville. 18°, pp. 7, with pp. 90 of Notes. (Anon.) Glens Falls, N. Y., 1832.

DAWES, (R.)

Rufus Dawes was born at Boston, January 26, 1803, studied at Harvard, but did not receive his degree, being charged with a violation of the college laws, of which it was subsequently proved that he was not guilty. He was admitted to the bar, but did not practice, preferring literature to law. He died November 30, 1859.

— Athenia of Damascus. A Tragedy. 12°, pp. 118. New York, 1839.

— The Valley of the Nashaway, etc. 18°, pp. 96. Boston, 1830.

DAWES, (T.)

Thomas Dawes was born at Boston in 1757, graduated at Harvard in 1777, became a lawyer, was appointed Judge of the Supreme Court in 1792, resigned in 1802, then was made Judge of Probate for the county of Suffolk, and Judge of the Municipal Court in Boston. He retained the former office till his death in July, 1825.

— The Law Given at Sinai. The name of the author does not appear on the title-page. (By a Young Gentleman.) The Poem is dedicated to President Langdon of Harvard College. 4°, pp. 7. Boston, 1777.

DAY DREAMS. By a Butterfly. In Nine Parts. 12°, pp. 156. Kingston, C. W., 1854.

DAY, (H. W.) Revival Hymns. 18°, pp. 72. Boston, 1842.

DAY, (S. M.) Pencillings of Light and Shade. 12°, pp. 70. Schenectady, 1850.

DEANE, (E.) A Poetical Oration. Pronounced at Tiverton, July 4, 1804. 12°, pp. 23. Dedham, 1804.

DEANE, (S., D. D.)

Samuel Deane was born at Norton, Mass., not far from 1741, graduated at Harvard in 1760, settled as colleague of Rev. Thomas Smith, pastor of the First Parish at Falmouth, now Portland, Me. After preaching forty-five years to this church, he received as colleague Rev., afterward Dr., Ichabod Nichols. Brown University conferred on him, in 1790, the degree of D. D. He died November 12, 1814.

— Pitchwood Hill. 18°, pp. 11. Written in the year 1780, and appeared originally in the Cumberland, Me., *Gazette*, March 5, 1795. Portland, 1806.

De Chatelain, (Chevalier.)   Evangeline; Suivie des Voix de la Nuit;
Poèmes Traduits de H. Longfellow.   16°, pp. viii, 92.   London,
Paris, New York, 1856.

De Costa, (B. F.)
Benjamin Franklin De Costa, D. D., a well-known minister of the Protestant Episco-
pal Church, at this date (1880) Rector of the Church of St. John the Evangelist, New York
city.
— Hiawatha.   The Story of the Iroquois Sage in Prose and Verse.
Sm. 8°, pp. 32.   New York, 1873.

Deems, (C. M. F.)   Devotional Melodies.   12°, pp. x, 48.   Raleigh,
1841.

De Grasse, (Will.)   Swallows on the Wing, etc.   12°, pp. 80.   New
York, 1866.
Several poems in the volume.

De Kay, (C.)   Hesperus, etc.   8°, pp. 269.   New York, 1880.
— The Vision of Nimrod.   8°, pp. 261.   New York, 1881.

Deluge, The.   A Demi-Serious Poem.   By a Mr. Smith.   Canto the
First.   8°, pp. 50.   Philadelphia, printed for the Author, 1830.

D'Elville, (Ben.)   The Hermitage; or, Alphonso and Agnes.   24°, pp.
44.   New York, 1813.

Demarest, (Mary Lee.)   My Ain Countree, etc.   18°, pp. vi, 146.
New York, 1882.

Democracy.   An Epic Poem.   By Aquiline Nimble Chops, (pseud.)
Canto First.   12°, pp. 20.   New York, no date.

Demos in Council; or, 'Bijah in Pandemonium.   Being a Sweep of the
Lyre.   In close imitation of Milton.   (Anon.)   16°, pp. 16.
Boston, 1799.
The imitation is of the addresses of Satan and others to the vanquished spirits in hell.

Denis, (A.)   "Tammany Hall," etc.   12°, pp. 46.   New York, 1847.

Denison, (C. W.)   The American Village, etc.   18°, pp. 143.   Boston, 1845.

Denison, (E.)   The Lottery, etc.   (St. Denis le Cadet, pseud.)   12°,
pp. 71.   Baltimore, 1815.

Denison, (F.)

Frederic Denison was born at Stonington, Conn., September 28, 1819, graduated at Brown University in 1847, has been pastor of Baptist Churches in Westerly, R. I., Norwich, Conn., Central Falls, R. I., New Haven, Conn., Woonsocket and Providence, R. I., was Chaplain in the army three years, with the First Rhode Island Cavalry and Third Rhode Island Heavy Artillery. Present residence (1886), Providence, R. I.

— Canonicus Memorial. Poem delivered September 21, 1883, at the Erection of "The Boulder Memorial" in honor of Canonicus. pp. 18-23 of the Account of the Exercises. Providence, 1883.

— Demons in Council; A Temperance Lyric. 16°, pp. 12. Providence, 1878.

— Home-Lay at the Denison Homestead, November 29, 1883. 8°, pp. 28.

— Soul-Liberty. 18°, pp. 12. Mystic, Conn., 1872.

Denny, (W. H.) Succotash. Written on the occasion of the Centennial Celebration of the Evacuation of Fort Duquesne. 18°, pp. 24. Pittsburgh, 1858.

Dénouement, The ; or, Apollo Cured of the Blue Devil. Recited at the Anniversary of the Union Book Society, 1807. (Anon.) 12°, pp. 11. Washington, 1807.

Denton, (W.)

William Denton was born at Darlington, Durham county, England, in 1823. His education was in an English Penny School, and, for six months, at the age of nineteen, he attended a Normal School in London. While residing at the West he has devoted himself to teaching and lecturing.

— Poems. 2d Edition. 12°, pp. 118. Cleveland, 1859.

D'Entremont, (C. H.) Shoemaker's Original Poems. (Anon.) 1 p. folio, folded 4°. No place, no date.

Derby, (J. B.)

John Barton Derby was born at Salem, Mass., in 1793, and graduated at Bowdoin College in 1811. He studied law, and interested himself much in political matters. For some time he held an office in the Boston Custom House. He died in 1867.

— Musings of a Recluse. 18°, pp. 180. Boston, 1837.

— The Sea. 18°, pp. 16. Boston, 1840.

— The Village. 18°, pp. 18. Boston, 1841.

Description, A Metrical, of a Fancy Ball at Washington, April 9. 1858. (Anon.) Dedicated to Mrs. Senator Gwin. 4°, pp. 40. Washington, 1858.

DESERET DESERTED; OR, THE LAST DAYS OF BRIGHAM YOUNG. As performed at Wallack's Theatre. (Anon.) 12°, pp. 28. New York, no date.

DE VERE, (MARY A.) Love Songs. Sq. 16°, pp. 103. New York, 1870.

DE VERE, (VEY.) You Know How it is Yourself, Sir. A Humorous Poem. 18°, pp. 35. Boston, 1871.

DEVEREAUX, (MRS. R.) Poems. 8°, pp. 29. New York, 1803.

DEVEREUX, (G. H.) Literary Fables; or, Yriarte. Translated from the Spanish. 12°, pp. viii, 144. Boston, 1855.

DEVIL, THE, AND THE GROG-SELLER. (Anon.) 18°, pp. 15. Allegheny, 1842.

DEVIL'S SHAVING MILL. (Anon.) 18°, pp. 44. Taunton, 1813.

DEVIL'S, THE, NEW WALK. A Satire. (Anon.) 12°, pp. 12. Boston, 1848.

DE WITT, (SUSAN A.) The Pleasures of Religion. 18°, pp. 72. New York, 1820.

DE WOLF, (ABBY.) Poems for Children. 12°, pp. 33. Providence, 1855.

DE WOLF, (W.) Poems. 8°, not paged. Providence, privately printed, 1883.

Presented to "The Harris Collection" by Dr. J. J. De Wolf, a well-known physician of Providence.

DEXTER, (C.) Versions and Verses. 12°, pp. 156. Cambridge, 1865.

DIALOGUE BETWEEN A SOUTHERN DELEGATE AND HIS SPOUSE, ETC. (Mary V. V., *pseud.*) 8°, pp. 14. No place, 1774.

DICK, (A.) Splores of a Hallowe'en, Twenty Years Ago. 18°, pp. 22. Woodstock, C. W., 1867.

DICK SHIFT; OR, THE STATE TRIUMVIRATE. (Anon.) 16°, pp. 81. New York, 1819.

DICKINSON, (A.) The City of the Dead, etc. 18°, pp. iv, 108. New York, 1845.

Dickinson, (Mary Lowe.) Edelweiss. An Alpine Rhyme. Sq. 18°,
pp. 102. New York, 1876.

Dimmock, (C. H.) The Modern: A Fragment. 8°, pp. 24. Richmond, Va., 1866.

Dimond, (W.) Native Land; or, The Return from Slavery. An Opera
in Three Acts. 18°, pp. 71. New York, 1824.

Diogenes, The New. (Anon.) 18°, pp. 100. Philadelphia, 1848.

Discipline of Earth and Time, for Freedom and Immortality. Four
Books of an Unpublished Poem. (Anon.) 16°, pp. vi, 147.
Boston, 1854.

Discovery, The, of America. (Anon.) 8°, pp. 35. Richmond, 1835.
On p. 35 appears the name, "John Headlam, Durham University."

Dix, (J. A.) Dies Iræ. 12°, pp. 15. Cambridge, 1863.

Dix, (J. R.) Teaching and Teachers. In the "Massachusetts Teacher,"
for March, 1855. 8°, pp. 12.

Dix, (W. G.) Pompeii and other Poems. 12°, pp. 160. Boston, 1848.
— The Deck of the Crescent City. 12°, pp. 46. Boston, 1852.

Doane, (G. W., D. D.)
George Washington Doane was born at Trenton, N. J., in 1799, graduated at Union
College in 1818, ordained an Episcopal clergyman, Deacon 1821, and Priest 1823, Rector of
Trinity, New York, for three years, Professor in Washington, now Trinity, College, Hart-
ford, 1824-28, Rector of Trinity, Boston, 1828-32, consecrated Bishop of New Jersey, 1832,
died in 1859.

— Songs by the Way. 3d Edition. 8°, pp. viii, 196. Albany, 1875.

Doane, (H.) Poems. 18°, pp. 71. Boston, 1826.

Doddridge, (J.) Logan, etc. 12°, pp. 46. Buffalo Creek, Brooke
Co., Va., 1823.
— Same. 4°, pp. 76. Reprinted from the Virginia Edition of 1823.
Cincinnati, 1868.

Dodge, (Mrs. H. M.) Hesselrigge; or, The Death of Lady Wallace,
etc. 8°, pp. 158. Utica, 1827.

Dodge, (Mary M.) Along the Way. 12°, pp. 135. New York, 1879.
Well-known editor of "Saint Nicholas."

Domestic Industry. (Anon.) 18°, pp. 24. No place, no date.

Don Paez, and other Poems. (Anon.) 12°, pp. vii, 150. New York, 1847.

Donaldson, (S. J., Jr.) Lyrics and other Poems. 12°, pp. 208. Philadelphia, 1860.

Donnelly, (I. L.) The Mourner's Vision. 12°, pp. 80. Philadelphia, 1850.

Doxorio, (T. S.) Mœna, etc. 12°, pp. 144. Washington, 1847.

Doolittle, (J. C.) Poems. 18°, pp. 68. Toledo, Ohio, 1858.

Dorgan, (J. A.) Studies. 12°, pp. 223. Philadelphia, 1862.

Dorr, (Julia C. R.) Friar Anselmo, etc. 12°, pp. 178. New York, 1879.

— Vermont. A Centennial Poem. 8°, pp. 12. Boston, 1877.

Dorsey, (Mrs. Anna H.) Flowers of Love and Memory. 12°, pp. 137. Baltimore, 1849.

Dow, (J. E.) Autumn: A Prize Poem. 12°, pp. 87. Washington, 1848.

Dow, (P.)

Peggy Dow was the wife of the eccentric preacher, Lorenzo Dow.

— A Collection of Methodist Hymns. Selected by Peggy Dow. Second Edition. 24°, pp. iv, p. i being the title, and pp. iii and iv, "A Short Account of the Rise and Progress of the Camp Meetings in the United States." pp. 5–8, "Cosmopolite's Muse." pp. 8–128, Hymns. Philadelphia, 1816.

So rare and valuable that it was sent to London and bound by F. Bedford.

Downey, (S. W.) The Immortals. Published in *Congressional Record*, 4°, pp. 15. Washington, April 22, 1880.

Downing, (Mrs. ——.) Pluto: Being the Sad Story and Lamentable Fate of the Fair Minthe. 8°, pp. 35. Raleigh, 1867.

Do You Remember? No title-page. 18°, pp. 13.

Drake, (J. R.)

Joseph Rodman Drake was born in the city of New York, August 7, 1795, studied medicine and was admitted to practice, but did not follow his profession. He wrote the first four of "The Croaker Pieces," published in the *New York Evening Post*, March 10-20, 1819. His two poems, the "American Flag" and "Culprit Fay," have secured for their author a well-deserved reputation. He died in New York, September 2, 1820.

Drake; (J. R.) — (*Continued.*)
— American Flag. Illustrated by Darley. 4°, pp. 4. New York, 1861.
— The Culprit Fay. 12°, pp. 62. New York, 1859.
— Same. With One Hundred Illustrations. Lg. 12°, pp. 118. New York, 1867.

Dramatic Pieces. Three volumes bound in one. 12°, each piece paged by itself. New Haven, 1791.

Dream, A, of a Happier Time, etc. Lg. 8°, pp. 40. New York, 1855.

Drinkwater, (M.) The United Worlds. 12°, pp. 250. Hamilton, N. Y., 1834.

Drown, (D. A.) Fragrant Flowers, etc. 12°, pp. xii, 236. Boston, 1860.

Drunkard, The; or, The Fallen Saved. (Anon.) 12°, pp. 50. Boston, 1847.

Duane, (W. N.) (Phineas Camp, *pseud.*) Poems of the Mohawk Valley, etc. 12°, pp. vi, 204. Utica, N. Y., 1859.

Duboccage, (Madame.) La Columbiade; ou, La Foi Portée Au Nouveau Monde. Poëme. 12°, pp. 184. Paris, 1756.

Duffield, (S. W.) The Heavenly Land. 12°, pp. xv, 12. New York, 1867.

Duganne, (A. J. H.)
> Augustine Joseph Hickey Duganne was born at Boston in 1823, and devoted his life mainly to literary pursuits. He died in New York City, July 14, 1875.

— Massachusetts, etc. 32°, pp. 64. Boston, 1843.
— Parnassus in Pillory. A Satire by Motley Manners, Esq., (*pseud.*) 12°, pp. 96. New York, 1851.
— The Mission of Intellect. Delivered at the Metropolitan Hall, New York, December 20, 1852. 12°, pp. 33. New York, 1853.
— The Poetical Works. 8°, pp. x, 407. Philadelphia, 1855.

Dulcken, (H. W.) The Book of the German Songs, from the Sixteenth to the Nineteenth Century. 12°, pp. xxi, 324. London, 1856.

DUNLAP, (W.)

William Dunlap was born February 19, 1766, at Perth Amboy, N. J. For many years he was manager of the Park Theatre, New York, and was a voluminous writer of plays. He was also a popular portrait painter. For details see "Duyckinck's Cyclopedia," vol. I, pp. 537–544.

— Archers of Switzerland. 8°, pp. 94. New York, 1796.

— André. A Tragedy in Five Acts, etc. In which are added Authentic Documents respecting Major André, consisting of Letters to Miss Seward, The Cow Chase, Proceedings of the Court Martial, etc. 12°, pp. viii, 109. New York, 1798.

The "Letters" were written to Miss Julia Seward, of Litchfield, England, a sister of Honora Steward, to whom André was greatly attached.

— Blue Beard. A Dramatic Romance. 18°, pp. 46. New York, date indistinct, 1802(?).

— Darby's Return. A Comic Sketch. 12°, pp. 14. New York, 1789.

— Same. 18°, pp. 9. New York, 1807.

— False Shame. (The original MS.) 4°, not paged. New York, 1799.

— Fontainville Abbey. A Tragedy. 18°, pp. 209. New York, 1807.

— Fraternal Discord. A Drama. 18°, pp. 67. New York, 1809.

— Leicester. A Tragedy. 16°, pp. 150. New York, 1807.

— Lovers' Vows. A Play. 18°, pp. 74. New York, February, 1814.

— Peter the Great; or, The Russian Mother. A Play. 18°, pp. 56. New York, 1814.

— Ribbemont; or, The Feudal Baron. A Tragedy. 18°, pp. 72. New York, 1803.

— Tell Truth and Shame the Devil. A Comedy in Two Acts. 12°, pp. 44. New York, 1797.

— Trip to Niagara. A Farce. 18°, pp. 54. New York, 1830.

— The Father of an Only Child. A Comedy. 18°, pp. 81. New York, 1807.

— The Glory of Columbia Her Yeomanry. 18°, pp. 56. New York, May, 1817.

— The Good Neighbor. 18°, pp. 12. New York, 1814.

— The Italian Father. 18°, pp. 63. New York, May, 1810.

— The Voice of Nature. 18°, pp. 41. New York, 1803.

— Same. 2d Edition. New York, 1807.

— Wife of Two Husbands. 18°, pp. 55. New York, February, 1881.

Dunlap, (W.) — *Continued.*
— Yankee Chronology. 18°, pp. 16. New York, December, 1812.

Durfee, J., (LL. D.)

Job Durfee was born at Tiverton, R. I., September 20, 1790, graduated at Brown University in 1813, was admitted to the bar, was Representative to Congress 1820-25, elected Associate Judge of the Supreme Court of Rhode Island in 1833, and Chief Justice in 1835, "a position which he held with peculiar honor to himself and to the State through the trying period of the Dorr ' Rebellion,' and until his death." The principal poem, " What Cheer," was published in 1832, and was most favorably received in this country and in England. He died July 26, 1847.

— Complete Works. Edited by his son, Hon. Thomas Durfee, LL. D., Chief Justice of the Supreme Court, Rhode Island. 8°, pp. 523. Providence and Boston, 1849.

Durivage, (O. E.) The Lady of the Lions. 12°, pp. 20. New York, no date.
— The Stage Struck Yankee. A Farce. 12°, pp. 18. Boston, no date.

Dutcher, (J. W.) Narrative of the Mysterious Can. A Temperance Poem. 18°, pp. 104. Amenia, N. Y., 1854.

Dutton, (T.) A Christmas Hymn, December 25, 1810. 12°, pp. 22. Brattleborough, 1811.

Dwight, (T.)

Timothy Dwight, D. D., was born at Northampton, Mass., May 14, 1752, graduated at Yale College in 1769, was licensed to preach in 1777, was Chaplain for about two years in the Continental army, became pastor of the Greenfield, Conn., Congregational Church in 1783, and was President of Yale College from 1795 to 1817. He died January 11, 1817.

— Greenfield Hill. Poem in Seven Parts. 8°, pp. 181. New York, 1794.

Earnest Call, An, from a Schoolmaster, etc. 18°, pp. 8. No place, no date.

Earning a Living. (Anon.) A Comedy. 8°, pp. 62. New York, 1849.

Eastburn, (J. W., and his Friend.)

James Wallis Eastburn, an Episcopal clergyman, was born in England in 1797, and was a son of James Eastburn, the well-known bookseller of New York, and a brother of the late Bishop Manton Eastburn of Massachusetts. He was a graduate of Columbia College, New York, studied theology under Bishop Griswold, and in 1818 became Rector of an Episcopal Church in Accomac county in Virginia, and soon after died at the early age of

14

EASTBURN, (J. W., AND HIS FRIEND.) — *Continued.*

twenty-two. The "Friend" alluded to in the title was Robert C. Sand. For a deeply interesting account of the part taken by each of these intimate friends in the authorship of "Yamoyden," see "Griswold's Poets and Poetry of America," 1860, pp. 249–50.

EASTER VERSES FROM FAIRLEIGH COTTAGE. (Anon.)　Sq. 18°, pp. 11. No place, no date.

EASTMAN, (C. G.)

Charles G. Eastman was born in Oxford county, Me., in 1810. In 1846 he became editor of the *Vermont Patriot*, published in Montpelier, Vt. "He has been highly commended as a successful delineator of the rural life of New England." His death occurred at Burlington, Vt., in 1861.

— Poems.　12°, pp. 208.　Montpelier, 1848.

EATON, (B. A.)　The Minstrel, etc.　18°, pp. 54.　Boston, 1833.

EATON, (N. W.)　Alberto and Matilda. A Drama.　18°, pp. 17.　Boston, 1809.

EATON, (TH.)　Review of New York.　24°, pp. 144.　New York, 1813. — Same.　2d Edition.　1814.

EBERLE, (MRS. ELIZA.)　The Pilgrim's Progress in Verse.　18°, pp. 306. Berlin, N. Y., 1854.

— Same.　4th Edition.　18°, pp. x, 322.　New Haven, 1856.

ECHO, THE.　(Richard Alsop, Lemuel Hopkins, Theodore Dwight, etc.) 8°, pp. xv, 331.　No place, 1807.

See sketch of Richard Alsop, p. 9.

The series of papers entitled "The Echo," was originally published in Hartford, in the *American Mercury*, in 1791. It has its title "from the last of these productions, which are parodies or exaggerations of newspaper narratives, popular addresses, governors' speeches and proclamations of the time, which offered numerous specimens with abundant provocation for the witty treatment which they secured at the hands of the Hartford wits."

Duyckinck, from whom the above is quoted, says: "'The Echo' caught the noise, fury and rhodomontade of orators and the press, and resounded them in louder measure. If a penny-a-liner grew more maudlin and drunken in his style than usual; if an office-holder played his 'fantastic tricks,' a politician vapored, or a scientific pretender bored the public with his ignorance, or a French democratic procession moved at the heels of Genet, it was sure to be heard of from the banks of the Connecticut. Metaphors with politics ran high. As the Conservative party of the country, the Federalists had an advantage, at least in the assumption of authority in the matter, for the force and talent employed being equal, the entrenched party will always laugh loudest. What began in 'The Echo' with the mirthful travesty of a newspaper article, soon rose to the bitter sarcasm of political controversy. The democracy of the day supplied the motive. In some of the eccentricities of John Hancock there was enough ready material for amusement, while the downright western humour of Brackenridge offered more resistance to the treatment.

Echo, The.—(*Continued.*)

> The naiveté of the former invited ridicule, while the intentional drollery of the other already occupied the ground of satire. It is easy to ridicule a fool, unconscious of his simplicity, but a rival satirist is more difficult game. The New England echo, however, with its strongly reverberating powers, receiving voices from all parts of the country, was well worth listening to. It had, too, a guarantee for a certain decorum in the necessities of verse. If it fell into railing, the poetical 'Echo' was at least bound to choice words and harmonious numbers — though indifferent enough at times to such refinements — while occasionally the victims were under obligation to the wits for embalming their nonsense."
>
> To any one who has a fit of the " blues," we commend the reading of the parody, which was No. 1 of the " The Echo," on a highflown description which appeared in a Boston newspaper, July 14, 1791, of a storm of thunder and lightning, "on Tuesday last, about 4 o'clock P. M."

Echoes of Infant Voices. Dedicated to " The Bereaved and Sorrowing Parent." (M. A. H. Anon.) 16°, pp. 144. Boston, 1849.

Echoes of Nature. (Anon.) 12°, pp. 140. Philadelphia, 1848.

Eclogues. (By Hengist Hobnail, *pseud.*) 18°, pp. 16. New York, 1820.

Edgarton, (S. C.) The Flower Vase. 32°, pp. 157. Lowell, 1844.

Edmund's Lyre. With his Life, by W. A. R. (Anon.) 8°, pp. 350. Washington, 1826.

Edwards, (Amelia B.) Ballads. 18°, pp. x, 127. New York, no date.

Edwards, (C.)

> Charles Edwards was born in England in 1797, came to the United States and was counsellor-at-law in New York. Among his writings may be mentioned his " History and Poetry of Finger Rings." " A curious and interesting volume."

— Feathers From My Own Wings. 8°, pp. 200. New York, 1832.

Effort, The Humble. (Anon.) 8°, pp. 29. Baltimore, 1848.

Effusions of Female Fancy. (Anon.) Sm. 8°, pp. 59. New York, 1784.

Effusions, Patriotic. (By Bob Short, *pseud.*) 18°, pp. 46. No place, 1819.

Egg Thief, The. (By Bricktop, *pseud.*) 12°, pp. 47. New York, 1879.

Egmont. A Tragedy, translated from Goethe. 16°, pp. iv, 150. Boston, 1841.

EJECTED ADDRESSES, CONTAINING EPISCOPO PUNCH, ETC.  (Anon.)  12°,
pp. 21.  No place, 1845.

> Scene—Rooms in the *Herald* Building, 28th December, full meeting of Carriers:
> Senior Carrier in the Chair.  Meeting called in consequence of a failure on the part of the
> poets at large in responding to the offer of twenty-five dollars, made on the 9th inst., for
> the best New Year's Address.  Senior Carrier anticipating the failure, had, at the first
> meeting, advised each member of his corps to come to the call meeting prepared to con-
> tribute to an address himself.  He was secretly in favor of the corps of carriers doing its
> own poetry from the beginning.

ELEGAIC POEM ON DR. BENJAMIN RUSH.  (Anon.)  12°, pp. 32.  Philadelphia, 1813.

> In the same volume are "The Portrait," by J. Pierpont, "Apologetic Postscript," by
> Peter Pindar, and "The Minister Impregnable," Anon.

ELEGIES AND OTHER LITTLE POEMS.  (Anon.)  12°, not paged.  Baltimore, 1800.

ELEGY, AN.  On the Death of Daniel Oliver, Esq., Brother-in-law of
Gov. Belcher, of Massachusetts, who died in England, July 5,
1726.  12°, pp. 4.  No place, no date.

ELEGY, AN, TO THE INFAMOUS MEMORY OF SR. F. B.  (Anon.)  8°, pp.
14.  Not published, 1769.

ELEGY, FUNERAL, TO THE MEMORY OF MR. SAMUEL JACOMB.  (Anon.)
Sq. 12°.  No place, no date.

ELIOT, (J.)  Poems.  12°, pp. vi, 106.  Greenfield, Mass., 1798.

ELEGY ON THE DEATH OF JONATHAN MAYHEW, D. D.  4°, pp. 15.  Boston, no date, probably 1766.

ELIOT, (S. A.)  Schiller's Song of the Bell.  8°, pp. 16.  Boston, 1839.
Rev. Dr. W. E. Channing's copy.

ELLET, (MRS. E. F.)  Poems.  Translated and Original.  16°, pp. xi,
229.  Philadelphia, 1835.
— White Lies.  A Drama.  12°, pp. 36.  New York, 1858.

ELLIOT, (MARY.)  Gems in the Mine.  18°, pp. 104.  Lancaster, 1828.

ELLIS, (T. B.)  Poetic Fillings on the Warp of Trade.  12°, pp. 120.
New York, 1851.

ELLIS, (G. W., M. D.)  Poem on the Catastrophe on the United States
Steam Frigate Princeton.  18°, pp. 4.  Boston, 1844.

EMBLEMS OF MORTALITY. Death Represented by Numerous Engravings. (Anon.) 18°, pp. 102. Charleston, S. C., 1846.

EMERSON, (N. S.) A Thanksgiving Story; Embodying the Ballad of "Betsey and I Are Out," etc. 12°, pp. 200. New York, 1872.

EMERSON, (R. W.)

Ralph Waldo Emerson was born at Boston, May 25, 1803, graduated at Harvard College in 1821, taught in his brother's Ladies' School in Boston five years, in 1826 was "approbated to preach," ordained in March, 1829, colleague with Rev. Henry Ware of the Second Unitarian Church, Boston, resigned in 1832, and for the remainder of his life devoted himself to literary pursuits, lecturing, etc. He died April 27, 1882.

— Class Poem. 8°, pp. 52. Concord, 1838.
— May-Day, etc. 16°, pp. iv, 205. Boston, 1867.
— Poems. 18°, pp. 254. Boston, 1865. Blue and Gold Series.

EMMONS, (R., M. D.) Battle of Bunker Hill. 2d Edition. 16°, pp. 144. Boston, 1841.
— Defence of Baltimore, and Death of General Ross. 16°, not paged. Washington, 1831.
— The Fredoniad. 4 vols. 12°, pp. 357, 371, 326, 350. Philadelphia, 1830.

A fine copy. Bound in red morocco, with gilt edges, etc.

— The National Jubilee, etc. 12°, pp. 47. Washington, 1830.

EMMONS, (W.) An Oration and Poem. 8°, pp. 18. Boston, 1826.
— Tecumseh; or, The Battle of the Thames. A National Drama. 12°, pp. 36. New York, 1836.

ENGLAND. History of Kings and Queens of, in Verse. (Published by W. T. Smithson.) 12°, pp. 27. New York, 1869.

ENGLISH, (T.) Rest for the Weary. 18°, pp. 15. Newburyport, 1809.

ENGLISH, (T. D.) The Mormons. A Drama. 12°, pp. 43. New York, no date.
— Zephaniah Doolittle. 12°, pp. 24. Philadelphia, 1838.
— Same. 2d Edition.

EPHEMERA; OR, THE HISTORY OF COCKNEY DANDIES. (By H. Buzz, pseud.) 18°, pp. 14. Philadelphia, 1819.

EPISTLE, A FAIR. From a Little Poet to a Great Player. 12°, pp. 12. New York, 1818.

EPISTLE, AN, TO ZENAS. (Anon. In pencil, Gardiner's.) 12°, pp. 15. Boston, no date.

ESTABROOK, (J. E.) The Golden Wedding. 8°, pp. 7. Worcester, 1862.

ESTLACK, (R.) Ethick Diversions, in Four Epistles, etc. 12°, pp. 79. New York, 1807.

ESTWICK, (S., LL. D.) Maniacs, The; or, Fantasia of Bos Bibers. (By a West-Indian. Anon.) 12°, pp. 128. No place, 1824.

The author was an English clergyman.

EUGENIA; OR, EARLY SCENES. (By Marshall, *pseud.?*) 18°, pp. 59. New York, 1823.

EULOGIUM, AN, ON MAJOR GENERAL JOSEPH WARREN. (Anon.) 12°, pp. 21. Boston, 1781.

EUROPE, THE CONQUEST OF. In 14 Short Cantos. By Confucius, (*pseud.*) Edited by John Smith in the office of the "Congressional Library," in 1875. No place, 1876.

EUSTAPHIEVE, (A.) Alexis. A Tragedy. 8°, pp. 127.

Bound in volume containing "Reflections on Peter the Great." 12°, pp. 272. Boston, 1814.

EVEREST, (C. W.)

Charles William Everest was born at East Windsor, Conn., May 27, 1814, graduated at Trinity College in 1838, was ordained Priest in the Protestant Episcopal Church in 1842, and became Rector of the Episcopal Church of Harnden, near New Haven, Conn. Here he remained thirty-one years, having under his charge for most of that period a prosperous select school. Most of his published works are referred to below. He died at Waterbury, Conn., January 11, 1877, while in the service of the "Society for the Increase of the Ministry."

— Babylon. 8°, pp. 48. Hartford, 1838.

— Poets of Connecticut. 8°, pp. 468. Hartford, 1843.

— The Hare Bell. 3d Edition. 32°, pp. x, 192. Hartford.

— The Moss Rose. 24°, pp. 192. Hartford, 1843.

— The Primrose. 32°, pp. 128. Hartford, 1850.

— The Snow Drop. 32°, pp. 128. New York, 1848.

— Vision of Death. 12°, pp. 16. Hartford, 1837.

— Same. 32°, pp. 127. Hartford, 1845.

EVERETT, (A. H.)

Alexander Hill Everett was born at Boston, March 10, 1790, graduated at Harvard in 1806, taught one year in the Phillips Exeter Academy, studied law in the office of J. Q. Adams, whom he accompanied to Russia, residing in St. Petersburg 1809–12, subsequently

Everett, (A. H.) — *Continued.*

was Secretary of Legation, and then Chargé d'Affaires to the Netherlands until 1824. From 1825 to 1829 was Minister to Spain. Returned to United States, and was editor of the "North American Review," 1830–35. While serving as Minister Plenipotentiary to China, died in Canton, June 28, 1847. One of the most accomplished of American scholars.

— Poems. 12°, pp. 105. Boston, 1845.

Everett, (D.) Common Sense in Dishabille, etc. One or two poems in the volume. 12°, pp. 120. Worcester, 1799.

Everett, (W.) Hesione; or, Europe Unchained. Phi Beta Kappa Poem. Harvard, July 16, 1868. Lg. 12°, pp. 28. Boston, 1868.

Everhart, (J. B.)

James Bowen Everhart, of German descent on his father's side, was born near Westchester, Chester county, Pa., graduated at Princeton College in 1842, studied law and practiced in Westchester until 1849, when he went abroad and was absent about three years, engaged in extensive travel and study. Returning home he resumed practice. In the late civil war he was engaged for some time in active service. From 1877 to 1883 he was a member of the Pennsylvania Senate, when he left it for a seat in Congress, which position he now (1886) holds. His "Miscellanies," published in 1863, were favorably received.

— Poems. 12°, pp. 144. Philadelphia, 1868.
— The Fox Chase. 12°, pp. 30. Philadelphia, 1874.

Excursion, An, of Mr. John E. Reyborn, etc. Members of the Courtland Saunders' Institute, June 22, 1867. Sq. 16°, pp. 16. Philadelphia, 1867.

Excursion, An, of the Dog-Cart. 8°, pp. 24. New York, 1822.

Excursions on the River Connecticut. (Anon.) 12°, pp. 48. Boston, 1826.

Exile's Lay, The. (Anon.) 18°, pp. 122. Boston, 1855.

Fagan, (Fanny). In Memoriam. A Selection from her Poems. Lg. 12°, pp. xii, 224. Philadelphia. Published for private distribution, 1878.

She wrote over the signature "F." and "F. F." Some of her "Poems of the War" and "Songs of Freedom" are full of spirit. She died January 30, 1878.

Fair Epistle, A. (Anon.) 18°, pp. 12. New York, 1818.

Fair, The Ladies'. (Anon.) 16°, pp. 11. Brooklyn, 1836.

Fairbanks, (Cassie.) The Lone House. 12°, pp. 15. Halifax, 1859.

FAIRFIELD, (S. L.)

Sumner Lincoln Fairfield was born at Warwick, Mass., June 25, 1803. He studied for a time in Brown University, but failing health compelled him to leave college. For two years he was tutor in a private family at the South. In 1825 he went abroad and remained one year. Returning home he devoted his life to literary pursuits with varied and chequered fortunes, and died in New Orleans, March 6, 1844.

— Abbadon. 8°, pp. 133. New York, 1830.
— Lays of Melpomene. 12°, pp. 122. Portland, 1824.
— Mina. A Dramatic Sketch, etc. 12°, pp. v, 120. Baltimore, 1825.
— Poetical Works. Lg. 8°, pp. viii, 400. Philadelphia, 1842.
— The Cities of the Plain. 18°, pp. 58. Boston, 1827.
— The Heir of the World, etc. 12°, pp. 166. Philadelphia, 1829.
— The Last Night of Pompeii. 8°, pp. 309. New York, 1832.

FALES, (R.)   Peregrinus in His Childhood.   18°, pp. 296.   Boston, 1848.

FALL OF BRITISH TYRANNY. (Anon.)   Tragi-Comedy.   12°, pp. 64. Philadelphia, 1776.
— Same.   12°, pp. 66.   Providence, no date.

FALLEN WOMAN, SOLILOQUY OF.   18°, pp. 13.   New York, 1868.

FALSE SHAME; OR, THE AMERICAN ORPHAN IN GERMANY. A Comedy. From the German of A. Von Kotzebue. (Anon.)   12°, pp. 76. Charleston, 1800.

FAMILY TABLET.   Selection of Original Poetry.   18°, pp. 81.   Boston, 1796.

FAMILY, THE, AND GUEST, IN THE UNITED STATES.   (By the Father. Anon.)   12°, pp. 164.   New York, 1850.

FANATICISM, SPIRIT OF.   (Anon.)   12°, pp. iv, 12.   New York, 1842.

FANATICISM UNVEILED.   (Anon.)   8°, pp. 14.   New York, 1834.

FARMER, (H. T., M. D.)

Henry T. Farmer was born in England, removed in early life to Charleston, S. C., where he engaged in commercial pursuits. He studied medicine in New York, was admitted to practice in 1821, and returned to Charleston, where he practiced his profession until his death at the age of 46.

— Imagination; The Maniac's Dream, etc.   12°, pp. 163.   New York and London, 1819.

FARMER, (MRS. P.) The Captives, etc. 18°, pp. 236. La Porte, Ind., 1856.

FARMERS' MUSEUM, THE SPIRIT OF. 12°, pp. 318. Walpole, N. H.
Several short poems in the volume.

FASHION'S ANALYSIS. (Sir A. Avalanche, *pseud.*) 12°, pp. 84. New York, 1807.
Ascribed to Blauvelt, an American poet.

FASHION; OR, THE ART OF MAKING BREECHES. (By Solomon Irony, Esq., *pseud.*) 18°, pp. 19. Philadelphia, 1800.

FASHION, THE SCOURGE OF. (Anon.) 18°, pp. 23. New York, 1800.

FAUGÉRES, (MARGARETTA V.)
Margaretta V. Bleeker was born near Albany, N. Y., in 1771. Her husband, Dr. Peter Faugères, an infidel physician, was a worthless fellow, who abused her and dissipated her fortune. She died January 9, 1801.

— Belisarius. A Tragedy. 12°, pp. 53. New York, 1795.
— John Young, The Ghost of. A Monody. 12°, pp. 6. No place, no date.

FAWCETT, (E.)
Edgar Fawcett, a poet of New York City, and editor of the "Family Star Paper," has contributed many articles to literary periodicals of the day.

— Fantasy and Passion. 12°, pp. 191. Boston, 1878.
— Short Poems for Short People. 12°, pp. 95. New York, 1872.

FAY, (T. S.)
Theodore Sedgwick Fay was born in the city of New York, February 10, 1807, was admitted to the bar in 1828, but did not practice; became editor of the *New York Mirror;* published in 1832, "Dreams and Reveries of a Quiet Man," and subsequently was the author of several novels, etc. From 1837 to 1853 he was Secretary of Legation at Berlin, and for a number of years was United States Minister to Switzerland. He ranks high among American authors.

— Ulric; or, The Voices. A Tale. 12°, pp. 189. New York, 1827.

FAYETTE IN PRISON; OR, MISFORTUNES OF THE GREAT. A Modern Tragedy. By a Gentleman of Massachusetts. 8°, pp. vi, 40. Worcester, 1802.

FELCH, (W.) Supplement to Lecture on the Stars. 12°, pp. —. Southbridge, 1828.
— The Manufacturer's Pocket Piece. 12°, pp. 23. Medway, Mass., 1816.

15

FELLOWES, (J.)  Reminiscences.  Moral Poems, etc.  16°, pp. xii, 275.
Exeter, N. H., 1824.

FELTON, (J. B.)  The Horse-Shoe.  Phi Beta Kappa Poem, Harvard,
July 19, 1849.  Cambridge, 1849.

FELTUS, (REV. DR.)  Lines occasioned by his Death.  By a Friend.  8°,
pp. viii, 80.  New York, 1829.

FENN, (J.)  A Poem on Friendship and Society.  12°, pp. 132.  Schenectady, 1815.

FENNER, (C. G.)  Poems of Many Moods.  12°, pp. iv, 87.  Boston,
1846.

FENNO, (J.)  Original Compositions in Prose and Verse.  18°, pp. 216.
Wrentham, Mass., 1803.

FERGUSON, (L. D.)  Occasional Poems.  12°, pp. 206.  Rochester, N.
Y., 1857.

FESSENDEN, (T. G.)

Thomas Green Fessenden was born at Walpole, N. H., April 22, 1771, graduated at
Dartmouth College in 1796, went abroad on business, and while there published his "Terrible Tractoration," a satire on the medical profession, which proved a great success.  It
was subsequently enlarged to "The Minute Philosopher."  His life was devoted to literary
and agricultural pursuits.  He died November 11, 1837.

— Original Poems.  12°, pp. xiii, 197.  London, 1804.
— Same.  Philadelphia, 1806.
— Pills.  Poetical, Political and Philosophical, etc.  16°, pp. 136.
Philadelphia, 1809.

An elegantly bound copy.

— Terrible Tractoration !!  2d Edition.  12°, pp. xxxv, 186.  Lon-
don, 1803.
— Same.  3d American Edition.  Boston, 1836.
— The Ladies' Monitor.  12°, pp. xii, 180.  Bellows Falls, Vt., 1818.

FEZLER, (MRS. FRANCES.)  Hymns and Spiritual Songs.  18°, pp. 32.
New York, 1836.

FIELD OF ORLEANS, THE.  (Anon.)  18°, pp. 31.  Philadelphia, 1816.

FIELD, (KATE)

A daughter of Joseph M. Field.  He was born in England, and at an early age came
to this country, where he was actor, editor, etc.  The daughter is celebrated as a writer
and actress.

— Mad on Purpose.  A Comedy.  12°, pp. 48.  New York, 1868.

FIELD, (M. B.)  Trifles in Verse.  Sq. 8°, pp. 40.  New York, 1869.
— Vivé La France.  Translation into French of O. W. Holmes's Toast
at the Prince Napoleon Dinner at the Revere House, Boston, September 25, 1861.  12°, pp. 3.  No place, no date.

Copy presented by Mr. Field to Richard Grant White.

FIELD, (S.)

Samuel Field was born at Deerfield, Mass., September 14, 1743, graduated in 1762, studied law, practicing for a time in his native place, then removed to Greenfield, where he remained till 1774, when he took up his residence in Conway, Mass.  In 1776 he returned to Deerfield, residing there till 1794, when he went back to Conway, where he died September 17, 1800.  Mr. F. was an "elder" in the Sandemanian church, for an account of whose "Tenets and Practices" see the volume whose title is given below, pp. 21–49.

— Poetry and Prose.  18°, pp. 284.  Greenfield, Mass., 1818.

FIELD, (T. W.)  The Minstrel Pilgrim, etc.  Sq. 8°, pp. 50.  New York, 1848.

FIELDS, (J. T.)

James T. Fields was born at Portsmouth, N. H., December 31, 1817.  For many years he was a partner in the well-known publishing house of Ticknor & Fields, the warm and liberal friend of authors, himself having marked literary tastes, and was a writer of ability, both in prose and poetry.  He died April 24, 1881.

— A Few Verses to a Few Friends.  12°, pp. 78.  No place, no date.
— Poems.  Sq. 16°, pp. vi, 99.  Boston, 1849.
— Same.  Sq. 18°, pp. 128.  Cambridge, 1854.

FILIOLA.  A Drama.  (Anon.)  12°, pp. 24.  Baltimore, 1873.

FINCH, (F. M.)  Senior Class Poem, Yale, July 3, 1849.  8°, pp. 52.  New Haven, 1849.
— Linonian Society, Yale.  Poem.  8°, pp. 55.  New Haven, 1853.

FIRST VOYAGE, THE SAILOR BOY'S.  A Ballad.  (Anon).

FISH, (F. W.)  Poems.  Sq. 18°, pp. 124.  New Haven, 1855.
— The Mind and the Heart.  12°, pp. xii, 72.  New York, 1851.

FISHER, (G. W.)  Poem.  Yale.  Senior Class Presentation Day, June 15, 1859.  8°, pp. 15.  New Haven, 1859.

FISHER, (J.)  Short Poems.  16°, pp. 143.

FISHER, (T.)  Song of the Sea Shells, etc.  8°, pp. 64.  Philadelphia, 1850.

FITCH, (E.)

Rev. Elijah Fitch was born in 1745, graduated at Yale College in 1765, received the degree of A. M. from Harvard College in 1770, and was minister of the Congregational Church in Hopkinton, Mass., 17 years. He died in 1778.

— The Beauties of Religion.　Providence, 1789.

FLAGG, (W.)　Analysis of Female Beauty.　12°, pp. vi, 108.　Boston, 1834.

— The Tailor's Shop.　Intended Chiefly for Politicians.　12°.　Boston, 1844.

FLEA, THE.　(By You.　Anon.)　12°, pp. 22.　New York, 1869.

FLAMBEAU, THE INTELLECTUAL.　(Anon.)　18°, pp. 143.　Washington, 1816.

FLASH, (H. L.)　Poems.　12°, pp. 168.　New York, 1860.

FLEMING, (J.)　Hymns in the Muskokee or Creek Language.　18°, pp. 35.　Boston, 1835.

FLINT, (M. P.)　The Hunter, etc.　12°, pp. 141.　Boston, 1826.

FLORENCE, THE MAID OF ; OR, A WOMAN'S VENGEANCE.　A *pseud.* historical Tragedy.　(Anon.)　12°, pp. 92.　Charleston, 1839.

FLOWERS OF AUTUMN, THE.　18°, pp. 108.　Philadelphia.

FOGG, (MRS. F. B.)　Poems.　12°, pp. 57.　No place, no date.

FOLLEN, (MRS. E. L.)

Eliza Lee Cabot was born at Boston in 1787, and in 1828 married Professor Follen. Most of her poetical productions will be found in "Poems on Occasional Topics," Boston, 1839. She died in Brookline, Mass., 1860.

— Hymns, etc., for Children.　2d Edition with additions.　18°, pp. 51.　Boston, 1833.

— Hymns, etc., for Young People.　18°, pp. viii, 99.　Boston, 1847.

— Nursery Songs.　Sq. 24°, pp. 114.　New York, 1843.

FONTAINE LA.　Translated.　(Anon.　Entered by J. S. Wright.)　18°, pp. 108.　Boston, 1839.

Elizur Wright, the translator of Fontaine's Fables, was born at South Canaan, Conn., in 1804, graduated at Yale in 1826, in 1829 was appointed Professor of Mathematics and Natural Philosophy in the Western Reserve College. He has taken an active part as a journalist, etc., in the anti-slavery and other reforms. His home in 1885 was in Medford, Mass.

— Same.　3d edition.　2 vols.　18°, pp. 247, 290.　Boston, 1842.

— Same.　2 vols.　12°, pp. 245, 351.　New York, 1860.

FOOTBALL, THE DEVIL'S. A Satire. (Anon.) 8°, pp. 23. Boston, 1879.

FOOTPRINTS; OR, FUGITIVE POEMS. (Anon.) 12°, pp. 92. Philadelphia, 1843.

FOOTSTEPS ON THE SEAS. (By A. D. T. W. Anon.) 18°, pp. 50. Boston, 1857.

FOREST VOICES. Translations from the German, edited by C. A. Smith, D. D. 12°, pp. 102. Albany, 1866.

FORGET-ME-NOTS FROM DEW DROP DALE. (By Ruth Rustic, *pseud.*) 12°, pp. 212. Washington, 1855.

FORREST, (M.) Travels Through America. 12°, pp. 50. Philadelphia, 1793.

FOSDICK, (W. W.) Ariel, etc. 12°, pp. xv, 316. New York, 1855.

FOSTER, (W. C.) Poems. 12°, pp. xii, 137. Salem, N. Y., 1805.
He wrote under the title of "Timothy Spectator."

FOWLER, (G.) The Examiner. 24°, pp. 78. Washington, 1835.

FOWLER, (M. B.) The Prophecy; or, Love and Friendship. A Drama. 18°, pp. 34. New York, 1821.

FOXTON, (E.) Prémices. 16°, pp. iv, 196. Boston, 1855.
— Sir Pavon and St. Pavon. Sq. 12°, pp. 84. Boston, 1867.

FRANCIS, (V. M.) The Fight for the Union. 8°, pp. 63. New York, 1863.

FRANK; OR, WHO'S THE CROAKER? 12°, pp. 41. New York, 1820.

FRANKENSTEIN, (J.) American Art. A Satire. 12°, pp. viii, 112. Cincinnati, 1864.

FREEDOM'S GIFT; OR, SENTIMENTS OF THE FREE. (Anon.) 12°, pp. 108. Hartford, 1840.

FREEMAN, (F. W.) A Scotch Ballad. 8°, pp. 14. Boston, 1869.

FREEMAN, (N. C.) The Twilight Dream, and Moments of Solitude. 12°, pp. vi, 141. Philadelphia, 1853.

FRELIGH, (J. S.) Poems. 12°, pp. 163. St Louis, 1852.

FRENCH ARROGANCE; OR, "THE CAT LET OUT OF THE BAG." A Poetical Dialogue between the Envoys of America and X. Y. Z. and the Lady. 12°, pp. 31. Philadelphia, 1798.

FRENEAU, (P.)

> Philip Freneau was born in the city of New York, January 2, 1752, graduated at Princeton in 1771, and in 1774–75 began to write his poetical satires. For two or three years he resided in the West Indies. The "United States Magazine," published in Philadelphia, was for a time under his editorial supervision. Subsequently he was a sea-captain. His life was, in some respects, spent in a desultory way. He died by freezing to death in a severe snow storm near Freehold, N. J., December 18, 1832.

— A Laughable Poem. 12°, pp. 24. Philadelphia, 1809.

— Miscellaneous Works. 18°, pp. 429. Philadelphia, 1788.

— Poems. 18°, pp. 407. Philadelphia, 1786.

— Same. 8°, pp. 455. Monmouth, N. J., 1795.

> An elegant copy.

— Same. 2 vols. 18°, pp. 188, 176. New York, 1815.

— Same. 3d Edition. 2 vols. pp. 280, 302. Philadelphia, 1809.

— Same. Reprinted from the rare Philadelphia edition of 1786. Sm. 8°, pp. xxii, 362. London, 1861.

— Same. With Memoir by E. A. Duyckinck. 8°, pp. xxxviii, 288. New York, 1865.

— The British Prison Ship. 18°, pp. 23. Philadelphia, 1781.

— The Village Merchant. 12°, pp. 16. Philadelphia, 1794.

FRESH FLOWERS FOR CHILDREN. (By a Mother. Anon.) New Edition. 12°, pp. 176. Boston, 1852.

FRIENDSHIP'S ECHO. (H. J. K. Anon.) 24°, pp. 59. Baltimore, 1853.

FRISBIE, (FANNIE.) Songs of the Flowers. 32°, pp. 96. New York, 1855.

FRISBIE, (L.)

> Levi Frisbie was born at Ipswich, Mass., in 1784, graduated at Harvard in 1802, and after teaching for a year at Concord, Mass., commenced the study of law, but was obliged, on account of an affection of his eyes, to abandon the profession. He was appointed Latin tutor in Harvard in 1805, retaining the position for six years, and then was chosen Professor of Latin, and was in office till 1817, when he was called to the chair of Moral Philosophy. He died July 9, 1822.

— Miscellaneous Writings, with some notices of his Life and Character, by Andrews Norton. 8°, pp. lxi, 235. Boston, 1823.

> The poetry in the volume is pp. 207–35. The longest of the poems is a translation of Horace's "Epistola ad Florum."

FRONTIER MAID; OR, THE TALE OF WYOMING. In Five Cantos. 12°, pp. 208. Wilkesbarre, Pa., 1819.

FROTHINGHAM, (ELLEN.) Nathan the Wise. A Dramatic Poem by Gotthold Ephraim Lessing. Translated by Miss F. 16°, pp. xxii, 258. New York, 1868.

— Translation of Goethe's Hermann and Dorothea. 16°, pp. 165. Boston, 1870.

FROTHINGHAM, (N. L.) Metrical Pieces. Translated and Original. 12°, pp. 362. Boston, 1855.

FUDGE FAMILY, THE, IN WASHINGTON. (Harry Nimrod, *pseud.*) 12°, pp. 109. Baltimore, 1820.

FUGITIVE POEMS. (Anon.) 18°, pp. 74. Philadelphia, 1824.

FUGITIVE, THE. An Epic Poem in one Canto, by P. Virgilius Maro. (Translated by John Dryden Bags, Esq., *pseud.*) 12°, pp. 44. Boston, 1854.

Refers to the rendition of Anthony Burns, June 2, 1854.

FULLER, (E. W.) The Angel in the Cloud. 12°, pp. 107. New York, 1871.

FULLER, (FRANCES A. AND METTA V.) Poems, etc. Lg. 8°, pp. x, 264. New York, 1851.

FULLERTON, (MRS. ELIZABETH A., of Baltimore.) Original Poetry. 16°, pp. 64. London, 1870.

FURMAN, (G.) Rural Hours. 8°, pp. 70. No place, 1824.
— The Maspeth Poems. Sq. 18°, pp. 128. New York, 1837.

FURMAN, (R.) The Pleasures of Piety, etc. 12°, pp. viii, 220. Charleston, S. C., 1859.

FURNESS, (W. H.) Translation of Schiller's Song of the Bell. 8°, pp. 48. Philadelphia, 1850.

Bound with F. H. Hedge's Poems and Ballads.

GAGE, (MRS. FRANCES D.)

Frances Dana Barker was born at Marietta, Ohio, in 1808; married, in 1828, James L. Gage, of McConnelsville, Ohio, where she resided for twenty-five years. In 1853 the family removed to St. Louis, Mo. She wrote under the signature of "Aunt Fanny."

— Poems. 12°, pp. 252. Philadelphia, 1867.

GAIAMAZ, (YUSEF EBN's.)  Story of the Young and Beautiful Carcmsil.
A Poem in Three Cantos.  18°, pp. ix, 58.  Philadelphia, 1833.

GALLAHER, (W. D.)

William Davis Gallaher was born at Philadelphia, August, 1808, removed to Cincinnati in 1816, where for many years he was engaged in literary pursuits, and especially distinguished himself as the editor of the *Cincinnati Mirror*, and of the " Western Literary
Journal" and " Monthly Review."  Many productions of his pen have been published.

— Erato No. II.  16°, pp. 60.  Cincinnati, 1835.

— Poem.  Hanover College, August 17, 1846.  8°, pp. 12.  Cincinnati,
1846.

GALLERY, A, OF FAMOUS ENGLISH AND AMERICAN POETS.  With an
Introductory Essay by Henry Coppée, LL. D., President of the
Lehigh University.  Richly illustrated with nearly One Hundred and
Fifty Steel Engravings.  4°, pp. 488.  Philadelphia, 1873.

GAMBOL, THE JIMS'; OR, HOW WE WENT TO RONDOUT.  (Anon.)  Not
published.  Sq. 8°, pp. 16.  1858.

GANILH, (A.)  Odes, etc.  12°, pp. 36.  Boston, 1830.

GARDINER, (J. S.)  An Epistle of Zenas.  12°, pp. 15.  Boston, no date.

GARDINER, (MARY L.)  A Collection from the Writings of.  Poems.
12°, pp. vi, 122.  New York, 1843.

GARLAND, THE.  A General Repository of Fugitive Poetry.  Vol. I,
No. 1.  Selected by G. A. Gamage.  Lg. 8°, pp. 48.  Auburn,
N. Y., 1825.

GARRISON, (W. L.)

William Lloyd Garrison was born at Newburyport, Mass., December 12, 1804, his
parents being natives of New Brunswick.  He was apprenticed, when a boy, to a shoe-
maker, and subsequently became a printer.  In 1827 he started the " National Philanthropist " in Boston, and January 1, 1831, issued the first number of the " Liberator."  From
that time forward he was the bold, uncompromising advocate of anti-slavery.  After a life
of unwearied devotion to the reforms which he advocated, he died at New York, May 26,
1879.

— Sonnets, etc.  16°, pp. vi, 96.  Boston, 1843.

GAUDALOUPE.  A Tale of Love and War.  12°, pp. 156.  Philadelphia,
1860.

GAY, (J.)  Gay's Chair.  16°, pp. 100.  Boston, 1320.

GAYLOR, (C.)  The Love of a Prince, etc.  12°, pp. 45.  New York,
no date.

Gaylor, (C.) — *Continued.*

— The Son of the Night.    A Drama.    12°, pp. 42.    New York, no
date.

Gem, The.    (Anon.)    18°, pp. xii, 360.    Boston, 1843.

Genevese.    (Anon.    Initials, E. C. M.)    A Collection of Brief Poems,
etc.    12°, pp. 32.    Geneva, 1847.

Genin, (T. H.)

Thomas Hedges Genin was born near Agnebogue, Suffolk county, on Long Island,
March 23, 1796.  His father, John Nicholas Genin, a native of Labeurville, in the Diocese
of Verdun, France, came to the United States in 1780, and was a clerk in the commissary
department of General Rochambeau's army.  His first wife lived but a short time after
marriage.  His second wife was Sarah Hedges, of East Hampton, L. I., to whom it may
literally be said that he "looked up," as she was a lady six feet and one inch in height,
three inches taller than her husband, "and was well proportioned and straight as an
arrow."  The son, without the training of a college course, studied law and made such progress that at the age of twenty he was admitted to the bar in New York, and having married, took up his residence at St. Clairville, Ohio, in 1817, and entered upon the practice of
his profession.  At once he became an earnest, outspoken opponent of slavery, and hence-
forth his life was consecrated to the cause which he had so warmly espoused.  He was
also a vigorous advocate of protection as against free trade, of reform in postal laws, of
railroads, etc.  Reference will be made to his poetical writings in a note under the next
title.

— Selections from the Writings of the late Thomas Hedges Genin, with
a Biographical Sketch.    A Memorial Work.    8°, pp. 613, viz:
Biography, 3–87; Prose Writings, 91–222; Poems, 225–613.
New York, 1869.

— The Napolead in 12 books.    18°, pp. ix, 342.    St. Clairsville, 1833.

The following communication to Mr. Harris from Mr. John F. Genin, of New York, a
nephew of Mr. Genin, accompanied the gift of a copy of the works of his uncle to Mr.
Harris:

115 East 60th Street, City N. Y.,<br>September 30, 1871.

Dear Sir:—Last June I sent a copy to Rhode Island State Library.  John R. Bartlett, Esq., Secretary of State, acknowledged its receipt and suggested to "send a copy of
this volume to Hon. C. F. Harris, of Providence, R. I., in whose collection it would seem
very appropriate, as Mr. H. has the largest collection of the writings of American Poets
of any one in the United States."  Accordingly it gives me great pleasure in presenting
this volume to add to your collection.

The Napolead was written before my uncle, T. H. G., was 21.  The likeness in front
of Napolead is from an oil painting taken at that time.  The first 5 Cantos of the Napolead
were handed to De Witt Clinton for his opinion as to whether the young author should
complete it.  He strongly urged him on.  A warm friendship always existed between them.

Yours respectfully,

John N. Genin.

16

Genin, (T. H.) — *Continued.*

— The Fatal Disunion. Written during the Hartford Convention. 24°, pp. 24. New York, 1816.

Genius of America, The. A MS. (Anon.) No place, no date.

Geraldine. A Souvenir of the St. Lawrence. (Anon.) 12°, pp. 321. Boston, 1882.

Gerard, (J. W.)

James Watson Gerard, LL. D., a lawyer in New York City.

— Aquarelles; or, Summer Sketches. (By Samuel Sombres, *pseud.*) 12°, pp. 95. New York, 1858.
— (Shelley, A Fishe, *pseud.*) Ostrea. 12°, pp. 72. New York, 1857.

Giant, The Little. (Anon.) 24°, pp. 10. Chicago, 1860.

Gibson, (H. S.) The Vision of War. 18°, pp. x, 152. Philadelphia, 1835.
— Poems. 16°, pp. iv, 154. Philadelphia, 1834.
— Same. 12°, pp. 156. Philadelphia, 1834.

Gibson, (W., U. S. N.) A Vision of Færy Land, etc. 16°, pp. iv, 214. Boston and Cambridge, 1853.
— Poems of Many Years and Many Places. 18°, pp. 166. Boston, 1881.

Gildea, (J. R.) Poems on Ireland. 8°, pp. 35. New Haven, 1871.

Gilder, (R. W.)

Richard Watson Gilder was born at Bordentown, N. J., in 1844. As a journalist, he wrote under the signature of "Old Cabinet." In 1870 he became associate editor of the "Century," and has been editor since 1881.

— The New Day. Lg. 12°, pp. 112. New York, 1876.
—. The Poet and His Master, etc., 12°, pp. 67. New York, 1878.

Giles, (C.) Drunkards, The Convention of. 32°, pp. 79. New York, 1839.

Giles, (Daphne S.) Scriptural and Miscellaneous Poems. 32°, pp. 172. Ann Arbor, 1845.

GILMAN, (CAROLINE.)

Caroline Howard was born at Boston, October 8, 1794, married Rev. Dr. Samuel Gilman in 1819, and took up her residence in Charleston, S. C., where her husband was a Unitarian clergyman. She is well known by her numerous writings. In 1883 she removed to Cambridge, Mass.

— Tales and Ballads. 12°, pp. 190. New York, 1839.

— Verses of a Life Time. 12°, pp. 263. Boston and Cambridge, 1849.

— AND (CAROLINE HOWARD.) Oracles for Youth. 12°, pp. 81. New York, 1853.

GILMAN, (S., D. D.) Pleasures and Pains of the Student's Life. 4°, pp. 271. Boston, 1852.

GILPIN, THE MODERN. (Anon.) A Ballad of Bull Run. 12°, pp. 19. New York, 1866.

GLANCE, A, AT THE NATIONS, ETC. (Anon.) 16°, pp. 60. Boston, 1835.

GLASS, THE. (Anon.) 16°, pp. 12. New York, 1791.

GLAZIER, (W. B.) Poems. 12°, pp. 168. Hallowell, Me., 1853.

GLEANINGS FROM THE FIELD OF TRUTH. (By Foxhall?) 12°, pp. 24. Baltimore, 1866.

GLEASON, (H.) Anniversary Poems. Boston Mechanic Apprentices Library Association. 35th Anniversary. 8°, pp. 12. Boston, 1855.

GLEE HIVE, THE. By Lowell Mason and George J. Webb. Lg. 8°, pp. 112. New York, 1853.

GLENN, (J.) The City and Country Compared. 8°, pp. 8. New York, 1845.

GLIMPSE, A, AT WATERTOWN. 2d Edition. 16°, pp. 42. Boston, 1851.

GLORY, THE MILITARY, OF GREAT BRITAIN. An Entertainment given in Nassau Hall, September, 1762. Sm. 4°, pp. 15. Philadelphia, 1762.

GLOVER, (S. E.) The Cradle of Liberty. 12°, pp. 39. Boston, no date.

GOBRIGHT, (L. A.)  Jack and Gill for Old and Young.    8°, pp. 29.
Philadelphia, 1873.

GODDARD, (ABBA A.)  The Trojan Sketch Book.    12°, pp. viii, 180.
Troy, 1846.

> A few poems in the volume.

GODFREY, (T., JR.)

> Thomas Godfrey was born at Philadelphia in 1736.  In 1758 he was Lieutenant in the
> Pennsylvania troops in the Fort Du Quesne expedition.  Afterwards he was engaged in
> commercial pursuits.  The following is said to have been the first dramatic work written in
> America.  He died in 1763.

— Juvenile Poems, with the Prince of Parthia.  A Tragedy.    Sq. 8°,
pp. xxvi, 223.  Philadelphia, 1765.

GOGGLES, (P.)  Bro-de-hed-da.   A Song of Slaughter.   12°, pp. 15.
Philadelphia, no date.

GOLDSMITH, (O., a Descendant of the author of " The Deserted Village.")
The Rising Village, etc.   18°, pp. x, 144.   St. John, N. B., 1834.

GOODALE, (ELAINE AND DORA REED.)  All Around the Year.  Verses
from Sky Farm.   Illustrated.   Sq. 16°, pp. 204.   New York,
1881.

— In Berkshire with the Wild Flowers.   Sq. 12°, pp. 92.   New York,
1879–80.

GOODRICH, (F. B.)   Flirtation, and What Comes of It.   A Comedy.
12°, pp. 92.   New York, 1861.

GOODRICH, (S. G.)

> Samuel Griswold Goodrich, the celebrated "Peter Parley," was born at Ridgefield,
> Conn., August 19, 1793, and for a number of years from 1824 edited " The Token," an
> annual, in which some of the finest of Hawthorne's "Twice-Told Tales" were originally
> published.  A list of his numerous productions will be found in Duyckinck and Allibone.
> He died in 1860.

— The Outcast, etc.   12°, pp. vi, 200.   Boston, 1836.

GOODWIN, (J. A.)  Poem at Bridgewater, before the Normal Association, August 15, 1849.   12°, pp. 11.   Providence, 1850.

GOOSE.  Old Mother's Daughter.   (Anon.)   Lg. 8°, pp. 32.   Boston,
etc., 1856.

GORDON, (H. L.)  Pauline, etc.   Sq. 12°, pp. 140.   New York, 1878.

GORTON, (S.)  Simplicities Defence against Seven-Headed Policy, etc.
Lg. 16°, pp. 111.  London, 1646.

For a full account of Gorton, see his life by Mackie, in "Sparks's American Biography," vol. xv.  A few pages of poetry at the beginning of the book gives it a place in the "Harris Collection."

GOULD, (E. S.)

Edward S. Gould was born at Litchfield, Conn., in 1808, and became a merchant in New York.  He translated several works from the French of Dumas, Balzac, etc., and wrote an abridgment of "Alison's History of Europe."

— "The Very Age."  A Comedy.  12°, pp. 153.  New York, 1850.

GOULD, (T. A.)  A Bouquet of Poesy.  12°, pp. 144.  New York, 1848.

GOULD, (HANNAH F.)

Hannah Flagg Gould was born at Lancaster, Vt., and when young removed to Newburyport.  Her poetical works have met with great favor.  (See "Griswold's Female Poets of America.")

— Hymns, etc.  12°, pp. 160.  Boston, 1854.
— New Poems.  12°, pp. 287.  Boston, 1850.
— Poems.  18°, pp. 174.  Boston, 1832.
— Same.  Vol. III.  12°, pp. 240.  Boston, 1841.
— Same.  2d Edition.  18°, pp. 224.  Boston, 1833.
— Same.  3d Edition.  16°, pp. 239.  Boston, 1835.
— Same.  2 vols.  12°, pp. 239, 240.  Boston, 1839.
— The Diosma.  A Perennial.  12°, pp. 287.  Boston, 1851.
— The Golden Vase.  A Gift for the Young.  16°, pp. 224.  Boston, 1843.
— The Mother's Dream, etc.  16°, pp. —.  Boston, 1853.
— The Youth's Coronal.  12°, pp. 200.  New York and Philadelphia, 1851.

GOULD, (SARAH.)  Asphodels.  12°, pp. xi, 236.  New York, 1856.
— Poems.  18°, pp. 180.  New York, 1860.

GOULD, (T. A.)  Bouquet of Poesy.  16°, pp. vi, 144.  New York, 1848.

GOULD, (T. R.)  The Tragedian: An Essay on the Histrionic Genius of Junius Brutus Booth.  12°, pp. 190.  New York, 1868.

GRAHAM, (J.)  The Flowers of Melody.  In two volumes.  Vol. I.  18°, pp. xi, 384.  New York, 1823.  Vol. II.  18°, pp. 388.  New York, 1828.

GRAHAM, (W. S.)

William Sloan Graham was born near New London, Chester county, Pa., April 23, 1816, graduated with the valedictory honors of his class from Delaware College in 1836, was tutor in the college from three to four years, then became Principal of the New London Academy, and in less than two years was called to take charge of the Preparatory Department of Delaware College, entering upon the discharge of his duties in 1841, and holding the position not far from four years, then became Principal of an Academy at Harrisburg, Pa., and died in office October 3, 1847.

This volume was edited by Professor George Allen, Professor of Languages in the University of Pennsylvania. pp. 13–156 contain a Memoir of Mr. Graham by his wife. The poems are pp. 159–250. The remainder of the volume is made up of Essays on Coleridge, pp. 253–66, and Rhythm, pp. 269–78.

— Poetical Remains.  12°, pp. viii, 94.  Philadelphia, 1849.
— Remains.  Prose and Poetry.  12°, pp. viii, 278.  Philadelphia, 1849.

GRANT, (C.)  Poem on the Restoration of Learning in the East.  8°, uncut, pp. 39.  Salem, 1807.

GRANT, (R.)  The Lambs.  A Tragedy.  12°, pp. 61.  Boston, 1883.
— The Little Tin-Gods on Wheels; or, Society in our Modern Athens. 2d Edition.  12°, pp. 21.  Cambridge, 1879.

GRATE, (C.)  Eugene.  In Two Cantos.  Sm. 16°, pp. 63.  Philadelphia, 1842.

GRATTAN, (H. P.)  The Bottle.  8°, with eight plates.  New York, 1848.

GRAVE, (J.)  A Song of Sion.  Written by a Citizen thereof, whose outward Habitation is in *Virginia;* and being sent over to some of his friends in *England*, the same is found fitting to be Published, for to warn the Seed of Evil-doers.

> "The seed is sown, from which rare fruits do spring,
> The Plant is grown, that heavenly virtues bring;
> The dead now lives, that's risen from the graves,
> That praises gives, to him that sinners saves.
> The morning of that day is dawned clear,
> Wherein men may walk in Celestial Sphere.
> Nations partake of Gospel Tidings found,
> Sins to forsake, and in Christ to be found.
> And happy's he, that's lived to see this day,
> And blessed be, the living God alway.
>                                         BY THE PUBLISHER."

With an additional Postscript from another hand [M. M., that is, Martin Mason(?)]. Sm. 4°, pp. 12.  No place.  Printed in the year 1662.

A choice and richly bound copy of a very rare and curious tract, the production of a Quaker pen. Sabin says that "a copy of it sold at Puttick's in 1860 for two guineas." The closing lines are as follows:

GRAVE, (J.) — *Continued.*

> " Glory to God, whose goodness doth increase,
> Praise him ever, who gives to us his peace.
> Not else I feel, that now to say I have,
> But that I am, your fellow-friend, John Grave."

GRAVES OF THE INDIANS. (Anon.) 18°, pp. 72. Boston, 1827.

GRAY, (A.) Shades of the Hamlet, etc. 12°, pp. 57. Woburn, Mass., 1852.

GRAY, (ANNIE.) A Child's Poem. (Anon.) Sold for the benefit of St. Peter's Church, Cambridgeport, Mass. 8°, pp. 8. Cambridge, 1869.

GRAY, (F. C.) Phi Beta Kappa Poem. Harvard, August 27, 1840. 12°, pp. 36. Boston, 1840. .

GRAYSON, (W. J.) The Hireling and Slave. Lg. 8°, pp. xv, 106. Charleston, 1854.

— Same. 2d Edition. 12°, pp. 85. Charleston, 1855.

GREEN, (J.) Entertainment for a Winter's Evening. 12°, pp. 12. Boston, 1750. Reprinted 1795.

GREEN, (J. W.) Satan Conquered ; or, The Son of God Victorious. A Poem in Five Books. 12°, pp. 166. Albany, 1844.

GREENE, (AELA.) Rhymes of Yankee Land. 12°, pp. 91. Boston and New York, 1872.

GREENE, (A. G.)

See " Introduction " for sketch.

— Anniversary Poem. Philermenian Society, Brown University. 8°, pp. 24. Providence, 1829.

— Old Grimes. Illustrated by A. Hoppin. 4°, pp. 12. Providence, 1867.

GREENE, (C. W.) Versified Chronology of the Sovereigns of Great Britain. 8°, pp. 17. Middleboro, Mass., 1875.

GREENE, (N.) Improvisations and Translations. 12°, pp. 133. Boston, 1852.

GREENLEAF, (L. N.) King Sham, and other Atrocities, in Verse ; including a Humorous History of the Pike's Peak Excitement. 16°, pp. iv, 139. New York, 1868.

He wrote under the signature, " Peter Punever."

GREENS FOR CHRISTMAS. Collected by Charles T. Moreau. Sq. 8°, not paged. 1874.

GREENWOOD, (GRACE.)

Sarah Jane Clark was born at Pompey, Onondaga county, N. Y., and in 1853 married Mr. Leander K. Lippincott, of Philadelphia. Under the *nom de plume* of "Grace Green-wood" she has been a welcome, gifted author, her writings having had an extensive cir-culation.

— Poems. 12°, pp. 190. Boston, 1851.
— Same. New Edition. 12°, pp. 196. Boston, 1858.

GREGOIRE, (MONS.) Critical Observations on Barlow's Columbiad. (Not a Poem.) 8°, pp. 15. Washington, 1809.

GRENVILLE, (A. S.) Original Poetic Effusions. 18°, pp. 180. Ded-ham, Mass., 1823.

GRIDLEY, (S., M. D.) The Mill of the Muses. 16°, pp. vii, 267. Exeter, 1828.

GRIEVOUS, PETER, JR. (A *pseud.*) A Congratulatory Epistle to "Peter Porcupine," etc. 8°, pp. 39. Philadelphia, 1796.

GRIFFIN, (E. D.) Reverendo Viro, etc. Translations from Latin into English Verse. 8°, pp. 16. New York, 1822.

GRIFFITH, (ARABELLA.) The Little Blind Girl of Normandie. 12°, pp. 40. New York, 1868.

GRIFFITH, (MATTIE.) Poems. 12°, pp. viii, 167.. New York, 1853.

GRIGGS, (H. N.) With Introduction by Rev. W. R. Williams, D. D. Songs for the Sorrowing. 16°, pp. xviii, 284. New York, 1861.

GRILLPARZER, (F.) Sappho. A Tragedy. Translated by Ellen Froth-ingham. 18°, pp. 136. Boston, 1876.

GRIMES, (G., AN INMATE OF THE LUNATIC ASYLUM OF TENNESSEE.) The Lily of the West. Prose and Poetry. 8°, pp. 96. Nashville, 1846.

GRISWOLD, (D. O.) Isaac N. Arnold. A Satire in Two Cantos. 4°, p. 1. Chicago, 1843.

GRISWOLD, (R. W.)

Rufus Wilmot Griswold, D. D., was born at Benson, Rutland county, Vt., February 15, 1815. He studied theology and became a minister in the Baptist denomination. Early in life he was connected with the press, being associate editor of the *New Yorker, Brother*

GRISWOLD, (R. W.) — *Continued.*

*Jonathan,* etc. In 1842 he took the editorial charge of " Graham's Magazine," which was very successful. Dr. G. will always be known as the "Collector of American Poetry." He died in 1857.

— Gems from American Female Poets. 24°, pp. vii, 92. Philadelphia, 1844.

— Readings in American Poetry. 12°, pp. x, 264. New York, 1843.

— The Female Poets of America. 8°, pp. 400. Philadelphia, 1860.

A fine copy.

— The Poets and Poetry of America. 8°, pp. xxxiii, 621. Philadelphia, 1842.

An elegant copy.

— Same. pp. 476. Philadelphia, 1843.

— The Poetry of the Sentiments. 18°, pp. 320. Philadelphia, 1846.

GROSS, (MRS. J. MASON.) In Memoriam. 12°, pp. 4. No place, no date.

GUERIN, (M.) Satire against Satire. French and English. 12°, pp. 25. Baltimore, no date.

GUEST, (M.) Poems. 1st Edition. 12°, pp. iv, 160. Cincinnati, 1823.
— Same. 2d Edition. 12°, pp. 160. Cincinnati, 1824.

GUILD, (R.) Poem in volume containing an account of Exercises at the Birthday Anniversary of the 80th year of his age. 12°, pp. 21. Providence, 1872.

GUSTAFSON, (Z. B.) Meg: A Pastoral, etc. 12°, pp. 280. Boston, 1879.

GUTHRIE, (W. E.) The Betrothed. A Nation's Vow. 12°, pp. 62. Philadelphia, 1867.

HADCOCK, (J. W.) Science Illustrated and Applied. 12°, pp. 186. Utica, 1851.

HAGAR IN THE DESERT. Translated from the French. 18°, pp. 24. Newburyport, no date.

HAGEN, (J. C.) Foot-Prints of Truth; or, Voice of Humanity. Lg. 8°, pp. 144. New York, 1853.

17

HALE, (MARY W.)  Poems.  12°, pp. 216.  Boston, 1840.

HALE, (E. E.)  Silhouettes and Songs.  Illustrated by Maria Hinds. Lg. 8°, not paged.  Boston, 1876.

HALE, (MRS. S. J.)

Sarah Josepha Buell was born at Newport, N. H., became the wife of David Hale, an eminent lawyer, who died in 1822.  In 1828 she became the editor of "The Ladies' Magazine," Boston, which, in 1837, was united with the "Lady's Book" of Philadelphia, and she continued to have charge of the periodical.  Mrs. Hale has performed an extraordinary amount of literary labor, for the details of which see Allibone, p. 758.

— Alice Ray.  Sq. 8°, pp. 37.  Philadelphia, 1845.

— The Genius of Oblivion, etc.  12°, pp. 146.  Concord, 1823.

— The Ladies' Wreath.  Selections from English and American Female Poetic Writers.  2d Edition.  12°, pp.   .  Boston, 1839.

— Three Hours ; or; The Vigil of Love, etc.  16°, pp. x, 216.  Philadelphia, 1848.

HALL, (A. O.)  The Downfall of Tammany Hall.  12°, pp. 24.  New York, 1871.

HALL, (J. E.)  The Philadelphia Souvenir.  18°, Philadelphia, 1826.

HALL, (MRS. E. B.)

Louisa Jane Park was born at Newburyport, Mass., February 7, 1802.  Her father removed to Boston in 1804, and for several years was editor of *The Repertory*, a journal of the Federal party.  In the spring of 1811 he opened a Ladies' School, in which for twenty years he was eminently successful.  The daughter, at the age of twenty years, began to publish the productions of her pen anonymously in the *Literary Gazette*, etc.  In 1831 her father removed his family to Worcester, where, although suffering from an affection of the eyes, she continued to pursue her studies.  In 1840 she became the wife of Rev. Dr. E. B. Hall, of Providence, R. I.  Dr. Hall died March 3, 1866.  Mrs. Hall continued to reside in Providence for a few years, and then removed to Boston, which is now (1886) her home.

— Miriam.  A Dramatic Poem.  12°, pp. 124.  Boston, 1837.

— Same.  12°, pp. 122.  Boston, 1843.

— Same.  2d Edition.  12°, pp. 122.  Boston, 1849.

— Same.  12°, pp. 155.  In the volume is Joanna of Naples, and other prose productions.  Whole number pp. 403.  Boston, 1850.

— The Cross and Anchor.  For Mariners' Fair.  Sq. 24°, pp. 31. Providence, 1844.

HALL, (MRS. JAMES.)  Phantasia, etc.  8°, pp. 144.  New York, 1849.

HALLECK, (F. G.)

Fitz-Greene Halleck was born at Guilford, Conn., in August, 1795, entered a bank-ing-house in New York in 1813, and was engaged in business pursuits in that city till 1849, when he returned to Guilford, where he died November, 1867. His life was published by J. G. Wilson, 1869.

— Alnwick Castle, etc.  8°, pp. 64.  New York, 1827.
— Same.  Lg. 8°, pp. 98.  New York, 1837.
— Same.  12°, pp. 104.  New York, 1845.
— Fanny.  12°, pp. 49.  New York, 1819.
— Same.  24°, pp. 48.  New York, 1833.
— Same.  From the edition of 1821.  12°, pp. 130.  New York, 1846.
— Same.  4°, pp. 84.  New York, 1866.

No. 24 of an edition of 70 copies.

— Lines to the Recorder.  Lg. 8°, pp. 25.  New York, 1866.
— Poetical Works.  New Edition.  12°, pp. 232.  New York, 1852.
— Same.  New York, 1854.
— Same.  New Edition.  12°, pp. 238.  New York, 1858.
— Same.  With Extracts from poems of Joseph Rodman Drake.  Edited by James Grant Wilson.  12°, pp. xvi, 389.  New York, 1869.
— Young America: A Poem.  16°, pp. 49.  New York, 1865.

HALLOCK, (B.)  Poems.  12°, pp. 204.  New York, 1856.

HALM, (F.)  Baron Münch-Bellinghausen.  Translated from the German by C. E. Anthon.  The Song of the Wilderness.  A Dramatic Poem.  8°, pp. 166.  New York, 1848.

HALPINE, (C. G.)

Charles Graham Halpine was born in Ireland in November, 1829, and graduated at the University of Dublin in 1846. He came to this country in 1847, and was a journalist in New York, 1847–69. In 1861 he enlisted in the Union army, and was made Brigadier-General of Volunteers in 1864. That year he became editor and proprietor of the Citizen newspaper. He died August 3, 1868. His most famous production is "The Miles O'Reilly Papers."

— Lyrics by the Letter H.  12°, pp. vi, 228.  New York, 1854.
— The Poetical Works.  12°, pp. xxi, 352.  New York, 1869.

HAMILTON, (J.)  Drifted Snow Flakes; or, Poetical Gatherings from Many Authors.  12°, pp. 208.  Philadelphia, 1864.

HAMILTON, (MAJ. A.)  Thomas A'Becket.  A Tragedy in Five Acts.  12°, pp. 106.  New York, 1863.

HAMLET, THE MODERN.  (Anon.)  12°, pp. 12.  No place, 1850.

HANCOCK, (SALLIE J.)  Rayon d'Amour.  Poems.  12°, pp. xii, 159.
Philadelphia, 1869.

HANNA, (ABIGAIL S.)  Withered Leaves from Memory's Garland.  12°,
pp. 390.  Providence, 1857.

HANNAH, THE MOTHER OF SAMUEL.  A Sacred Drama.  (Anon.)  12°,
pp. xiii, 94.  Boston, 1839.

HAPPINESS.  The Uses of Domestick, etc.  (Anon.)  18°, pp. 316.
Pittsburg, 1817.

HAPPY CHANGES.  (Anon.)  24°, pp. 62.  New York, no date.

HARBAUGH, (H.)  Poems.  12°, pp. 285.  Philadelphia, 1860.

HARBINGER, THE.  A May Gift.  (Anon.)  12°, pp. 96.  Boston, 1833.

HARBY, (I.)

Isaac Harby was born at Charleston, S. C., in 1788.  He was of Jewish descent.  His
father, Solomon Harby, came originally from Barbary, where he enjoyed a post of honor
in the palace of the Emperor of Morocco, that of Royal Lapidary.  (See " North Ameri -
can Review," New Series, No. xxvii, p. 73.)  The subject of this sketch received his education in his native city, where, for a time, he was a successful teacher.  Here also
he commenced his career as a journalist and dramatic writer.  In 1828 he removed to New
York, where he became a literary contributor to the *Evening Post* and other journals.
As a dramatic critic he took a high rank.  His death occurred November 14, 1828.

— Alberti.  A Play.  12°, pp. 55.  Charleston, 1819.

— Prose and Poetry.  8°, pp. 287.  Charleston, 1869.

" Alberti " occupies pp. 1-55 of the " Writings " of Mr. Harby collected in this volume.

HARDCASTLE, (J.)  Masonic Museum, The.  Songs for Chapters, etc.
12°, pp. 76.  New York, 5816.

HARDY, (D., JR.)

David Hardy was born at Westminster, Vt., July 25, 1520, removed in early life to
Hancock, N. H., and then to Preble, N. Y., graduated from Courtlandt Academy at
Homer, N. Y., in 1854, in which institution he became a teacher.  Subsequently he had
charge of the Preparatory Department of Bethel College, Ky., and died in office October
3, 1857.

— Poems.  18°, pp. 260.  New York, 1858.

HARLEQUIN BLUE BEARD.  A Comedy.  (Anon.)  12°, pp. 16.  New
York, 1857.

HARNEY, (J. M.)

John M. Harney was born in Sussex county, Delaware, in 1789, lived in Bardstown,
Ky., and subsequently in Savannah, Ga.  This poem, in six cantos, was enthusiastically
commended by John Neal.  Mr. Harney died in 1823.

HARNEY, (J. M.) — *Continued.*
— Crystalina. A Fairy Tale. 12°, pp. 142. New York, 1816.

HAROLDSON, (J.) The Lay of. Printed for Private Circulation. (Edition 63 copies. No. 17.) 8°, pp. 5. Philadelphia, 1866.

HARP AND PLOW, THE. By the " Peasant Bard." 12°, pp. 204. Greenfield, 1852.

HARP OF PELHAM, THE. (Anon.) 18°, pp. viii, 106. New York, 1844.

HARP, THE ÆOLIAN. (Anon.) 2 vols. 32°, pp. 124, 124. New York, 1817.

HARPER, (MRS. F. E. W.) Moses: A Story of the Nile. 12°, pp. 48. Philadelphia, 1869.
— Same. 2d Edition.
— Poems. 18°, pp. 48. Philadelphia, 1871.

HARRIS, (S. B., M. D.) Remains. 12°, pp. 312. Plymouth, Mass., 1829.

HARRIS, (S. M.) The Life Boat. (Bound up with Discourse before the Humane Society of Massachusetts.) 8°, pp. 6. Boston, 1806.

HARRIS, (T. L.) A Lyric of the Golden Age. 12°, pp. xxxiv, 381. New York, 1856.
— An Epic of the Starry Heavens. 12°, pp. 210. New York, 1855.
— Hymns of Spiritual Devotion. Part I. 18°, pp. vi, 139. New York, 1857.

HARRIS, (T. M., D. D.)
> Thaddeus Mason Harris was born at Charlestown in 1768, graduated at Harvard in 1787, was Librarian 1791-93, became pastor of the Congregational Church in Dorchester in 1793, holding the office forty-nine years. He died in 1842.

— Hymns for the Lord's Supper. 24°, pp. 54. Boston, 1820.
— Same. 2d Edition. 1821.
— Triumphs of Superstition. Sq. 8°, pp. 16. Boston, 1790.

HARRISON, (G.) John Howard Payne, Dramatist, Poet, Actor, and Author of " Home, Sweet Home." His Life and Writings, with Illustrations. 8°, pp. 404. Philadelphia.

HARRY. By the Author of "Mrs. Jerningham's Journal." (Anon.) 12°, pp. 145. New York, 1877.

HART, (C. W.) Imaginary Debate, etc. 12°, pp. 24. Boston, 1839.

HART, (S.) Poems. 3d Edition Revised. 18°, pp. 120. Fall River, Mass., 1855.

HARTE, (B.)

Francis Bret Harte was born at Albany, August 25, 1829, went to California in 1854, and was engaged in various occupations for several years. In 1868 commenced "The Overland Monthly" Magazine. Some poems which were published in this periodical became very popular, for example, "The Heathen Chinee." In 1871 he removed to New York, and subsequently was appointed United States Consul at Glasgow.

— East and West Poems. 16°, pp. 171. Boston, 1871.

— Poems. 12°, pp. 152. Boston, 1871.

— The Heathen Chinee. Illustrated by Joseph Hull. Sq. 8°, not paged. Chicago, 1870.

— Same. Illustrations by S. Eytinge, Jr. 12°, pp. vi, 17. Boston, 1871.

HARVEST FESTIVAL, THE. (F. S. H. Anon.) 18°, pp. 79. Boston, 1826.

HARVEY, (M. J.) Poems for the Drawing-Room. No. 1. 12°, pp. 45. Concord, 1851.

HARWOOD, (J. E.) Poems. 12°, pp. 107. New York, 1809.

HASKELL, (B. D.) Zethar, the Celestial Visitant. 12°, pp. 71. No place, no date.

HASKINS, (J.)

James Haskins, the son of a wealthy Dublin gentleman, was born in 1805. His father "was the beau ideal of the generous, warm-hearted, whole-souled Irishman. He was distinguished for humour; and from him his son inherited that quality in a very high degree." The subject of this sketch took his degree in Arts and in Medicine at Trinity College in his native city. For several years he was a private tutor in several families in Ireland, and taught for a time in England. In 1834 he came to America and took up his residence in Belleville, Upper Canada, where he practiced his profession, and in other places, Trent, Loughborough and Frankford. He was also a physician. He died at Frankford in the fall of 1845.

— Poetical Works. 12°, pp. xvii, 320. Hartford, 1848.

HASLETT, (A.) Original Poems. 12°, pp. 95. Baltimore, 1812.

HASSAN, (A. B., U. S. A.) Contributions to the Rhymes of the War. 12°, pp. 29. No place, no date.

HASTINGS, (SALLY.) Poems. 12°, pp. 220. Lancaster, 1808.

HASTINGS, (T.) The Mother's Nursery Songs. 12°, pp. 60. New York, 1835.

— Devotional Hymns. 18°, pp. 220. New York, 1850.

HATHAWAY, (B.) The League of the Iroquois, etc. 12°, pp. x, 316. Chicago, 1882.

HAWES, (MRS. ELIZABETH.) The Harp of Acushnet. Poems. 12°, pp. 172. Boston, 1838.

HAWKINS, (M.) The Saw-Mill; or, A Yankee Trick. A Comic Opera. New York, J. & J. Harper, 1824.

HAWKS, (F. L., D. D.)

Francis Lester Hawks was born at Newbern, N. C., June 10, 1798, graduated at the University of North Carolina in 1815, was admitted to the bar in 1819, in 1827 was ordained clergyman in the Protestant Episcopal Church, was Assistant Minister of St. James's Church, Philadelphia, in 1820, Rector of St. Stephen's Church, New York, 1830, St. Thomas's, New York, 1832-43, elected Bishop of Mississippi in 1844, but for various reasons was not consecrated; Rector of Christ Church, New Orleans, 1844-49, of Calvary Church, New York, 1849-66, the year of his death, which event occurred September 27, 1866.

— Poems Hitherto Uncollected. Lg. 8°, pp. 27. New York, 1873.

Privately printed. No. 56 of 60 copies.

HAWLEY, (W. F.) Quebec, The Harp, etc. 18°, pp. viii, 172. Montreal, 1829,

HAWSER, (HARRY, *pseud.*) Buds and Flowers. 8°, pp. 132. Philadelphia, 1844.

HAY, (J.)

John Hay was born at Salem, Ill., October 8, 1838, graduated at Brown University in 1858, and was admitted to the bar in Springfield, Ill., 1861. From 1861 to 1865 he was Private Secretary and Aide to President Lincoln, performing military service a part of the time, and attaining the rank of Colonel. From 1865 to 1870 he was in the diplomatic service, was on the editorial staff of the *New York Tribune* 1870-76, and again in 1881; was Assistant Secretary of State 1870-81.

— Little Breeches. Illustrations by Engel. 8°, pp. 14. New York, 1871.

— Jim Bludso of the Prairie Bell and Little Breeches. Illustrated by S. Eytinge, Jr. 12°, pp. 23. Boston, 1871.

— Pike County Ballads and Other Pieces. 18°, pp. 167. Boston, 1871.

HAYDN, ETC.  By the Author of " Life Below."  (Anon.)  16°, pp. 161. New York, 1870.

HAYDEN, ESTHER.  Account of Life, etc.  (Anon.)  18°, pp. 12.  Boston, 1759.

HAYES, (J.)  Rural Poems.  12°, pp. 182.  Carlisle, Pa., 1807.

HAYNE, (P. H.)

> Paul Hamilton Hayne was born at Charleston, S. C., January 1, 1831.  He was for a time editor of " The Southern Literary Magazine," etc., and he was known as " The Poet Laureate of the South."  His residence was near Augusta, Ga.  He died July 9, 1886.

— Avolio: A Legend of the Island of Cos, etc.  12°, pp. viii, 244. Boston, 1860.
— Poems.  16°, pp. 108.  Boston, 1855.

HAYNES, (J., M. D.)  Poems.  12°, pp. 152.  Quebec, 1864.
— Savannah.  A Poem.  12°, pp. 48.  Savannah, 1855.

HEAD, (J., JR.)  Enthusiasm.  Phi Beta Kappa, Harvard, 1809.  8°, pp. 10.  Boston, 1809.

HEART-SONGS.  (Anon.)  12°, pp. 144.  Boston, 1856.

HEART, THE CITY'S.  (By a Daughter of New York.  Anon.)  Sq. 18°, pp. 60.  New York, 1866.

HEAVENLY FRIEND, THE; OR, RECOLLECTIONS OF MY MINISTER.  A few Poems in the volume.  18°, pp. 112.  Portland, 1841.

HEAVYSEGE, (C.)  Saul.  A Drama.  12°, pp. 436.  Boston, 1869.

HEBBARD, (W. W.)  The Night of Freedom.  8°, pp. 43.  Boston, 1857.

H. (E. D.)  (Anon.)  Temperance Poems.  No. II.  18°, pp. 72. Philadelphia, 1844.

HELMS, (W. T.)  Moses Resisted.  In 12 Cantos.  12°, pp. 129.  Nashville, 1881.

HEDGE, (F. H.)

> Frederic H. Hedge, son of Professor Levi Hedge, Professor of Logic and Metaphysics in Harvard University, was born at Cambridge, Mass., December 5, 1805, pursued his preparatory studies chiefly in Germany, under the care of George Bancroft.  He graduated at Harvard in 1825, and was ordained a Unitarian minister in 1829.  In 1835 he became pastor of a church in Bangor, Me., and in 1850 of the Westminster Church in Providence, R. I.  In 1858 he was chosen Professor of Ecclesiastical History in the Harvard Divinity School. His present residence (1880) is Cambridge.

Hedge, (F. H.) — *Continued.*

— Poems and Ballads from the German.  Bound with Furness's Song of the Bell.  8°.  Philadelphia, 1850.

Helmer, (C. D.)  The Stars and Stripes.  8°, pp. 23.  New Haven, 1862.

A poem pronounced before the Phi Beta Kappa Society, Yale College, July 30, 1862. The oration of Charles Tracy, Esq., on " The True and the False," delivered on the same occasion, is bound up in the same volume.

Hemenway, (Abby M.)  Editor of "Poets and Poetry of Vermont." 12°, pp. xii, 400.  Rutland, 1858.

Hempstead, (T.)  Poems.  12°, pp. 190.  New York, 1859.

Henck, (E. C.)  Spirit Voices : Odes Dictated by Departed Spirits.  18°, pp. 108.  Philadelphia, 1853.

— Same.  Philadelphia, 1855.

Hentz, (Mrs. C. L.)  De Lara ; or, The Moorish Bride.  A Tragedy. 12°, pp. viii, 79.  Tuscaloosa, Ala., 1843.

Henderson, (M. A.)  The Song of Milkanwatha.  3d Edition.  12°, pp. 99.  Albany, 1883.

Henry, (G. W.)  The Golden Harp ; or, Camp-Meeting Hymns.  18°, pp. 154.  New York, 1853.

Herbert, (H. W.)

Henry William Herbert, a son of the Hon. and Rev. William Herbert, and a descend-ant from the Earl of Pembroke and Percy, was born in London, April 7, 1807, graduated at Caius College, Cambridge, came to New York in 1831, and for eight years was principal Greek teacher in a Classical Academy in that city.  After his marriage, in 1839, he took up his residence at " The Cedars," near Newark, N. J., and devoted himself to literary pur-suits.  For a notice of his works, see Allibone, p. 830, and " New York International Magazine," vol. iii, pp. 280–91.  He died at New York, May 17, 1858.

— The Prometheus and Agamemnon of Æschylus, translated into English Verse.  12°, pp. xii, 156.  Cambridge, 1849.

Hermes, (P.)  The Confessions of Hermes, etc.  8°, pp. 153.  Philadelphia, 1884.

Herre, (B. G.)  Voyage in the Air, etc.  18°, pp. 65.  Harrisburg, Pa., 1870.

Hersey, (A. G.)  Dew-Drops.  12°, pp. 24.  Boston, 1836.

HESTON, (J. F.) Moral and Political Truth. 12°, pp. 401. Philadelphia, 1811.

— Poems on Political and Other Subjects. 18°, pp. 257. Philadelphia, 1854.

HEWETT, (J. D.) The Votary. 12°, pp. 123. New York, 1867.

— Miscellaneous Poems. 12°, pp. 235. Baltimore, 1838.

— Flora's Festival. A Pastoral Oratorio. 12°, pp. 12.

Sung by the pupils of the "Baltimore Musical Institute," May 1, 1838. No place, no date.

HEWITT, (MARY E.)

Mary Elizabeth Moore was born at Malden, Mass., in 1808, married Mr. James L Hewitt, of New York, and in 1854 Mr. R. Stebbins. She wrote in the "Knickerbocker" and other periodicals under the signature of "Jane." For criticisms on her writings, see Griswold's and Mrs. May's "Female Poets," etc.

— Poems. Sacred, Passionate and Legendary. 16°, pp. 196. New York, 1864.

— The Memorial. Written by Friends of the late Mrs. Osgood. 8°, pp. vi, 346. New York, 1851.

HEYDE, (C. L.) Louie and Marie. A Tale of the Heart, etc. 18°, pp. 88. New York, 1844.

HEYES, (H.) Hymns, Psalms, etc. 18°, pp. 123. Albany, 1849.

HEYWOOD, (J. C.) Antonius. A Dramatic Poem. 12°, pp. 272. New York, 1867.

— Salome, the Daughter of Herodias. 12°, pp. 251. New York, 1862.

— Same. 16°, pp. 222. New York, 1867.

"H. G." Horace Greeley at Chappaqua. (Anon.) 18°, pp. 32. New York, 1872.

HILL, (F. S.) The Six Degrees of Crime. A New Drama. 12°, pp. 50. Boston, 1856.

— The Shoemaker of Toulouse. A Drama. 12°, pp. 48. Boston, no date.

HILL, (G.)

George Hill was born at Guilford, Conn., in 1796, graduated at Yale in 1816, served the United States Government for several years, entered the Navy, in 1827, as teacher of Mathematics, was Librarian of the State Department at Washington 1831-55, and for a time United States Consul for the southern portion of Asia Minor. The closing years of his life were spent in his native town. He died in St. Vincent Hospital, New York, in 1871.

Hill, (G.) — *Continued.*

— Ruins of Athens, etc.   8°, pp. 160.   Boston, 1839.

Hill, (T.)   Christmas, and Poems on Slavery for Christmas, 1843.   12°, pp. 16.   Cambridge, 1843.

— Poetical Works.   Vol. I.   12°, pp. 32.   Worcester, 1851.

Hill, (T. H.)   Hesper, etc.   16°, pp. 96.   Raleigh, 1861.

Hill, (W.)   The Rise and Fall of the Jews.   32°, pp. 40.   Albany, 1859.

Hillard, (I.)   Poetical History of Fragments.   12°, pp. 84.   Danbury, Conn., 1803.

Hiller, (O. P.)   American Lyrics.   12°, pp. 80.   Boston, 1860.

Hillhouse, (J. A.)

James Abraham Hillhouse was born at New Haven, Conn., September 26, 1789, graduated at Yale College in 1808.   For a time he resided in Boston, and after the war of 1812 removed to New York, and was actively engaged in commerce for several years.   Shortly after his marriage, in 1824, he took up his residence at "Sachem's Wood," near New Haven, and as "a man of letters" devoted himself to literary pursuits.   He died January 4, 1841.

— Dramas, Discourses, and other Pieces.   2 vols.   12°, pp. xiv, 296, 247.   Boston, 1839.
— Hadad.   A Dramatic Poem.   8°, pp. x, 208.   New York, 1825.
— Sachem's Wood.   A Short Poem.   8°, pp. 30.   New Haven, 1838.
— The Judgment.   8°, pp. 46.   New York, 1821.

"This poem was rewarded, shortly after its appearance, by the enthusiastic commendation of one of the most accomplished of English critics."

Hine, (B.)   Miscellaneous Poetry ; or, The Farmer's Muse.   12, pp. x, 273.   New York, 1835.

Hine, (C. C.)   A Legend of Chicago.   Mrs. Leary's Cow.   8°, pp. 14.   New York, 1872.

A poetical account of the cause of the great Chicago fire, October 8, 1871.

Hine, (E. C.)   The Haunted Barque and other Poems.   8°, pp. 109.   Auburn, 1848.

"Most of the poems in this volume were composed at sea, while the author was attached to an American frigate cruising in the Pacific ocean, to while away the tedious hours, monotony and *ennui* of a life on board a ship-of-war."

**HIRST, (H. B.)**

Henry B. Hirst was born at Philadelphia, August 23, 1813, was admitted to the bar in 1843. "The Coming of Mammoth" was originally published in "Graham's Magazine." Among his other writings are "Endymion, a Tale of Greece," in Four Cantos, and "The Penance of Roland," a Romance.

— Endymion. A Tale of Greece. 12°, pp. 122. Boston, 1848.

— The Coming of Mammoth, etc. 12°, pp. 168. Boston, 1845.

— The Penance of Roland. A Romance of the Peine Fort et Dure, etc. 12°, pp. 128. Boston, 1849.

— A Poetical Dictionary; or, Popular Terms. Illustrated in Rhyme. 12°, pp. vi, 113. Lenox, Mass., 1808.

**HITCHCOCK, (D.)**

David Hitchcock was born at Bethlehem, Litchfield county, Conn., in 1773. He worked at farming and shoe making most of his life, and was always in straitened circumstances. The date of his death is not given.

— Christ not the Minister of Sin. A Dialogue between a Universalist and his Neighbor. 12°, pp. 35. Hartford, 1832.

— The Shade of Plato, etc. 18°, pp. 107. Hudson, 1805.

Duyckinck says: "'The Shade of Plato' is certainly a remarkable production under the circumstances, to have been hammered out between the blows of the lapstone."

— The Social Monitor. 16°, pp. v, 158. Stockbridge, Mass., 1812.

**HODGES, (LAURA JANE.)** Panorama of the Heart; or, The Four Prayers of Life. 12°, pp. 12. Worcester, 1870.

**HODGKINS, (T. G)** Time on the Iron Horse. 12°, pp. 12. New York, 1847.

**HODSON, (J.)** Miscellaneous Poems, in 2 vols. Vol. I. 18°, pp. 151. Wellesville, Ohio, 1866.

**HOEY, (G.)** Mary Leigh. 8°, pp. 12. New York, 1874.

**HOFFMAN, (C. F.)**

Charles Fenno Hoffman was born in the city of New York in 1806, entered Columbia College at the age of fifteen, and was admitted to the New York bar at twenty-one. Literary pursuits having for him greater attractions than the practice of his profession, he decided to devote himself to letters. In 1849 his mind became deranged, and he was forced to retire from the work. He died at Harrisburg, Pa., in 1884.

— Love's Calendar, etc. 24°, pp. 221. New York, 1847.

— The Echo. 8°, pp. 48. New York, 1844.

— The Vigil of Faith, etc. 12°, pp. 84. New York, 1842.

— Same. 4th Edition. 18°, pp. 164. New York, 1845.

Hogg, (E.)  The Lay of the First Minstrel, etc.  12°, pp. iv, 46.  New York, 1834.

Holcombe, (W. H., M. D.)  Poems.  12°, pp. x, 360.  New York, 1860.

Holden, (O.)  Sacred Dirges, etc.  Commemoration of the Death of General George Washington.  Lg. 8°, pp. 24.  Boston, 1800.

Holiday Exercises ; or, The Christian A, B, C.  12°, pp. 36.  Philadelphia, 1785.

Holland, (E. G.)

Elihu G. Holland was born at Solon, Cortlandt county, N. Y., April 14, 1817, and was the author of "The Being of God," etc., 1846, and "Memoir of Rev. Joseph Badger," 1853.

— The Highland Treason.  A Drama, bound in a volume containing Essays.  12°, pp. 152.  Boston, 1852.

Holland, (J. G.)

Josiah Gilbert Holland, M. D., was born at Belchertown, Mass., July 24, 1819, devoted himself to journalism, having been connected with the *Springfield Republican* seventeen years, 1849–66, and was editior of "Scribner's Monthly" eleven years, 1870–61, and died in New York City in 1881.  For a discriminating article on Dr. Holland, see "The Nation," October 20, 1881.

— Bitter Sweet.  16°, pp. 220.  New York, 1859.
— Poems.  12°, pp. 108.  Boston, 1858.
— Same.  With illustrations by E. J. Whitney.  12°, pp. 208.  New York, 1863.
— Same.  15th Edition.  12°, pp. 220.  New York, 1863.
— Kathrina ; Her Life and Mine.  20th Edition.  12°.  New York, 1867.
— The Marble Prophecy, etc.  12°, pp. iv, 112.  New York, 1872.
— The Mistress of the Manse.  12°, pp. 187.  New York, 1881.

Hollister, (G. H.)  Senior Class Poem, Yale, July 1, 1840.  8°, pp. 15.  New Haven, 1840.

Holloway, (W.)  The Peasant's Fate, etc.  12°, pp. x, 128.  Wilmington, 1808.

Holmes, (Alice A.)

Alice Holmes was born in the county of Norfolk, England, in February, 1821, and came to the United States in 1830.  On the passage over she had the small-pox and was left blind by the disease.  In 1837 she became an inmate of the "New York Institution for the

HOLMES, (ALICE A.) — *Continued.*

Blind," where she remained seven years. After leaving the institution she was enabled to gain a precarious livelihood by means of plain sewing and other handiwork. "To poetry she only turned as a solace in her darker hours."

— Arcadian Leaves. 18°, pp. 122. New York, 1858.

— Poems. 12°, pp. x, 53. New York, 1849.

— Stray Leaves. 12°, pp. 60. New York, 1868.

HOLMES, (O. W.)

Oliver Wendell Holmes, M. D., son of Rev. Dr. Abiel Holmes, was born at Cambridge, August 29, 1800, graduated at Harvard University in 1820, studied law for a year and a half, and then decided to study medicine, was in Europe between two and three years, his time being occupied chiefly in the hospitals of Paris, took his medical degree at Cambridge in 1836, was elected Professor of Anatomy and Physiology in Dartmouth College in 1838, and to the same office in the Harvard Medical school in 1847, relinquishing general practice in 1840. Since 1882 he has been Professor *Emeritus.* For a fuller sketch of his life and of his works than can be given in this note, see Allibone, pp. 868–70.

— Astrea : The Balance of Illusions. Phi Beta Kappa, Yale, August 14, 1850. 12°, pp. 39. Boston, 1850.

— Grandmother's Story of Bunker Hill Battle. 4°, pp. 16. Boston, 1875.

— Poem at the Dinner given to Prince Napoleon, Boston, September 25, 1861. 8°, pp. 2. Bound with the address of Edward Everett. Cambridge, privately printed, 1861.

— Poem. Dedication of Pittsfield Cemetery, September 9, 1850. 8°, pp. 8. No place.

— Poems. 12°, pp. xiv, 163. Boston, 1836.

— Same. 12°, pp. xx, 175. London, 1846.

— Same. New and enlarged Edition. 12°, pp. vi, 212. Boston, 1849.

— Same. pp. 286. 1850.

— Same. pp. 286. 1851.

— Same. pp. 286. 1858.

— Same. 18°, pp. 410. Boston, 1864.

— Same. 18°, pp. 410. Boston, 1866.

— Same. 18°, pp. 410. Boston, 1869.

— Songs in Many Keys. 12°, pp. x, 308. Boston, 1862.

The author's presentation copy to Richard Grant White.

— Urania. 8°, pp. 31. Boston, 1846.

HOME BALLADS. By Our Home Poets. 18°, pp. 96. New York, 1865.

HONEYWOOD, (ST. J.)  Poems.  12°.  New York, 1801.

HOOD, (C.)  Gonzaloo ; or, The Fall of Grenada.  12°, pp. 377.  Boston, 1845.

HOOD, (C.)  Poem at the Dedication of the Dorchester High School, December 7, 1852.  8°, pp. 12.  Boston, 1852.

HOOPER, (LUCY.)

Lucy Hooper was born at Newburyport, Mass., February 4, 1816, and removed in 1831 to Brooklyn, N. Y., which was her residence till her death.  Soon after her removal to Brooklyn she became an occasional contributor to the columns of the *Long Island Star*, under the signature of her initials, " L. H," her articles attracting attention by their merit.  Among her published writings were " Scenes from Real Life," " Essay on Domestic Happiness," and " The Poetry of Flowers."  She died August 1, 1841.

— Complete Poetical Works.  8°, pp. 404.  New York, 1848.

— Poetical Remains.  Collected by John Keese.  12°, pp. 291.  New York, 1842.

— The Lady's Book of Flowers and Poetry.  12°, pp. 263.  New York, 1842.

— Same.  1843.

HOOPER, (LUCY H.)  Poems.  With Translations from the German of Geiber, etc.  18°, pp. 96.  Philadelphia, 1864.

HOOPER, (R.)  Class Poem, Harvard, 1811.  Songs by Edward Everett and N. L. Frothingham are in the volume.  Also, Oration by John T. Cooper.  12°, pp. 24.  Cambridge, 1811.

HOPE, (J. B.)  A Collection of Poems.  12°, pp. 139.  Richmond, Va., 1869.

— A Poem pronounced on the 250th Anniversary of the Settlement of Jamestown, Va.  8°, pp. 16.  Richmond, 1857.

— Elegaic Ode.  On the occasion of completing the Monument erected over the remains of Ann Carter Lee.  12°, pp. 29.  Richmond, 1866.

— Leoni di Monota, etc.  12°, pp. 226.  Philadelphia, 1857.

HOPKINS, (J. H., D. D., LL. D.)

John Henry Hopkins was born at Dublin, Ireland, January 30, 1792, came to this country in 1800, was admitted to the bar at Pittsburg, Pa., in 1818, subsequently studied for the ministry, became Rector of Trinity Church, Pittsburg, in 1824, assistant Rector of Trinity, Boston, in 1831, and in 1832 was consecrated the first Bishop of Vermont.  A strong High-churchman.  He died January 9, 1868.

— The History of the Church in verse.  12°, pp. 256.  New York, 1867.

HOPKINS, (J. S.)  The Poetical Works of.  12°, pp. 215.  Baltimore, 1842.

HOPKINS, (L.)

> Lemuel Hopkins, M. D., was born at Waterbury, Conn., June 19, 1750, was a physician in Litchfield, 1770-84, and in Hartford, 1784-1801.  He died in the latter year, April 14.  He was the literary associate of Trumbull, Barlow, Humphrey, Dwight, and others.

— The Democratiad.  A Poem in Retaliation for the "Philadelphia Jockey Club."  12°, pp. iv, 22.  Philadelphia, 1796.

— The Guillotina; or, A Democratic Dirge.  8°, pp. 14.  Philadelphia, no date.

HOPKINSON, (F.)

> Francis Hopkinson was born at Philadelphia in 1737, and educated at what is now the University of Pennsylvania.  Subsequently he studied law.  He was one of the signers of the Declaration of Independence, and held high civil offices under the government.  He died May 9, 1791.

—Miscellaneous Works, in which are several Poems.  8°.  3 vols.  Philadelphia, 1792.

— Poems on several Subjects.  8°, pp. 204.  No place, no date.

— The Battle of the Kegs.  Lg. 8°, not paged.  No place.

> 100 copies in the edition.  18 Lg., 82 Sm.

HOPPER, (E.)  Old Horse Gray, and The Parish of Grumbleton.  12°, pp. 82.  New York, 1869.

— One Wife Too Many; or, Rip Van Bigham.  A Tale of Tappan Zee.  12°, pp. 262.  New York, 1867.

— The Dutch Pilgrim Fathers, etc.  12°, pp. vi, 216.  New York, 1865.

— The Fire on the Hearth in Sleepy Hollow.  12°, pp. 105.  New York, 1864.

HOPPIN, (A.)  Carrot-Pomade.  With twenty-six illustrations.  8°, not paged.  New York.

HORACE, IMITATIONS OF.  (Anon.)  18°, pp. 46.  Albany, no date.

HORNE, (A. G., M. P., pseud.)  The New Temple of Ceres.  8°, pp. 15.

HORNER, (J. M.)  The Rights of Adopted Citizens.  12°, pp. 24.  New York, 1844.

HORNER, (S. S.)  Thoughts in Verse.  2d Edition.  12°, pp. 130.  Paris, 1864.

Horse-Car Poetry. (Anon.) 18°, pp. 14. New York, 1876.

Horsford, (Mary G.) Indian Legends, etc, 12°, pp. viii, 167. New York, 1855.

Horton, (Mary L.) Poetical and Prose Compositions. 18°, pp. 88. Salem, 1832.

Horton, (F.) Memorials of Brookfield, Mass. 8°, pp. 20. Springfield, 1868.

This poem was delivered by Rev. F. Horton, October 16, 1867, at the 150th Anniversary of the West Brookfield Congregational Church.

— Temperance Poem. Brookfield, Mass., January, 1833. 12°, pp. 40. Brookfield, 1833.

Hosmer, (W. H. C.)

William Henry Cuyler Hosmer was born at Avon, N. Y., May 25, 1814, graduated at Genesee College, practiced law in Avon, moved to New York in 1854, where for a number of years he held an office in the Custom House. He died in his native town, May 23, 1877.

— Later Lays and Lyrics. 12°, pp. 168. Rochester, N. Y., 1873.
— Poetical Works. 2 vols. 12°, pp. ix, 374, 377. New York, 1854.
— The Months. 12°, pp. 71. Boston, 1847.
— Yonnondio; or, Warriors of the Genesee. A Tale of the 17th Century. 12°, pp. vi, 239. New York, 1844.

Hosmot, (H.) The Saturniad: Being a full and true account of the Rise, Progress, and Downfall of the University of Quillsyvane. 18°, pp. 63. Philadelphia, 1832.

Hough, (G. W.) Puritan. 12°, pp. 94. Cincinnati, 1868.

Hough, (L. S.) The Wanderer. 18°, pp. 64. Cleveland, 1847.

Houghton, (G.) Niagara, etc. 18°, pp. 130. Boston, 1882.
— The Legend of St. Olaf's Kirk. Sm. 4°, pp. 64. Boston, 1880.
— Same. 2d Edition. Sq. 18°, pp. 92. Boston, 1881.

Hours of Childhood, etc. (Anon.) 18°, pp. vi, 94. Montreal, 1820.

Hours, The, of Childhood. (Anon.) 12°, pp. 24. New York, 1837.

House, The, That Jeff Built. (Anon.) 8°, pp. 16. New York, 1868.

House, The, That Jonathan Built. A Poetical Primer for 1832. (Anon.) 8°, pp. 16. Philadelphia.

House, The, That Old Nick Built. (Anon.) 16°, pp. 16. Baltimore, 1834.

House, The, That Tweed Built. (Anon.) 8°, pp. 23. New York, no date.

How, (H. K.) The Battle of Trenton. 8°, pp. 15. New Brunswick, N. J., 1865.

How Little Katie Knocked at the Door of Heaven. (By Aunt Fanny, *pseud.*) 18°, pp. 15. New York, 1864.

How to Try a Lover. A Comedy. (Anon.) 18°, pp. 67. New York, 1817.

Howard Hynes; or, The Enthusiast of Nature, etc. (By Fulkerson, the Eccentric, *pseud?*) 12°, pp. 192. Louisville, 1831.

Howarth, (Ellen C.) Poems. 18°, pp. 112. Newark, N. J., 1868.
— The Wind Harp, etc. 12°, pp. 244. Philadelphia, 1864.

Howe, (J. B.) The British Slave. 12°, pp. 43. Boston, no date.
— Woman of the World, The. 12°, pp. 36. New York, no date.

Howe, (Mrs. Julia Ward.)

Julia Ward was the daughter of Samuel Ward, the eminent banker of New York, and was born in 1819. Her mother was Julia Rush Cutler, of Boston, the maternal ancestors of Miss C. being natives of South Carolina, and her grandmother, the only sister of the famous General Marion. The subject of this sketch was married in 1843 to the distinguished philanthropist, Dr. Samuel G. Howe. Her poems have been warmly commended.

— Leonore. A Tragedy. 8°, pp. 63. New York, 1857.
— Passion Flowers. 16°, pp. iv, 186. Boston, 1854.
— The Golden Eagle; or, The Privateer of '76. A National Drama. 12°, pp. 37. New York, no date.
— The World's Own. 12°, pp. 141. Boston, 1857.
— Words for the Hour. 16°, pp. iv, 165. Boston, 1857.

Howell, (J. E.) Poems in 2 vols. 12°, pp. 862, 514. New York, 1857.

Howland, (A.) Rhode Island Tales. Sq. 18°, pp. 171. New York, 1839.

Hoyt, (R.)

Rev. Ralph Hoyt was born in the city of New York and became Rector of the Church of the Good Shepherd in that city. He devoted himself with great earnestness and self-denial to his ministerial work.

Hoyt, (R.) — *Continued.*

— Chaunt of Life, etc., in Six Parts. Part I. 8°, pp. 32. New York, 1844.

— Same. Part II. New York, 1845.

— Echoes of Memory and Emotion. 12°, pp. 167. New York and London, 1859.

— Same. 1862.

— Sketches of Life and Landscape. Julia, etc. 8°, not paged. New York, 1847–48.

— Same. New Edition. 12°, pp. 134. New York, 1849.

— The True Life. 8°, pp. 15. Hartford, 1849.

Hubbard, (H.) Ixion, etc. 12°, pp. viii, 165. Boston, 1852.

Hubbard, (S.) The New Temperance Melodist. 12°, pp. 152. Boston, 1859.

Hubbell, (M. E.)

Mary Elizabeth Hubbell was born at Hamden, Conn., December 5, 1833, her father, Rev. Stephen Hubbell, being the minister of the parish of Mt. Carmel in that town. The closing years of her educational life were spent in Ipswich, Mass., and New Haven. In 1851 she became an assistant teacher in a Young Ladies' school in New Haven, where she remained one year, and then accepted an appointment as principal English teacher in a school in Baltimore. She died of consumption at North Stonington, Conn., June 10, 1854. The poems in the volume are pp. 207-57.

— Prose and Poetical Writings, in a Memorial by her Mother. 12°, pp. 384. Boston, 1857.

Huber, (S.) The Rose of Innichen; or, The Tailor and Barber. 12°, pp. 23. Philadelphia, 1870.

Hubner, (C. W.) Poems and Essays. 12°, pp. 172. New York, 1881.

Hudson, (H. R.) Poems. 12°, pp. 214. Boston, 1874.

Huerta de la, (J. G.) La Aurora, etc. 18°, pp. 153. Mexico, 1869.

Huggins, (J. R. D.) Huggiana. 12°, pp. viii, 288. New York, 1808.

Hulbert, (F. R.) Wandering Strains. 8°, pp 52. New York, 1850.

Hull, (J.) What I Know of Farming. Founded on the Experience of Horace Greeley. 12°, pp. 14. New York, 1871.

Humboldt, (G.) Poems and Letters. 12°, pp. x, 252. Albany, 1857.

Humbugs, The Age of. The Grand Tour, etc. By the author of the
" Snowy Daughter." (Anon.)   16°, pp. 52.   Wheeling, Va.,
1837.

Humorist, The. From June 21 to August 9, 1834.   4°, not paged.
New York.

Humphreys, (D.)

David Humphreys was born at Derby, Conn., in 1753, educated at Yale College, was
attached as Major to Putnam's staff, subsequently was on Washington's staff, and for
several years sustained most intimate relations with him.   In 1784 he was appointed Secretary of Legation, and was abroad two years.   In 1794 he was sent as United States
Ambassador to Lisbon, and in 1797 became Minister to the Court of Spain.   He was a
somewhat voluminous writer, and the productions of his pen were popular in his day.   He
died in 1818.

— A Poem on Industry.   8°.   Philadelphia, 1794.
— A Poem Addressed to the Armies of the United States.   8°, pp. 28.
New Haven, 1784.   Paris, reprinted 1785, and London, same
year.
— A Poem on the Happiness of America.   Sm. 4°, pp. 51.   London
and Hartford, 1786.
— Miscellaneous Works.   8°, pp. 348.   New York, 1790.
— Same.   12°.   Portsmouth, 1790.
— Same.   8°, pp. 294.   New York, 1804.

Hunker Lament.   (Anon.)   12°, pp. 24.   Concord, 1855.

Hunt, (C. M.)   Greenbacks and Tin.   8°, pp. 12.   Washington, 1864.

Hunt, (J., M. D.)   Hours of Reflection.   16°, pp. 324.   No place,
1845.

Huntington, (D.)   Pleasures and Advantages of True Religion.   United
Brothers' Society Poem, Brown University, August 31, 1819.   12°,
pp. 23.   Providence, 1819.
— Same.   Boston, 1830.

Huntington, (G.)   The Guests of Brazil; or, The Martyrdom of
Frederic.   12°, pp. 70.   New York, 1844.
— The Shadowy Land, etc.   8°, pp. 506.   New York, 1860.

Huntington, (J., Rev. and M. D.)   Poems.   12°, pp. 231.   New York,
1843.

HUNTINGTON, (J. V.)

Jedediah Vincent Huntington, M. D., was born in the city of New York, January 20, 1815, graduated at the New York University in 1835, received M. D. at the University of Pennsylvania, took orders in the Episcopal Church, subsequently became a Roman Catholic, and as a journalist was devoted to Roman Catholic interests. He died at Pau, France, March 10, 1862.

— America Discovered. A Poem Delivered before the Association of Alumni of the University of the City of New York, June 29, 1852. 12°, pp. xi, 32. New York, 1852.

HUNTLEY, (L.) Moral Pieces. 12°, pp. xii. Hartford, 1815.

HURLBUT, (W. H.) Wealth and Beauty. Phi Beta Kappa Poem, Harvard, July 19, 1855. 12°, pp. 31. Cambridge, 1855.

HUSBAND VS. WIFE. With designs by A. Hoppin. 12°, pp. 44. New York, 1858.

HUTTON, (F. R.) Seventy-Three. Junior Class Poem, Columbia College. 8°, pp. 4. New York, 1872.

HUTTON, (I. G.) The Vigneron; The Culture of the Grape, etc. 18°, pp. 60. Washington, 1827.

HUTTON, (J.) Leisure Hours. 18°, pp. 305. Philadelphia, 1812.
— School for Prodigals. A Comedy. 18°, pp. 62. New York, 1809.

HYDE, (NANCY MARIA.)

Miss Hyde was born at Norwich, Conn, March 1, 1792, and early in life developed poetic talent. She died March 26, 1816. The volume of which the title is here consists chiefly of her Journal and Letters.

— Writings of. A few Poems in the volume. 12°, pp. 252. Norwich, 1816.

HYER, (W. G.) Rosa. A Melo-Drama. 12°, pp. 44. New York, 1822.

HYMNS, ETC. Collected. (Anon.) 24°, pp. 182. Newport, R. I., 1766.

HYMNS AND POEMS. (Anon.) In *pseud.* William Durkee.) Sq. 24°, pp. 90. Baltimore, 1790.

HYMNS AND SACRED SONGS. (Anon.) 12°, pp. 106. Andover, 1823.

This collection was made by the late Rev. Leonard Bacon, D. D., of New Haven.

HYMNS AND TWILIGHT STORIES. By Cousin Hattie. (Anon.) Sq. 24°, pp. 64. Boston, 1852.

HYMNS, CHEROKEE.  Compiled by S. A. Worcester and E. Boudinot.
4th Edition.  24°, pp. 46.  New Echota, 1833.

HYMN BOOK, CHOCTAW.  3d Edition.  (Anon.)  24°, pp. 172.  Boston, 1844.

HYMNS EXHIBITING THE CHRISTIAN'S DUTY.  Recommended by the Fraternity of Baptists.  3d Edition.  18°, pp. 331.  Philadelphia, 1813.
— Same.  Germantown, 1825.

HYMNS FOR LUTHERAN CHURCH.  (Anon.)  32°, pp. 344.  Hagerstown,
1822.

HYMNS FOR OPEN-AIR MEETINGS IN BLOOMFIELD, N. J.  (Anon.)  24°,
not paged.  No place, 1873.

HYMNS, ORIGINAL, FOR SABBATH SCHOOLS.  (J. S. W.)  18°, pp. 96.
Boston, 1833.

HYMNS FOR UNIVERSALIST CHURCHES.  2d Edition.  18°, pp. 360.
Charlestown, Mass., 1810.
— Same.  By Sebastian Streeter and Russell Streeter.  9th Edition.
Boston, 1833.

HYMNS, GERMAN AND ENGLISH.  32°.  German, pp. 115.  English, pp.
41.  Ephrata, Pa., 1858.

> Mr. Harris makes the following note: "The Ephrata press was for some time on
> storage with J. E. Pfautz, a farmer at or near Ephrata, and whilst in his hands he printed
> this book. It was the last thing printed on the press."
> Pfautz was not a professional printer. The Press is now in the rooms of the Pennsylvania Historical Society.

— Gospel.  Bliss and Sankey.  24°, pp. 96.  New York, etc., no date.
— Illustrative of the Life of a Christian Child.  18°, pp. 54.  New York,
1858.
— Methodist.  Selected by Peggy Dow.  2d Edition.  24°, pp. 128.
Philadelphia, 1816.

> A perfect copy.  Bedford's binding.

— Of the Ages.  Second Series.  12°, pp. vii, 336.  Boston, 1861.
— Same.  Third Series.  Compiled by C. S. H. and A. E. G., of
Roxbury, Mass.  12°, pp. iv, 331.  Boston, 1865.
— On Various Subjects.  (Anna Beeman, etc.)  Imperfect.  No place,
no date.

HYMNS.—*Continued.*

— Selection of.  (Anon.)  24°, pp. 207.  Brooklyn, 1817.

— Social, for the Use of the Friends of Universal Reform.  (Anon.)  18°, pp. 32.  Boston, 1843.

— Sung in Drama of Uncle Tom's Cabin by Cordelia Howard.  24°, pp. 6.  New York, no date.

— The Hartford Selection.  Compiled by Rev. Messrs. Strong, Flint and Steward.  5th Edition.  24°, pp. 359.  Hartford, 1816.

HYNEMAN, (MRS. REBEKAH.)  The Leper, etc.  12°, pp. viii, 216.  Philadelphia, 1853.

IDA.  (Anon.)  12°, pp. 68.  Boston, 1851.

— Same.  12°, pp. 69.  Philadelphia, 1857.

IDEALINA, ETC.  (By Harry Quillem, *pseud.*)  12°, pp. 123.  San Francisco, 1853.

IDEALS, AND OTHER POEMS.  (By Algernon, *pseud.*)  12°, pp. 102.  Philadelphia, 1842.

I DINE WITH MY MOTHER.  A Comedietta.  (Anon.)  12°, pp. 15.  New York, no date.

INFIDELITY, THE TRIUMPH OF.  8°, pp. 40.  No place, 1788.

The author's name, Timothy Dwight, not on title-page.

INGERSOL, (C. J.)

Charles Jared Ingersoll was born at Philadelphia, October 3, 1782, received a liberal education, elected Representative to Congress in 1812, and, for the greater part of his life, was devoted to the public service.  He was a voluminous writer on political subjects.  He died January 14, 1862.

— Edwy and Elgiva.  A Tragedy in Five Acts.  8°, pp. 84.  Philadelphia, 1801.

INNOCENT POETRY.  (Anon.)  18°, pp. 104.  New York, no date.

INTEMPERANCE, EVILS OF.  (Anon.)  16°, pp. 24.  Boston, 1829.

IOOR, (W.)  Independence.  A Comedy.  8°, pp. 70.  Charleston, 1805.

IRISH-OFFICE-HUNTER-ONIAD.  A Heroic Epic.  (By Blarney O'Democrat, *pseud.*)  18°, pp. 72.  New York, 1838.

IRVINE, (J. P.) Concerning Washington and His Monument. Lg. 8°, not paged. Washington, 1875.

ITALIAN BRIDE. A Play. (Anon.) Yates[?]. 12°, pp. 132. Savannah, 1856.

ITALIAN HUSBAND, THE, ETC. (Anon.) 16°, pp. 107. Philadelphia, 1825.

ITALIAN IN ALGIERS, THE. A Play. (Anon.) 18°, pp. 71. New York, 1832.

IVES, (C.) Chips from the Workshop, etc. 12°, pp. 152. New Haven, 1843.

IXION, THE SPAWN OF; OR, "THE BITER BIT." (Anon.) (Forge of Vulcan, *pseud.*) 12°, pp. 15. No place, 1846.

The writer was Leon N. Salmon.

JACK THE PIPER, ETC. (Anon.) 16°, pp. 23. New York, 1831.

JACKSON, (H. R.) Tallulah, etc. 12°, pp. 229. Savannah, 1850.

JACKSON, (MRS. H. H.)

Helen Maria Fiske, daughter of Professor N. W. Fiske, was born at Amherst, Mass., in 1831, and married Major E. B. Hunt, of the United States Engineers, in 1822. Her husband was killed in 1863. Subsequently she married Mr. Jackson. She died in San Francisco in 1885. She wrote under the signature of "H. H." She was among the most popular of American female writers.

— Verses. 18°, pp. viii, 191. Boston, 1874.

JACKSON, (J. W.) Universal Peace. Poem delivered before the Biennial Convention of the Sigma Chi Fraternity in Washington, December 27, 1866. 8°, pp. 17. Washington, 1867.

JAIMSON, (G.) The Revolutionary Soldier. A Farce. 12°, pp. 22. Boston, no date.

JAMES, (MARIA.)

Maria James was born in Wales not far from the year 1795, and came to America in the seventh year of her age. For a number of years she lived as a trusted and loved domestic in different families, her marked intellectual abilities securing for her great respect. Bishop Alonzo Potter wrote the introduction to the following named volume, in which he warmly commended the genius and piety of the author.

— Wales and other Poems. 12°, pp. 170. New York, 1839.

JANE AND ELIZA. (Anon.) 12°, pp. 12. Newark, 1840.

JANE EATON; OR, THE SUNDAY SCHOOL. In Four Books. (Anon.) 16°, pp. 82. Philadelphia, 1858.

JANVIER, (F. DE H.) The Sleeping Sentinel. 12°, pp. 19. Philadelphia, 1863.

> The incidents in the poem relate to William Scott, a young Vermont soldier, who, while on duty, fell asleep. He was condemned to die, and was pardoned by President Lincoln. James E. Murdoch read the poem with great effect on several occasions.

JANNEY, (S. M.) The Last of the Lenapé, etc. 12°, pp. 180. Philadelphia and Boston, 1839.

JEANNETTE. (By Æsculapius Non Vinctus, *pseud.*) 8°, pp. 92. New York, 1857.

JERAULD, (MRS. CHARLOTTE A.)

> Charlotte A. Fillebrown was born at Cambridge, Mass., April 16, 1820, and in early life removed to Boston, in the excellent common schools of which city she received her education. For a time, after leaving school, she worked in a bookbindery, meanwhile contributing to the " Ladies' Repository," a literary and religious periodical of the Universalist denomination. She married Mr. J. W. Jerauld, November 10, 1843. Her death occurred August 2, 1845.
>
> In the volume with the title here given, there is a Memoir of Mrs. Jerauld, by Henry Bacon, pp. 17–97. Her poetry is included in pp. 100–196, and her prose writings, pp. 198–440.

— Poetry and Prose. 8°, pp. viii, 196 of poetry. Boston, 1850.

JEROME, (A. B.) 11–11–11–5. A Signal Song. 18°, pp. 8. Washington, no date.

JESTER, THE CAMP. (Anon.) 12°, pp. 71. Augusta, Ga., 1864.

JESUS, THE HOLY. The History of, in Rhyme. (Anon.) 24th Edition. 32°, pp. 46. Boston, 1771.

> An elegantly bound copy.

JEWETT, (SUSAN.) The Parent's Gift. Sq. 16°. New York, 1843.

JILSON, (C.) Progress Attributed to the Laboring Classes. Delivered before the Worcester County Mechanics Association, March 3, 1853. 12°, pp. 36. Worcester, 1853.

JOAN OF ARC. L. H. S., a Member of the Graduating Class of Wake Forest College, N. C., 1856. 8°, pp. 20. Richmond, 1856.

20

JOB, COMMENT UPON SOME PASSAGES IN. (Anon.) 12°, pp. 15. Boston, 1783.

JOBSON, (C.) The World; or, Instability. 2d Edition. 12°, pp. 249. Philadelphia and London, 1836.

JOBSON, (D. W.) The Poetry of the Flag. 8°, pp. 20. New York, 1858.

JOHNSON, (E. R.) The Dame of Ossipee. 8°, pp. 17. Concord, N. H., 1870.

JOHNSON, (J.) The Rape of Bethesda; or, The Georgia Orphan House Destroyed. 12°, pp. 16. Charleston, 1792.

JOHNSON, (ROSA V.) Poems. 12°, pp. 334. Boston, 1857.

JOHNSON, (R.)
> Rossiter Johnson was born at Rochester, N. Y., January 27, 1840, and graduated at Rochester University in 1863. Besides the "Idler and Poet," he has written "Phæton Rogers," "History of the War of 1812," and has edited several books and serial works.

— Idler and Poet. 8°, pp. iv, 126. Boston, 1883.

JOHNSON, (S. D.) In and Out of Place. 12°, pp. 13. New York, no date.
— Our Gal. A Farce. 12°, pp. 9. New York, no date.
— The Fireman. 12°, pp. 36. Boston, no date.
— The Shaker Lovers. 12°, pp. 10. Boston, no date.

JOHNSTON, (A.) The Mariner. A Poem in Two Cantos. 12°, pp. 152. Philadelphia, 1818.

JOHNSON, (N. P.) Poetry. Original and Compiled. 12°, pp. 54. Boston, 1835.

JOKEBY. A Burlesque on Rokeby. (Anon.) 16°, pp. 218. Boston and New York, 1815.

JONATHAN AND VIRGINIA, THE LIVES OF. By Boswell, (*pseud.*) 12°, pp. 120. Philadelphia, 1873.
> "Boswell" is the *pseudonym* of W. B. Johnson, of Virginia.

JONATHAN, ST. The Lay of a Scald. (Anon.) Canto II. 8°, pp. 103. New York, 1838.

JONATHAN IN ENGLAND. (Anon.) 12°, pp. 32. Boston, no date.

Jones, (A.)  Melodies of the Church.  8°, pp. 440.  New York, 1832.

Jones, (Amanda T.)  Ulah, etc.  8°, pp. viii, 309.  Buffalo, 1861.

Jones, (C. A.)



— The Outlaw, etc.  18°, pp. 72.  Cincinnati, 1835.

Jones, (C. L. S.)  American Lyrics.  12°, pp. 306.  Mobile, 1834.
— Translation of Voltaire's Henriad.  12°, pp. vii, 304.  Mobile, 1834.

Jones, (C. S.)  Captain Kyd.  12°, pp. 44.  Boston, no date.

Jones, (D. M.)  Lethe, etc.  Sm. 12°, pp. 92.  Philadelphia, 1882.

Jones, (E. C.)  Echoes of the Heart.  Original Poems.  8°, pp. 168.  Philadelphia, 1850.
— The Harp of Sylvia.  12°, pp. viii, 218.  Philadelphia, 1841.

Jones, (J. H.)  Heaven's Golden Treasures.  Sm. 12°, pp. 18.  Carbondale, Pa., 1871.

Jones, (J. S.)  Moll Pitcher; or, The Fortune Teller of Lyme.  12°, pp. 64.  Boston, 1855.
— The Carpenter of Rouen.  12°, pp. 32.  New York, no date.
— The Green Mountain Boy.  12°, pp. 29.  Boston, no date.
— The People's Lawyer.  12°, pp. 36.  Boston, 1856.
— The Surgeon of Paris.  12°, pp. 41.  Boston, 1856.

Jones, (Mrs. Eliza G.)  A Memoir of, with a few of her Poems.  12°, pp. 212.  Philadelphia, 1853.

Jones, (Mrs. Elizabeth C.)  Fugitive Poems.  12°, pp. 59.  Providence, 1826.
— Original Poem.  12°, pp. 48.  Providence, 1819.
— Same.  Part II.  12°, pp. 47.  Providence, 1821.

Jones, (P. F.)  "No Sect in Heaven," etc.  A Wide Awake Reply.  12°, pp. 8.  New York, 1875.

JONES, (JULIA CLINTON.)  Valhalla, the Myths of Norseland.  12°, pp. 156.  New York, 1880.

JORDAN, (CORNELIA J. M.)  Corinth, and other Poems of the War.  12°, pp. 31.  Lynchburgh, 1865.

JOSEPH AND HIS BRETHREN, THE STORY OF.  (Anon.)  12°, pp. 18.  No place, 1854.

JOSSELYN, (JEP.[?])  Tar-Heel Tales.  12°, pp. 69.  New York, 1873.

JOSSELYN, (R.)  The Faded Flower, etc.  16°, pp. 167.  Boston, 1849.

JOURNEY, THE POPE'S, TO HEAVEN.  18°, pp. 32.  (Anon.)  Philadelphia, 1845.

JOVELLANOS, (DEL SENOR.)  Epistola Moral sobre Los Vanos Descos y Los Estudios de los hombres.  8°, pp. 12.  Lima, 1815.

JOYCE, (R. D.)  Blandid.  12°, pp. 240.  Boston, 1879.

JUBA.  (Anon.)  United We Stand : Divided We Fall.  24°, pp. 74·  New York, 1812.

JUBILEE, THE SAINTS'.  (Anon.)  16°, pp. 24.  St. Louis, 1866.

JUDAH, (S. B. H.)  A Tale of Lexington.  18°, pp. v, 60.  New York, 1823.

He wrote under the signature of " Terentius Phlogambus."

— Gotham and the Gothamites.  24°, pp. 93.  New York, 1823.
— Odofried, the Outcast.  Sq. 8°.  No date.
— Rose of Arragon.  16°, pp. 38.  New York, 1822.
— The Mountain Torrent.  A Melo-Drama.  18°, pp. v, 54.  New York, 1820.

JUDD, (S.)

Sylvester Judd was born at Westhampton, Mass., July 23, 1813, graduated at Yale in 1836, and pursued his theological studies at Cambridge.  He was pastor of a Unitarian Church in Augusta, Me., 1840-53, his ministry being terminated by his death, January 20, 1853.  His life was written by Mrs. A. Hall, 1854.  He was the author of a romance, " Margaret," 1845, a remarkable production.

— Philo : An Evangeliad.  16°, pp. 244.  Boston, 1850.

JUDITH, ESTHER, ETC.  (Anon.)  16°, pp. 112.  Boston, 1820.

Judson, (Mrs. Emily.)

Emily Chubbuck was born at Eaton, N. Y., in 1817. Under the signature of "Fanny Forrester" she attained to much popularity as a writer of both prose and poetry. In June, 1846, she married Rev. Dr. Adoniram Judson, the distinguished missionary to Burmah. After his decease, in 1850, she returned to the United States, and died at Hamilton, N. Y., in 1854.

— An Olio of Domestic Verses. 12°, pp. 232. New York, 1852.

Julap, (*pseud?*) The Glosser. A Poem in Two Books. 18°. No place, 1802.

Julian. A Tragedy. (Anon.) 12°, pp. 59. Baltimore, 1843.

Julius, (Julia M.) Hoboken, etc. Sq. 12°, pp. 112. New York, 1866.

Jumbo-Jum. A Farce. (Anon.) 12°, pp. 16. Boston, no date.

Juniper Hill Cemetery, Bristol, R. I. (Anon.) 12°, pp. 16. No place, no date.

Junkin, (D. X., D. D.) The Class of 1831, Jefferson College, Pa. A Memorial. 12°, pp. 31. Pittsburg, 1861.


Kah-Ge-Ga-Gah-Bowh, or Copway, (G.) The Ojibway Conquest. A Tale of the Northwest. 12°, pp. 91. New York, 1850.

Kalewala and Hiawatha. 8°, pp. 21. Lancaster, Pa., no date.

Kalewala is an epic poem, "unique and thoroughly national in its character, among the people of Finland." The resemblance of Longfellow's "Hiawatha" to this poem is pointed out.

Kansas War, The; or, The Conquests of Chivalry in the Crusades of the Nineteenth Century. A Heroic Poem. 12°, pp. 164. New York, 1856.

Kause, (J. C.) Poems. 16°, pp. 132. Philadelphia, 1778.

Keefer, (J.) Slavery, etc. 12°, pp. 120. Baltimore, 1864.

Keese, (J.) The Poets of America. 12°, pp. 284. New York, 1840.
— Same. Vol. II of the Series. 12°, pp. 320. New York, 1842.
— Same. 5th Edition. Vol. II of the Series. 12°, pp. 284. Boston, no date.

KEIMER, (S.)

> Samuel Keimer was, according to Franklin's statement, " one of the French prophets, and could act their enthusiastic agitations." His elegy on " Aquila Rose " is a noted production. He employed Franklin as a printer. Subsequently he went to the West Indies, and was editor of the *Barbadoes Gazette.* See on the above, Duyckinck, vol. I, p. 100.

— Caribbeana. Prose and Poetry. 2 vols. 4°, pp. 404, 358. London, 1741.

KEMBLE, (F. A.) Francis the First. A Tragedy in Five Acts. 6th American Edition. 8°, pp. 72. New York, 1833.

> See sketch under F. K. Butler.

— Poems. 12°, pp. ix, 312. Boston, 1859.

KENDALL, (E. H.) Poems. 12°, pp. 32. No place, 1850.

KENDRICK, (A. C.)

> Asahel C. Kendrick, D. D., LL. D., was born at Poultney, N. Y., December 7, 1809, graduated at Hamilton College, Clinton, N. Y., in 1831, was elected Professor of Greek and Latin in Madison University in 1832, and subsequently, dropping the Latin Professorship, retained the Greek until 1850, when he was elected to the Greek chair in the new University of Rochester, N. Y. Dr. K. is the author of several classical and other works, and takes high rank among American scholars. His present residence (1880) is in Rochester, N. Y.

— Echoes; or, Leisure Hours with the German Poets. 12°, pp. iv, 148. Rochester, New York and Chicago, 1855.

KENNEDY, (C.) Corn in the Blade. Poems and Thoughts in Verse. 12°, pp. xv, 213. New York, 1860.

KENNEDY, (J.) The Night Vision. 12°, pp. vii, 152. Philadelphia, 1859.

KENNEDY, (T.) Poems. 12°, pp. 334. Washington, 1816. ♪
— Songs of Love and Liberty. 12°, pp. 96. Washington, 1817.

KENYON, (W. A.) Poetry of Observation, etc. 12°, pp. iv, 104. Boston, 1851.
— Same. Part II, etc. 12°, pp. 104. Boston, 1853.

KERR, (H.) Texas, Poetical Description of. 18°, pp. 122. New York, 1838.

KETCHUM, (ANNIE C.) Benny: A Christmas Ballad. 12°, pp. 9. New York, 1870.

KETCHUM, (MRS. CHAMBERS.) Lotos Flowers, gathered in Sun and Shadow. 12°, pp. 205. New York, 1877.

KETELTAS, (CAROLINE M.)  The Last of the Plantagenets.  A Tragic
	Drama.  12°, pp. iv, 56.  New York, 1844.

KETTELL, (S.)

> Samuel Kettell was born at Newburyport, Mass., August 5, 1800.  He is said to have
> been an accomplished linguist, and to have mastered no less than fourteen languages.
> Mr. Goodrich employed him as his assistant in preparing his " Peter Parley " books.  For
> seven years (1848–55) he was chief editor of the *Boston Courier*.  He published several
> books, the best known of which is the one referred to below.  His death took place at
> Malden, Mass., December 3, 1855.

— Specimens of American Poetry.  3 vols.  12°.  Vol. I, pp. xlviii,
	253.  Vol II, pp. x, 408.  Vol. III, pp. x, 406.  Boston, 1829.

KEY, A, TO THE GRAND MAXIMS OF REPUBLICAN LIBERTY.  (By a
	Yankee Lawyer.  Anon.)  16°, pp. 72.  Philadelphia, 1844.

KEY, (F. S.)

> Francis Scott Key was born in Frederic county, Md., August, 1779, educated at St.
> John's College, Annapolis, studied law, and commenced practice in 1801 in his native
> county.  Subsequently he removed to Washington, where he was appointed District Attor-
> ney.  He died January 11, 1843.  He was the well-known author of the " Star Spangled
> Banner," a national song, inspired by the author's position as a prisoner held by the Bri-
> tish in 1814, when Fort McHenry was unsuccessfully bombarded.

— Poems.  12°, pp. ix, 203.  New York, 1857.

KEYES, (F. J.)  A Life Poem, etc.  12°, pp. 120.  Boston, 1855.

KIDD, (A.)  The Huron Chief, etc.  12°, pp. 216.  Montréal, 1830.

KIDDER, (J.)  The Drama of Earth.  12°, pp. 360.  New York, 1857.

KIDNEY, (J. S.)

> John Steinfort Kidney was born in Essex county, N. J., in 1819, was educated in part
> at Union College, studied law, then theology, received orders in the Episcopal Church, and
> was settled at Saratoga Springs, N. Y.

— Catawba River, etc.  16°, pp. 119.  New York, 1847.
— The Conflict of the Age.  8°, pp. 22.  Hartford, 1856.

KILBOURN, (P. K.)  The Sceptic, etc.  12°, pp. 180.  Hartford, 1843.

KILTON, (CHANCELLOR F.)  Homer.  A Burlesque Translation.  A
	Folio Manuscript.

> The " copy," with the author's memoranda for editor and printer.  The manuscript is
> very neatly written out, apparently by a copyist, in a stout folio volume, which is in good
> condition.  A pencil memorandum on the fly-leaf ascribes the work to Chancellor Kilty,
> of Maryland.  He was the author of " Report of all such English Statutes as are applicable
> to the United States."  Annapolis, 1811.

KIMBALL, (S. C.)  Poems.  18°, pp. 139.  Albany, 1858.

Kimmens, (H.)  The Number of the Beast.  8°, pp. 31.  New York, 1806.

King, (D. S.)  Fireside Poetical Readings.  12°, pp. 313.  Boston, 1843.

King, The, and His Cabinet.  (Th. Horatius Delpho, *pseud.*)  12°, pp. 23.  No place, no date.

Kinney, (Elizabeth C.)  Felicitá.  A Metrical Romance.  12°, pp. 188.  New York, 1855.

— Poems.  8°, pp. 226.  New York, 1867.

Knapp, (J.)  Revival Melodies.  Sq. 18°, pp. 60.  Boston, 1842.

Knapp, (S. L.)  Advice in the Pursuits of Literature.  Several poems in the volume.  12°, pp. 296.  Granville, Middletown, N. J., 1837.

Kneeland, (A.)  National Hymns for the use of those who are " Slaves to no Sect."  24°, pp. 140.  Boston, 1834.

Knight, (A.)  Miracles of God and the Prophets.  18°, pp. 18.  Newburyport, 1829.

Knight, (H. C.)

Henry Coggswell Knight was born at Newburyport, Mass., not far from 1788, graduated at Brown University in 1812, took orders in the Protestant Episcopal Church, but was never settled.  He died in 1835.

— Poems.  2 vols.  18°, 192, 195.  Boston, 1821.

— The Broken Harp.  18°, pp. x, 176.  Philadelphia, 1815.

Knight, The, of the Rum Bottle & Co.  A Musical Farce.  (Anon.)  32°, pp. 16.  New York, 1818.

Know Nothing.  A Poem for Natives and Aliens.  12°, pp. 38.  Boston, 1854.

Kormak, An Icelandic Romance of the Tenth Century.  In Six Cantos.  (Anon.)  16°, pp. vi, 118.  Boston, 1861.

Kossuth Coppered.  (Anon.)  8°, pp. 32.  New York, 1852.

Krause, (W. E. F.)  Four Poems.  The Destiny of Mankind; or, The Redeemed Savage. — The Christian's Cross, borne by Faith, Hope and Charity. — The Advance of the United States; or, The Test of Brotherly Love. — Heaven's Record of Mankind; or, The Birth of a Child.  8°, pp. 16.  San Francisco, 1868.

Krause, (W. E. F.) — *Continued.*
— The Sanctity of Marriage. 12°, pp. 16. San Francisco, 1869.

Knowles, (Sarah E.) Orlean Lamar, etc. 12°, pp. 167. New York and London, 1864.

Knowles, (W. J.) Features of Inauguration of the Franklin Statue in Boston, September 17, 1856. 12°, pp. 12. Boston, 1856.
— Poetical Expression of the Gospels. 12°, pp. 96. Boston, 1858.

Knowlton, (J. M.) The Prize of Life. 12°, pp. 12. Sing Sing, N. Y., 1850.
— Beauty. 12°, pp. 15. Sing Sing, 1848.

La Araucana. Rimera. Segundo y Tercera Parte de Don Alonzo de Ercilla y Zuniga Caballero de la Ordre de Santiago, etc. Folio, pp. 167. Madrid, 1733.

La Bree, (L.) Ebenezer Venture. A Farce. 12°, pp. 18. New York, no date.

Ladd, (J. B.)

Joseph Brown Ladd was born at Newport, R. I., in 1764. While studying medicine he wrote under the signature of "Arouet," his poems being addressed to "Amanda," a name by which he designated the lady who subsequently became his wife. In 1783 he removed to Charleston, S. C., where he had an extensive medical practice. Having become involved in a political controversy he was killed in a duel in 1786.

— Arouet. Poems of. 12°, pp. viii, 128. Charleston, S. C., 1786.
— Literary Remains. Poems. 8°, pp. xxvi, 163. New York, 1832.

La Déesse. An Elssler-atic Romance. (Anon.) 12°, pp. 44. New York, 1841.

Lady Elgiva, The. A Christmas Myth, by M. L. B. (Anon.) Sq. 18°, pp. 47. New York, 1866.

La Gazza Ladra. A Melo-Drama. 18°, pp. 101. New York, 1833.

Laighton, (A.) Poems. 16°, pp. 133. Boston, 1859.

Lake, (W.)

William Lake was born at Kingston, Penn., in 1787, and died in 1805, at the early age of 18 years.

— The Parnassian Pilgrim. 12°, pp. 184. Hudson, 1807.

Lamar, (M. L.) Verse Memorials. Lg. 8°, pp. 224. New York, 1857.

LAMENT, THE, OF QUINTIN MCKELL. Sq. 16°, pp. 48. New York, 1858.

LAMENTATIONS OF A BEREAVED MOTHER. (Anon.) 12°, pp. 99. Farmville, Va., 1849.

LAMENTATION, THE, OF MARY MAGDALENE. 18°, pp. 11. No place, 1793.

LAMPLIGHTER PICTURE BOOK. (Anon.) 8°, pp. 30. Boston, 1856.

LANCEY, (S. H.) The Native Poets of Maine. Lg. 8°, pp. 324. Bangor, 1854.

LANDER, (META.) Fading Flowers. 12°, pp. xiv, 288. Boston, 1860.

LANDIS, (J. )

> Mr. John Landis, "poet, painter and prophet," informs the *New York Post*, that being without a home, he is willing to accept contributions towards settling him in life. Under date of October, 1854, he says: "My heroic poem, 'Life of the Messiah,' fifth edition, is out of print, and I am out of money, sojourning at a shilling lodging house, while foreign theatrical celebrities live at the St. Nicholas, &c., at times accumulating fortunes. I expect success from the citizens, particularly of our country."

— Messiah. Sq. 16°, pp. 64. Chambersburg, 1838.

LANDIS, (R. W.) Liberty's Triumph. 12°, pp. 544. New York, 1849.

LA NEUVILLE, (M. J.) Elégie Sur La Mort de George Washington. 8°, pp. 6. Philadelphia, 1800.

LARCOM, (LUCY.)

> Lucy Larcom was born at Beverly Farms, Mass., in 1826. She worked in early life in the Lowell mills, and subsequently was a teacher in Illinois and Massachusetts. Her compilations of prose and verse are valuable.

— Wild Roses of Cape Ann, etc. 3d Edition. 12°, pp. 272. Boston, 1881.

LASH, THE ; OR, TRUTHS IN RHYME. (Eustacius Swamerdam, *pseud.*) 8°, pp. 35. No place, 1840.

LATHROP, (J.)

> John Lathrop was born at Boston in January, 1772, graduated at Harvard in 1789, commenced the practice of law, removing to Dedham in 1797. Here he remained but a short time. Returning to Boston he practiced his profession and devoted his spare hours to literary pursuits. In 1790 he went to Calcutta and started an English school in that city. He remained abroad about twenty years, then returned to Boston, was teacher, lecturer, periodical writer, etc. Having obtained a situation in the Post Office Department, he took up his residence in Georgetown, D. C., where he died January 30, 1820.

LATHROP, (J.) — *Continued.*

— The Speech of Caunonicus ; or, An Indian Tradition.   A Poem, with Explanatory Notes.   4°, pp. xi, 25.   Calcutta, 1802.

A presentation copy by the author to "Mr. W. Oliver."  It has been put into elegant binding by Bedford.

LATHY, (T. P.)

Thomas Pike Lathy, who wrote under the signature of "Piscator," was born at Exeter, England, in 1771.  He was brought up as a trader, but gratified his taste for letters instead of devoting himself exclusively to business.

— Reparation ; or, The School for Libertines.   12°, pp. 46.   Boston, 1800.

LATROBE, (J. H. B.)

John Hazelhurst Boneval Latrobe was born at Philadelphia in 1803, and was admitted to the Baltimore bar in 1825.  He has taken much interest in the Maryland Historical Society, and devoted himself to historical and other literary work.

— Odds and Ends.   Sq. 8°, pp. 72.   Baltimore, 1864.

— Ode.   Sesqui-Centennial Anniversary of the Settlement of Baltimore, October 18, 1880.   8°, pp. 10.   No place, no date.

LAUREL, THE.   A Gift for all Seasons.   (Anon.)   18°, pp. 251.   Baltimore, 1837.

— Same.   (Anon.)   18°, pp. 252.   Boston, 1836.

LAUS PATRIAE CELESTIS.   Translation of an Ancient Hymn.   (By O. A. M.)   12°, pp. 16.   Albany, 1867.

LAWRENCE, (I.)   Shadows of the Metropolis.   8°, pp. 8.   New York, 1859.

LAWRENCE, (J., JR.)

Jonathan Lawrence, Jr., was born in the city of New York, November 19, 1807, graduated from Columbia College at the early age of fifteen, studied and practiced law, devoting his leisure hours to literary pursuits.  He died April 26, 1833.

— A Selection from the Writings of.   12°, pp. v, 172.   Poetry, pp. 75–172.   New York, 1833.

LAWSON, (J.)

James Lawson was born at Glasgow, Scotland, November 9, 1799, and was educated in the University in that city.  He came to America in 1815, and entered his maternal uncle's counting-house in the city of New York.  He began early to interest himself in literary pursuits, and was the means of introducing several of the most distinguished authors to the British people by his correspondence with the editor of the *Greenock Advertiser*.  In 1827 he was associate editor of the *New York Courier and Enquirer*, remaining in that position until 1829.  For about four years he was connected with the *Mercantile Advertiser*.  For many years he pursued the business of marine insurance in New York City.

Lawson, (J.) — *Continued.*

— Giordano.  A Tragedy.  8°, pp. 102.  New York, 1832.

— Same.  8°, pp. 102.  New Haven, 1859.

— The Maniac, etc.  18°, pp. 101.  Philadelphia, 1811.

Lay of the Bed-Chamber, The.  A Farce.  (Anon.)  12°, pp. 17.
     New York, no date.

Lay, The, of the Last Pilgrim.  (Anon.)  12°, pp. 48.  Charleston,
     S. C., 1832.

Lay of the Wilderness, The.  A Poem in Five Cantos.  (Anon.)
     12°, pp. x, 163.  Saint John, 1833.

Lays of Liberty.  (Anon.)  18°, pp. 55.  Boston, 1854.

Leadbeater, (J., Jr.)  Literary Remains.  12°, pp. 106.  Philadel-
     phia, 1850.

Leaves Gathered in the Daily Walks of Life.  (Anon.)  Sq. 18°,
     pp. 223.  Philadelphia, 1867.

Leavitt, (J. M.)  Afranius and the Idumean, etc.  12°, pp. 255.  Bos-
     ton, 1869.

— The Siege of Babyton.  16°, pp. 47.  New York, 1869.

Le Baron, (F.)  The Poet and His Song.  12°, pp. 118.  Charleston,
     1848.

Le Cato, (N. J. W.)  Theodora, etc.  12°, pp. 67.  Baltimore, 1871.

— Same.  12°, pp. 61.  New York, 1872.

Lecraw, (J. B.)  Reformed Man.  Life, Travels and Sufferings of.
     12°, pp. 36.  Pawtucket, R. I., 1844.

Lee, (A. M.)  Fashion, etc.  12°, pp. 52.  New York, 1864.

Lee, (C.)  Scriptural Hymns.  12°, pp. 72.  Middletown, Conn., 1824.

Lee, (C. C.)  Virginia Georgics.  8°, pp. 121.  Richmond, 1858.

Lee, (Jean.)  Nothing but Leaves.  Illustrated.  4°, pp. 5.  Philadel-
     phia, 1868.

Lee, (Leila.)  Wee-Wee Songs.  18°, pp. 203.  Boston, 1859.

— Same.  12°, pp. 200.  New York, 1878.

LEE, (M. E.)

Mary Elizabeth Lee was born at Charleston, S. C., March, 23, 1813, and commenced to write for "The Southern Rose" when she was about twenty years of age, and soon began to attract attention. Among the earlier productions of her pen was a volume for which she received a prize from the Massachusetts Board of Education, entitled "Social Evenings; or, Historical Tales for Youth." Her contributions to journals, of which "Graham's Magazine," "Godey's Lady's Book" and the "Southern Literary Messenger" were representatives, were very numerous. She possessed a happy faculty for translation, and was able to lay before her English readers many gems from German poetry. For a notice of her works see the "Southern Quarterly Review," vol. xix, pp. 518. She died September 23, 1849.

— Poetical Remains. Memoir by S. Gilman, D. D. 12°, pp. xl, 224. Charleston, 1851.

LEES, (T. J.) The Musings of Carol. 18°, pp. viii, 178. Wheeling, Va., 1831.

LEGEND OF THE CASTLE OF DRACHENFELS. In Humorous Verse. (J. M. S. Anon.) 8°, pp. xi, 100. Washington, 1881.

LEGGETT, (W.)

William Leggett was born in the city of New York in 1802, became midshipman in the United States Navy in 1822, resigned in 1826, was associated in 1829, with W. C. Bryant in the editorial management of the *New York Evening Post*, holding the position till 1836. For a short time he edited *The Plaindealer*, which was continued only ten months. In May, 1839, he was appointed by Van Buren, diplomatic agent to the Republic of Gautemala. He died, however, before entering upon the duties of his office, May 29, 1839.

— Poems. 16°, pp. 46. MS. Edwardsville, 1822.

LE GUIRE, (A.) The Heliad. 12°, pp. vii, 53. Haverstraw, 1828.

LEHMANOWSKI, (L. F.) The Fall of Warsaw. A Tragedy. 18°, pp. 59. Annapolis, 1840.

LEIBER, (F.) Ein Ergnk. 8°, pp. 3. St. Louis, 1872.

LEIGH, (LARRY.) The True Grecian Bend. A Story in Verse. 12°, pp. 48. New York, 1868.

LEIGHTON, (R., JR.) Character. 12°, pp. 35. Boston, 1859.

LEISURE HOURS. Desultory Pieces in Prose and Verse. (By E. L., Anon.) Lg. 8°, pp. 320. Calcutta, 1846.

The author's name was Mrs. Lydia Lillybridge Simons, a missionary in Burma.

LEISURE HOURS. (By Tacita, *pseud.*) 18°, pp. 106. Utica, 1855.

LELAND, (C. G.)

Charles Godfrey Leland was born at Philadelphia, August 15, 1824, graduated at Princeton in 1845, and studied three years in European Universities. He has been a busy

LELAND, (C. G.) — *Continued.*

writer during his literary career. Lippincott, in his last Pronouncing Biographical Dictionary, 1886, refers to thirteen of his publications, bringing the date down to 1862. See
Allibone, pp. 1081-82.

— Breitmann and his Philosopede. Illustrated by Frank Beard. 12°,
pp. 22. New York, 1869.

— Hans Breitmann about Town, and other new Ballads. Second Series
of the Breitman Ballads. 8°, pp. 62. Philadelphia, 1869.

— Hans Breitman in Politics. 8°, pp. 13. Philadelphia, 1869.

— Hans Breitman's Party. With other Ballads. 8°, pp. 32. Philadelphia, 1868.

— Same. 8°, pp. 48. Philadelphia, 1869.

— The Music Lesson of Confucius, etc. 18°, pp. 168. London, 1872.

— The Poetry and Mystery of Dreams. 12°, pp. xi, 271. Philadelphia, 1856.

LELAND, (O. S.) Beatrice; or, The False and the True. 12°, pp. 64.
Boston, 1858.

— Caprice. A Comedy. 12°, pp. 50. Boston, 1857.

— The Rights of Man. A Comedy. 12°, pp. 30. Boston, no date.

LESCARBOT, (M.)

Marc Lescarbot was born of a noble family at Vervins, France, not far from the middle of the 16th century, for a time was an advocate in Parliament, resided for several years
in New France, now Canada, and published an account of that country. Subsequently he
attended Peter de Castille, the Ambassador of Louis XIII. to Switzerland, and published
a description of the Thirteen Cantons in French heroic verse. The "Biographie Univer-
salle," Paris, 1810, says: " Ou ignore les autres particularités de la vie de Lescarbot; et ce
n'est que par conjecture qu'on place sa mort vers l'an 1630."

— Les Muses de la Nouvelle France. A Monseigneur Le Chancellier,
etc. Sm. 8°, pp. 6 (not numbered), 66. Paris, 1609.

This elegantly bound volume was presented to Mr. Harris by John Carter Brown,
for sundry tracts about the Lancaster Massacre.

LESDERNIER, (MRS. EMILY P. DE.) Voices of Life. 12°, pp. 38. New
York, 1853.

— Same. 18°, pp. 104. Paris, 1862.

L'ESTRANGE, (CORINNE.) Woman's Witchcraft; or, The Curse of
Coquetry. A Dramatic Romance. 12°, pp. 73. Philadelphia,
1854.

Lewis, (A.)

Alonzo Lewis, who wrote under the signature of "The Lynn Bard," was born in 1794, in Lynn, Mass., which was his permanent residence. He was a teacher, had the editorial charge of a paper, made maps, was a surveyor, and for a term of years filled the office of Justice of the Peace. He died in 1861.

—Poems. 12°, pp. 203. Portsmouth, 1823.

Lewis, (E.) Eulogy on Washington, in verse. Delivered at Lenox, February 22, 1800. 16°, pp. 20. Pittsfield, 1800.

Lewis, (Estelle Anna.)

Estelle A. B. Robinson was born near Baltimore, educated at the Troy Seminary, and married Mr. S. D. Lewis, of Brooklyn, N. Y. She has been a large contributor to the periodical literature of the day.

— Poems. 8°, pp. 420. New York, 1857.
— Myths of the Minstrel. 12°, pp. x, 95. New York, 1852.

Lewis, (Eliza G.) Poems. 12°, pp. 148. Brooklyn, 1850.

Lewis, (Mrs. S. Anna.) Child of the Sea, etc. 12°, pp. 179. New York, 1848.

Leypoldt, (F.) Copperheads, Ye Book of. pp. 24. Philadelphia, 1863.

Liberty. A Poem by Rusticus. (Anon.) Sm. 4°, pp. iv, 26. Philadelphia, 1768.

A note says "lately found in a bundle of papers."

— Same. 2d Edition. 4°, pp. 21. Charlestown, 1770.

Liberty Bell, The. 12°, pp. 208. Boston, 1843.
— Same. 12°, pp. 231. Boston, 1844.
— Same. 12°, pp. 256. Boston, 1845.
— Same. 12°, pp. 268. Boston, 1846.
— Same. 12°, pp. 292. Boston, 1848.
— Same. 12°, pp. 292. Boston, 1849.
-- Same. 12°, pp. 315. Boston, 1853.
— Same. 12°, pp. 200. Boston, 1856.

Liberty, Property and No Excise. A poem compos'd on occasion of the Light seen on the Great Trees (so called) in Boston, New England, on the 14th of August, 1765. 12°, pp. 8. Boston, 1765. (Price, 6 cop.)

LIDDESDALE, LORD; OR, THE BORDER CHIEF. A Tragedy. (Anon.)
Lg. 8°, pp. 101. Yonkers, N. Y., 1874.

The name of James Lawson is given as having entered this volume.

LIDSTONE, (J. T. S.) Bostoniad. 12°, pp. 86. Boston, 1853.

LIEBER, (F.)

Francis Lieber was born at Berlin, March 18, 1800. For a time he was in the German
Army, and at the battle of Waterloo was wounded. After various fortunes in the old
world he came to the United States in 1827, and entered upon the work of editing the
"Encyclopædia Americana," which was completed in 13 volumes 8°, published in Philadelphia 1828–32. For a number of years he was engaged in important literary work, the
best known of his productions being "Manual of Political Ethics," "Legal and Political
Hermeneutics," and "Civil Liberty and Self-Government." He was professor in South
Carolina College 1835–56, and was chosen professor in Columbia College in 1857, and
remained in office till his death, October 2, 1872.

— The West. Sq. 16°, pp. 31. New York, 1848.

LIÉS, (E.) The Preludes. 12°, pp. 56. New York, 1846.

LIFE-WAKE, THE, OF THE FINE ARKANSAS GENTLEMAN WHO DIED BE-
FORE HIS TIME. 8°, pp. 54. Washington, 1859.

A report that Albert Pike, the Arkansas poet had died, led to the observance of this
"wake" or entertainment given by J. F. Coyle, Esq. A memorial which had been prepared by Professor Alexander Dimitry was read on the occasion. A song was then sung
by the host, entitled "The Second Fytte of the Fine Arkansas Gentleman who died Before
His Time," which was followed by a speech from the supposed decedent, who had been
invited to be present at his own "wake." Songs deemed appropriate to the occasion were
sung, and the combination of the grave and the humorous gave great zest to the entertainment, an account of which, written by Dr. R. Shelton Mackenzie, appeared in the *Philadelphia Press*, January 22, 1859. On the fly-leaf of the volume, which has been attractively
bound, is the following: "This private print is excessively rare. Very few copies were
printed. I never saw but one other copy even in private hands.—B. M."

LIGHT, (G. W.) Keep Cool, etc. 18°, pp. 35. Boston, 1851.

LILLIBRIDGE, (G. R.) Tancred. A Drama. 18°, pp. 68. Providence,
1824.

LINCOLN, (E.) A Poem. 18°, pp. 180. Portland, 1816.

LINDSEY, (W. M.) Poems. 12°, pp. 197. New York, 1856.

LINDSLEY, (A. B.) Love and Friendship. A Comedy. 18°, pp. 58.
New York, 1809.

LINEN, (J.) Poems. 12°, pp. 212. New York, 1866.

— Poetical and Prose Writings. 12°, pp. 423. New York and San
Francisco, 1865.

— Songs of the Seasons and other Poems. 12°, pp. vi, 165. New
York, 1852.

Linn, (J. B.)

John Blair Linn was born at Shippensburg, Pa., March 14, 1777, graduated at Columbia College, studied law for a time, then theology, and then became assistant minister of the First Presbyterian Church, Philadelphia. He died in 1804. His brother-in-law, the novelist, Charles Brockden Brown, wrote his memoir.

— Miscellaneous Works. 12°, pp. 351. New York, 1795.
— The Powers of Genius. 16°, pp. 127. Philadelphia, 1801.
— Same. 2d Edition. 16°, pp. 191. Philadelphia, 1802.
— Same. 16°, pp. 155. London, 1804.
— Valerian. A Narrative Poem, intended in part to describe the Early
    Persecutions of the Christians, etc. 4°, pp. xxvi, 97. Philadel-
    phia, 1805.

Linton, (W. J.) Ireland for the Irish. Lg. 12°, pp. 95. New York,
    1867.

Little, (Sophia L.)

A daughter of Hon. Asher Robbins, she was born at Newport in 1799, and in 1824 married Mr. William Little, Jr., of Boston. She has contributed many articles to the periodicals of the day.

— Pentecost. Sq. 16°, pp. 49. Newport, R. I., 1869.
— The Branded Hand. Commemorative of the Tragedies at the South
    in the Winter of 1844-5. 18°, pp. 46. Pawtucket, R. I., 1845.
— The Last Days of Jesus, etc. 2d Edition. 12°, pp. 162. New-
    port, R. I., 1877.

Litchfield County, Conn., Celebration, August 13th and 14th, 1851.
    Several Poems in the volume, one by Rev. J. Pierpont. pp. 26.
    Lg. 8°, pp. 212. Hartford, 1851.

List, A, of the Members of the Assembly. (Anon.) 8°, pp. 16.
    Albany, 1806.

Littlefield, (Mrs.) The Wreath. 12°, pp. 132. Richmond, 1828.

Live Woman in the Mines; or, Pike County Ahead. By "Old
    Block." (Anon.) 12°, pp. 36. New York, no date.

Livermore, (Harriet.) The Harp of Israel. 18°, pp. 180. Philadel-
    phia, 1835.

Livingston, (Ann H. S.) Sacred Records. Abridged in Verse. 12°,
    pp. 124. Philadelphia.

22

LIVINGSTON, (J. H., D. D.)　Psalms and Hymns, etc., for the Reformed Dutch Church.　18°, pp. 610.　Philadelphia, 1829.

LIVINGSTON, (MRS. O. M.)　Poems.　12°, pp. 242.　Cambridge, 1868.

LIVINGSTON, (W.)

William Livingston was born at Albany, N. Y., graduated at Yale College 1741, was elected member of the National Congress in 1774, and was Governor of New Jersey from 1776 to his death.　(See Memoir, New York, 1833.)

— America.　Sq. 8°, pp. 12.　New Haven, no date.
— Philosophic Solitude.　8°, pp. 45.　Boston, 1762.
— Same.　3d Edition. 12°, pp. 40.　New York, no date.
— Same.　13th Edition.　New York, 1790.

LLOYD, (S. H.) Glimpses of the Spirit Land.　12°, pp. 145.　New York, 1867.
— Same.　8°, pp. 174.　New York, 1869.

LOCKE, (MRS. E. J.)　Daniel Webster.　A Rhymèd Eulogy.　Sm. 4°, pp. 24.　Boston, 1854.

LOCKE, (MRS. J. E.)

Jane Ermina Stockweather was born in Worthington, Mass., and has published many periodical articles.

— Boston and Boston People in 1850.　16°, pp. 45.　Boston, 1850.
— Miscellaneous Poems.　12°, pp. 300.　Boston, 1842.
— Rachel; or, The Little Mourner.　Sq. 32°, pp. 16.　Lowell, 1844.
— The Recalled; In the Voices of the Past, and Poems of the Ideal. 12°, pp. vii, 246.　Boston, 1854.

LOCKE, (MRS. M. J. E.)　Boston.　A Poem.　8°, pp. 15.　Boston, 1803.

LOCKERBY, (E. N.)　The Wild Brier.　16°, pp. 96.　Charlottetown, P. E. I., 1866.

LOCKWOOD, (J.)　Palermo.　8°, pp. 36.　New York, 1861.

LODGE, (H. C.)　Ballads and Lyrics.　12°, pp. xii, 387.　Boston, 1880.

LOGAN, (C. A.)　Yankee Land.　A Comedy.　12°, pp. 31.　Boston, no date.

LOMAX, (JUDITH.)　Notes of an American Lyre.　18°, pp. 70.　Richmond, 1813.

LONG, (MRS. ELIZABETH W.)　The Parallel.　8°, pp. 8.　Baltimore, 1848.

LONGFELLOW, (H. W.)

Henry Wadsworth Longfellow was born at Portland, Me., February 27, 1807. The house in which he was born is in the northeast section of the city, and was long known as "The Stephenson House." It is now an Irish tenement house. He graduated at Bowdoin College in 1825, and studied law for a short time. In 1826, having been appointed Professor of Modern Languages in Bowdoin College, he went abroad and spent three and a half years in fitting himself for the duties of the chair to which he had been elected. He began to teach in his *alma mater* in 1829, was married in 1831, was chosen Professor of Belles Lettres in Harvard College in 1835, went abroad the second time, and on his return entered upon his task in Harvard, and continued at his post for twenty years, resigning in 1855, and devoting the remainder of his life to literary work. He died at his home, the famous "Craigie House," the headquarters of Gen. Washington, in Cambridge, Mass., March 24, 1882. No one author is more largely represented in the Harris Collection than Longfellow, the number of volumes, including duplicates and different editions of his works, being not far from eighty. For a full and most satisfactory account of Longfellow and his works, see Allibone's Dictionary of Authors, pp. 1123–30.

— Aftermath. 16°, pp. 144. Boston, 1878.

— Ballads and other Poems. 3d Edition. Lg. 8°, pp. xxv, 132. Cambridge, 1842.

— Same. 4th Edition. 16°, pp. xxiv, 132.

— Same. 8th Edition. 1844.

— Same. 9th Edition. 1845.

— Same. 10th Edition. 1848.

— Coplas de Don Jorge Manrique. 12°, pp. vi., 89. Boston, 1833.

At the time this volume was published, the title of Prof. Longfellow was "Professor of Modern Languages and Literature in Bowdoin College."

— Dante's Divine Comedy. Translated. 8°, 3 vols. I. Inferno, pp. vii, 413. II. Purgatorio, pp. vi, 410. III. Paradiso, pp. vi, 452. Boston, 1867.

— Same. 11th Edition. 8°, pp. 760. Boston, 1884.

— Estray, The: A Collection of Poems. 12°, pp. vii, 144. Boston, 1847.

— Evangeline. A Tale of Acadie. 12°, pp. 163. Boston, 1847.

— Same. 2d Edition. 1848.

— Same. 9th Edition. 1854.

— Same. 12°, pp. viii, 112. Illustrated with 45 wood engravings. London, 1866.

— Excelsior. 12 Illustrations. 12°, not paged. New York, 1872.

Published by the Excelsior Life Insurance Company, of New York.

— Flower-de-Luce. With Illustrations. Small 4°, pp. 72. Boston, 1867.

LONGFELLOW, (H. W.) — *Continued.*

— Kavanagh. A Tale. 16°, pp. 188. Boston, 1849.
 Not a poem.  A few poetical extracts in the volume.

— Poems. 18°, pp. 124. London, no date.

— Same. Illustrated by D. Huntington. 8°, pp. 387. Philadelphia, 1845.

— Same. 2 vols. 12°, pp. vi, 475 ; 452. Boston, 1850.

— Same. 2 vols. 16°, pp. xiv, 475 ; 452. Boston, 1856.

— Same. 2 vols. 18°, pp. 375 ; 467. Boston, 1857. Blue and Gold Series.

— Same. 2 vols. 18°, pp. 420 ; 405. Boston, 1864. Blue and Gold Series.

— Editor. Poems of Places. England. 3 vols. (Vol. I. wanting.) 18°, pp. ix, 264 ; x, 280. Boston, 1876.

— Ireland. 18°, pp. ix, 260. Same place and date.

— Scotland. 2 vols. 18°, pp. x, 246 ; xi, 266. Same place and date.

— France. 2 vols. 18°, pp. viii, 265 ; vii, 266. Boston, 1877.

— Poems on Slavery. 2d Edition. 12°, pp. 31. Cambridge, 1842.

— Same. 3d Edition. Lg. 8°, pp. 31. Cambridge, 1843.

— Poetical Works. 16°, pp. 256. London and New York, 1854.

— Same. 16°, pp. 256. Edinburgh, London and New York, 1855.

— Same. 2 vols. 18°, pp. viii, 399 ; 322. Leipzig, 1856.

— Tales of a Wayside Inn. 12°, pp. v, 225. Boston, 1863.

— Same. 16°, pp. v, 140. London, 1864.

— Same. With Illustrations by John Gilbert. 8°, pp. 160. Boston, 1866.

— Same. Illustrated with 15 engravings on wood. 12°, pp. vi, 119.. London, 1867.

— The Belfrey of Bruges, etc. 2d Edition. 12°, pp. vii, 151. Boston, 1846.

— Same. 3d Edition. 12°, pp. vii, 151. Boston, 1846.

— Same. 4th Edition. Lg. 8°. Cambridge, 1846.

— The Courtship of Miles Standish, etc. 12°, pp. iv, 215. Boston, 1859.

— Same. With 25 Illustrations by John Gilbert, engraved by the Brothers Dalziel. Lg. 12°, pp. 119. London, 1859.

— The Divine Tragedy. 16°, pp. iv, 150. Boston, 1871.

— The Golden Legend. 16°, pp. iv, 336. Boston, 1851.

Longfellow, (H. W.) — *Continued.*

— The Golden Legend.  16°, pp. iv, 336.  Boston, 1856.

— Same.  1857.

— The Masque of Pandora, etc,  16°, pp. iv, 146.  Boston, 1875.

— The New England Tragedies.  I. John Endicott.  II. Giles Corey, of the Salem Farms.  16°, pp. 179.  Boston, 1868.

— The Seaside and the Fireside.  16°, pp. iv, 141.  Boston, 1850.

— The Song of Hiawatha.  16°, pp. iv, 316.  Boston, 1855.

> This copy of Hiawatha (there are several others in the collection) belongs to the Anthony part of the "Harris Collection." The original cover in the volume was removed, or it was procured in sheets, and some sixty blank pages added. Upon these blank pages have been pasted clippings from the papers. Most of them are parodies on Hiawatha, and some are favorable criticisms. For future reference these clippings will be invaluable.

— The Song of Hiawatha.  Tenth thousand.  18°, pp. iv, 252.  London, 1856.

— The Spanish Student.  A Play in three parts.  12°, pp. vi, 183.  Cambridge, 1843.

— Same.  3d Edition.  1843.

— Same.  4th Edition.  1843.

— Same.  6th Edition.  1844.

— Voices of the Night, etc.  2d Edition.  12°, pp. vi, 144.  Cambridge, 1840.

— Same.  3d Edition.  Lg. 8°, pp. vi, 144.

— Same.  4th Edition.  12°, pp. vi, 144.

— Same.  8th Edition.  12°, pp. vi, 144.  1843.

— Same.  10th Edition.  16°, pp. vi, 144.  1844.

— Same.  18°, pp. xxviii, 140.  London, 1844.

Look, (H. M.)  A Poem for the New Year.  12°, pp. 4.  Pontiac, Mich., 1865.

Look Before Ye Loup ; or, A Healin' Sa' for the Crackit Crowns of Country Politicians.  By Tam Thrum, (*pseud.*)  18°, pp. 40.  Philadelphia, 1798.

Lord, (W. W.)

> William W. Lord was born in Western New York not far from the year 1818, and became Rector of a church (Protestant Episcopal) in Vicksburg, Miss.

— Christ in Hades.  12°, pp. xv, 183.  New York, 1851.

— Poems.  12°, pp. 158.  New York and Philadelphia, 1845.

LORING, (F. W.)  The Boston Dip, etc.   Sq. 16°, pp. 63.  Boston, 1871.

LOOSJES, (A.)  Gedenkzuil, ter gelegenheid der Vry-verklaaring.  Noord-
America.  8°, pp. 49.  Amsterdam, 1782.  A Dutch Poem.

> The following, separately paged, is in the same volume:
>
> BYLAAGEN TER OPHELDERING VAN DE GEDENKZUL. DER VRYVERKLAARING VAN
> DE DERTIEN VEREENIGDE STAATEN VEN NORD AMERICA BESTAANDE IN REQUESTEN,
> BENCHTEN, RESOLUTIEN, ENZ.  8°, pp. 176.
>
> This volume was presented to Mr. Harris by John Carter Brown, Esq., March 15, 1873.
> At the end of the volume are two songs printed in English.  The first has this title:  "A
> Song, made by a *Dutch* Lady at the *Hague*, for the Sailors of the VIII American vessels
> at Amsterdam."  The title of the second is:  "Another Song, made by a *Dutch* Gentleman
> at *Amsterdam*, to be sung by the same, on the 4th of July, 1779."  Both may be sung to the
> tune "America."
>
> The following note is appended:  "This is a true copy of two Songs, made at the
> *Hague* and at *Amsterdam*, with a most hearty wish that they may add fuel to the precious
> fire which is burning in every true *American* heart."  Attest:  "The steady friends of Amer-
> ica at the Hague."
>
> > "Endure, dear Brethren, what remains of labour,
> > To get the Part of Freedom's heav'nly favour."

LOST SPADE, THE ; OR, THE GRAVE DIGGER'S REVENGE.  With Appendix.  A great Political, Martial, Serio-Comic Legendary, Romantic and Farcial Drama.  Written by the Happy Democratic Family expressly for the Peace Democracy.  16°, pp. 13.  New York,
1864.

LOUD, (MRS. M. ST. LEON.)

> Marguerite St. L. Barstow was born at Bradford county, Pa.  In 1824 she married Mr.
> Loud, of Philadelphia.  She has made many contributions to the periodical literature of
> the day.

— Wayside Flowers.  12°, pp. xii, 276.  Boston, 1851.

LOUISA.  A Domestic Tale.  (Anon.)  8°, pp. 4.  No place, no date.

LOVE, (C.)  Death of General George Washington.  12°.  Alexandria, Va., 1800.

LOVE OF NATURE.  An Anniversary Poem, delivered before the I. K. A.
of Washington.  16°, pp. 12.  Hartford, 1837.

LOVELL, (J.)

> John Lovell, the famous "Master Lovell" of the Boston Latin School, was born in
> 1718, graduated at Harvard, and for more than forty years, 1734–75, was Master of the
> Latin School, Boston.  Being a Loyalist, he went with the British to Halifax, where he
> died in 1778.

Lovell, (J.) — *Continued.*

— A Tribute to Washington for February 22, 1800.  Lg. 12°, pp. 15.
     Troy, 1800.

— The Seasons.  Read June 26, 1765, the day of the Annual Visita-
     tion of the Schools in Boston.  Lg. 12°, pp. 8.  Boston, 1765.

— Washington's Birthday.  Sm. 4°, pp. 55.  Albany, 1812.

Low, (S.)

> Samuel Low was born December 12, 1765.

— Poems.  2 vols.  12°, pp. 147, 168.  New York, 1800.

— Winter Displayed.  12°, pp. 40.  New York, 1784.

— Ode, July 4, 1800, sung in St. Paul's Church, before the General
     Society of Mechanics and Tradesmen, etc.  12°, pp. 3.  The vol-
     ume contains the Oration of M. L. Davis.  New York, 1800.

Lowe, (Mrs. Charles.)

> Martha A. Perry was born in Keene, N. H., and became the wife of Rev. Charles
> Lowe, and for many years was a resident in Somerville, Mass.

— The Olive and The Pine.  12°, pp. 156.  Boston, 1859.

Lowell.  The Offering.  Vol. I.  8°, pp. 380.  Lowell, no date.

> Original articles, some of them poems, written by females actively employed in the
> mills.

Lowell, (J. R.)

> James Russell Lowell was born at Cambridge, Mass., February 22, 1819, graduated at
> Harvard College in 1838, studied law and was admitted to the bar, but chose the profession
> of letters, and in 1855 succeeded Professor Longfellow in the department of Modern Lit-
> erature in his *alma mater;* was editor of "The Atlantic Monthly" 1857–62.  He was Uni-
> ted States Minister to Spain 1878–80, and to the Court of St. James 1880–85.  He is recog-
> nized as one of the most cultivated and accomplished scholars of America.  The signatures
> under which he has written are "J. R. L.," "Hosea Bigelow," "Elmwood," "Columbus
> Nye," "Homer Wilbur," and "A Wonderful Quiz."  His residence at this date (1886) is
> Cambridge.

— A Year's Life.  16°, pp. 182.  Boston, 1841.

— Conversations on some of the Old Poets.  16°, pp. viii, 263.  Cam-
     bridge, 1845.

— Fable for Critics.  12°, pp. 80.  New York, 1848.

— Poems.  3d Edition.  12°, pp. 279.  Cambridge, 1844.

— Same.  2d Series.  12°, pp. 184.  Cambridge and Boston, 1848.

— Same.  In 2 vols.  12°, pp. xii, 251, 254.  Boston, 1849.

— Same.  In 2 vols.  18°, pp. xi, 315, 322.  Boston, 1861.  Blue and
     Gold Series.

LOWELL, (J. R.) — *Continued.*
— The Biglow Papers. (Homer Wilbur, *pseud.*)   12°, pp. 163.
    Cambridge and New York, 1848.
— Same. Lg. 18°, pp. 140.   London, 1859.
    This edition has a preface by the author of "Tom Brown's School Days."
— Same. 2d Series. 12°, pp. lxxvi, 258.   Boston, 1867.
— The Cathedral. 12°, pp. 53.   Boston, 1870.
— The Vision of Sir Launfal. 12°, pp. 27.   Cambridge, 1848.
— Same. 2d Edition. 1849.
— Same. 4th Edition. 1851.
— Three Memorial Poems. Sq. 12°, pp. 92.   Boston, 1877.
— Under the Willows, etc. 12°, pp. viii, 286.   Boston, 1869.

LOWELL, (R. T. S.)   Fresh Hearts that Failed Three Thousand Years
    Ago ; with Other Things.   16°, pp, vi, 121.   Boston, 1860.

LUCAS, (A.)   The Shaving Mill.   12°, pp. 21.   Freetown, 1831.

LUCAS, (D. B.)   The Wreath of Eglantine, etc.   12°, pp. 169.   Balti-
    more, 1869.

LUCREZIA ; OR, THE BAG OF GOLD.   A Dramatic Sketch.   (Anon.)
    18°, pp. 82.   Philadelphia, no date.

LUMSDEN, (C.)   Mountain Buds and Blossoms.   12°, pp. viii, 204.
    Petersburg, Va., 1825.

LUNT, (G.)
    George Lunt was born at Newburyport, Mass., in 1803, graduated at Harvard College
    in 1824, became a lawyer and practiced in his native town.   In 1848 he removed to Boston,
    and was appointed by President Taylor, United States Attorney for the District of Massa-
    chusetts, 1849–53.   He died May 17, 1885.
— Culture. 12°, pp. 44.   Boston, 1843.
— Poems. 12°, pp. 160.   New York, 1839.
— Lyric Poems. 12°, pp. iv, 108.   Boston, 1854.
— The Dove and the Eagle. 12°, pp. 27.   Boston, 1851.
— The Grave of Byron, etc. 18°, pp. 84.   Boston, 1826.

LUTE, (——.)   Poems. 18°, pp. 204.   Dayton, Ohio, 1858.

LUTTON, (ANNE.)   Poems. 12°, pp. 136.   New York, 1842.

LYDE, (A. F.)
    Augustus Foster Lyde was born at Wilmington, N. C., February 4, 1813, graduated at
    Washington, now Trinity, College, Hartford, in 1830, with the honors of his class, entered

Lyde, (A. F.) — *Continued.*

the Protestant Episcopal Theological Seminary in 1831, taking the usual course of study in that institution. He decided to offer himself as a missionary to China. The Sabbath after his graduation he was ordained Deacon in St. Thomas's Church, New York, by Bishop Brownell. His plans for future labor were frustrated by illness, which proved fatal, his death occurring November 10, 1834.

— Buds of Spring. Poetical Remains, with Addenda by Thomas H. Vail. 12°, pp. xliii, 149. Boston, 1838.

Lynch, (Anne C.)

Anne Charlotte Lynch was born at Bennington, Vt. She was of Irish descent, her father being an active participant in the rebellion of 1798. After an imprisonment of four years he came to this country. His daughter was educated in Albany, removed to Providence, where, in 1841, she edited the "Rhode Island Book." In 1855 she married Mr. Vincenzo Botta, an Italian statesman. She died November 16, 1870.

— Poems. With Illustrations. 8°, pp. vi, 189. New York, 1849.
— Same. New Edition. 8°, pp. 203. New York, 1853.
— The Rhode Island Book. Prose and Poetry. 12°, pp. viii, 352. Providence, 1841.

Lyons, (J. G., D. D.) Christian Songs. 8°, pp. 59. Philadelphia, 1848.

Lyrics. By W. A. W. (Anon.) 12°, pp. 59. Boston, 1841.

Lyrics, Modern American. 12°, pp. 308. Edited by Carl Knortz and Otto Dickmann. Leipzig and Boston, 1880.

Luckey, (S., D. D.) Ethic Hymns, etc. 18°, pp. 132. Rochester, N. Y., 1868.

Lyons, (J. G.) Christian Songs. 8°, pp. 76. 4th Edition. Philadelphia, 1849.
— Same. 1861.

Lyrics. Words by W. H. Bellamy. Music by C. W. Glover. 8°, pp. 51. New York, 1853.

Lyte, (E. O.) School-Room Songs. 8°, pp. 48. Philadelphia.


Macbeth, (J. W. V.) The Might and Mirth of Literature. A Treatise on Figurative Language. 16°, pp. xxxvi, 542. New York, 1875.

McBride, (F.) The Robber: A Drama. 18°, pp. 18. New York, 1842.

23

M'Cabe, (J. C.)  Scraps.  12°, pp. 192.  Richmond, 1835.

McCabe, (W. G.)  Real and Ideal.  8°, pp. 22.  Richmond, Va., 1861.

McCaleb, (Mary Hunt.)  Poems.  12°, pp. 310.  New York, 1884.

McCall, (J. C.)  Fleurette, etc.  18°, pp. 68.  Philadelphia, 1828.
— The Troubadour, etc.  12°, pp. ix, 64.  Philadelphia, 1822.

McCall, (J. C. M.)  Savanarola.  8°, pp. 77.  Harrisburg, 1831.

McCord, (Louisa S.)

Louisa S. Cheves, daughter of Hon. Langdon Cheves, was born at Columbia, S. C., in December, 1810, married Colonel D. M. McCord in 1840, a distinguished lawyer of Columbia.  Her prose and poetical productions have received warm commendation.  During the civil war her residence was in Columbia, where she performed excellent service in the hospitals.

— Caius Gracchus.  A Tragedy in Five Acts.  12°, pp. 128.  New York, 1851.

McDermott, (H. F.)

Hugh F. McDermott was born in 1833, and wrote under the signature of "Pax."  He is a journalist residing in Boston.

— Lavona.  12°, pp. 75.  New York, 1860.

McDonald, (Mrs. Mary Noel.)

Mary Noel Bleecker was born in New York City.  Her poetical effusions were published in the New York Mirror.  She was married, first to P. E. F. McDonald in 1834, and in 1848 to Mr. Henry Meigs, of New York.  She has contributed much to periodical literature.

— Poems.  8°, pp. 208.  New York, 1844.

McDougal, (F. G.)  The Genius of American Liberty.  8°, pp. 32.  San Francisco, 1867.

Maceuen, (M.)  A Mosaic from Italy.  12°, pp. 69.  Philadelphia, 1867.

M'Henry, (J., M. D.)

James M'Henry, of Philadelphia, who wrote under the signature of "Solomon Second-Sight," was a contributor to the "American Quarterly Review," 1827-37.  His writings were severely criticised in "Blackwood's Magazine."

— The Antediluvians.  In Ten Works.  18°, pp. xv, 272.  Philadelphia, 1840.
— Feelings of Age, etc.  24°, pp. 36.  Philadelphia, 1830.
— The Pleasures of Friendship, etc.  12°, pp. 96.  Philadelphia, 1825.

M'HENRY, (J., M. D.) — *Continued.*

— The Pleasures of Friendship, etc. 18°, pp. 216. Philadelphia, 1836.
— Waltham. A Revolutionary Tale. 18°, pp. 70. New York, 1823.

M'JILTON, (J. N.) Poems. 12°, pp. xi, 360. Boston, 1840.
— The Triumph of Liberty. Poem. July 4, 1838. 12°, pp. 29. Baltimore, 1838.

McJIMSEY, (W.) Hebrew Melodies. 8°, pp. 260. New York, 1859.
— The Lessons of Nature and of Life. 8°, pp. 20. Nyack, 1867.
— The Memory of the Sabbath. 8°, pp. 96. Baltimore, 1837.
— Thompsonville; or, The Valley of the Connecticut. 16°, pp. 22. New York, 1847.

MACK, (E., M. D.) The Cat-Fight. A Mock Heroic Poem. 12°, pp. 276. New York, 1824.

Dr. Ebenezer Mack wrote a Life of General La Fayette. 12°, Ithaca, N. Y., 1841.

MACK, (R.) Kyle Stuart, etc. Vol. I. 18°, pp. 200. Columbia, T., 1834.

MACKELLAR, (T.)

Thomas Mackellar was born in the city of New York, August 12, 1812. After a partial education in a Classical Academy, he entered the printing office of the Harpers. Early in life he developed a taste for literary pursuits, and with other lads in New York organized an Association, from which sprang some able lawyers, such as Chief Justice Charles P. Daly, and other men of some note. Having removed to Philadelphia in 1833, he suggested and assisted in organizing a similar society in that city. After serving as a proof-reader and foreman in the type and stereotype foundry of Lawrence Johnson, Philadelphia, for several years, he was admitted into the firm in 1845. He began, at once, the preparation of the unique Specimen Books which made the house known world-wide, and finally brought it to the highest place among the type-foundries of the world. He began and edited a trade periodical in 1855, the "Typographical Advertiser," the forerunner of a multitude of its class, which is still published under the control of his son. He prepared the "American Printer," which has reached its sixteenth edition. In 1884 the degree of Ph. D. was conferred upon him by Wooster University, Ohio. Mr. Mackellar's present residence (1886) is Philadelphia.

— Hymns and a few Metrical Psalms. 12°, pp. 169. Philadelphia, 1883.

"Some of the hymns in this volume," says the author, "were written before a busy life had passed its noontide; others when the rays of the westering sun were falling slantwise. The latest were the outcome (as well as the alleviation) of times of anguish and bereavement."

— Rhymes Atween-Times. 12°, pp. 336. Philadelphia, 1873.
— Tam's Fortnight Ramble, etc. 12°, pp. ix, 216. Philadelphia, 1847.

M'KINNON, (J. D.)  Descriptive Poems.  12°, pp. 79.  New York, 1802.

McKNIGHT, (G.)  Life and Faith Sonnets.  Sq. 12°, pp. 136.  New York, 1878.

M'LAUGHLIN, (E. A.)

Edward A. M'Laughlin was born at West Stamford, Conn., January 9, 1798.  In early life he was a sailor, and passed through many adventures; then, for three years and a half, was in the United States Navy, being discharged from the service on account of ill health.

— The Lovers of the Deep.  In Four Cantos, etc.  12°, pp. x, 312.  Cincinnati, 1841.

McLELLAN, (I.)

Isaac McLellan was born at Portland, Me., in 1806, graduated at Bowdoin College in 1826, having among his classmates the celebrated S. S. Prentiss, of Mississippi.  Having been admitted to the bar, he practiced his profession for a few years in Boston, and engaged in journalistic work.  At the end of a two-years' tour in Europe he returned home, abandoned his profession, and returned to a country life.  "Devoted, as ever before, to field sports," says Professor Packard, "he wrote on subjects which they suggested.  This taste especially made him familiar with resorts on the Massachusetts coast, and brought him into intercourse with lovers of the sports, and especially with Daniel Webster at his summer retreat at Marshfield, where he passed two seasons at one of the farm-houses of the statesman.  He removed to New York, exercising his inveterate passion in its neighborhood, passing a part of the season for several years on the Virginia and North Carolina coasts."  For several years his residence was at Greenport, L. I.

— Mt. Auburn, etc.  12°, pp. 156.  Boston, 1843.
— The Year, with other Poems.  By the Author of " The Fall of the Indians," etc.  A New Year's Gift.  8°, pp. 60.  Boston, 1832.

McLELLAN, (R. C.)  The Foundling.  A Drama.  18°, pp. 68.  Philadelphia, 1839.

McMASTERS, (JULIA R.)  Silver Pictures.  12°, pp. 64.  Philadelphia, 1856.

MACMULLEN, (J.)  Poem before Alumni Association of Columbia College, October 27, 1858.  8°, pp. 31.  New York, 1858.

McNAIR, (JOHN, D.D.)  Eighty Original Poems, Secular and Sacred.  12°, pp. 263.  Lancaster, Pa., 1865.

M'NAUGHTON, (J. H.)

John H. M'Naughton, a poet of Caledonia, N. Y.

— Babble Brook Songs.  12°, pp. 235.  Boston, 1864.

Macon, (J. A.)  Uncle Gabe Tucker; or, Reflection, Song and Sentiment in the Quarters.  12°, pp. 181.  Philadelphia, 1883.

Madden, (R. R., M. D.)

Dr. Madden was born in Ireland.  He is known as an author and traveller.  (See Allibone, p. 1199.)

The poems in this volume were translated from the Spanish by Dr. M.  They were
written by a slave who had been liberated in the island of Cuba.  An interesting autobiography of the author precedes the poems.  Dr. M. has also introduced into the volume two
poems of his own, entitled "The Sugar Estate," and "The Slave Trade Merchant."  A
valuable Appendix, containing matter having reference to slavery in Cuba, may be found
in the volume.  There is also a Glossary of Creole terms in common use in Cuba.

— Poems.  8°, pp. v, 145.  London, 1840.

Mad-House Lyrics.  (By Cole, *pseud?*)  Vol. I.  18°, pp. 48.  Concord, N. H., 1852.

Maelstrom, The.  (Anon.)  Entered by John Hammond.  8°, pp. 68.
San Francisco, 1861.

Maffitt, (J. N.)

John Newland Maffitt, a noted Methodist preacher, was born at Dublin, Ireland, in
1794, came to the United States in 1819, and attained great celebrity as a preacher.  In
1833 he was appointed associate editor of the *Western Methodist*, Nashville, Tenn.  In
1837 he was chosen Professor of Elocution in La Grange College, Ala.  He died at Mobile
in 1850.

— Ireland: A Poem.  12°, pp. 79.  Louisville, 1839.
— Literary and Religious Sketches.  Poems in the volume.  12°, pp.
240.  New York, 1832.

Magazine, Columbian.  The number for July, 1848, contains Anna
Blackwell's "Tambounna," Mrs. Sigourney's "The Emigrant,"
and Wallace's "Perditi."  4°.

Magdalen Report, The.  A Farce.  (Peter Pendergrass, Sr., *pseud.*)
12°, pp. 25.  New York, 1831.

Mahomet.  (Anon.)  A Bouquet for Jenny Lind.  8°, pp. 39.  New
York, 1850.

Maid of Midian.  A Tragedy.  (Anon.)  3d Edition.  12°, pp. iv, 36.
Philadelphia, 1836.

Man, (T.)

A native of Rhode Island, familiarly known as "Tom Man."

— Woonsocket, A Picture of; or, The Truth in its Nudity, etc.  12°,
pp. 108.  No place, 1835.

A few poems in the volume.

MANGUM, (A. W.)   Myrtle Leaves; or, Tokens at the Tomb.   12°, pp. 132.   Raleigh, N. C., 1864.

MANNERS, (G.)   The Conflagration.   4°, pp. 18.   Boston, 1825.

> This poem was written and published for the benefit of the sufferers by disastrous fires in the Province of New Brunswick.

MANNERS, THE, OF THE TIMES.   (Philadelphiensis.)   Sq. 12°, pp. 16.   Philadelphia, 1762.

MANNING, (J. B.)

> Joseph Bolles Manning was born at Gloucester (now Rockport), Mass., in 1787, graduated at Harvard in 1808, and, for several years, was a lawyer in Ipswich, Mass., and Gloucester.   He died in Ipswich in 1854.

— The Voice of Letters.   12°, pp. vii, 135.   Boston and Cambridge, 1844.

MANSFIELD, (J.)   Hope.   Poem delivered at Commencement, Harvard, July 8, 1800.   18°, pp. 10.   Fitchburg, 1871.

MARCH, (D.)

> Daniel March, D. D., was born at Millbury, Mass., July 21, 1816, graduated at Yale in 1840, was ordained in 1845, and has been pastor of Congregational and Presbyterian churches.   Among his published writings are "Night Scenes in the Bible," "Walks and Hours of Jesus," etc.   He is at this time (1886) pastor of the Congregational Church in Woburn, Mass.

— Yale.   Phi Beta Kappa Poem.   8°, pp. 12.   New Haven, 1846.

— Yankee Land and the Yankee.   A Poem delivered at the Centennial Celebration of the Connecticut Historical Society, April 21, 1840.   12°, pp. 33.   Hartford, 1840.

MARCH FLOWERS.   (Miss E. C. Greene[?])   12°, pp. 36.   Providence, 1836.

MARCH OF SCIENCE.   (Anon.)   12°, pp. 36.   Philadelphia, 1846.

MARIE, (P.)   A Midsummer's Fête at Woodland Hall.   12°, pp. 30.   New York, 1850.

— A Tribute to the Fair.   Comprising a Collection of Vers de Societé.   12°, pp. xiii, 253.   New York, 1864.

— The Bandit's Daughter.   12°, pp. 54.   New York, 1834.

MARRIOTT, (J.)   Poems.   18°, pp. 141.   New Bedford, 1805.

MARKOE, (P.)

> Peter Markoe wrote under the signature of "*A Native of Algiers.*"   He died in Philadelphia in 1792.

MARKOE, (P.) — *Continued.*

— Miscellaneous Poems.  12°, pp. 30.  Philadelphia, 1787.
— The Patriot Chief.  8°, pp. 70.  Philadelphia, 1783.
— Reconciliations.  Comic Opera.  12°, pp. 48.  Philadelphia, 1790.
— The Times.  8°, pp. iv, 22.  Baltimore, 1788.
> Two copies in the Collection.

MARKS, (E., M. D.)  Elfreide of Guldal.  A Scandinavian Legend, etc.
12°, pp. vi, 186.  New York, 1850.

MARKWELL, (W. R. S.)  On Parole.  From the Spanish of Moraton.
4°, pp. 33.  The original MS.  No place, no date.

MARSDEN, (J.)  Leisure Hours.  12°, pp. 160.  New York, 1842.

MARSH, (MRS. GEORGE P.)
> Constance Crane, the wife of Hon. George P. Marsh, was born at Berkely, Mass., in
> 1816.  She translated from the German, among other things, "The Halig; or, The Sheep-
> fold in the Waters," etc.

— Wolfe of the Knoll, etc.  12°, pp. 327.  New York, 1860.

MARSH, (W.)  England, etc.  12°, pp. 112.  New York, 1839.

MARSHALL, (H.)  The Aliens.  Occasioned by the Alien Bill before the
Senate, May 15, 1798.  8°, pp. v, 71.  Philadelphia, 1798.
Rare.

MARTIN, (A. LL. D., supposed to be the author of.)  A New Scene
Interesting to the Citizens of the United States of America.  Additional to the Historical Play of Columbus.  8°, pp. 8.  Philadelphia, 1798.

MARTIN, (J. L.)
> Mr. Martin was for some time Chargé d'Affaires of the United States to the Pontifical
> States.  He died at Rome; date not learned.

— Native Bards.  A Satirical Effusion, etc.  12°.  Philadelphia, 1831.

MARTIN VAN BUREN.  A Miniature of.  (Anon.)  18°, pp. 54.  No
place, no date.

MARTYN, (MRS. S. T.)  Ione.  A Dramatic Sketch.  8°, pp. 35.  No
place, no date.

MARY'S VISION.  (Anon.)  16°, pp. 180.  Hartford, 1874.

MASON, (H. B.)  Poem.  Senior Class, Yale.  Presentation Day, June
29, 1870.  8°, pp. 15.  New Haven, 1870.

MASONRY, FREE.  By a Citizen of Massachusetts.  (Anon.)  A Poem in
Three Cantos.  12°, pp. 216.  Leicester, 1830.

An attack on Masonry.

MASQUE OF POETS, A, INCLUDING GUY VERNON.  A Novellette in Verse.
12°, pp. 301.  Boston, 1878.

MATHER, (C.)

Cotton Mather was born at Boston, February 12, 1662–3, graduated at Harvard in 1678,
at the early age of fifteen years, two only in the long list of the graduates of that venerable
University, completing the regular course of study at an earlier age than he, namely, Paul
Dudley, of the class of 1690, and the Rev. Dr. Andrew P. Peabody, of the class of 1826.
He preached his first sermon August 22, 1680, at the age of seventeen, was ordained colleague of his father, Rev. Dr. Increase Mather, May 13, 1685.  To attempt even to give the
simple titles of all the works he published would be impossible in a sketch like this.  Sibley,
in his "Graduates of Harvard," vol. iii, devotes 116 pages to an enumeration of the published writings of Cotton Mather, under 450 distinct heads.  Professor M. C. Tyler gives
the number of his published writings as exceeding 383.  It is an interesting circumstance that in "The Harris Collection" are copies of the first and the third productions
of his pen, which are believed to be the only copies extant.  The great work on whic h
his fame rests is his "Magnalia Christi Americana; or, The Ecclesiastical History of
New England, from its planting in the year 1620, unto the year of our Lord 1698."  It
has been well said of him: "His character exhibits a remarkable compound of ardent
piety, (which, however, was not without a tincture of self-conceit), uncommon activity
and force of intellect, joined to a credulity, which, even in that age, had scarcely any parallel among educated men."  He died February 13, 1827–8.

— A Poem Dedicated to the Memory of the Reverend and Excellent Mr.
Urian Oakes, the late Pastor to Christ's Flock, and Præsident of
Harvard College, in Cambridge, who was gathered to his People on
25ᵈ 5ᵐᵒ 1681.  In the Fifty-th Year of his Age.  1 Sam. 25 1.
And Samuel dyed and all the Israelites were gathered together,
and Lamented him.

Scindentur Vestes, Gemmae Frangentiur, et Aurum ;
Carmina quam tribuunt Fama perennis erit.   Ovid.
Magna dabit qui magna potest ; mihi parva potenti
Parvaq. ; poscenti, parva dedisse sat est.

Boston in New England
Printed for *John Ratcliff*, 1682.

This was Cotton Mather's first published work, the only copy known and believed to
be unique.  It has the autograph of N(athanael) Mather on the last page.  The little volume, purchased at the "Brinley sale," is in every respect perfect and is elegantly bound.
It is one of the rare treasures of "The Harris Collection."  On a fly-leaf at the end of the
volume is written in pencil, $300.  Whether this was the price paid for this rare book by
Mr. Harris, the compiler of this catalogue does not know.

If worthy Cotton Mather had been to Mount Helicon, in old Bœotia, to drink from the
pure rills of the Muses, before he sat down to write this delectable poem, we fear the

Mather, (C.) — *Continued.*

water must have become muddy, or in some way lost its inspiring power. The following lines will hardly compare with even the poorest stanzas of the least poetical of all the writers whose productions are represented in this collection.

—— Lord! from thy lofty Throne
Look down upon thy *Heritage!* Lett none
Of all our *Breaches* bee unhealed! Lett
This dear poor Land be our Immanuels yett!
Lett's be a Goshen still! Restrain the *Boar*
That makes *Incursions!* Give us daily more
Of thy All-curing Spirit from on High
Let all thy *Churches* flourish! And supply
The almost *Twenty Ones,* that thy just Ire
Has left *without Help* that their needs require!
Lett not the *Colledge* droop and dy! O Lett
The Fountain run! A *Doctor* give to it!
Moses's are to th' *Upper Canaan* gone!
Lett Joshua's Succeed them! goes when one
Elijah, raise Elisha's! Pauls become
Dissolv'd! with Christ! Send Tim'thees in their room.
Avert the Omen, that *Teeth* apace
Fall out. No new ones should supply their place!
Lord! Lett us *Peace* on this our *Israel* see!
And still both *Hephsibah,* and Beulah bee!
Then will thy People Grace! and Glory! Sing,
And every wood with Hallelujah's ring.

N. R.

Says Sibley, in his notice of Cotton Mather, "Harvard Graduates," vol. iii, pp. 43: "The letters N. R. subscribed to this poem are the last letters of the name Cotton Mather."

— An Elegy on the much-to-be-deplored Death of that never-to-be-forgotten Person, the Reverend Mr. Nathanael Collins, who after he had been many years a faithful Pastor to the church at *Middletown* of *Connecticut* in *New England* about the *Forty-third* year of his age expired; on 28th. 10. moneth 1684.

Testor, Christianum his de Christiano vera proferre

Hier. Epis. Paulæ

Sic oculos, sic ille manus, sic ora ferebat.

Dignum laude virum musa vetat mori.

Horat.

Boston in New England
Printed by Richard Pierce for Obadiah Gill.
Anno Christi 1685.

The full title is given of a book which is claimed to be, and without doubt was, among the earliest, probably the third, of the exceedingly voluminous writings of Cotton Mather, published when he was not far from twenty-two years of age. It has also the merit of

24

MATHER, (C.) — *Continued.*

being, so far as is known, the only copy in existence.  Brinley, who was the highest authority in such matters, writes: "Not in any public library.  Have never *heard of another copy.*"
Even his own son, Samuel Mather, who professes to have made out a complete list of all his
father's known writings, did not include in it this "Elegy" of Cotton Mather.  No reference is made to it by the best writers on early New England literature.  Mr. Harris purchased this rare little volume, 24°, of twenty pages, paying for it $205, at the Brinley sale.

— Corderius Americanus——An Essay upon the Good Education of
Children.  And what may Hopefully be Attempted, for the *Hope
of the* FLOCK.  In a Funeral Sermon upon Mr. Ezekiel Cheever.
The *Ancient* and *Honourable* MASTER of the FREE-SCHOOL
in Boston.  Who left off, but when Mortality took him off, in
August, 1708, the Ninety Fourth year of his Age.  With an
ELEGY and an EPITAPH upon him —— By one that was made
a scholar by him—— *Vester* [CHEEVERUS] *cum sic moritur,
non moritur.*  Boston.  Printed by *John Allen,* for *Nicholas Boone,*
at the sign of the Bible in *Cornhill,* near the corner of School street,
1708.

This copy of the "Coderius Americanus" purchased at the Brinley sale is in perfect condition and binding.  In his "Harvard Graduates," Sibley calls the volume an
8°.  In the Harris Collection it has been trimmed down to an 18°.  The Poetical Essay
and Epitaph are pp. 26–34.

— Psalterium Americanum.  The Book of Psalms, in a Translation
Exactly conformed unto the Original, but all in Blank verse fitted
unto the Tunes commonly used in our Churches.  Which pure
offering is accompanied with Illustrations, digging for Hidden
Treasures in it, and Rules to employ it upon the Glorious and
Various Intentions of it..  Whereto are added some other portions of
the Sacred Scriptures to enrich the Cantional.  12°, pp. xxxv, 426.
Boston in N. E.  Printed by *S. Kneeland* for *B. Eliot, F. Ger-
rish, D. Henchman & J. Edwards,* and sold at their shops.  1718.

It could hardly be expected that Cotton Mather, who, in those early colonial times,
touched life on so many sides, would fail to turn his thoughts to so important a matter as
"the service of song, in the House of the Lord."  His laudable aim in this book is to
improve what he regarded as the careless, untrustworthy translation of the Psalms then
current, and produce something that should bear a closer resemblance to the original.  In
this version we do not have lines beginning with capitals, whether they do or do not rhyme,
but the entire matter is "run out," the proper syllabization to suit the metre being made
by upright parallel lines.  Mather says: "Our Poetry has attempted many editions of the
Psalms in such *Numbers* and *Measures* as might render them capable of being *Sung* in
those grave *Tunes* which have been prepared and received for our *Christian Psalmody.*
But of all the more than twice Seven Versions which I have seen, it must be affirmed, That
they *leave out* a vast heap of those rich things which the Holy Spirit of God Speaks in the

**MATHER, (C.)** — *Continued.*

Original Hebrew; and that they *put in* as large an Heap of poor Things which are entirely *their own.* All this has been meerly for the sake of preserving the *Clink* of the *Rhime:* Which after all is of small consequence unto a Generous *Poem,* and of none at all unto the Melody of *Singing;* But of how little then, in Singing unto the Lord!" An illustration of the way in which the "Psalterium" was prepared is taken from Psalm LI. By omitting the words in BLACK LETTER, the verse is adapted to another metre. "The Director of the Psalmody need only say 'Sing with the BLACK LETTER, or sing without the BLACK LETTER,' and the tune will be sufficiently directed."

9. From the beholding of my Sins || [kindly] hide thou away thy face; || and all of my Iniquities || [wholly] do thou obliterate.

10. O God, Create in me an heart || that shall be [judged] thoroughly clean; || and in the midst of me do thou || renew a Spirit right [and firm].

**MATHER, (S.)**

Samuel Mather, a son of Cotton Mather, was born in 1706, graduated at Harvard in 1723, for ten years was colleague pastor with Rev. Mr. Gee in the Old North Church, Boston, and then of a colony which withdrew from that church. He died in 1785. Professor Tyler says of him: "He left no successor to continue the once splendid dynasty of his tribe. He was the last and the least of the Mathers."

— An attempt to show, that America must be (have been?) known to the Ancients; made at the request, and to gratifiy the curiosity, of an inquisitive gentleman. To which is added an Appendix concerning the American colonies, and some modern managements against them. By an American Englishman, Pastor of a church in Boston, New England. 8°, pp. 35, 1773.

A very rare and curious volume, so rare that Rich, the celebrated bibliographer, had never seen a copy, but refers to the catalogue of Harvard College Library. There is a copy in the John Carter Brown Library, also one in the Library of Bowdoin College, and two copies in the Library of the Massachusetts Historical Society. Thomas, in his History of Printing, vol. I, p. 20, says: This is "a work of equal learning and patriotism. It maintains that the posterity of Japhet by Magog were the primary inhabitants of America, a warlike people, well qualified to make those Ancient Encampments which have been discovered at the West."

The claim of this book to be in a "Collection of American Poetry" is found in the circumstance that there are in it two or three poetical quotations.

— The Sacred Minister. A new Poem in Five Parts, representing his qualifications for the Ministry, and his Life and Death in it. By Aurelius Prudentius, Americanus. 8°, pp. 22. Boston, 1783.

**MATHEWS' LECTURE ON AMERICA, ETC.** 16°, pp. 35. Baltimore, 1824.

**MATHEWS, (C.)**

Cornelius Mathews was born at Port Chester, N. Y., October 28, 1817, graduated at the University of New York, 1835, was admitted to the bar in 1837, has been editor of several journals and a frequent contributor to periodicals, etc.

MATHEWS, (C.) — *Continued.*

— Poems on Man, in his Various Aspects under the American Republic. 12°, pp. viii, 112.  London, 1842.

— Man in the Republic.  A New Edition.  24°, pp. 96.  New York, 1846.

— Witchcraft.  A Tragedy.  18°, pp. 99.  London, 1852.

MATHIES, (J.)  Rochester.  A Satire, etc.  18°, pp. 130.  Rochester, 1830.

MATRIMONY, THE ROMANCE OF.  (Anon.)  12°, pp. 122.  Philadelphia, 1865.

MATTHEWS, (J. B.)

James Brander Matthews was born in Louisiana in 1852, and removed to New York City.  He wrote under the signature of *Arthur Penn.*

— Poems of American Patriotism.  12°, pp. xiii, 285.  New York, 1882.

MATURIN, (E. S.)

Edward S., son of Charles Robert Maturin, of Dublin, Ireland, was born in that city in 1812, and was educated at Trinity College, in his native city  He came to New York in 1832, where he practiced law.  Subsequently he resided as a teacher in South Carolina, then returned to New York, where he died May 25, 1881.

— Lyrics of Spain and Erin.  12°, pp. 208.  Boston, 1851.

— Viola.  12°, pp. 32.  New York, no date.

MAXWELL, (W.)  Poems.  24°, pp. 144.  Philadelphia, 1812.

— Same.  18°, pp. 168.  Philadelphia, 1816.

MAY, (CAROLINE.)

The daughter of Rev. E. H. May, a clergyman of the Reformed Church in America, in the city of New York.  She is well known as the compiler of " The American Female Poets."

— The American Female Poets, with Biographical and Critical Notices. 12°, pp. 532.  Philadelphia, 1848.

— Poems.  12°, pp. 223.  New York, 1865.

MAY, (EDITH.)  Poems.  12°, pp. 52, 324.  Philadelphia, 1856.

This is the *pseud.* of Anna Drinker, a native of Philadelphia.  (See Griswold's " Female Poets of America."  1860, pp. 302.)

MAYFIELD, (MILLIE.)  Progression ; or, The South Defended.  12°, pp. 226.  Cincinnati, 1860.

MAYLEM, (J.)

> John Maylem was born not far from 1695, graduated at Harvard College in 1715, and died 1742. His memory is not very fragrant. (See Duyckink, vol. 1, pp. 432.)

— The Conquest of Louisberg. 18°, pp. 16. No place, no date.

MAYLIN, (ANNE W.) Lays of Many Hours. 12°, pp. 168. Philadelphia, 1847.

MAYO, (MRS. SARAH C. E.)

> Sarah C., Edgarton was born at Shirley, Mass., in 1819, became the wife of Rev. A. D. Mayo, a Universalist minister, in 1846, for nine years edited "The Rose of Sharon," was editor also of "The Ladies' Repository," contributed many articles to "The Knickerbocker," "The New Yorker," etc. She died in 1848.

— Selections from her Writings. Prose and Poetry. 12°, pp. 432. Boston, 1849.

MAZARO AND LELLAH; OR, THE VICTIMS OF LOVE. (Anon.) 12°, pp. 21. Cincinnati, 1840.

MEACHAM, (A. G.) Sumner. 24°, pp. 16. Rushville, Ill., 1856.

MEAD, (—— ?) Wall Street; or, Ten Minutes before Three. A Farce. 3d Edition. 18°, pp. 34. New York, 1819.

MEAD, (C.) American Minstrel. 18°, pp. viii, 174. Philadelphia, 1828.
— Mississippian Scenery. A Poem, descriptive of the interior of North America. 12°, pp. ix, 113. Philadelphia, 1819.

MEDINA, (LOUISA H.) Ernest Maltravers. A Drama. 12°, pp. 37. New York, no date.
— Nick of the Woods. A Drama. 12°, pp. 30. Boston, no date.
— The Last Days of Pompeii. A Dramatic Spectacle. 12°, pp. 31. New York, no date.

MEDLEY, A, OF JOY AND GRIEF. (Anon.) 12°, pp. iv, 298. New York, 1822.

MEDLEY, THE. 8°. New Haven, 1833.

MEGIA, (F.) Lafayette en Monte Vernon. Drama. 18°, pp. 30. Filadelfia, 1825.

**MEEK, (A. B.)**

Alexander Beaufort Meek was born at Columbia, S. C., July 17, 1814, graduated at the University of Alabama in 1833, was admitted to the bar in 1835, filled many important offices of civil trust, and originated the free school system of Alabama. He died at Columbus, Miss., November 30, 1865.

— Songs and Poems of the South. 12°, pp. x, 282. Mobile, 1857.

— Same. 2d Edition. New York, 1857.

— The Red Eagle. 12°, pp. 108. New York, 1855.

**MEGRATH, (G.)** The New Dido. 12°, pp. 92. New York, 1851.

**MEIGS, (R. J.)**

Return Jonathan Meigs was born at Middletown, Conn., December 17, 1740, and rose to distinction as an officer in the American army in the Revolutionary war. He died at the Cherokee Agency, January 28, 1823. (See Johnson's Universal Encyclopædia, vol. iii, p. 398.)

— A Poem Delivered at Yale, March 9, 1784. Sm. 8°, pp. 16. New Haven, 1784.

**MEIGS, (MRS. MARY N.)** Lays of a Lifetime. Sq. 8°, pp. 157. New York, 1857.

**MELLEN, (G.)**

The name of the author, Grenville Mellen, is not given on the title-page. He was born at Biddeford, Me., June 19, 1799, graduated at Harvard in 1818, studied law and practiced for several years in North Yarmouth (now Yarmouth), Me. For five years he resided in Boston. In 1823 he began in New York a "Monthly Miscellany," which had only a brief existence. He died in 1840.

— Our Chronicle of '26. A Satirical Poem. 8°, pp. 40. Boston, 1827.

— Poem at Amherst College, delivered August 27, 1839. 8°, pp. 35. Amherst, 1839.

— The Martyr's Triumph, Buried Valley, etc. 12°, pp. vi, 297. Boston, 1833.

— The Passions. Lg. 8°, pp. 44. Boston, 1836.

— The Rest of the Nations. Pronounced before the Peace Society of Maine, May 10, 1826. 8°, pp. 28. Portland, 1826.

**MELLEN, (J., JR.)** The Fall of the Indian, etc. 12°, pp. 99. Boston, 1830.

**MELMOTH, (S.)** The Confessions of Cuthburt, etc. 18°, pp. xviii, 124. Boston, 1827.

MELODIES, SACRED. (Anon.) 12°, pp. 111. New York, 1841.

MELODIST REVIVAL, Y. M. C. A. Ob. 18°, pp. 51. Providence, no date.

MEMORIAM, IN. Sarah Hills Hall, b. November 12, 1777, d. September 21, 1866. (Anon.) Sq. 12°, pp. 16. No place, no date.

MENKEN, (ADAH ISAACS.) Infelicia. Sq. 18°, pp. v, 141. London, Paris, New York, 1868.

MERING, (ANN S.) Songs in the Night. 12°, pp. 62. Cincinnati, 1855.

MERRY, (R.)

Robert Merry was born at London in 1755, and was educated at Christ's College, Cambridge. For many years he resided in Florence. In 1796 he came to America. His death occured at Baltimore, January 24, 1798.

— The Pains of Memory. Sq. 8°, pp. 39. Boston, 1797.

MERRY'S ILLUSTRATED BOOK OF RHYMES. (R. Merry and H. Hatchet, pseud.) 12°, pp. 108. 1859.

METHODISM, THE SPIRIT OF. (Anon.) 18°, pp. 94. New York, 1831.

METAMORPHOSIS; OR, A TRANSFORMATION OF PICTURES, ETC. 18°, pp. 6. Wilmington, 1814.

MEXITLI; OR, THE CONQUEST OF MEXICO. (By T. C. R. Anon.) 12°, pp. 24. No place, date in pencil, 1863.

MAYER, (M.) Translation of Karl Gutzkow's Uriel Acosta. A Tragedy. 12°, pp. 104. New York, 1860.

MICHARD, (J.) Religio Poetæ. A Trilogy. 12°, pp. 119. Richmond, 1860.

MICHEL BONHAM; OR, THE FALL OF BEXAR. A Tale of Texas. (Anon. By a Southron.) 8°, pp. 35. Richmond, 1852.

MICROCOSMUS PHILADELPHICUS, IN TWO EPISTLES, ETC. 12°, pp. 60. Philadelphia, 1825.

MIDDLETON, (EDDA.) Sappho. A Tragedy. 4°, pp. 159. New York, 1858.

After the German of Francis Grillparzer, born in 1790. "Sappho" appeared in 1818. It was a great favorite with Rachel.

MIDNIGHT, ETC. (Anon.) 12°, pp. 90. New York, 1858.

Miles, (G. H.)  Christine : A Troubadour's Song.  12°, pp. 285.  New
York, 1866.

— Mary's Birthday ; or, The Cynic.  12°, pp. 36.  Boston, no date.

— Senor Valiente.  A Comedy.  12°, pp. 52.  Boston, no date.

Millefleur's, Miss Milly, Career.  (Anon.)  In Fifteen Sketches.  4°.
New York, 1869.

Miller, (J.)

Cincinnatus Heine, or Joaquin Miller, was born in the Wabash District, Ind., Novem -
ber 10, 1841, went to the Pacific coast in 1854, had all sorts of adventures in California, was
with Walker in his Nicaragua Expedition, and for a time lived among the Indians, subsequently studied law, was a County Judge in Oregon, 1866–70, went to England in 1870,
where he attracted much attention.  Besides his poetry he has published several prose
productions.

— Poems.  12°.  Songs of the Sierras, pp. 277.  Songs of the Sun
Lands, pp. 178.  Fallen Leaves, pp. 209.  The Ship in the
Desert, pp. 205.  Songs of Italy, pp. 178.  Boston, 1882.

— Songs of Italy.  12°, pp. 186.  Boston, 1878.

— Songs of the Sierras.  12°, pp. 299.  London, 1872.

— The Ship in the Desert.  12°, pp. xii, 205.  Boston, 1875.

Miller, (J. W.)  Poems and Sketches.  12°, pp. 165.  Boston, 1830.

Mills, (H.)  Horæ Germanicæ : A Version of German Hymns.  16°,
pp. 274.  Auburn, 1845.

— Same.  2d Edition.  12°, pp. 368.  New York and Auburn, 1856.

Mills, (J. H.)  Poetic Trifles.  12°, pp. 116.  Baltimore, 1808.

Mines, (J. F.)  The Heroes of the Last Lustre.  16°, pp. 135.  New
York, 1858.

Minshall, (J.)  Rural Felicity.  8°, pp. 68.  New York, 1801.

Minstrelsy of Edmund, the Wanderer.  Collected by R. T. Spence.
8°, pp. 340.  New York, 1810.

Minstrel's Cabinet.  (Anon.)  24°, pp. 187.  Title-page gone.

Misanthrope, The, of the Mountain.  (Anon.)  12°, pp. 48.  New
Haven, 1833.

Miscellaneous Poems.  (By a Lady.  Anon.)  12°, pp. 143.  Woodstock, 1820.

MISCELLANIES. Prose and Verse. (Compiled. Anon.) 2d Burlington Edition. 12°, pp. 198. Burlington, Vt., 1796.

MISSING LINKS, THE, TO DARWIN'S ORIGIN OF SPECIES. Large 12°, not paged. No place, no date.

MISTRAL, (F.) Mirèio. A Provencal Poem. Translated by Harriet W. Preston. 12°, pp. 241. Boston, 1872.

MITCHELL, (AGNES W.) The Smuggler's Son, etc. Prose and Verse. 12°, pp. viii, 299. Philadelphia, 1842.

MITCHELL, (CATHERINE.) , The Downfall of Jerusalem, etc. 18°, pp. 70. Philadelphia, 1845.
— The Minstrel's Bride; or, The Shepherd of Hazel Glen. 12°, pp. 237. Philadelphia, 1859.

MITCHELL, (J. K., M. D.) Indecision. A Tale of the Far West. 12°, pp. x, 212. Philadelphia, 1839.

MITCHELL, (S. W.) The Hill of Stones, etc. 16°, pp. 98. Boston, 1883.

MITCHELL, (W.) Poems. 18°, pp. 35. New York, 1860.

MOCK AUCTION, THE. Ossawatomie Sold. A Mock Heroic Poem. 12°, pp. 261. Richmond, 1860.

MODERN BATTLE, THE, OF THE KEGS. (Anon.) 12°, pp. 12. Philadelphia, 1854.

MOELLING, (C. E.) Faust's Death. A Tragedy. 12°, pp. 136. Philadelphia, 1865.

MOISE, (P.) Fancy's Sketch Book. 18°, pp. 159. Charleston, S. C., 1833.

MOLE FAMILY, THE. (E. P. Anon.) 12°, pp. 39. Poughkeepsie, 1870.

MOLLINEUX, (MARY.)

Mary Southworth, the wife of Henry Mollineux, was an English Friend, born not far from the year 1650. She shared with her husband the severe persecutions to which the Quakers were subjected in the period in which she lived. She died 11th month, 3d day, 1695.

25

MOLLINEUX, (MARY.) — *Continued.*

— Fruits of Retirement; or, Miscellaneous Poems, Moral and Divine,
etc.   18°, pp. 182.   Philadelphia, 1729.
An elegant, richly bound copy from the Brinley sale, for which $26 was paid.

MONEGHAN, (J. C.)   Emmet; or, The Hero of 1803.   12°, pp. 70.
Providence, 1879.

MONGRELITES; OR, THE RADICALS, SO CALLED.   (Anon.)   12°, pp.
viii, 52.   New York, no date.

MONIAD, THE.   A Satire.   (Anon.)   18°, pp. 112.   Philadelphia, 1867.

MONITOR, THE.   An Earnest Appeal to Merchants and Other Business
Men.   (Anon.)   12°, pp. 22.   New York, 1863.

MONTCLAIR, (J. W.)   Real and Ideal.   12°, pp. x, 119.   Philadelphia,
New York, Boston, London, 1865.

MONTGOMERIES, MEMORABLES OF THE.   8°, pp. iii, 7.   New York,
printed for the King of Clubs, 1866.
Edition, 60 copies 8°, 40 copies 4°.

MONTGOMERY, GENERAL.   The Death of, etc.   (Anon.)   12°, pp. 68.
Norwich, 1777.

MONTGOMERY, (H. P.)   Tadmor, the Pride of the Desert.   12°, pp. 67.
Boston, 1865.

MONUMENTAL GRATITUDE, A, ATTEMPTED, ETC.   12°, pp. 10.   New London, 1727.

MOODS AND EMOTIONS IN RHYME.   (By H. A. R., *pseud.*)   12°, pp. 181.
Boston, 1855.

MOORE, (C. C., LL. D.)
Clement Clarke Moore, son of Bishop Benjamin Moore, was born in the city of New
York, July 15, 1779, graduated at Columbia College in 1798, was appointed Professor of
Biblical Learning in the New York General Theological Seminary in 1821, and subse-
quently filled the chair of Hebrew and Greek, and then that of Greek and Oriental Liter-
ature.   He died at Newport, R. I., July 10, 1863.

— Poems.   12°, pp. viii, 216.   New York, 1844.
— Santa Claus.   Sq. 8°, pp. 9.   New York, no date.
— The Night before Christmas.   Lg. 8°, pp. 15.   Philadelphia, no date.

Moore, (F.)

Frank Moore was born at Concord, N. H., December 17, 1828. He has published " The Rebellion Record," 11 vols., 8°, 1862-68, an invaluable work for reference. For some time he was Secretary of Legation at Paris.

— Songs and Ballads of the American Revolution. 16°, pp. xii, 394. New York, 1856.

Moore, (F. A.)

Frederic A. Moore wrote under the signature of "Eugene Sinclair." He resided at one time in Manchester, N. H., where he was engaged in literary work, and subsequently in Washington, D. C.

— Gems for You; from New Hampshire Authors. Prose and Poems. 12°, pp. 312. Manchester, 1850.

Moore, (J., M. D.)

A Philadelphia physician.

— Happiness. 12°, pp. 24. Philadelphia, 1878.
— Mad Dogs : A Farce. 12°, pp. 15. New York, no date.
— Meditations on the Divine Attributes. 12°, pp. 23. Philadelphia, 1879.
— Our Redeemer's Kingdom. 12°, pp. 24. Philadelphia, 1877.
— Saint Paul. 12°, pp. 22. Philadelphia, 1878.
— The City of God. 12°, pp. 23. Philadelphia, 1877.
— The Kimeliad. 18°, pp. 65. Philadelphia, 1867.
— The Necklace. 12°, pp. 24. Philadelphia, 1880.
— What is Man? 12°, pp. 24. Philadelphia, 1879.
— Willard Glazier, the Cavalier, etc. 12°, pp. 24. Philadelphia, 1880.

Moore, (J. M.) Lord Nial, etc. 12°, pp. 276. New York, 1834.

Moore, (J. S.) Abrah : The Conspirator. A Tragedy. 12°, pp. 51. Washington, 1847.
— The Oracle of Delphos, etc. 24°, pp. 87. Washington, 1844.

Moos, (H. M.) Mortara ; or, The Pope and His Inquisitors. 12°, pp. 171. Cincinnati, 1860.

More, (Innis.) The Twa Rats. After Burns. 16°, pp. 12. Washington, 1868.

Moreton, (———.) Miscellaneous Poems. 12°, pp. 288. Printed for Private Circulation. Philadelphia, 1875.

Morey, (A. C.)  Charlotte Corday.  A Tragedy in Five Acts.  12°, pp. 48.  New York, 1844.

Morford, (H.)  Music of the Spheres.  12°, pp. 12.  Granville, Middletown, N. J., 1840.
— Rhymes of an Editor.  12°, pp. 303.  London and New York, 1873.
— Rhymes of Twenty Years.  12°, pp. xii, 240.  New York, 1859.

Mormoniad.  (Anon.)  16°, pp. 95.  Boston, 1858.

Morning Watch, The.  (Anon.)  12°, pp. 175.  New York, 1850.

Moron.  A Tale of the Alhambra.  In Three Cantos, etc.  12°, pp. iv, 111.  Philadelphia, 1829.

Morris, (T. H.)  Mariana; or, The Coquette.  A Comedy.  12°, pp. 50.  Baltimore, 1868.

Morris, (G. P.)

George P. Morris was born at Philadelphia, October 10, 1802, removed to New York in early life and devoted himself to literary pursuits.  The periodicals with which he was connected were the *New York Mirror* and *Ladies' Literary Gazette*, 1823–42.  *New Mirror*, 1843–44, *Evening Mirror*, 1844 to close of '45.  *Home Journal* late in 1845 to his death, July 6, 1864.  He was distinguished, among other things, as a song-writer.  (See Allibone, pp. 1371–72.)

— Poems.  4th Edition.  18°, pp. 366.  New York, 1860.
— The Deserted Bride, etc.  8°, pp. 80.  New York, 1838.
— Same.  1843.
— Same.  With Illustrations, 1853.
— The Maid of Saxony.  12°, pp. 16.  New York, 1842.
— The Whip-Poor-Will.  Illustrated.  8°, pp. 62.  Philadelphia and New York, no date.

Morris, (Maria and Catherine M.)  Metrical Musings.  12°, pp. 188.  New York, 1856.

Morrison, (J. M.)  Clarsach Albin, etc.  12°, pp. 108.  Philadelphia, 1847.

Morse, (O. A.)  A Vindication of the Authorship of the Poem, "Rock Me to Sleep, Mother."  Sq. 8°, pp. 72.  New York, 1867.

The claimants to the authorship of this poem are Elizabeth A. C. Akers and Alexander M. W. Ball.  Mr. Morse favors the claim of Mr. Ball.

Mortimer, (J.)  The Theban Club; or, The Wall Street Critics.  24°, pp. 15.  Philadelphia, 1824.

Morton, (J. W.) The Pleasures of Home. 12°, pp. 132. Pittsburgh, 1841.

Morton, (Mrs. S. W.)

Sarah Wentworth Apthorpe was the wife of Hon. Perez Morton, Attorney General of Massachusetts. She wrote under the signature of " Philena."

— Beacon Hill. 4°, pp. 56. Boston, 1797.

— Ouabi. 8°, pp. viii, 52. Boston, 1790.

— My Mind and its Thoughts. Prose and Poetry. 8°, pp. xvii, 295. Boston, 1823.

— The Virtues of Society. 4°, pp. 46. Boston, 1799.

Morton, (T.) The Blind Girl. A Comic Opera. 18°, pp. 60. Boston, 1808.

Moses; or, The Man who Supposes Himself to be Moses no Moses at All. (Anon.) 24°, pp. 24. New York, 1866.

Moses, Song of. Written by the Columbia Warrior. (Anon.) 12°, pp. 11. No place, no date.

Moses, (T. P.) Leisure Thoughts in Prose and Verse. 12°, pp. 192. Portsmouth, N. H., 1849.

Mother Goose for Grown Folks. Illustrated by Billings. 12°, pp. 111. New York, 1868.

Motley Assembly. A Farce. 12°, pp. 15. Boston, 1779.

Mott, (A.) Biographical Sketches, etc., of Persons of Color. A few Poems in the volume. 12°, pp. 190. New York, 1826.

Moulton, (Louise Chandler.)

Ellen Louise Chandler was born at Pomfret, Conn., April 10, 1835, and in 1855 married William U. Moulton, a journalist, of Boston. She has been a frequent contributor to the periodicals of the day.

— Poems. 18°, pp. 153. Boston, 1878.

Mount Vernon. (Anon.) 8°, pp. 19. No place, no date.

A Dutch poem.

Mountain, (G. J., D. D.)

George Jehoshaphat Mountain was born at Norwich, England, July 27, 1789, educated at Trinity College, Cambridge, ordained Deacon in the Established Church in 1812, and Priest in 1813, was a clergyman in Frederickton and Quebec for several years, was Bishop of Montreal 1836–50, and of Quebec 1850–03, and died January 0, 1803.

— Songs of the Wilderness. 12°, pp. xxvi, 153. London, 1846.

Moving Times and no Friends. (Anon.) Sq. 12°. No place, 1765[?].

Mowatt, (Anna C.)

Anna Cora Ogden was born of American parents at Bordeaux, France, in 1819, was first married at the age of fifteen to Mr. Mowatt, a lawyer of New York, and subsequently to W. Ritchie, of Richmond, Va. She commenced her career as an actress about 1845. Her death occurred in 1870.

— Armand; or, The Peer and the Peasant. A Play. 12°, pp. 60. New York, 1851.

— Fashion; or, Life in New York. A Comedy. 12°, pp. 62. London, 1830.

— Same. 12°, pp. 62. New York, no date.

— Pelayo; or, The Cavern of Covandonga. (By Isabel, *pseud.*) 8°, pp. 204. New York, 1836.

— Plays. New and Revised Edition. 12°, pp. 60, 62. Boston, 1855.

— Reviewers Reviewed. 12°, pp. xii, 72. New York, 1837.

Mudge, (E.) Temperance Address to Seamen. 12°, pp. 12. New Bedford, 1837.

Muhlenberg, (W. A.)

William Augustus Muhlenberg, D. D., was born at Philadelphia, September 16, 1796, graduated at the University of Pennsylvania in 1814, was ordained in the Protestant Episcopal Church in 1817, and after preaching for several years he founded, in 1828, at Flushing, N. Y., the school which subsequently became St. Paul's College. The Church of the Holy Communion. N. Y., St. Luke's Hospital, N. Y., and the Colony of St. Johnland, on Long Island, were founded by him. He died April 8, 1877.

— I Would Not Live Alway, etc. 12°, pp. 66. New York, 1860.

Muller, (A. A.)

Rev. Albert A. Muller, an Episcopal clergyman, was Rector of Christ Church, Charleston.

— Gospel Melodies, etc. 12°, pp. 104. Charleston, 1823.

Multiplication Table in Rhyme. (By a Lady. Anon.) 18°, pp. 15. Boston, 1830.

Munday, (Lurania A. H.) Acacian Lyrics, etc. 12°, pp. 178. Cincinnati, 1860.

Munford, (R.)

Robert Munford was an officer in the Revolutionary army, and the author of one or two political dramas. This Collection of Plays and Poems was made by his son William.

Munford, (R.) — *Continued.*

— Collection of Plays and Poems. 12°, pp. xii, 206. Petersburg, 1798.

— Same. 12°, pp. 189. Richmond, 1798.

Munford, (W.)

William Munford was born at Mecklenberg county, Va., August 15, 1775, graduated at William and Mary College, studied law, for several years, served in the House of Delegates, was elected a member of the Privy Council of State, and for several years occupied important posts of trust and honor in his native State. The work of the leisure years of his life was " Homer's Iliad." He died at Richmond, June 21, 1825.

— Homer's Iliad. 2 vols. 8°, pp. xii, 452, 524. Boston, 1846.

Munson, (A. D.) Lyrics of Trade. 12°, pp. 73. New York, 1865.

Murden, (Mrs., married name of Miss Eliza Crawley.) Poems. 2d Edition. 12°, pp. 155. Charleston, 1827.

Murdock, (J.) The Triumphs of Love ; or, Happy Reconciliation. A Comedy. 1st Edition. 12°, pp. 83. Philadelphia, 1795.

Murdock, (J. E.)

James Edward Murdock, the well-known actor and elocutionist, was born at Philadelphia, January 25, 1811, and has attained to a high rank in his profession. For some time, during the civil war, he was on the staff of General Rousseau. He did good service by his readings in raising funds for hospitals, etc. After the war he returned to his profession.

— Patriotism in Poetry and Prose. Selections. 12°, pp. 172. Philadelphia, 1866.

Murdock, (W.) Poems and Songs. 12°, pp. 150. St. John, N. B., 1860.

Murphy, (W. D.) The Burial of W. Colgate. 8°, pp. 8. New York, 1857.

Musings at an Evening Club in Boston. (Anon.) 16°, pp. 53. Boston, 1819.

Musical Miscellany, The Boston. 18°, pp. 192. Boston, 1811.

Muzzy, (Mrs. Harriet.) Poems. 12°, pp. iv, 200. New York, 1821.

Myers, (P. H.)

Peter Hamilton Myers was born at Herkimer, N. Y., in August, 1813, and for some time was a member of the Brooklyn bar. He was the author of several historical romances. His later residence was in Auburn, N. Y., where he died in October, 1878. Mr. M. was the author of other poems, and of several prose productions.

— Ensenore. 8°, pp. 104. New York, 1840.

MYNEHIEUR VON HERRICK HEIMELMAN, THE DANCING MASTER; OR,
THE CONFLUENCE OF NASSAU STREET AND MAIDEN LANE, AS IT
WAS WHILOM, ETC.  (Anon.)  12°, pp. 19.  New York, 1824.

MYSTERIES OF ODD FELLOWSHIP.  A Farce.  12°, pp. 32.  Philadelphia, no date.

MYSTICAL CRAFT, THE.  (Anon.)  12°, pp. 24.  New York, 1844.


NACK, (J.)

James Nack was born in the city of New York about the year 1807.  In consequence
of an accident he became deaf at the age of nine.  He early developed remarkable mental
ability, especially in the acquisition of languages.  He published a volume of poems written between the fourteenth and seventeenth years of his age which showed a singular
poetical talent.

— Earl Rupert, etc.  12°, pp. xx, 219.  New York, 1839.
— Legend of the Rocks, etc.  12°, pp. 204.  New York, 1827.
— The Immortal, etc.  12°, pp. vi, 172.  New York, 1850.
— The Romance of the Ring, etc.  12°, pp. 232.  New York, 1859.

NAHANT: THINGS TO BE SEEN BY THE SEA, ETC.  (Anon.)  8°, pp. 6.
Boston, 1862.

NAPOLEON BONAPARTE, THE SECOND DOWNFALL OF.  (Anon.)  16°,
pp. 11.  No place, no date.

NATURE, ETC.  (Anon.)  12°, pp. 36.  Boston, 1839.

NATURE, THE TEACHINGS OF.  (Anon.)  18°, pp. 84.  Boston, 1845.

NAUTILUS, THE.  Contributions for the Seamen's Missions.  (Anon.)
12°, pp. 63.  Philadelphia, 1855.

NEAL, (J.)

John Neal was born at Portland, Me., October 25, 1793, was in commercial business
for a time in Baltimore, then studied law, and was admitted to the bar.  His reputation
rests upon his writings, which have been very numerous and of a varied character, for an
account of which see Allibone, p. 1804.  He died June 20, 1876.

— Niagara, etc.  12°, pp. xiii, 143.  Baltimore, 1818.

NEBRASKA: PERSONAL AND POLITICAL.  (Anon.)  12°, pp. 42.  Boston
and Cleveland, 1854.

NEEDHAM, (J. R.)  The Pleasures of Poverty.  12°, pp. 12.  New
York, 1837.

NELLIE GREY.  (By S. C. S.  Anon.)  Sq. 24°, pp. 7.  Philadelphia,
1869.

Nelmes, (T. E.)  The Lays of a Wanderer.  12°, pp. 117.  New York, 1856.

Neptune, The Court of, etc.  18°, pp. 106.  New York, 1817.

Nettleton, (A.)  Village Hymns.  24°, pp. 452.  New York, 1828.

New Bedford Traders in Rhyme.  (Anon.)  18°, pp. 23.  New Bedford, 1860.

Newell, (R. H.)

Robert Henry Newell, whose *nom de plume* was Orpheus C. Kerr, was born in the city of New York, December 13, 1830, was liberally educated, and for a time was in business. He was the literary editor of the *New York Mercury*, 1858–63, moved to California in 1863, was an editor of the *New York World*, 1869–74, and subsequently took charge of *The Hearth and Home*.

— The Martyr President.  12°, pp. 43.  New York, 1865.

— The Palace Beautiful, etc.  12°, pp. 178.  New York, 1865.

— Versatilites.  12°, pp. iv, 266.  Boston and New York, 1871.

New England Drama, The.  Founded on Incidents contained in the New England Tale.  12°, pp. 72.  Dedham, 1825.

New England; or, The Age of Brass.  Dedicated to the President and Gentlemen of the Society of Plymouth.  (Anon.)  Sq. 16°, pp. 28.  New York, 1875.

New Fashioned Girl, The.  A Story of To-Day.  12°, pp. 30.  New York, 1870.

New Hampshire Book, The.  Names of Editors not given.  Prose and Poems.  12°, pp. x, 391.  Nashua, 1842.

New Hampshire, Festival of the Sons of.  November 7, 1849.  Several Poems in the volume.  8°, pp. 178.  Boston, 1850.

Newman, (B. J.)  The Eagle of Washington.  A Story of the Revolution.  12°, pp. xiv, 152.  Louisville, 1859.

Newman, (J. C.)  The Harmonies of Creation.  16°, pp. xvi, 256.  Baltimore, 1836.

New Orleans Book, The.  (Edited by Robert G. Barnwell.)  Prose and Poetical Extracts.  12°, pp. xii, 348.  New Orleans, 1851.

New Orleans, The Battle of.  (Anon.)  16°, pp. 36.  Baltimore, 1825.

New Year's Address, A. A Circular, etc. (Anon.) 12°, pp. 24. Providence, 1857.

New York. A Glance at. (Anon.) 12°, pp. 32. New York, no date.

New York Book of Poetry, The. A Compilation. (Anon.) 8°, pp. 353. New York, 1837.

New York. The Streets of. ("Sphinx.") 12°, pp. 95. Florence, Italy, 1856.

Niagara. By a member of the Ohio Bar. (Anon.) 8°, pp. 11. New York, 1848.

Niagara, The Falls of. (Anon.) 8°, pp. 30. New York, 1829.

Nicholas, (S. H.) Monte Rosa. The Epic of the Alp. 12°, pp. 148. Boston, 1883.

Nichols, (J. H.) Poem delivered before the Association of the Alumni of Washington College, August 3, 1842. 8°, pp. 16. New Haven, 1842.

Nichols, (J. N.) The New England Coquette, from the history of the celebrated Eliza Wharton. 12°, pp. 44. Salem, no date.

Nichols, (Mrs. Louisa H.) Poems. 12°, pp. 110. New York, 1859.

Nichols, (Mrs. Rebecca S.)

Rebecca S. Reed, born at Greenwich, N. J., married in 1838 to Willard Nichols, publisher of a paper in St. Louis. She assisted him in the editorial department, and subsequently lived ten years, 1841–51, in Cincinnati, where she engaged in literary pursuits. She acquired a justly deserved reputation for her poetical productions.

— Bernice; or, The Curse of Minna, etc. 12°, pp. 216. Cincinnati, 1844.

— Songs of the Heart, etc. 8°, pp. 319. Philadelphia and Cincinnati, 1851.

Nicholson, (E. G.) The Votaries of Twilight. 8°, pp. 32. 1840.

Nicholson, (G. W. H.) The Ages of Sin; or, Hints for Critics. A Satire. 12°, pp. 82. Philadelphia, 1851.

Mr. Nicholson was a Baltimore lawyer.

Nicholson, (G. W. S.) A Budget of Youthful Fancy. 12°, pp. 195. Philadelphia, 1850.

— Poems of the Heart. 12°, pp. 120. Philadelphia, 1850.

NICOLAUS, (J. SECUNDUS.) Epithalmium, The; or, Nuptial Song. Translated by Dr. John Nott. 4°, pp. 64. Philadelphia, privately printed, 1856.

Only twenty copies.

NIGHT. (Anon.) 8°, pp. 60. New York, 1845.

NIGHT, A FOGGY, AT NEWPORT. (Anon.) 12°, pp. 39. St. Louis, 1860.

NIGHT WATCHES; OR, THE PEACE OF THE CROSS. (By E. L. Anon.) 12°, pp. xii, 248. Philadelphia, 1853.

NILES, (S.) .

Samuel Niles was born in 1674, graduated at Harvard in 1699, and for some time preached in a district in Rhode Island called "Ministerial Lands." He was ordained Pastor of the Second Congregational church in Braintree, Mass., May 23, 1711. He died May 1, 1762.

— Essay on God's Wonder-Working Providence for New England, etc. 18°, pp. 34. London, 1747.

NINE MUSES, FAGNINI'S. Sq. 16°, pp. 21. No place, no date.

NOAH, (M. M.)

Mordecai Manuel Noah was born at Philadelphia, July 19, 1785, removed to Charleston, S. C., studied law, and interested himself in politics, was consul to Morocco 1813-16, settled in New York, and for many years was actively engaged in journalism. His attempt to establish a Jewish Colony on Grand Island, in the Niagara river, is well known. He died in New York City, March 22, 1851.

— The Fortress of Sorrento. 18°, pp. 28. New York, 1868.

— The Grecian Captive; or, The Fall of Athens. 18°, pp. iv, 48. New York, 1822.

NOBLE, (L. L.)

Louis Legrand Noble was born in Ostego county, N. Y., in 1812, became, in 1840, a clergyman in the Protestant Episcopal Church, preached in North Carolina, then at Catskill, N. Y., and in 1854 was called to be Rector of a church in Chicago. He published a memoir of Thomas Cole, the painter.

— The Lady Angeline. A Lay of the Apalachians, etc. 12°, pp. viii, 118. New York, 1856.

NOCTE COGITATA. Latin of Young's Night Thoughts. 12°, pp. 21. Caroloppidii, Mass., 1786.

NORTHAU, (W. K.) Macbeth Travestie. 12°, pp. 36. New York, 1848.

NORTHMORE, (T.)

Thomas Northmore was an English poet, born near Exeter, and received his education at Jesus College, Cambridge. He resided on his estate, occupying his time, in part, in literary pursuits. (See "London Review," ii, pp. 305-75, for a severe criticism of the following poem.)

Northimore, (T.) — *Continued.*

— Washington; or, Liberty Restored.  A Poem in Ten Books.  12°, pp. viii, 253.  Baltimore, 1809.

Norton, (A.)

Andrews Norton, the eminent Biblical scholar, was born at Hingham, Mass., December 31, 1786, graduated at Harvard in 1804, and, for many years, was connected with the University as tutor, professor and librarian.  (See Allibone, pp. 1437–38.)  He died at Newport, R. I., September 18, 1853.

— Verses.  8°, pp. 55.  No place, 1853.

North Star, The.  The Poetry of Freedom.  By Her Friends.  (Anon.)  18°, pp. vi, 118.  Philadelphia, 1840.

Norwich, Conn., Jubilee, September 7th and 8th, 1859.  Several Poems in the volume.  Lg. 8°, pp. 304.  Norwich, Conn., 1859.

Nothing to Do.  (Anon.)  Illustrated.  12°, pp. 48.  Boston, 1857.

Nothing to Eat.  (Anon.)  Illustrated.  12°, pp. 117.  New York, 1857.

Nothing to Wear.  (Anon.)  Sq. 18°, not paged.  Philadelphia, no date.

Nothing to You.  (Anon.)  Illustrated by Howard.  12°, pp. 68.  New York, 1857.

Notice sur la vie et Les Ecrits de M. Joel Barlow, Ministre Plenipotentaire des Etats Unis d'Amerique, etc.  4°, pp. 31.  No place, 1813.

This volume is a French translation of Book I. of Barlow's Columbiad.

Nowell, (E. P.)  Ballad of Jefferson D.  24°, pp. 14.  Portsmouth, 1865.

Nowell, (Sarah A.)  Poems.  12°, pp. 208.  Boston, 1850.

Nourse, (J.)  The Book of Psalms.  24°, pp. 224.  New York, 1842.

Noyes, (G. R.)

George Rapall Noyes was born at Newburyport, Mass., March 6, 1798, graduated at Harvard in 1818, and after preaching several years, was appointed, 1840, professor in his *alma mater*, and continued in office till his death, June 3, 1868.

— Amended Version of the Book of Job.  Lg. 8°, pp. ix, 116.  Cambridge, 1827.

Nunes, (J. A., U. S. A.)  Day Dreams.  12°, pp. 134.  Philadelphia, 1863.

Nutall, (W.)  Wayside Flowers.  32°, pp. 82.  Philadelphia, 1845.

Nye, (J. W.)  Offering of Friendship.  12°, pp. 168.  Lynn, Mass., 1860.

Oakes, (R. A.)  Poems.  12°, pp. 72.  New York, 1859.

Oakes, (U.)

Urian Oakes, the fourth President of Harvard College, was born in England about the year 1631, was brought to America when a child by his parents, graduated at Harvard in 1649, returned to England, and for some time was a preacher there, under the Protectorate, having charge of the living of Titchfield, Hampshire. This position he held till the Restoration of Charles II, when he was compelled to give up his parish. In 1671 he came back to this country, and was called to the pastorate of the church in Cambridge, Mass. Having been elected President of Harvard, he entered upon the duties of his office April 7, 1675, still retaining his connection with the church in Cambridge. He died July 25, 1681. (See "Sibley's Harvard Graduates," vol. i, pp. 173–185.)

— An Elegy upon the Death of the Reverend Mr. Thomas Shepard, late Teacher of the Church at Charlestown, in New England, etc.  Lg. 16°, pp. 16.  Cambridge, printed by Samuel Green, 1677.

The copy in "The Harris Collection" is No. 835 of the Brinley sale, and was purchased for $57.50, is in every respect perfect, and bound in the highest style of the binder's art.

President Oakes held a high place in the regards of his cotemporaries. Professor Tyler says of him: "He was distinguished in his day for the unsurpassed elegance and fluency of his Latin; and with respect to his English, it is, perhaps, the richest prose style; it furnishes the most brilliant examples of originality, breadth and force of thought, set aglow by flame of passion, by flame of imagination, to be met with in our sermon-literature from the settlement of our country down to the Revolution." He adds that "the one example that is left to us of his verse, reaches the highest point touched by American poetry during the same era. It was within a few days after the death of 'Mr. Shepard' that Oakes published his elegy, a poem in fifty-two six-lined stanzas; not without some mechanical defects; blurred also by some patches of the prevailing theological jargon; yet upon the whole, affluent, stately, pathetic; beautiful and strong with the beauty and strength of true imaginative vision." Dr. Abiel Holmes says: "This elegy of considerable length . . . . rises, in my judgment, far above the poetry of the day. It is of Pindaric measure, and is plaintive, pathetic and replete with imagery."

This is high praise, but if the Harvard President be judged by the poetic standard of those early Puritan days, probably it is not exaggerated.

Oakley, (J.)  Our Village.  Delivered at Flatbush, N. Y., February 23, 1863.  12°, pp. 36.  New York, 1863.

O'Brien, (Lieut. L., 8th U. S. Infantry.)  The Unpublished Writings. Transcribed from the Original by his Son.  12°, pp. 17.  Leavenworth, 1867.

OBERHOLTZER, (MRS. S. L.)

Sarah Louisa Vickers was born at Unchlan, Christie county, Pa., May 20, 1841, married John Oberholtzer in 1801, and resides, as the season of the year may be, at Norristown, Pa., and Longport, N. Y.   She has contributed not a little to the periodical literature of the day.

— Come for Arbutus, etc.   12°, pp. 147.   Philadelphia, 1882.
— Daisies of Verse.   12°, pp. 152.   Philadelphia, 1886.
— Violet Lee, and other Poems.   12°, pp. 143.   Philadelphia, 1873.

OCCURRENCES OF THE TIMES; OR, THE TRANSACTIONS OF FOUR DAYS.   A
    Farce.   16°, pp. 23.   Boston, 1789.

OCEAN WAVES IN LYRIC STRAINS.   (Anon.)   8°, pp. viii, 88.   Pitts-
    burgh, Pa., 1856.

ODE SUGGESTED BY REMBRANDT PEALE'S NATIONAL PORTRAIT OF WASH-
    INGTON.   8°, pp. 8.   Philadelphia, 1824.

ODELL, (J.[?])   The Times.   A Satirical Poem, written during the Ameri-
    can Revolution, by the Rev. Mr. Odell.   Sm. 4°, pp. 40.   New
    Jersey.   Printed but not published.   No date.
— Same.   12°, pp. 26.   No place, no date.

ODIORNE, (T.)

Thomas Odiorne was born about the year 1780, and died in 1851.

— The Progress of Refinement and Influence of Nature.   18°, pp. x,
    176.   Boston, 1792.

In its outward dress, one of the most attractive books in the collection.

OEHLSCHLAEGER, (C. J.)   The Tragedy of Reason and other Poems.
    12°, pp. 103.   Utica, 1882.

OGEE, (QUIRK, LL. D., *pseud.*)   Extracts from Humbugiana, etc.   12°,
    pp. 24.   Gotham, 1847.

OJEBWAY AND ENGLISH HYMNS.   (Compiled.)   18°, pp. 236.   Toronto,
    1860.

OLAVIDE, (D. P.)   El Escandalo.   Poema Christiano.   18°, pp. 11.
    Guayaquil, 1839.
— El Fin del Hombre.   Poema Christiano.   18°, pp. 12.   Guayaquil,
    1839.

OLD BUCK'S FEAST ; OR, THE POWER OF OFFICE.　By Dryden, JR., (*pseud.*)
　　12°, pp. 15.　No place, no date.

OLD FASHIONED 'LECTION, AND THE CAKE.　(Anon.)　32°, pp. 12.
　　Hartford, 1869.

OLIO ; OR, SATIRICAL HODGE PODGE.　(Anon.)　8°, pp. iv, 46.　1801.

> A satirical poem written at a period of intense political excitement by a warm admirer
> of Jefferson.
> In an "Introductory Letter to a Friend," the writer says : "The characters of the
> Poem are drawn from *real* Life and Conduct ; no fancied Production of the Pen or Mind, as
> you know. And if the Lights and Shades, or, as the Artist would term it, the Claraobscura
> had been well managed, the whole would have appeared to greater advantage. You may
> call it a Family Picture, if you please, or at least the whole are politically related, and the
> only variation you will find, is where the change of matter has produced it, merely as a
> relief to the Reader by way of contrast."

OLIO, THE.　(Anon.)　18°, pp. 104.　New York, 1823.

OLIVER, (I.)

> Miss Isabella Oliver was the daughter of James Oliver, Esq., of Cumberland county,
> Penn., "a worthy citizen, an eminent mathematician, of whom she was deprived when
> about fourteen years of age." Her opportunities for acquiring an education were of the
> most limited character, and these poems were composed while she was engaged in the
> common affairs of life, or while taking a walk, and finished without putting pen to paper.
> The copy in " The Harris Collection " is richly bound, and is one of the varieties of the
> Collection.

—Poems on Various Subjects.　12°, pp. 220.　Carlisle, 1805.

OLIVER, (J. E.)　Class Poem of 1849, Harvard.　12°, pp. 12.　"Printed
　　not published."

OLIVER, (ISABELLA.)　Poems.　16°, pp. 220.　Carlisle, 1805.

OLIVER, (P.)

> Peter Oliver was born at Boston March 26, 1713, and graduated at Harvard in 1730.
> Subsequently he filled several stations of important civil trust in Plymouth county, Mass.
> Although not a professional lawyer he was made a Judge, September 14, 1756, and after
> serving in a subordinate capacity for fifteen years, he was, in 1771, made Chief Justice. It
> was a time of great excitement in the Commonwealth in consequence of what were
> regarded as the oppressive acts of the Mother Country. The House of Representatives, in
> March, 1774, voted salaries for the Superior Judges, and forbade them to receive anything
> from the royal treasury. Four of the Judges acquiesced in the new arrangement, but
> Oliver refused compliance. The House impeached him and he was suspended from office.
> Openly siding with the Tories, when the British troops evacuated Boston he left with
> them, and after various fortunes went to England. He resided chiefly in Birmingham,
> where he died October 13, 1791.
> Judge Oliver received from Oxford, in 1776, the degree of J. C. D. He is supposed to
> have been the author of No. xxix of the famous "Pietas et Gratulatio," the elegant quarto
> volume in which were celebrated the death of George II, the accession of George III,

OLIVER, (P.) — *Continued.*

with the Epithalamia on the marriage of the Princess Charlotte. The subject of the poem referred to below was the son of Rev. Samuel Willard, the pastor of the Old South Church, and was born in Boston in 1680, and graduated at Harvard in 1698. For a time he was Tutor and Librarian in the college. Having made a somewhat exteded tour in Europe, he returned to his native land, and was appointed Secretary of the Colony, which office he held for thirty-nine years. He was also Judge of Probate and a member of the Council. "He was as remarkable for his aimable manners as for his piety." His death took place in 1756.

— Poem sacred to the memory of the Honorable Josiah Willard, late Secretary of the Province of the Massachusetts Bay, etc. (Anon.) Lg. 18°, pp. 16. Boston, 1757.

A choice copy richly bound.

OPDYKE LIBEL SUIT, THE. (Anon.) 8°, pp. 62. New York, 1865.

OPPRESSION. By an American, with notes by a North Briton. 8°, pp. 20. Boston, 1765.

ORGALLEZ, (M.) Poesias. Sq. 16°, pp. 110. Habana, 1858.

ORMUSD's TRIUMPH. (Anon.) 12°, pp. 100. New York, 1842.

ORNE, (CAROLINE F.) Sweet Auburn, etc. 12°, pp. 196. Cambridge, 1844.

ORPHAN TWINS, THE. (Anon.) 12°, pp. 100. New York, 1849.

ORPHAN's SOUVENIR. A Rochester Book. (Anon.) 16°, pp. 200. Rochester, 1843.

ORTON, (J. R.) Arnold, etc. 12°, pp. 144. New York, 1854.

OSBORNE, (L.)

Laughton Osborne was born in New York City not far from 1806, and graduated at Columbia College in 1827. He died in 1878.

In his "Sketches of the Literati," Edgar A. Poe, whose genius in some respects was akin to that of Osborne, alludes to this poet. Duycklink says that all his books which were published anonymously "have been of a character to excite attention. They are bold, discursive, play some tricks with good taste and propriety, and upon the whole are not less remarkable for their keenness of perception than for their want of judgment in its display. With more skill and a just proportion, the writer's powers would have made a deeper impression on the public. As it is, he has rather added to the curiosities of litera - ture than to the familiar companions of the library."

In addition to the three volumes referred to below, Laughton wrote *Sixty Years of the Life of Jeremy Lewis, The Dream of Alla-ad-Deen, from the Romance of Anastasia, The Confessions of a Poet, The Vision of Rubeta, an Epic Story of the Island of Manhattan, with Illustrations done on Stone.* This last satire, which was published in Boston in 1838, and brought out in an elegant octavo form, was especially aimed at Colonel Stone, of the *Commercial Advertiser.* It contains also a fierce onslaught on Wordsworth. "Arthur Carryll" is considered the most creditable of the author's works.

Osborne, (L.) — *Continued.*

— Arthur Carryl. Cantos First and Second, etc. 8°. New York, 1841.

— Bianca Lapello. A Tragedy. 12°, pp. 419. New York, 1868.

— Calvary, Virginia. Tragedies. 12°, pp. 200. New York, 1867.

Osgood, (Frances S.)

Frances S. Locke was born at Boston, June 18, 1811, and passed the early part of her life in Hingham, Mass. Under the signature of "Florence," she wrote a number of short poems which attracted considerable attention. In 1835 she married Mr. S. S. Osgood, a then rising artist to whom she sat for her portrait. They went to London soon after their marriage and remained abroad four years, both husband and wife gaining well deserved reputation by the productions of pencil and pen. In 1840 they returned to the United States, and passed most of the remainder of their lives in the city of New York. Her death from consumption took place at Hingham, May 12, 1850. The last production of her pen was prophetic of the near approach of death:

> "I'm going through the eternal gates
> Ere June's sweet roses blow;
> Death's lonely angel leads me there,
> And it is sweet to go."

Thomas Buchanan Read, one of the frontispieces of whose beautiful volume "The Female Poets of America" is a portrait of Mrs. Osgood, says: "A charming naivete, an exquisite simplicity, an inimitable peace, with at times a thrilling and impassioned earnestness are Mrs. Osgood's characteristics as a writer."

— A Letter About the Lions. 24°, pp. 24. New York, 1849.

— A Wreath of Wild Flowers. 2d Edition. 12°, pp. 364. London and Boston, 1842.

— Poems. 8°, pp. 466. Philadelphia, 1849.

— Same. Lg. 8°. Philadelphia, 1850.

— Same. 18°, pp. 252. New York, 1861. Blue and Gold Series.

— The Casket of Fate. 32°, pp. 67. Boston, 1840.

— The Snow Drop. Sq. 24°, pp. 88. Providence, 1842.

Our Book. A Call from Salem's Watch-Towers in behalf of Unitarian Churches. A few Poems in the volume. 12°, pp. iv, 72. Salem, 1844.

Outcroppings. Selections of California Verses. Sq. 16°, pp. 144. San Francisco and New York, 1866.

Outarson, (F. J.) Poem. Tribune Dinner, January 14, 1855. Report of the Proceedings. 8°, pp. 32. New York, 1855.

Owen, (M.) Ballads of Portland. 24°, pp. 160. Portland, 1874.

27

## OWEN, (R. D.)

Robert Dale Owen was born at Glasgow, Scotland, November 7, 1801, came to the United States in 1823, and was identified with the New Harmony, Indiana, Communistic Colony. He was a member of Congress two terms, and distinguished himself by introducing the bill for the establishment of the Smithsonian Institution. For five years he was United States Minister to Naples. He rendered valuable service to the country in the Civil War. His death took place June 24, 1872.

— Pocahontas.	8°, pp. 47.	New York, 1837.

## PABODIE, (W. J.)

William Jewett Pabodie was born at Providence, R. I., not far from the year 1815. He was a lawyer by profession and practiced in his native city. He died in 1870.

— Calidore : A Legendary Poem.	8°, pp. 48.	Boston, 1859.

## PACKARD, (HANNAH J.)

She was born at Duxbury, Mass., April 15, 1815, and in early life developed remarkable poetic talent, and ranked high as a scholar. She died August 10, 1831. For notice of her poems see American Monthly Review, ii. 73.

— The Choice.	A Tragedy, etc.	18°, pp. 142.	Boston, 1832.

## PAGE, (ANN.)	A Tribute for Pupils designed for Sabbath Schools.	Vol. 1.	18°, pp. 119.	Providence, 1842.

## PAINE, (R. T., JR.)

Robert Treat Paine, Jr., originally bore the name of Thomas. As this was the name of "Tom" Paine, the well-known author of "The Age of Reason," the subject of this sketch, at the age of twenty-eight, pleading that he had no *Christian* name, presented a petition to the Massachusetts Legislature asking that he might be allowed to take that of his distinguished father, Robert Treat Paine, celebrated in American History as one of the signers of the Declaration of Independence. Hence the Jr. attached to his name. He was born in Taunton, Mass., December 9, 1773, and graduated at Harvard in 1792. Among his classmates were Professor Levi Hedge, and that eminent Greek scholar Professor John Snelling Popkin, and the Hon. William Sullivan. It is related that he became aware of his possession of the poetic gift in the following way : "One of his classmates wrote a squib on him in verse, on the college wall, and Paine on consultation with his friends was advised to retaliate in kind." He found on making the attempt that he could do it, and thereafter he wrote many productions in verse. So accusomed did he become to write in rhyme that having entered a counting house to fit himself for a business career, "he made entries in his day-book in poetry, and once made out a charter-party in the same style." He found time while occupied with the duties of his apprenticeship to prepare a number of articles for the "Seat of the Muses," of the "Massachusetts Magazine." When the Federal street theatre was opened, February 4, 1794, he wrote the prize prologue for the occasion. Among the actresses was Miss Baker, a young lady of sixteen, with whom he fell in love, and subsequently, to the very great displeasure of his father, who, for the act, turned him out of doors, he married her. He now abandoned his purpose to enter mercantile life, and gave himself up to literary pursuits, the productions of his pen being very popular and for a time lucrative. In 1800 he was a student at law under Mr., afterwards Chief Justice, Parsons, and was admitted to the bar, but drawn away by the fascinations of the

Paine, (R. T., Jr.) — *Continued.*

theatre he gave up his profession and for several years lived a somewhat shiftless sort of life, and died in Boston, November 13, 1811. His song, "Adams and Liberty, " was very famous, and yielded him a profit of more than seven hundred and fifty dollars.

— Monody on the Death of Sir John Moore. 8°, pp. 32. Boston, 1811.
— The Hasty-Pudding, etc. 18°, pp. 32. Hallowell, 1815.
— Works. 8°, pp. lxxxiv, 454. Boston, 1812.
— The Invention of Letters. 8°, pp. 10. Boston, 1819.

This poem was delivered at commencement at Harvard in 1795, on the occasion of his taking the degree of A. M. In the poem were some lines referring to Jacobinism which the college authorities erased. Paine however spoke them just as they were written, and, perhaps, partly as the result of his boldness, the poem became very popular. Two large editions of it were published and yielded the author the generous sum of fifteen hundred dollars.

— The Ruling Passion. 8°, pp. 32. Boston, 1797.

This poem delivered befor the Phi Beta Kappa Society was also a source of pecuniary profit to Paine, yielding him some twelve hundred dollars.

Paine's, Tom., Jests. 8°, pp. 72. Philadelphia, 1796.

Pains of Memory, etc. 12°, pp. 115. New York, 1808.

Palmer, (B. F.) Poem before the Society of the Sons of New England in Pennsylvania, December 22, 1858. 8°, pp. 16. Philadelphia, 1859.

Palmer, (J. C., U. S. N.) Thulia: A Tale of the Antarctic. 8°, pp. 72. New York, 1843.

Palmer, (J. W.) The Poetry of Compliment and Courtship. A Selection. 12°, pp. xx, 219. Boston, 1868.

Palmer, (R.)

Ray Palmer was born at Little Compton, R. I., November 12, 1808, graduated at Yale College in 1830, having among his classmates Henry Barnard, LL. D., and Professor Elias Loomis, received his theological education at the divinity school in Yale, was ordained a Congregational Minister in 1835, and preached in Bath, Me., Albany, N. Y., etc. Union College, in 1852, conferred on him the degree of D. D. The Devotional Hymns of Dr. Palmer take very high rank in English Hymnology. His present residence (1880) is Newark, N. J.

— Hymns and Sacred Pieces, etc. 8°, pp. 195. Albany, 1865.
— The Spirit's Life. 8°, pp. 16. Boston, 1837.

Palmetto Pictures. (Anon.) 12°, pp. 67. New York, 1863.

PANTHEON, THE NEW; OR, THE AGE OF BLACK.  12°, pp. 47.  New
    York, 1860.

PAPENDICK, (G.)  The Stranger.  12°, pp. 76.  Boston, no date.

PARADISE LOST; OR, THE GREAT DRAGON CAST OUT.  (By Lucian Redi-
    vivus, *pseud.*)  18°, pp. 138.  New York, no date.

PARAPHRASE OF THE FIRST FEW CHAPTERS OF THE BOOK OF GENESIS.
    (Anon.)  No place, no date.  Imperfect.  8°.

PARK, (R.)

> Roswell Park, D. D., was born at Lebanon, Conn., October 1, 1807, and graduated at
> the United States Military Academy, West Point, and at Union College, in July, 1831. He
> was appointed Lieutenant of Engineers and served in that capacity five years, 1831–36. The
> next six years, 1836–42, he was Professor of Natural Philosophy and Chemistry in the Uni-
> versity of Pennsylvania.  In 1843 he was admitted to orders in the Episcopal church,
> taught for a time in Annapolis, and subsequently in Connecticut.  For seven years, 1852–
> 59, he was President of Racine College, and Chancellor, 1859–63.  He removed in the
> latter year to Chicago where he founded a school, and died July 16, 1869.  He published,
> 1841, Pantology; 1840, Sketch of West Point, and in 1853, a Hand-book for European
> travel.

— Jerusalem, etc.  12°, pp. 309.  New York, 1857.

PARKE, (J.)  The Lyric Works of Horace, translated into English verse,
    to which are added a number of Original Poems.  By a Native of
    America.  8°, pp. xli, 334.  Philadelphia, 1786.

> The name of the author is not found on the title-page.  The compiler has given it as
> above, the name Colonel John Parke having been written by some one under the words
> "By a Native of America."  There is nothing to indicate who he was, and nothing about
> him can be learned from numerous sources of information at hand which treat of biographi-
> cal matters.  The volume is dedicated to George Washington, Esq., etc.  The author says:
> "Many of these translations were the work of my youthful days when I scarce had num-
> bered fifteen years in the scale of my existence; others were written at a more advanced
> period of life; some in the retirement of a winter cantonment; and others in the acciden-
> tal quietude of a camp."

PARKER, (D.)  Phrenology, etc.  8°, pp. 40.  Lowell, 1859.

PARKER, (H. W.)

> Henry Webster Parker was born at Danby, N. Y., in 1822, and graduated at Amherst
> College in 1843.  Mr. Parker has been a contributor to the "North American Review,"
> and other periodicals, and some time since was appointed a Professor in the Agricultural
> College at Amherst, Mass.

— Poems.  12°, pp. 238.  Auburn, 1850.

— The Story of a Soul.  8°, pp. 46.  New York, 1852.

PARMLY, (E.)  Poem.  Address to the Graduating Class of the Balti-
    more College of Dental Surgery.  8°, pp. 30.  Baltimore, 1847.

PARMLY, (E. AND A. M.)  Memorials Written During the Illness and After the Death of Three Little Boys.  (By those who love them. Anon.)  8°, pp. 52.  New York, 1843.

PARRIS, (S. B., M. D.)

Samuel Bartlett Parris was born at Kingston, Mass., January 30, 1806.  He commenced the study of the languages at the age of six years.  When he was ten he was presented for examination to enter college, and was admitted, but did not commence the course of study for about two years.  He graduated at Brown University in 1821, at the age of fifteen, with honors, the Greek oration having been assigned to him, and was admitted to the practice of medicine August 31, 1825, being a little more than nineteen years of age, and commenced his professional life in Attleborough, Mass., in October of the same year.  His death occurred September 21, 1827.

— Remains of.  Comprising Miscellaneous Poems, etc.  12°, pp. xii. Biographical Sketch, 13–58.  Poems, 59–168.  Prose, 169–312. Plymouth, 1829.

PARSONS, (T. W.)

Thomas William Parsons, M. D., was born at Boston, August 18, 1819, was educated at the Boston Latin school and in Europe, became a dentist and received from Harvard College, in 1853, the degree of M. D.  Some of his best poems appeared in the "Knickerbocker," etc., and were warmly praised.  Some of his works have been beautifully illustrated and elegantly bound, furnishing fine specimens of American typography and binding.

— Dante's Inferno.  8°, pp. viii, 83.  Boston, 1843.
— Poems.  Sq. 16°, pp. viii, 189.  Boston, 1854.
— The Magnolia.  4°, pp. 58.  Boston, 1866.
— The Old House at Sudbury.  12°, pp. 114.  Cambridge, 1870.
— The Willey House and Sonnets.  12°, pp. 42.  Cambridge. 1875.

PARTHENON, THE.  4°, pp. 40.  New York, 1851.

PASSING BELL, THE.  An Elegy.  (Anon.)  18°, pp. 15.  Boston, 1789.

PASSION FLOWERS.  (Anon.)  12°, pp. iv, 187.  Boston, 1854.

PASTOR, THE.  (Anon.)  12°, pp. xii, 50.  New York, 1821.

PATCH, (J.)

John Patch was born at Ipswich, Mass., in 1807, and graduated at Bowdoin College in 1831.  For a time he was a resident graduate at Harvard, studying German under Dr. Follen and reading the Greek poets under Professor Felton.  He studied law, was admitted to practice and opened an office in Boston.  After a residence of a year or two in Boston he removed to Beverly, Mass., and soon after to Nantucket, Mass., where he remained a year.  The *Literary Museum*, the responsibility of editing and publishing which he took upon himself, did not prove remunerative, and finding himself pecuniarily embarrassed, with the hope of retrieving his fortunes, he went to California in 1849.  After spending three years and over in the mining district he took up his residence in San Francisco, where he opened an office and practiced his profession for two or three years, and then returned to his native place which became his permanent home.

— The Poet's Offering.  12°, pp. xi, 372.  Boston, 1842.

PATERSON, (S. V. R. AND W.)

Stephan Van Rensselaer and William Paterson, twins by birth, were born at Perth Amboy, May 31, 1817. Their grandfather, William P., filled high and important civil positions: was the first United States Senator for New Jersey, was Governor of the State, and was appointed by President Washington, Associate Justice of the Supreme Court of the United States, and held this office till his death in 1800. The subjects of this sketch graduated at Princeton in 1835. The former became a civil engineer, and after having pursued his profession for a time on the Genessee Valley Canal, was appointed Surveyor General of the Council of Proprietors of East New Jersey. This position he resigned, but subsequently was re-appointed to the same office, holding the same till his death in 1872.

William Paterson was admitted to the bar in November, 1838. Among the offices of civil trust which he has held may be mentioned the Mayoralty of Perth Amboy in 1846, '50–60, '74–78, Presidential elector in 1864, Judge of the Appelate Court of New Jersey, having been appointed in 1882, and now (1886) in office.

— (S. V. R.)  Hierosolyma and Milton's Dream, etc.  12°, pp. 114. Princeton, 1850.

— (S. V. R. AND WILLIAM.)  Poems of Twin Graduates of the College of New Jersey.  8°, pp. v, 384.  Newark, N. J., 1882.

Presented to the Library of the University to be placed in "The Harris Collection," by Hon. W. Paterson, March 1, 1886.

PATRIOT, THE.  (By a Mechanic of Charlestown. Anon.)  12°, pp. vii, 24.  Charlestown, 1798.

PATRIOTS, THE, OF NORTH AMERICA.  (Anon.)  8°, pp. 47.  1775.

PATTEN, (G. W., U. S. A.)

George W. Patten was born at Newport, R. I., in 1808, graduated at Brown University in 1825, and at West Point in 1830. He served in the Florida and Mexican wars, lost his hand at Cerro Gerdo, April 18, 1847, and was retired from the service in 1864.

— Episodes of the Mexican War.  Sq. 18°, pp. v, 43.  New York, 1878.

— Voices of the Border.  12°, pp. 361.  New York, 1867.

PATTERSON, (A. M.)  Onward: A Lay of the West.  Sq. 16°, pp. 28. New York, and San Francisco, 1869.

PAULDING, (J. K. AND W. I.)

James Kirke Paulding's ancestor was among the early Dutch settlers of the State of New York, his name being Hendrick Pauldwick, or, as sometimes spelled Heinrick Paulden, which, anglecised, became Henry Pawling. The grandfather of James settled in Westchester county, N. Y., and his father took up his residence in Pleasant Valley, Dutchess county, N. Y., where the son was born, August 22, 1770. The war of the Revolution brought great pecuniary embarrassment to the family, which was reduced to great straits, and led to their removal, after peace was declared, to the old home in Westchester. The only school education which James received was acquired in a little log school house two miles from his home. In early manhood he went to New Yord and resided for a time

PAULDING, (J. K. AND W. I.) — *Continued.*

with his brother-in-law, Mr. William Irving, "a man of wit and genius, whose home was the familiar resort of a knot of young men of a similar stamp, who were members of the Calliopean Society, one of the first purely literary institutions established in the city." The society and influence of the men with whom he was thus associated was in itself an education to young Paulding. He was, moreover, brought into intimate relations with Washington Irving, the brother of his brother-in-law, with whom he made his first literary venture in the publication of the famous *Salmagundi; or, the Whim-Whams and Opinions of Launcelot Langstaff and others,* the first number of which appeared January 24, 1807. It had a brief existence of only one year. In 1814 he was appointed Secretary to the Board of Navy Commissioners, and subsequently was for twelve years Navy Agent for the port of New York, and for three years, 1838–41, was Secretary of the Navy. During all this time his pen was busy in the production of several works which secured popular favor The one of these on which perhaps his fame most securely rests is his "Dutchman's Fireside." At the close of his public service he took up his residence at Hyde Park, Dutchess county, N. Y., where he died April 6, 1860.

— American Comedies. 12°, pp. iv, 295. Philadelphia, 1847.

The contents of this volume are: The Bucktails; or, Americans in England. The Noble Exile. Madmen All; or, The Cure of Love. Antipathies; or, The Enthusiasts by the Ears. "The Bucktails" was written by the father soon after the war of 1812. The son, William Irving Paulding, was the author of the others.

PAYNE, (D. A.) The Pleasures, etc. 18°, pp. 43. Baltimore, 1850.

PAYNE, (J. H.)

John Howard Payne was born in the city of New York, June 9, 1791 (instead of 1792, as the Encyclopædias, etc., generally give the date), in a house pulled down in 1832, near the junction of Pearl and Broad streets. He spent a part of his early childhood in East Hampton, L. I., and then removed to Boston. His dramatic tastes were developed while he was a mere lad. At the age of thirteen, while a clerk in the store of an uncle in New York, who had recently died, he was the clandestine editor of a little paper bearing the title, *The Thespian Mirror,* the first number of which appeared December 28, 1805. It ran through fourteen numbers, the last appearing March 22, 1806. For about two years he was a student in Union College, Schenectady. Family reverses compelled him to abandon a college course of study. He first appeared on the stage in the character of *Young Norval* at the Old Park Theatre, New York, February 24, 1809, when he was under seventeen years of age. A brilliant success, reaching on through several years, followed his professional efforts in this country and in Great Britain. His career as a dramatic author commenced with his writing "Accusation," which was produced for the first time at the Drury Lane Theatre, February 1, 1816.

Various accounts have been given of the circumstances which led to the composition by John Howard Payne of the immortal song, "Home, Sweet Home."

The following is the story as related by his biographer, Gabriel Harrison. While temporarily residing in Paris, his services were secured by Mr. Charles Kemble, who had the management of the Covent Garden Theatre. Before leaving Paris the then dramatist sent to his employer "a batch of manuscript plays, setting the price at two hundred and fifty pounds upon the whole." One of these plays subsequently was produced on the stage under the name of "Clari." Its author asked and received for it from Mr. Kemble, fifty pounds. The plot of the play having been somewhat changed and several songs and duets introduced, it was brought out as an opera at Covent Garden Theatre "with prodigious success." The music was composed and partly founded on a Sicilian air, by Sir Henry

Payne, (J. H.) — *Continued.*

Bishop, the gentleman who arranged all the music for Mr. Payne's pieces. Mr. Harrison says: "This song has had a more universal circulation than any other song written before or since. It is a fact that upwards of one hundred thousand copies were issued by its publisher in London in less than one year after its publication. The profit yielded over two thousand guineas. It at once became so popular that it was heard everywhere."

That Sir Henry Bishop did not wholly compose the simple touching music of "Home, Sweet Home," appears from the following as related by Payne: "I first heard the air," he says, "in Italy. One beautiful morning as I was strolling along amid some delightful scenery my attention was arrested by the sweet voice of a peasant girl who was carrying a basket laden with flowers and vegetables. This plaintive air she trilled out with so much sweetness and simplicity that the melody at once caught my fancy. I accosted her, and after a few moments conversation I asked for the name of the song, which she could not give me, but having a slight knowledge of music myself, barely enough for the purpose, I requested her to repeat the air which she did, while I dotted down the notes as best I could. It was this air that suggested the words of 'Home, Sweet Home,' both of which I sent to Bishop at the time I was preparing the opera of 'Clari' for Mr. Kemble. Bishop happened to know the air perfectly well, and adapted the music to the words."

Mr. Payne returned to his native country in July, 1832, and was warmly received in several cities of the United States. It was his purpose to publish a weekly periodical to be issued in London, its contributors to be both English and American. The plan did not succeed in enlisting sufficient interest to warrant its being carried out. On the 23d of August, 1842, he was appointed by President Tyler Consul at Tunis, and remained in office until a change of administration led to his recall, official notice of the same being received November 20, 1845. In the spring of 1851, having been reappointed Consul, he returned to Tunis, where he died April 9, 1852. The body was exhumed January 5, 1883, sent to America at the expense of W. W. Corcoran, Esq., of Washington, D. C., and reinterred in Oak Hill Cemetery, Washington, June 9, 1883.

— Accusation. 18°, pp. vii, 76. Boston, 1818.

— Adeline. A Melo-Drama. 16°, pp. 41. New York, 1822.

— Algiers, The Fall of. 18°, pp. 47. London, no date.

— Ali Pacha; or, The Signet Ring. A Melo-Drama. 18°, pp. 36. New York, 1823.

— Same. 18°, pp. 28. London, no date.

— Brutus. A Tragedy in Five Acts. 18°, pp. 52. London, no date.

— Same. 8°, pp. vi, 56. London, 1819.

— Charles the Second; or, The Merry Monarch. A Comedy. 18°, pp. 45. London, no date.

— Same. Philadelphia, 1829.

— Clari; or, The Maid of Milan. 18°, pp. 40. London, no date.

The original of "Home, Sweet Home," appeared first in this play, which was brought out as an opera, in Covent Garden Theatre, in the spring of 1823.

— Lispings of the Muse: A Selection from Juvenile Poems, chiefly written at and before the age of sixteen. "He lisp'd in numbers, for the numbers came." Printed as a testimony of regard from the author to his personal friends. 8°, pp. viii, 30. London, 1815.

Payne, (J. H.) — *Continued.*

> The following was written on the short title-page in the handwriting of the author: "Isaac S. Clason, Esq., from his friend, John Howard Payne, London, Sept. 2, 1820." Written in pencil under the title referred to are the figures, $6.00.
>
> Another copy of these Juvenile Poems is published in Harrison's Memoirs of Payne, pp. 290–314.

— Love in Humble Life. A Comedy. 18°, pp, 31. London, no date.

— Richelieu. A Dramatic Tragedy. 18°, pp. 79. New York, 1826.

— The Lancers. 18°, pp. 27. London, no date.

— Therese. The Orphan of Geneva. 18°, pp. 46. London, no date.

— The Two Galley Slaves. A Melo-Drama. 18°, pp. 33. London, no date.

> The placing upon the pages of this Catalogue the titles of so many plays, which were written by Payne, renders it not out of place to allude to the very great interest which Mr. Harris took in dramatic literature. Almost all the dramatic works in the "Collection" were procured by him. The tastes of Judge Greene do not seem to have been in that direction. Of the numerous productions of Payne, for instance, only one, his "Brutus," is referred to in the Bangs, Merwin & Co.'s Catalogue. A cursory glance at this Catalogue will show that the dramatic volumes would, by themsleves, form no inconsiderable part of a library. The following authors are represented, and some of them largely so, in the "Collection:" G. H. Boker, J. B. Booth, C. T. Brooks, D. P. Brown, C. H. Calvert, C. J. Cannon, M. Carey, W. W. Clapp, Mary L. Cobb, H. J. Conway, J. Crowne, W. Dunlap (between twenty and thirty plays), F. A. Kemble, H. W. Longfellow, Mrs. A. C. Mowatt, H. Paul, J. H. Payne, C. Smith, C. Stearns, C. M. Walcot, N. P. Willis. These are a few of the writers of plays whose works are found in the "Harris Collection." The four volumes of Crowne's works, as they appear in a double form, the Philadelphia Edition compiled by Burton, and the Dramatists of the Restoration, are worthy of special note. More particular reference to these will be found under their own titles in the Catalogue. The large collection of dramatic works thus made by Mr. Harris make this part of the library of poetry of special value to lovers of the drama, and of great worth to the curious who may wish to inform themselves about American dramatic literature.

Peace, Dialogue on. (Anon.) Nassau Hall, Commencement, September 28, 1763. Philadelphia, 1763.

Pearce, (G. W.) A Poem recited before the Chester county, Pa., Cabinet of Natural Science, December 4, 1841. 8°, pp. 11. Philadelphia, 1841.

Peace, The Triumph of, etc. (Anon.) 12°, pp. 96. New York, 1840.

Peck, (J.)

> John Peck was born at Stanford, N. Y., in 1780, and was well known in the State of New York as an able minister of the Baptist denomination. He died November 15, 1849.

— A Descant on Universalism. 8°, pp. 21. New Haven, 1822.

28

PECK, (J.)—*Continued.*

— A Short Poem, etc.   3d Edition.   16°, pp. 23.   No place, 1813.

— The Spirit of Methodism.   18°, pp. 94.   New York, 1831.

— Poems on the Last Judgment and on Death.   12°, pp. 34.   Palmer, 1817.

PEET, (L. R.)   Experiences and Comments of a Fool About Town.   Sq. 18°, pp. 18.   Baltimore, 1876.

PEIRCE, (T.)

Thomas Peirce was born in Chester Co., Penn., August 4, 1786, and, in early life, was farmer, mechanic and school teacher.   In 1813 he went to Cincinnati, engaged in mercantile pursuits and was successful.   His literary tastes were of the most marked character, and he did much to elevate the standard of art and literature in his adopted home..   He died in 1850.

— The Odes of Horace in Cincinnati.   18°, pp. 117.   Cincinnati, 1822.

PEIRSON, (MRS. LYDIA J.)

Lydia J. Wheeler was born at Middletown, Conn., and resided for many years in Liberty, Tioga Co., where her husband, Mr. Peirson, had purchased a tract of land.   In the solitude of a home five miles from any other habitation, and twenty from any village, she beguiled her lonely hours with her pen, writing for *The New Yorker*, *The Southern Literary Messenger*, etc.

— Forest Minstrel.   12°, pp. xi, 264.   Philadelphia, 1846.

PELT, (D. V.)   The Hollanders in Nova Zembla, 1596–1597.   12°, pp. xvii, 120.   New York, 1884.

An Arctic Poem, translated from the Dutch of Hendrick Tollens.

PENNSYLVANIA GEORGICS.   No title page.   18°, pp. 60.

PEPPER, (G.)   Kathleen O'Neil.   A Melo-Drama.   A Picture of Feudal Times in Ireland.   18°, pp. vii, 84.   Philadelphia, 1832.

PEPPER, (H.)   Juvenile Essays.   8°, pp. 75.   Philadelphia, no date.

PERCIVAL, (J. G.)

James Gates Percival was born at Kensington, Conn., September 15, 1795, and graduated at Yale in 1815 with the honors of his class.   He published his "Prometheus" in 1820, a poetical production which was favorably received.   He chose for his profession that of his father, medicine, receiving his degree in 1820, and commencing practice in Charleston, S. C.   Here he published his "Clio," mostly of verse.   In 1824 he was appointed Assistant Surgeon in the army, and Professor of Chemistry at West Point, which position he held but a short time, and then took up his residence in Boston, where he was engaged in the recruiting service.   In 1827 he removed to New Haven, Conn., and for two years assisted in preparing for the press the first Quarto Edition of Webster's Dictionary.   His next literary work of special note was a translation of Malte Brun's Geography.   He performed excellent service as mineralogist and geologist in both

PERCIVAL. (J. G.) — *Continued.*

Connecticut and Wisconsin, reports of his labors in both these States being made by him. He was distinguished for his linguistic attainments. A great difference of opinion prevails as to his merits as a poet. The writer of the sketch of him prepared for "Johnson's New Cyclopædia," says "his poetry, though not without conspicuous merits, is nearly all crude and half written, and it has consequently been forgotten." In the "North American Review," January, 1822, a critic, said to be Edward Everett, in reviewing the volume of "Percival's Poems" published in 1820, and containing his "Prometheus," remarks: "These poems appear to contain decided indications of genuine poetical talent. This little volume contains the marks of an inspiration more lofty and genuine than any similar collection of fugitive pieces which has come to our notice from any native bard." There are, however, some serious drawbacks, which he proceeds to point out. The poem delivered before the Yale Phi Beta Kappa in 1825 is noticed in an article also in the "North American Review" for April, 1826. The criticism on the production, as a whole, is very severe, although the writer warmly commends isolated passages. In the July, 1860, No. of this same Review, is still another notice of "Percival's Poems," called out by the publication of the two volumes of his books published in the "Blue and Gold Series" of Ticknor & Fields, 1859. It is far more candid and favorable than either of the others referred to. It will repay perusal.

— Clio.  12°, pp. 203.  New York, 1827.

— Poems.  18°, pp. 346.  New Haven, 1851.

— Same.  2 vols.  18°, pp. li, 402–517.  Boston, 1859.  Blue and Gold Series.

— Yale.  Phi Beta Kappa Poem, September 13, 1825.  8°, pp. 40. Boston, 1826.


PERCY, (FLORENCE,) the *nom de plume* of Mrs. E. Akers.  Forest Buds from the Woods of Maine.  12°, pp. viii, 207.  Boston, 1856.

— Same.  18°, pp. 251.  Boston, 1866  Blue and Gold Series.

That the poems of Mrs. Akers were regarded as worthy a place in the carefully selected volumes which make up the "Blue and Gold" Series of Ticknor & Fields, is a sufficient endorsement of their general excellence. The compiler of that series would not have placed them in that series along with the productions of some of the best of American poets had he not deemed them worthy of such a place.


PERKINS, (ELIZA.)

She was born in New York, January 27, 1804, and died in 1820.

— Poems, etc.  12°, pp. 96.  New York, 1823.


PERRIN, (W.)  Hebrew Canticles.  18°, pp. 126.  Philadelphia, 1820.

Sixteen pages of this volume are devoted to "Preliminary Observations on the Song of Solomon," in which the writer dwells at some length on the arrangement of its parts, its antiquity, its authenticity, its nature and design. Pages 17–53 contain an English translation of the Song. Pages 57–78 contain a translation of the "Lamentations of Jeremiah." Pages 81–103 contain a translation of all the other "Songs," so called, of the Old and New Testaments.

PERRY, (NORA.)  After the Ball, and other Poems.  Sq. 16°, pp. vi, 192. Boston, 1875.

— Her Lover's Friend, etc.  12°, pp. 183.  Boston, 1880.

PERRY, (T.)  Then and Now.  A Poem delivered at New Ipswich, N. H.  8°, pp. 40.  New York, 1861.

PERSEVERANCE, ETC.  (Anon.)  Reply to the Rev. John Wesley.  An imperfect copy, beginning with page 11.  8°, pp. 65.

PETER, (MR., British Consul, Philadelphia.)  Leonore.  A Romance from the German of Bürger.  18°, pp. 15.  No place, no date.

PETERSON, (H.)  Poems, including "Modern Job."  Second Series. 12°, pp. 227.  Philadelphia, 1833.

PETERS, (G. W.)  Poem.  Centennial, Providence, July 4, 1876.  8°, pp. 13.  Providence, 1876.

PETTIS, (S.)  Boston and its Environs, as seen from the Cupola of the State House.  12°, pp. 47.  Boston, 1832.

PHANTASMAGORIA, THE.  (Anon.)  12°, pp. 12.  New York, date in pencil, 1831.

PHANTOM BARGE, ETC.  (Anon.)  18°, pp. 171.  Philadelphia, 1822.

PHELPS, (E.)  Modern Benevolence.  A Satire.  8°, pp. 37.  New York, 1860.

PHELPS, (ELIZABETH STUART.)

Miss Phelp-, the daughter of Rev. Dr. Austin Phelps, was born at Boston, August 31, 1844.  Her mother was Elizabeth, daughter of Moses Stuart, of Andover, who was the author of several moral and religious tales, which, in their day, were very popular.  Miss Phelps is the author of "Gates Ajar," which has had an extensive circulation.  Other productions of her pen are well known.

— Songs of the Silent World, etc.  12°, pp. 155.  Boston, 1885.

PHELPS, (MRS. A. C.)

Adaliza Cutter was born in Jaffrey, N. H., in 1823, became the wife of Gurley A. Phelps, M. D., and died June 3, 1852.

— The Life of Christ, etc.  12°, pp. 286.  Boston, 1852.

PHELPS, (S. D.)

Sylvanus Dryden Phelps was born at Suffield, Conn., 1816, graduated at Brown University in 1844, and was pastor of the First Baptist Church, New Haven, 1846–63.  Subsequently he became pastor of the Jefferson Street Church, Providence, R. I., and after serving this church for a time he became editor of The Christian Secretary, Hartford, of which he now (1880) has charge.

PHELPS, (S. D.) — *Continued.*

— A Song of Thanksgiving. A Sermon in Rhyme. Delivered November 18, 1869. 8°, pp. 16. New Haven, 1870.

PHELPS, (S. M.) Triumphs of Divine Grace. 12°, pp. 132. New York, 1835.

PHI BETA KAPPA POEM. Harvard Commencement, August 29, 1811. (By a Brother.) Salem, Mass., 1811.

> The author was Jacob Bigelow, M. D.

PHILADELPHIA BOOK, THE. 12°, pp. 380. Philadelphia, 1836.

> Poetical effusions in the volume.

PHILADELPHIAD, THE. 12°, pp. 48. An imperfect copy.

PHILLIPS, (H., JR.)

> Henry Phillips, Jr., an American lawyer, of Philadelphia, much interested in numismatics.

— Poems translated from the Spanish and German. 8°, pp. 76. Philadelphia, 1878.

> One hundred copies printed, exclusively for private circulation.

PHILLIPS, (J. B.) Camillus. A Tragedy. 18°, pp. 59. New York, 1833.

PHILLIPS, (W.) Alexander the Great; or, The Learned Camel. 18°, pp. 23. New York, no date.

PIATT, (J. J.,) AND HOWELLS, (W. D.)

> John James Piatt was born at Milton, Ind., March 1, 1835, educated at Kenyon College, and has published many pieces of marked poetic merit. He was a contributor to the "Atlantic Monthly."

— Poems of Two Friends. 12°, pp. viii, 132. Columbus, 1860.

— Poems in Sunshine and Firelight. 12°, pp. 127. Cincinnati, 1866.

PIATT, (MRS. S. M. B.)

> Sarah Morgan Bryan, the wife of J. J. Piatt, was born at Lexington, Ky., in 1835, was educated at Newcastle, Ky., and lived in Cincinnati, 1868, *et seq.*

— A Woman's Poems. 12°, pp. 127. Boston, 1871.

— (J. J. AND S. M. B.) The Nests in Washington, etc. 12°, pp. 150. New York and London, 1864.

PICKERING, (H.)

> Henry Pickering, the third son of Colonel Timothy Pickering, was born at Newburgh, N. Y., October 8, 1781, in what was the headquarters of General Washington, the famous Hasbrouck mansion. At the time of his birth his father was Quartermaster-General of

the American army.  At the age of twenty he removed to Massachusetts, and subsequently became a merchant in Salem, and acquired a fortune, which in large measure he lost, and in 1825 removed to the city of New York, where, and in Rondout and other places on the banks of the Hudson, he resided the remainder of his life.  He died in New York, May 8, 1831.

"The writings of Pickering," says Duyckinck, "take occasionally a sombre tint from the circumstances which shaded the later years of his life, although his natural temperament was cheerful.  He was a lover of the beautiful as well in art as in nature, and he numbered among his friends the most eminent poets and artists of our country."  The following is found in a graceful tribute which was paid to his memory in the *Salem Gazette* in May, 1838:  "With a highly cultivated and tasteful mind he imparted pleasant instruction to all who held intercourse with him, while his unobtrusive manners silently forced themselves on the affections and won the hearts of all who enjoyed his society."

— Athens, and other Poems.  8°, pp. 84.  Salem, 1824.

This poem was suggested by the writer's seeing a panorama of Athens, painted by Messrs. Barker & Burford, of London, and after "having been the object of admiration in England" for a year, was purchased by Theodore Lyman, with the intention of presenting it to Harvard University.  "It will readily be perceived," says Mr. Pickering, "that my little performance is a mere *panoramic sketch*, not a finished picture; which, indeed, I should in vain have attempted.  Still less can I flatter myself that I have been able to identify my own feelings with those of the fortunate man who has actually traced the banks of the Illissus and its sister stream, or who has knelt within the sacred precincts of the Parthenon."

In the notes, which occupy pp. 69-84, the author has brought together many interesting facts to explain and illustrate his text.  In a note on the Parthenon, he gives expression to a hope which, although more than sixty years have passed away since it was uttered, has not yet been realized, and it is doubtful if it ever will be.  "If the Greeks, in spite of the frowns of power and the apathy of mankind, should be able to achieve their independence" — (that hypothesis has become fact) — "one of the early acts of their government should be to decree the restoration of the Parthenon.  I do not mean that they should begin to labor upon it in that state of exhaustion in which they must be left after their sanguinary but glorious struggle; yet I should hope that the project would be kept steadily in view.  It is to be presumed, that in this event, the British Parliament would send back the sculptures of *Phidias*, and that the King of France would follow the laudable example.  Every *block* should be replaced.  The inscription (as translated) may then read thus :

ERECTED BY PERICLES<br>
DEFACED AND VIOLATED BY THE BARBARIANS<br>
RESTORED<br>
BY THE PEOPLE OF GREECE.

If the compiler may venture to refer to his own feelings, he would say that some years since, on returning from a visit to Athens, as he was wandering through the British Museum he saw one of the Caryatides which had been taken from its place on the Acropolis and transported to England.  He could not help saying to himself: "This statue has no right to be here; it ought to be sent back to Athens and set up in the place which for so many centuries it occupied."  He remembers when sitting on a prostrate column of the famous Temple of Jupiter, a little beyond the eastern base of the Acropolis, and not far from the Arch of Hadrian, that he was told that an enterprising Yankee had quite seriously thought of trying to buy that column and transporting it to New York!

In one of his notes Pickering says: "A Frenchman, some years since, conceived the thought of transporting the Temple of Theseus to France; what infatuation!  Yet an idea

**PICKERING, (H.) — *Continued.***

of this kind was not new. We are told that an Earl of Bristol, in the last century
seriously meditated the removal of the beautiful little Temple of the Sybil at Tivoli in order
that he might place it in his own park! He was only restrained from committing the
outrage by an absolute prohibition of His Holiness." It is thus that the poet apostro-
phises the sacreligious Frenchman:

> "Thou phrensied Gaul! Could'st thou the thought endure
> To wrest this dear relict from the soil,
> To plant it impious on a foreign strand?
> Shade of immortal Theseus, arise!
> In dreadful majesty appear once more
> And palsy with benumbing fear what hand
> Shall sacreligious dare attempt the deed!"

— Paestum. Ruins of. (Anon.) 4°, pp. 128. Salem, Mass., 1822.

— Poems. 8°, pp. 84. Boston, 1830.

An edition of only twenty-five copies was printed for private circulation. Among the
beautiful " gems " of this very rare volume is a poem of great sweetness, " The Death of
My Mother." Pickering was a most affectionate son.

— The Buckwheat Cake. 8°, pp. 14. Boston, 1831.

This charming little poem first appeared in the *New York Evening Post*. The volume
in its present form is exceedingly rare.

PICTURE POEMS. (Marian Douglas.) Lg. 12°, pp. 104. Boston, 1872.

PIERCE, (E. J.) A Poem. 18°, pp. 36. No place, no date.

PIERCE, (W. L.) The Year. A Poem in Three Cantos. 18°, pp. 191.
New York, 1813.

PIERPONT, (J.)

John Pierpont was born at Litchfield, Conn., April 6, 1785, graduated at Yale College
in 1804, having among his classmates Hon. John C. Calhoun, Bishop C. E. Gadsden, of
South Carolina, President Bennet Tyler, of Dartmouth College, and Rev. Drs. E. Stiles
Ely, T. C. Lansing, John Marsh and A. McEwen. He was admitted to the practice of law
in 1812, and resided for a time in Newburyport, Mass. Then he removed to Boston, and
afterwards to Baltimore, where he was in business with John Neal, as his partner. Having studied theology he was ordained as a Unitarian minister in 1819, and was pastor of
the Hollis Street Church, Boston, 1819–15, then of the church in Medford, Mass, 1849–50.
He was in the Treasury Department, Washington, 1861–64, and died at Medford, August
27, 1866.

— Airs of Palestine. 8°, pp. xxvi, 56. Baltimore, 1816.

— Same. 2d Edition. 18°, pp. 58. Boston, 1817.

— Same. 12°, pp. 334. Boston, 1840.

— Anti-Slavery Poems. 18°, pp. 64. Boston, 1843.

— Lays for the Sabbath. A Collection of Religious Poetry. 12°, pp.
288. Boston, 1850.

PIERPONT, (J.) — *Continued.*

— Sabbath Recreations.   12°, pp. 288.   Boston, 1839.
— The Pilgrims of Plymouth.   8°, pp. 30.   Boston, 1856.
— The Portrait.   A Poem delivered before the Washington Benevolent
    Society of Newburyport, October 27, 1812.   8°, pp. 36.   Boston,
    1812.

PIETAS ET CONGRATULATIO COLLEGII CANTABRIGIENSIS APUD NOVAN-
    GLOS.   Bostoni, Massachusettensium :  Typis *J. Green & J. Rus-
    sell*, 1761.   4°, pp. Dedication to the King, xiv.   Text 106.

This volume in Latin, Greek and English, and containing thirty-one pieces, exclusive
of the "dedication to the King," was designed to celebrate the death of George II. and the
accession of George III. The "dedication" was composed by Governor Bernard or
Lieutenant Governor Hutchinson. The poems were prepared in response to an invitation
sent to Harvard College, for which prizes were offered. "Under these circumstances," as
Duyckinck well says ("Cyclopædia American Literature," vol. i, p. 11,), "the inevitable
condition of such a work is eulogy; so the departing guest is sped, and the coming welcomed in the most rapturous figments of poetry. George II is elevated to the apotheosis
in the skies, in the long echoing wave of the exulting hexameter, while the ebbing flood
of feeling at so mournful an exaltation is couched in the subdued expression of the sink-
ing pentameter. All nature is called upon to weep, and again to rejoice; all hearts to
bleed, and again to live as one royal monarch ascends the skies and another the throne."

Four pages of the "Monthly Review" [London], for July, 1763, are devoted to a notice
of this volume. The writer says: "A poetical offering from a college in America, and the
first of the kind that a King of Great Britain has received from his Colonies, must be
esteemed a curiosity." He then proceeds to make quotations, speaking of the 'address'
to the King as 'very judiciously and elegantly drawn up.'" The following are the con-
cluding words of this notice: "It must be acknowledged that this New England Collection, like other public offerings of the same kind, contains some indifferent performances;
but these, though they cannot be well excused when they come from ancient and established seats of learning, may at least be connived at here; and what we could not endure
from an illustrious University, we can pardon in an Infant Seminary." The "Infant Seminary," of which this writer so patronizingly speaks, had, when he wrote the above, been
in existence one hundred and twenty-seven years!

(See Duyckinck, as above; also "Monthly Anthology," June, 1809, an article by A. H.
Everett; also, Justin Winsor's "Biographical Contributions," No. 4.

PIKE, (A.)

Albert Pike was born at Boston, December 29, 1809, his father being a poor shoe-
maker. He studied for a time at Harvard College, which, in 1859, conferred on him the
degree of A. M. He went to Santa Fé in 1831, travelling most of the way on foot; was a
journalist at Little Rock, Ark., 1834–36; subsequently practiced law; was in the Mexican
war, sided with the South in the Civil War, being a Brigadier-General; editor of the
*Memphis Appeal*, 1867–68, and is the author of Law Reports, etc. For years he has been
the head of the Ancient Accepted Masons of the South.

— Nugae.   12°, pp. 393.   Philadelphia, 1854.
— Prose Sketches and Poems.   12°, pp. viii, 200.   Boston, 1834.

PIKE, (M. S.) Creola. 8°, pp. 53. Boston, 1850.

PILSBURY, (A.) Sacred Songster. 5th Edition. 18°, pp. 252. Columbia, S. C., 1825.

PIMPELLY, (MARY H.) Poems. 8°, pp. 76. New York, 1852.

PINDAR, PETER. (Anon.) Letters to a Friend Relative to the Sunday Mail. 18°, pp. 36. New York, 1830.

PINKNEY, (E. C.)

Edward Coate Pinkney, son of the distinguished lawyer and diplomatist, the Hon. William Pinkney, of Maryland, was born in London, October, 1802, his father at the time being United States Minister to the Court of St. James. Returning to this country with his parents in 1811, he pursued his studies in St. Mary's College, Baltimore, and in 1816 became a midshipman in the navy. On the decease of his father in 1822, he threw up his commission, and devoted himself for a time to the practice of law and to literary pursuits. The small volume of poems referred to below, being a copy of the Second Edition, is "sufficiently large to preserve his memory with all generous appreciators of true poetry as a writer of exquisite taste and sensibility." William Leggett speaks of his shorter poems as "rich in beauties of a peculiar nature, and not surpassed by productions of a similar character in the English language." His critic had a special admiration for the poem "On Italy." Pinkney died in Baltimore, April 11, 1828.

— Miscellaneous Poems of. The Rococo, No. 2. New Mirror Extra. 4°, pp. 16. New York, 1844.

— Poems. 2d Edition. 18°, pp. 72. Baltimore, 1838.

PINKNEY, (W., D. D.)

A nephew of Hon. William Pinkney.

— Ernest Murray; or, A Dream of Life. 12°, pp. 96. New York, 1869.

PINDLE, (B. T.) Miscellaneous Poems. 18°, pp. 199. Baltimore, 1851.

PISE, (C. C., D. D.)

Charles Constantine Pise, D. D., the son of an Italian by an American mother, was born at Annapolis, Md., in 1802. He received his collegiate education at Georgetown, D. C. After graduation he went to Rome to complete his studies, where he was knighted and had conferred on him the doctor's degree. Returning to the United States, he was, for a time, an instructor in the college at Emmittsburg, Md. Having received ordination as a Priest in the Roman Catholic Church, he discharged his clerical functions in Maryland and the District of Columbia, also in the cities of New York and Brooklyn. Dr. Pise was the author of a "Church History," 5 vols., 1830; wrote much in the form of poetry, tales, etc., and was regarded as one of the ablest clergymen of his church in America. He died in Brooklyn, May 26, 1866.

— The Pleasures of Religion, etc. 18°, pp. vi, 251. Philadelphia, 1833.

PLATTSBURG, BATTLE OF.  In Three Cantos.  By an American Youth.
(Anon.)   16°, pp. 46.   Montpelier, 1819.

This volume was "entered" by John Woodworth, author of "Reminiscences of Troy
from its settlement in 1790 to 1810."  It was elegantly bound by W. Pratt for H. Stevens,
1876.

PLAYS AND POEMS OF H.  (Anon.)  Part I.  12°, pp. 150.  New York,
1859.

PLEASANTS, (A. P.)   Lilies of the Valley.  8°, pp. 56.

PLEASANTS, (MRS. J.)  Cinderella, etc.  8°, pp. 16.  Philadelphia, 1864.

PLUMB, (D.)   The Slaveholder's Rebellion.  Fiat Justitia.  8°, pp. 15.
Dated New York, May, 1865.

POE, (E. A.)

Edgar Allan Poe was born at Boston, February 19, 1809, and was sent to school at
Stoke Newington, near London, England, by his adopted father, Mr. John Allan, of
Richmond, Va.  In this school he remained not far from six years, then studied for a short
time at the University of Virginia, received an appointment as Cadet at West Point, was
expelled by sentence of Court Martial for "gross neglect of all duty and disobedience of
orders;" became editor of the *Southern Literary Messenger*, Richmond, removed to New
York in 1837, where he earned a precarious living by his pen; published "The Raven" in
"The American Review," February, 1845.  After various literary adventures he died at
Baltimore, October 7, 1849.

— Life and Poems.  Memoir by R. H. Stoddard.  12°, pp. xiv, 380.
New York, 1875.

The following, condensed from John H. Ingram's "The Bibliography of Edgar Allan
Poe," may properly find a place here.  After stating that he had spared no pains to make
the bibliography of Poe complete and exhaustive, Mr. Ingram says: "Doubtless translations have appeared and disappeared, without leaving any discoverable traces in the
somewhat imperfectly-kept registers of the past, whilst even distinct native publications,
anonymous and pseudonymous, as well as various editions of Poe's known works, may no
longer be recognizable.  The poet's name and works are well known in Poland, Hungary
and Russia, but whether by means of native or foreign versions, or by journals or books,
is unknown to us; in France and Spain Poe's tales have been frequently published in the
journals, *en feuilleton*."

Beginning with what is so rare, "Tamerlane, etc., Boston, 1827," Mr. Ingram gives
the titles of Poe's "Works," etc., to the number of eighteen, including different editions
of the same, the date being brought down to 1859.  Editions of the "Poetical Works," "in
all shapes and sizes, with or without memoir, illustrated or not, continued to be issued
from the press."  Mr. Ingram makes no reference to Mr. Stoddard's edition, published in
1875, which Mr. Stoddard says is "the first complete one that has ever been made, and contains, it is believed, all that he published in verse."

Mr. Ingram gives for the British publication of Poe's productions in different editions twenty-seven titles, the places of publication being London, Edinburgh and Halifax.
The last one referred to belonged to "The Emerald Series."  "The thirteenth thou-
sandth," says Mr. Ingram, "was announced a short time ago."

Five French translations of Baudelaire's Series of Poe's Works are referred to by Mr.

Poe, (E. A.) — *Continued.*

Ingram. Six others are mentioned, one of which is a magnificent *édition de luxe* of " The Raven," — " Le Corbeau," — a large folio, Paris, 1875, " Illustrè par E. Manet."

Nine titles are given in German, the volumes having been published in Leipsig, Stuttgart and Philadelphia.

Reference is made, also, to three Spanish, two Italian, and one Australian title of Poe's Works.

— Poems. 18°, pp. 124. New York, 1831.

— Same. 18°, pp. xxvi, 172. London and New York, 1881.

— Poetical Works. Illustrated. 8°, pp. xxx, 247. New York, 1858.

— The Raven. Illustrated by Gustave Doré. Comments by E. C. Stedman. Folio. Harper's Edition. Not paged. New York, 1883.

An elegant copy.

Poem, A. Addressed to a Young Lady. In Three Parts. I. Descriptive and Moral. II. On Love and Friendship. III. The Caution. Written at Antigua. (Anon.) Sq. 12°, pp. 33. Boston, 1773.

— Comprising a Few Thoughts suggested by the Assault on our Glorious Flag in 1860–61. (E. B. R. Anon.) 18°, pp. 32. New York, 1861.

— On Reading the President's Address, etc. 8°, pp. 6. Philadelphia, 1796.

— Written by a Virginia Clergyman in a Storm of Wind and Rain. pp. 3. Bound with " A Touch Stone for the Clergy." No place, 1771.

— Addressed to the Armies of the United States. (Anon.) 12°, pp. 16. New Haven, 1780.

— By a New England Lady. (Anon.) 8°, pp. 20. Washington, 1833.

— Commencement at Nassau-Hall, September 25, 1771. (Anon.) 18°, pp. 27. Philadelphia, 1772.

— The Poor Man's, to his Poor Neighbors. 8°, pp. 19. New York, 1774.

Poems. A Collection of. (By Several Hands. Anon.) 8°, pp. 55. Boston, 1744.

The names of none of the authors of these collected poems are given, nor is there anything to indicate who the compiler was. Some of these productions of the Colonial days of New England are very quaint and curious. One of them has this title: " *A full*

POEMS. — *Continued.*

and true *Account of how the lamentable wicked* French *and* Indian *Pirates were taken by the valient* English Men." The following is the doleful story of the fate of three of the pirates:

> "Three of the fellows in a fright
>    (that is to say in feares)
> Leaping *into* the sea *out-right*,
>    sows'd over head and ears.
>
> They on the waves in woful wise,
>    to swim did make a strife,
> [So in a pond a kitten cries,
>    and dubbles for his life;
>
> While boys about the border scud,
>    with brick-bats and with stones;
> Still dowse him deeper in the mud,
>    and break his little bones.]
>
> What came of them we cannot tell,
>    though many things are said;
> But this besure, we know full well,
>    if they were drown'd they're dead."

— AND TALES. By Mary Campbell, Mary Mell, etc., *noms de plume* of M. E. B. (Anon.) Mary E. Gellie[?] 12°, pp. 160. 1851.

— By a South Carolinian. (Anon.) 12°, pp. vi, 104. Charleston, 1848.

— By Croaker, Croaker & Co., and Croaker, Jr., as published in the *Evening Post.* 16°, pp. 36. New York, 1819.

   This is an untrimmed copy, elegantly bound by Bedford. These celebrated poems were written by Fitz-Greene Halleck and Joseph Rodman Drake, and published in the *New York Evening Post.* Several of them are satires of well-known characters of the day, while others were simply poetical effusions, some of which are among the most charming specimens of American poetry. "The World is Bright Before Thee," and "There is an Evening Twilight of the Heart," are very beautiful.

— 1830–1833. Compiler's name not given. Sq. 8°, pp. 112. Privately printed, 1862.

   Copy belonging to Henry Giles, Esq.

— By a Harvard Student. (Anon.) 12°, pp. 56. Boston, 1855.

— By Eaglestone, (*pseud.*) 12°, pp. 104. Albany, 1857.

— By Gold-Pen, (*pseud.*) 2d Edition. pp. 285. Philadelphia, 1856.

— Chiefly in the Scottish Dialect. (Anon.) 12°, pp. xii, 126. Washington, 1801.

   The author, a resident of Washington county, Pa., "was a fierce Federalist, and uses the lash with great vigor on all opposing factions. He wrote in the time of the Whiskey Rebellion, and brings upon the stage all the prominent actors in Pennsylvania politics of that period."

POEMS. — *Continued.*

— Miscellaneous. (By Osander, *psend.*) 18°, pp. 180. New York, 1812.

"Osander" was the *nom de plume* of Rev. Benjamin Allen.

— Miscellaneous. (Anon.) 12°, pp. 108. Place cut out, 1828.

— Miscellaneous. Selected from the *United States Literary Gazette.* (Compiler, anon.) 18°, pp. 172. Boston, 1826.

— Moral and Divine, etc. By an American Gentleman. 4°, pp. 106. Printed by Charles Rivington for John and James Rivington in St. Paul's Churchyard. London, 1756.

— On Different Subjects. By a Lady. (Anon.) 18°, pp. 117. Boston, 1813.

— On Several Occasions. (Anon.) 18°, pp. 141. Philadelphia, 1786.

— On Subjects Arising in England and the West Indies. 4°, pp. 108. London, 1783.

— Original. (Anon.) 12°, pp. x, 139. Baltimore, 1809.

— (Supposed to have been written by Mr. Fisher, an Englishman, editor of the *Albion* newspaper, New York.) 12°, pp. 63. Boston, 1820.

POESIE'S DREAM, ETC. (Anon.) 12°, pp. 72. Halifax, 1835.

POETICAL DESCRIPTION OF THE CHASTE VIRGIN, ETC. (Anon.) 16°, pp. 17. Boston, 1796.

POETICAL EPISTLE TO GEORGE WASHINGTON. By an Inhabitant of the State of Maryland. Anon.) 18°, pp. 10. London, 1781.

— Same. (Anon. Ascribed to C. W. Worster.) A Reprint. 4°, pp. 24. New York, 1865.

Seventy-five copies were printed, of which twenty-five were on large paper. This is No. 6 Lg.

— To the Enslaved Africans. 12°, pp. 24. Philadelphia, 1790.

POETICAL MISCELLANY, THE AMERICAN. 12°, pp. 304. Philadelphia, 1809.

POETS, AMERICAN. Selections from. 16°, pp. 356. Dublin and London, 1834.

POETS AND POETRY OF AMERICA. A Satire. (Anon.) 18°, pp. 33. Philadelphia, 1847.

POETRY OF ANIMATED NATURE. Illustrated. Vol. I. 8°, pp. 34. Philadelphia, 1846.

— The, of the Port-Folio. (Collected by Oliver Old School, *pseud.*) 24°, pp. 144. Philadelphia, 1818.

— Philosophical, of the Book of Nature. (Anon.) 12°, pp. 478. Albany, 1845.

POLITICAL DUENNA. Title page wanting. 16°, pp. 45.

POLITICAL GREEN HOUSE, THE. (Anon.) 16°, pp. 24. Hartford, 1799.

> The writers of this political satire were Richard Alsop, Theodore Dwight and Lemuel Hopkins. The copy in the "Harris Collection" is in perfect condition, very handsomely bound.

POLITICIANS, THE; OR, A STATE OF THINGS WRITTEN BY AN AMERICAN AND A CITIZEN OF PHILADELPHIA. 8°, pp. 37. Philadelphia, 1798.

POLLARD, (J.) The Decorative Sisters. A Modern Ballad. Illustrations by W. Satterlee. 8°, not paged. New York, no date.

POLYXENA. A Tragedy. (Anon. Copyrighted by W. R. Smith.) 12°, pp. 84. 1879.

POOR LITTLE HEARTS. Lines on some Deceased Hens. (Anon.) 8°, pp. 16. No place, 1860.

POOR, (J.) Collection of Psalms, Hymns, etc. 18°, pp. 48. Philadelphia, 1794.

POOR OF NEW YORK, THE. A Drama. (Anon.) 12°, pp. 45. New York, no date.

POOR YOUNG MAN. The Romance of A. From the French of Octavè Feuillet. 12°, pp. 53. New York, no date.

PORTER, (C. L.) Pebbles from the Lake Shore. 12°, pp. xii, 239. Philadelphia, 1855.

> Charles Leland Porter was born at Plattsburgh, New York, in 1820. He has furnished articles to "Knickerbocker," "Godey's," and other magazines.

PORTER, (J.) Poems. 8°, pp. 27. Hartford, 1818.

— Poems. 8°, pp. 27. Hartford, 1819.

PORTER, (J. A.)

John Addison Porter, M. D., was born at Catskill, N. Y., March 15, 1822, graduated at Yale in 1842, was appointed Professor in Delaware College, pursued chemical studies under Liebig at Giessen, was Professor of Chemistry in Brown University 1850–52, and was professor in Yale 1852–64. Professor Porter was the author of two chemical text-books, and of papers on scientific subjects. He edited the *Connecticut War Record*. He died at New Haven, August 25, 1866.

— Poem. Yale College, July 6, 1842. 8°, pp. 36. New Haven, 1842.

— Selections from the Kalevala. Translated from the German. 12°, pp. vi, 144. New York, 1868.

PORTER, (ROSE.) Foregleams of Immortality, etc. 12°, pp. 168. New York, 1884.

PORTSMOUTH, N. H. The Poets of. Compiled by A. M. Payson and A. Laighton. 8°, pp. 405. Boston, 1865.

POTOMAC MUSE, THE. (Anon.) 12°, pp. 172. Richmond, 1825.

POTTER, (R.) Phelles, King of Tyre. A Tragedy. 18°, pp. 76. New York, 1825.

POWELL, (I.) The Living Authors of America. First Series. In the volume are extracts from the principal poets of the United States. 8°, pp. viii, 365. New York, 1850.

POWER, (S. A.) Cinderella. 12°, pp. 12. Providence, 1867.

POWER, (T.) Secrecy. 8°, pp. 24. Boston, 1832.

POWERS OF FANCY, THE, ETC. (Anon.) 12°, pp. 93. Baltimore, 1822.

POWERS, (MRS. O. A.) High-Toned Sprees. A Series of Temperance Legends. 8th Edition. 18°, pp. 80. Middletown, N. Y., 1877.

POWHATTAN, THE LAND OF. (Anon.) 18°, pp. vi, 120. Baltimore, 1821.

POYAS, (C. G.) In Memory of Rev. C. P. Gadsden, Rector of St. Luke's Church, Charleston, S. C. 8°, pp. 6. Charleston, S. C., 1871.

— Year of Grace. 12°, pp. 242. Charleston, S. C., 1869.

PRAY, (I. C.)

Isaac Clark Pray was born at Boston in 1813, studied for a time at Harvard, and graduated at Amherst College in 1833, engaged in journalism in Boston and New York, and devoted many years to the management of theatres, being himself a professional actor, edited several magazines, and, 1855, wrote memoirs of James Gordon Bennett. He died at New York, November 28, 1869.

PRAY, (I. C.) — *Continued.*

— Julietta Gordini, the Miser's Daughter. 8°, pp. 40. New York, 1835.

— Poems. Lg. 8°, pp. 42. Boston, 1837.

— Prose and Verse. 12°, pp. 186. Boston, 1836.

PRENTISS, (C.) .

Charles Prentiss was born at Reading, Mass., October 8, 1774, graduated at Harvard 1795, and, for many years was a journalist and a Congressional reporter. He died at Brimfield, Mass., October 20, 1820.

— Child of Pallas. 12°, pp. 288. Baltimore, 1800.

— New England Freedom. 8°, pp. 28. Brookfield, 1813.

PRESCOTT, (HENRIETTA.) Poem Written in Newfoundland. 12°, pp. xiv, 311. London, 1839.

PRESTON, (H. C.) Poem. Homœpathic. 8°, pp. (with Dr. Payne's Address) 52. Boston, 1855.

PRESTON, (HARRIET P.) The Georgics of Virgil. Translated. 18°, pp. 153. Boston, 1881.

PRESTON, (HARRIET W.) Memoirs of Madame Desbordes-Valmore. By the late C. A. Sainte-Beuve. With a Selection from her Poems. Translated by Harriet W. Preston. 12°, pp. viii. Memoirs, 1. 18°. Poems, 183–287. Boston, 1873.

— Morèio. A Provençal Poem by Frédéric Mistral. Translated. 12°, pp. xvii, 249. Boston, 1872.

— Troubadours and Trouvères. New and Old. 12°, pp. viii, 280. Boston, 1876.

PRESTON, (MARGARET J.) Cartoons. 3d Edition. 16°, pp. 240. Boston, 1881.

PRESTY, PEGGY, AND OTHER BALLADS. Illustrated by Rosince Emmet. 4°, pp. 64. New York, 1880.

PREUSS, (H. C.) "God Save our Noble Union," etc. 8°, pp. 8. Washington, 1862.

PRICE, (C. A.) Poems. 12°, pp. 180. Charleston, 1850.

PRICE, (J. H.) Miscellany in Verse and Prose. 12°, pp. 168. Albany, 1813.

PRICE, (T. B.) Kissing a Soldier! A Drama. 12°, pp. 25. Baltimore, 1863.

PRIME, (B. Y.)

Benjamin Young Prime was born at Huntington, L. I., December 20, 1733, graduated at Princeton in 1751, and was tutor in the college 1756-57, having in the interim turned his attention somewhat to the study of medicine. He went to Europe in 1762 to pursue to better advantage his professional studies as a physician. After a residence abroad of not far from three years, he took his medical degree at the University of Leyden. He became, as we are told, "a highly accomplished scholar, eminent for his mathematical, philosophical and classical attainments. He was in the habit of writing with great facility both prose and poetry, in the Hebrew, Greek, Latin, French and Spanish languages; and in the opening of the Revolutionary struggle his patriotic and popular songs spread like wild-fire over the land, and helped to kindle the sparks of liberty into a flame." The curious reader will find some of these songs in the Curiosities of American Literature, appended by Griswold to D'Israel's Collection, and in Duyckinck, vol. I, pp. 433-34. Dr. Prime for several years practiced his profession in the city of New York, and then removed to Huntington to be with his father in his declining years. Here he died October 31, 1701. One of his sons, Rev. Dr. Nathaniel Scudder Prime, was the father of Dr. Prime, the "Irenæus" of the *New York Observer*.

— Columbia's Glory; or, British Pride Humbled. A Poem on the American Revolution : some part of it being a parody on an ode entitled Britain's Glory; or, Gallic Pride Humbled. Composed on the Capture of Quebec, A. D. 1759. 8°, pp. vi, 42. New York, 1791.

This poem, of 1,441 lines, "was ready for publication at the close of the war, but, as the author informs us, in consequence of a seven years' absence from the city, his affairs had become somewhat deranged, and as no printer could be found to execute the work on any but cash terms, he postponed publishing it for a few years."

— Muscipula, sive Cambromyomachia. The Mouse Trap, etc. 16°, pp. 96. New York, 1840.

PRIMER, NEW ENGLAND; OR, AN EASY AND PLEASANT GUIDE TO THE ART OF READING. Adorn'd with Cutts. To which are added, The Assembly of Divines' Catechism, etc. Boston : Printed and sold by J. White, near Charles River Bridge.

This is a small 32° book, not paged, printed probably in 1789. So far as is known the earliest copy of the Primer now in existence was printed in Boston in 1737. This, together with five other copies, brought at the Brinley sale, $612. It is not known who compiled the Primer, or the date of the first publication.

— Same. New York, 1829.

PRINCE, ERICK. (Anon.) A Satire. 8°, pp. 32. New York, 1872.

PRINCETON COLLEGE PRODUCTIONS. 1868. Several Poems in the volume. 8°, pp. 115. No date.

Prisoner, The. (Anon.) 16°, pp. 24. Trenton, 1802.

Prize Book, The. No. 1. Latin School, Boston. 8°, pp. 63. Boston, 1820.

> This volume contains a Latin Poem by William Newell; Latin Translation of Pope's Messiah, by Samuel Parker; English Translation of Juvenal's Satire III., by E. H. Derby; English Translation of Horace, Ode X., Book II., by J. H. Deblois, and an English Poem by E. H. Derby.

Proctor, (Ednah Dean.) Poems. 18°, pp. iv, 140. New York, 1866.

Progress, A Poet's. 16°, pp. 12. New York, 1818.
— The, of Society. (Anon.) 18°, pp. vii, 62. New York, 1817.

Prometheus' Diarial Account, etc. (Anon.) 8°. Chicago, 1869.
> Prose, with which several poems are bound.

Proser, A. Poems by. (Anon.) 18°, pp. 48. New York, 1831.

Ps and Qs. (Anon.) 18°, pp. 200. Boston, 1828.

Psalm-Book, The New England.
> An imperfect copy.
— Same. 18°, pp. 360. Boston, 1758.
— Same. 27th Edition. 18°, pp. 334. Boston, 1762.

Psalms. Allowed by the Synod of New York and Philadelphia. 24°, pp. 306. New York, 1790.
— Same. 24°, pp. 285. Philadelphia, 1792.

Psalms and Hymns. A Collection, etc. Revised Edition, with Supplement. (Anon.) 18°, pp. 508. New York, 1857.

Psalms, Hymns, etc. 2 vols. in 1. 24°, pp. 90, 90. London, 1719 and 1741.
> Bought at the Brinley sale. Small print, a clean, perfect copy, and richly bound.

Psalms, New England. 25th Edition. 18°, pp. 346. Boston, 1742.
> A perfect and elegantly bound copy.

Psalms, The, | Hymns, | and | Spiritual Songs | of the | Old and New Testament. | Faithfully Translated into | English Metre. | For the use, edification and comfort of the Saints in publick and private, especially in *New England.* | 2. Tim. 3. 16, 17. | Col. 3. 16. *Let the Word of God dwell in you richly in all wisdome, teaching and admonishing one another in Psalms, Hymns, and Spiritual Songs, Singing to the Lord with grace in your hearts.* |

Psalms, The, etc. — *Continued.*

> Ephes. 5. 18. 19. *Be filled with, &c.* | James 5. 13. | Cambridge. | Printed for Hezekiah Usher, of Bostoo. | No date.

"Bostoo" is evidently a misprint for Boston.

The above is an exact copy — the only change being in placing the word "the" after, instead of before, the word "Psalms" — of one of the most unique and most valuable volumes in "The Harris Collection." It is a 12°, pp. 100, printed at Cambridge, England. Just over the word Cambridge, a little to the right is written, H. M. There is nothing to indicate who H. M. was. At the bottom of the page is the letter C. Six of the originally blank pages at the beginning of the book are covered with short-hand writing. At the bottom of the sixth page some one has written in pencil 1650[?] The figures indicating the first fourteen pages are written, not printed, and are in Roman characters. Page i is the title page. Page ii is blank. Pages iii-vii is the Preface, which is a reproduction of the Preface in the Bay Psalm Book, with the exception that certain abbreviations in the Preface of the Bay Psalm Book are expanded in the later Psalm Book, and there are some changes in spelling. Occupying one-third of the middle of page viii, the remaining two-thirds being blank, is the address "To the Godly Reader" as follows: "We know that these Psalms, and Hymns, and Spirituall Songs, though in other Languages (and so consequently in other Poeticall Measures) were inspired by the Holy Ghost, to holy men of old, for the edification and comfort of the Church and People of God in all ensuing ages to the end of the world. And for these holy ends we have with speciall care and diligence translated them into such Meeters as are most usuall and suitable for such holy Poems, in our language, having special eye both to the gravity of the phrase of Sacred Writ and sweetness of the Verse. And for fuller satisfaction of the godly desires of all, we have added sundry interpretations, according to the latitude of the significations of the Hebrew Text, commonly noted with an asterisk thus [*], and some other various readings, though not so noted." On page ix are several passages translated from the Old Testament. The following is Hab. 3, 9:

> "His chariots of Salvation were,
> Streams by thy bow their channels
> leave:
> Th' oath words to th' tribes that thou
> didst swear
> Thou didst the earth with rivers
> cleave·"

Pages x-xiv contain Songs of Moses. 1. Exod. 15. After the passage through the Red Sea. 2. Deut. 32. The Prophetical Song,— The Song of Deborah and Barak. Judges 5. The Song of Hannah. I. Sam. 2. David's Elegie. II. Sam. 1, 17-27. We give one example of the remarkable versification of an old Puritan hymologist, selecting it from a famous passage in the Song of Deborah and Barak. Judges, v. 28—31.

> "28. Out of a window Sisera
>         his mother look'd and said,
> The lattess through, in coming why
> So long's his chariot stald?
> His chariot wheeles, why tarry they?
>
> 29. Her wise dames answered;
> Yea she turn'd answer to her selfe.
>
> 30. And what have they not sped?
> The prey by poll a Maid or twain
>         what parted have not they?

PSALMS, THE, ETC. — *Continued.*

> Have they not parted Sisera
>     a party-coloured prey?
> A party-coloured nield-work prey,
>     of nield-work on each side,
> That's party-coloured, meet for
>         necks
> Of them that spoiles divide?
>
> 31.   So perish let thine enemies all
>      O Lord; but let each wight
> That do him love, be like the Sun
>      that goes out in his might."

The Psalter is pp. 1—93. The Song of Songs, which is Solomon's, pp. 94-98. The Songs in the Prophet Isaiah, pp. 98-101, being selected from Chaps. v, xii, in two "Meeters," xxv, xxvi and xxxviii, "The Song of Hezekiah, after his recovery from sickness." The Lamentations of Jeremiah, Chap. iii, v. The Prayer of Jonah, Chap. ii. A Prayer of Habakuk, Chap. iii. Three Songs from Luke. 1. The Song of the blessed Virgin Mary, Luke i, 46. 2. The Song of Zacharias, verses 68-79. 3. The Song of Simeon, Luke ii, 29. Then follow several translations of short passages in the Book of Revelation. The foregoing are pp. 101-106.

At the bottom of p. xiv there is a blank space of about one-fifth of the page. On this blank space some one has pasted a small engraving of a monk, apparently with shaven head, and cowl thrown back, and face upturned to heaven, as if he were in the act of prayer.

On one of the fly leaves, at the end of the volume, is a written version of the 8th Psalm, in five verses, by whom made there is nothing to show.

A slip cut from Longman, 1830, is pasted on the bottom of the inside of the right cover. At the end of the title we read, "*extremely rare,* 8°, 18s."

For a valuable bibliographical note, prepared by Wilberforce Eames of the Lenox Library, on this very rare volume, see Sabin's Dictionary of Books relating to America, Parts xci-xcii, p. 30. Mr. Eames, who has devoted much time and research in ascertaining all that can be learned about "the Psalms, Hymns, etc.," in the different editions from 1651 to 1672, says: "The only copy of this edition that I know of was sold at the Brinley sale for $90, and is now in the library of Brown University at Providence."

PUMMILL, (J.)   Russet Leaves.   12°, pp. 213.   Philadelphia, 1870.

PUMPELLY, (M. H.)   Poems.   8°, pp. iv, 76.   New York, 1852.

PURDY, (S. S.)   Paul Pry Songster.   16°, pp. 64.   New York, 1865.

PUTNAM, (MRS. M. L.)

Mary Lowell, sister of James Russell Lowell, was born at Boston, December 3, 1810, distinguished in early life for her linguistic attainments, married in 1832 Samuel R. Putnam, a Boston merchant, who died in 1861. Mrs. Putnam is one of the most accomplished female writers in America.

— A Translation of "The Bondmaid."   By Frederika Bremer.   16°, pp. vi, 112.   Boston, 1844.

— Tragedy of Errors.   16°, pp. 249.   Boston, 1862.

— Tragedy of Success.   16°, pp. 191.   Boston, 1862.

QUAKER QUIDDITIES; OR, FRIENDS IN COUNCIL. A Colloquy. (Anon.)
12°, pp. 48. Boston, 1860.

The name of the author of this little volume, J. B. Congdon, is not given on the title
page. It is "dedicated to the Alumni of the Yearly-Meeting School, Providence, by an
Undergraduate." The writer, a birth-right Friend, while admitting the decline of Quakerism, says that "the vital questions are: 'Is it worth saving?' 'Can it be saved?' 'How
can it be saved?' One thing is sure, it must show its right to a distinctive place in the
world's civilization by something more significant and progressive than a formless method
in its meetings and a uniform costume. Its negations cannot give it a longer lease of life.
It must in some way grapple with the world and show its potency by helping the world
onward. The world is demanding aid from every organization that has for its object the
inculcation of moral and religious truth. It is not satisfied, it should not be satisfied, with
the plea of self-preservation. It seems to me that Quakerism is dying of isolation."

QUARTER DAY EXERCISES, YALE COLLEGE, MARCH 28, 1776. 12°, pp.
31. Hartford, 1776.

These "Exercises" are two dialogues, the second of which is entitled "On the Success of our Arms and the Rising Glory of America." The speakers are Count Massilon, a
French gentleman, and Narvon, an American. The piece is filled with the patriotic spirit
of Revolutionary times.

QUINCY, (J. P.)

Josiah Phillips Quincy, a grandson of President Quincy of Harvard College, was
born at Boston in 1830, and graduated at Harvard in 1850. In 1854 he published, as literary
curiosities, not as illustrations of the text, "Manuscript Corrections from a copy of the
Fourth Folio of Shakespeare's Plays." This is the pamphlet to which Professor F. Bowen
refers in an able article in the North American Review, April, 1854, on the "Restoration of
the Text of Shakespeare." He remarks: "Copies of the old folio editions of Shakespeare
containing manuscript corrections of the text made by some unknown hand are not rare
or difficult to be had." One "exists here in Boston." Mr. Quincy was a contributor to
the pages of "Sartain," "Putnam," etc.

— Charicles. A Dramatic Poem. 12°, pp. viii, 102. Boston, 1856.
— Lyteria. A Dramatic Poem. 16°, pp. 123. Boston, 1854.

The two works of which the titles are given above are warmly commended in the
North American Review, the latter in January No., 1855, and the former in January No.,
1857.

RADICAL CLUB. (Anon.) 18°, pp. 14. Boston, 1876.

RAKE, THE NASSAU. (Edited and Published by the Sophomore Class of
the College of New Jersey.) 8°, pp. 96. Princeton, June, 1858.

RALLING, (J.) Miscellaneous. 12°, pp. 24. Philadelphia, 1790.
— Miscellaneous Sketches in Prose and Verse. 12°, pp. 24. New-
buryport, 1796.
— The Time Piece. 8°, pp. vi, 170. Philadelphia, 1803.

RALPH, (J.)

James Ralph was born, as is supposed, at Philadelphia, not far from the year 1698. For a time he taught school in his native city, where he formed the acquaintance of Franklin, and accompanied him on his visit to England in 1724. He seems to have lived in a desultory sort of way, writing as a political pamphleteer, appearing as an actor on the stage, composing verses, etc. He published, in 1728, his "Night," referred to below, to which Pope, in his "Dunciad," alluded in severe terms. Subsequently he became the author of a number of works, prose and poetical, some of which were commended. He died at Chiswick, January 24, 1762.

— Clarinda; or, The Fair Libertine. 8°, pp. 64. London, 1729.
— Night. 12°, pp. x, 75. London, 1728.

The lines from Pope's "Dunciad" alluded to above, were as follows:
"Silence, ye wolves, while Ralph to Cynthia howls,
And makes night hideous: Answer him, ye owls."

— Sawney. 12°, pp. xvi, 45 London, 1728.
— The Fashionable Lady. 8°, pp. 94. London, 1730.
— The Muses' Address to the King. 12°, pp. 43. London, 1728. ·
— The Tempest; or, The Terrors of Death. 16°, pp. 27. London, 1727.
— Zeuma; or, The Love of Liberty. 8°, pp. vi, 136. London, 1729.

RAND, (E. S., JR.) Life Memories, etc. 12°, pp. 176. Boston, 1859.

RANDALL, (J. W., M. D.) Consolations of Solitude. 12°, pp. 261. Boston, 1856.

This copy contains many corrections and improvements in writing by the author.

RANDOLPH, (A. D. F.) Hopefully Waiting, etc. Sq. 16°, pp. 101. New York, 1867.

The well-known New York Publisher.

RANDOLPH, IDA, OF VIRGINIA. (Anon.) 12°, pp. 60. Philadelphia, 1860.

RANKIN, (MRS. S. B.) Centennial Poem. 8°, pp. 24. Peoria, Ill., no date.

RANKIN, (J. E.) Heather Bells. 8°, pp. 20. Washington, 1872.

A Congregational clergyman for several years settled in Washington, D. C.

RATCATCHER'S DAUGHTER, THE. (Anon.) Illustrated. Sq. 18°, not paged. London, no date.

RAY, (L.) Phi Beta Kappa Poem, Yale, August 18, 1847. 8°, pp. 16. New Haven, 1847.

RAY, (W.)

William Ray was born at Salisbury, Conn., December, 1771. When he was nineteen he took charge of a school in Dover, Dutchess county, N. Y., then embarked in business, was unfortunate, and after various fortunes, he enlisted June 13, 1803, in the maratime service of the United States, and on the 3d of July following embarked on board the Philadelphia, under command of Captain Bainbridge, to join the squadron against Tripoli. The frigate having run upon a shoal in the harbor of Tripoli, was taken by the pirates, and Ray and his companions were made prisoners, and endured the severest hardship from which they were not released until June 3, 1805. The subject of this sketch returned to the United States in 1800. For a time he engaged in mercantile pursuits, and when war was declared in 1812, he received an appointment as Major, serving, however, only for a short time. He finally settled in Onondaga, N. Y., where he was Justice of the Peace and Commissioner in Courts of Record. His death took place at Auburn, N. Y., in 1827.

Everest says : "His poems are characterised by melodious versification, and are often forcible."

— Poems. 12°, pp. 254. Title-page gone.
— Same. 8°, pp. viii, 254. Auburn, 1821.
— Poems on Various Subjects. 18°, pp. 252. New York, 1826.

READ, (H. F.)

Harriet Fanning Read was born at Jamaica Plain, near Boston, her father being a "book-seller and publisher, and a man of much intelligence and taste." Her grandfather on the mother's side was a distinguished officer in the British army in the Revolutionary war. When young she removed to Washington and became an inmate of her uncle Colonel Fanning's family. Upon the death of her uncle in 1846, she removed to New York. In February, 1848, she made her appearance as an actress at the Boston Theatre, and afterwards played in Washington. Of her subsequent career we have no information.

— Dramatic Poems. 8°, pp. vi, 297. Boston, 1848.

The poems in this volume are Medea, Erominia, and the New World.

READ, (MRS. M. S.) The Wild Flower. 32°, pp. 96. Portland, 1848.

READ, (T. B.)

Thomas Buchanan Read was born in Chester county, Penn., March 12, 1822. In 1636 he went to Cincinnati and entered the studio of the Sculptor Clevinger and learned the art of the chisel, and on the departure of his master to Europe he turned his attention to portrait painting, in which he soon achieved reputation and succes. In 1841 he removed to New York and the following year to Boston, where he married and resided for five years, practicing his profession and engaged in literary pursuits, the productions of his pen attracting attention from the literary world. In 1846 he took up his residence in Philadelphia, and in 1850 went to Florence, where, with occasional visits to the United States, he resided for twenty-five years. On his return to America early in 1872, he resided during the few remaining months of his life chiefly in Philadelphia and Cincinnati. He died in New York, May, 1872.

For notice of his works, (see Allibone, pp. 1752-53.)

— A Summer Story. Sheridan's Ride, etc. 12°, pp. ix, 154. Philadelphia, 1865.

READ, (T. B.) — *Continued.*

— Gems from his Poetical Works. Sq. 16°. " Drifting," not paged. " Brushwood," not paged. " Christine," pp. 45. Philadelphia, 1884.

— Lays and Ballads. 2d Edition. 8°, pp. 140. Philadelphia, 1849.

— Poems. 12°, pp. 124. Boston, 1847.

— Same. 2 vols. 8°, pp. 426–426. Boston, 1860.

— Sylvia, etc. 8°, pp. 158. Philadelphia, 1857.

— The Female Poets of America, with Portraits, Biographical Notices and Specimens of their Writings. 8°, pp. xvi, 420. Philadelphia, 1849.

— The Home by the Sea. 8°, pp. 152. Philadelphia, 1856.

— The New Pastoral. 8°, pp. xiv, 249. Philadelphia, 1855.

— Same. New Edition. 12°, pp. 249. Philadelphia, 1856.

— The Poetical Works. In 3 vols. 12°, pp. 426, 423, 420. Philadelphia, 1866.

— The Wagoner of the Alleghanies. 8°, pp. 276. Philadelphia, 1863.

— Same. Illustrated from Drawings by Hovenden, Fenn, Gaul and Low. 12°, pp. 74. Philadelphia, 1885.

    A beautiful copy. Bound, Alligator limp.

READ, (Y.) Masks. 12°, pp. 48. New York, 1838.

READE, (J.) The Prophecy of Merlin, etc. 16°, pp. 237. Montreal, 1870.

RED BOOK, THE. Prose and Poetry. A Serial. 2 vols. 18°, pp., vol. i, 171, vol. ii, continues 174–262, and this really completes vol. i. pp. 87 of vol. ii, are bound in the second of the two volumes. Baltimore, 1819–20.

    The first number is dated October 23, 1810.

RED ROVER, THE. A Drama founded on J. F. Cooper's Novel of that Name. 18°, pp. 52. Philadelphia, no date.

REDBURN ; OR, THE SCHOOLMASTER OF A MORNING. (Anon.) 12°, pp. 71. New York, 1845.

REDDEN, (LAURA C.) Idyls of Battle and Poems of the Rebellion. 16°. New York, 1864.

Rede, (W. L.)  The Flight to America; or, Ten Hours in New York
A Drama.  18°, pp. 47.  Philadelphia and New York, no date.

Reed, (P. F.)  The Voices of the Wind, etc.  12°, pp. 199.  Chicago,
1868.

Reed, (R. G.)  Thoughts from Scripture.  8°, pp. 64.  New York,
1843.

Rees, (J.)

James Rees was born at Morristown, Pa., in 1802, and was a journalist in Philadelphia,
and held office in the Post Office of that city.  He died in Pennsylvania in 1885.

— The Battle of Saratoga.  16°, pp. 20.  New York, 1839.
— The Dramatic Authors of America.  12°, pp. xi, 144.  Philadelphia, 1845.

Rees, (L. S. D.)  Theroique de Mericourt.  A Romance.  In Five Parts.
Parts I, II, 12°, pp. 32, 44.  Philadelphia, 1855.

Reiff, (D. P.)  Poems.  3d Edition.  8°, pp. 100.  St. Louis, 1865.

Reign of Reform, The; or, Yankee Doodle Court.  (Anon.)  16°,
pp. 146.  Baltimore, 1830.

Rejected Addresses.  Presented for the Cup offered for the best Address
at the Opening of the New Theatre, Philadelphia.  18°, pp. 107.
Philadelphia, 1823.

Relly, (J. and J.)  Christian Hymns.  8°. pp. iv, 235.  Burlington,
1776.
— Same.  12°, pp. 241.  Portsmouth, N. H., 1782.

Remains of My Early Friend.  (Anon.)  16°, pp. 55.  Keene, N. H.,
1828.

Remington, (A. G.)  Prose and Verse.  18°, pp. 106.  New York, no
date.

Reno, (Lydia M.)

She was born at Rochester, Penn., 1831, a contributor to several periodicals.

— Early Buds.  12°, pp. 309.  Boston and Cambridge, 1853.

Renville, (J. and Sons.)  Hymns in the Dakota or Sioux Languages.
18°, pp. 105.  Boston, 1842.

31

REPOSITORY, THE SONGSTERS'. (Anon.) 12°, pp. 286. New York, 1811.

REQUIER, (A. J.)

> Augustus Julian Requier was born at Charleston, S. C., May 27, 1825, and was of French extraction. He was admitted to the bar, 1844, and held the position of District Attorney for the southern district of Alabama, 1853–61, and held the same office under the Confederate Government.

— Poems. 12°, pp. 190. Philadelphia, 1860.

RESPONSE TO CHARLESTON. A Poem, etc. 12°, pp. 15. No place, 1848.

RETREAT, A, FROM TOWN. 8°, pp. 24. Boston, 1815.

RETROSPECT, ETC. (Anon.) 12°, pp. viii, 142. Boston, 1846.

REUNION GRADUATES. Senior Department of School No. 47, 12th Street, New York. Several Poems in the volume. 4°, pp. 73. New York, 1865.

REVELATION OF NATURE WITH THE PROPHECY OF REASON. (Anon.) 16°, pp. xxxix, 164. New York, no date.

REVERIES IN RHYME. (By "Nemo" of Louisiana—in pencil John L. Megee.) 12°, pp. 88. New York, 1846.

REVOLUTION IN ORCUS. (By Piang Pu, *pseud.*) 12°, pp. vi, 112. New York, 1848.

REVOLUTIONARY WAR, HISTORY OF. 12°, pp. 243. Title-page gone.

REYNOLDS, (D. C.) A Romance in Smoke. 4°, pp. 26. . Providence, 1876.

> Illustrations by W. F. Brown.

REYNOLDS, (J. P.) Poems. 24°, pp. 20. Freehold, N. J., 1851.

REYNOLDS, (T.) A Poem Spoken on the Summit of Wamang Mountain, August 16, 1820. 18°, pp. 12. New Haven, 1820.

RHAND, (TALLY. A *pseud.*) Guttle and Gulpit. A Farce. 12°, pp. 36. New York, 1854.

RHAPSODY, A. (Anon.) 8°, pp. 19. New York, 1789.

RHODE ISLAND COTTAGE. (Anon.) 18°, pp. 108. New York, 1835.

RHODES, (W. H.)  Poem.  Twenty-first Anniversary of the Corporate Society of California Pioneers, September 9, 1871.  8°, pp. 7.  San Francisco, 1871.

— The Indian Gallows, etc.  8°, pp. 153.  New York, 1846.

RHODOMANTHUS, ETC.  (Anon.)  12°, pp. 23.  No place, 1858.

RHYME, STORIES IN.  (Anon.  Entered by S. S.)  8°, pp. 48.  New York, 1850.

RHYME, THE AGE OF ; OR, A GLANCE AT THE POETS.  By a Southerner.  8°, pp. 30.  Charleston, 1830.

RHYMED TACTICS.  (By "Gov.," *pseud.*)  18°, pp. 144.  New York, 1862.

RHYMERS' CLUB, THE.  (By an Honorary Member.  Anon.)  12°, pp. 71.  New York, 1859.

RHYMES FOR MY CHILDREN.  (By a Mother.  Anon.)  18°, pp. 108.  Boston, 1837.

RHYMING STORY BOOK.  (Anon.)  Sq. 12°, pp. 64.  New York, 1867.

RICE, (G. E.)

George Edward Rice was born at Boston in 1822, and graduated at Harvard in 1840. He was admitted to the bar and practiced in Boston for several years.  His death occurred at Roxbury, Mass., in 1863.

— An Old Play in a New Garb.  Hamlet.  12°, pp. 59.  Boston, 1852.

— Blondel : A Historic Fancy.  12°, pp. 51.  Boston, 1854.

— Myrtilla.  A Fairy Extravaganza.  12°, pp. 35.  Boston, 1854.

"These dramatic pieces," *i. e.*, the above, says Allibone, "display a very uncommon species of talent."

— Nugamenta ; A Book of Verses.  12°, pp. viii, 145.  Boston, 1860.

The North American Review, July, 1860, p. 273, says : "With these *Nugamenta* there are several pieces of altogether higher order, which evince in the author true poetic sensibility and an easy command of imagery, language and rhythm."

— (AND J. H. WAINWRIGHT.)  Ephemera.  12°, pp. 112.  Boston, 1852.

RICE, (H.)

Harvey Rice was born at Conway, Mass., in 1800, graduated at Williams College in 1820, removed to Cleveland, Ohio, in 1824, was a teacher for a short time, admitted to the bar in 1826, started the Cleveland *Plaindealer* in 1829.  As a member of the State Senate he took a prominent part in school legislation.

— Mount Vernon, etc.  12°, pp. 184.  Boston, 1858.

RICE, (J.)   The Battle Fields of the Revolution.   8°, pp. 15.   Palmer, Mass., 1859.

RICE, (R.)   Orations and Poetry.   12°, pp. 362.   Albany, no date.

RICHARDS, (G.)   The Declaration of Independence, by a Citizen of Boston.   8°, pp. 24.   Boston, 1793.

RICHARDS, (W. C.)

William C. Richards, Ph. D., was born at London, England, in 1817, came to this country in 1831, was a graduate of Madison University, N. Y., in 1848, was a Baptist preacher in Georgia and South Carolina, and in Providence, R. I.   He has given courses of lectures on Chemistry, and been a frequent contributor to the periodicals of the day. His residence is now (1886) in Chicago.

— Electron ; or, The Pranks of the Modern Puck.   12°, pp. 84.   New York, 1858.

— Retrorsum :  Madison  University Alumni School, August 4, 1869.   12°, pp. 48.   New York, 1869.

RICHARDSIANA.   (Anon.)   8°, pp. 40.   New York, 1841.

RICHMOND, (C. R.)

Cyrus Richmond Richmond was born at Maryland, N. Y., March 14, 1814, removed in 1829 with his father, a Baptist minister, to Rome, Ohio, was ordained in 1843, and was pastor of the church in his adopted home for ten years, occupying, for a part of the time, offices of civil trust.   After ministering to several churches in Ohio, identifying himself in the most decided way with the great reform movements of the day, he died at Geneva, Ohio, December 19, 1885.

— Selections from Poetical Writings.   12°, pp. 43.   Privately printed.   Cambridge, 1886.

Prefixed to the Poem is a MS. Biographical Sketch of Mr. Richmond prepared by Mr. R. H. Ferguson of the Newton Theoligical Institution.

RICORD, (MRS. ELIZABETH.)

She was born in 1787, was a teacher in Genesee, N. Y., 1828–48, and for a number of years, in the city of New York, where she died in 1865.

— Zamba ; or, The Insurrection.   A Dramatic Poem.   12°, pp. 139.   Cambridge, 1842.

RIDER, (G. T.)

George Thomas Rider was born at Coventry, R. I., in 1829, graduated at Trinity College, Hartford, 1850, and took orders in the Episcopal church.

— Lyra Americana.   12°, pp. x, 295.   New York, 1865.

— "Now and Then."   A Poem Delivered at the Junior Exhibition, Trinity College, Hartford, August 1, 1849.   8°, pp. 8.   No place.

— Reminiscences.   8°, pp. 15.   Hartford, 1848.

RIFLE SHOTS AT PAST AND PASSING EVENTS. (Anon.) 8°, pp. 112. Philadelphia, no date.

RIGGS, (L. G.) The Anarchiad. Sq. 18°, pp. 120. New Haven, 1861.

RICHMOND, (J. C.)

James Cook Richmond was born at Providence, R. I., in 1808, graduated at Harvard in 1828, and took orders in the Episcopal Church. After preaching several years, he came to an untimely end, being murdered in Poughkeepsie, N. Y., in 1866.

— Metacomet. First American, from the London Edition. 12°, pp. 47. London, New York and Providence, 1851.

— The Country Schoolmaster in Love. 8°, pp. 16. New York, 1845.

RICHMOND, (W. E.) Mount Hope. An Evening Excursion. 16°, pp. 69. Providence, 1818.

RICKEY, (ANNA S.)

She was born at Philadelphia in 1827, and in 1851 became the wife of an eminent civil engineer, Solomon W. Roberts. She died in 1858.

— Forest Flowers of the West. 12°, pp. 138. Philadelphia, 1851.

RINALDO RINALDINI; OR, THE GREAT BANDITTI. A Tragedy. (Anon.) 18°, pp. 82. New York, 1810.

RING, (J.) Book of Rhymes. 12°, pp. 94. Clinton, 1853.

RINGGOLD, (G. H., U. S. A.) Fountain Rock, etc. New York, 1860.

RIPPON, (J., D. D.) Hymns. 24°, not paged. Baltimore, 1814.
— Same. With additions by Rev. W. Stoughton. 24°. Philadelphia, 1826.

RITCHIE, (A. T.) The Columbiad. 12°, pp. xi, 228. New York, 1849.

The Columbiad was originally published in London, 1843.

ROACH, (SALLIE NEILL.) Theon. A Tale of the American Civil War. 12°, pp. 220. Philadelphia, 1882.

ROATH, (D. L.) Zara. A Romance. 18°, pp. 160. Athens, 1851.

ROBBINS, (J. W.) Progress. Read before Roxbury Mechanics Institute, February 19, 1861. No place, no date.

ROBERTSON, (J.) Riego; or, The Spanish Martyr. A Tragedy. 12°, pp. 67. Richmond, Va., 1872.

ROBERTSON, (W.)  Sacred Harmony.  18°, pp. 36.  New York, 1831.

ROBINS.  The Christmas Eve (C. E. B.), with a Translation in French Poetry, by J. Gustave Bonnet.  8°, pp. 11.  New York, 1869.

ROBINSON, (ANNE S.)  Poetic Reveries.  8°, pp. 171.  Baltimore, 1848.

ROBINSON, (J. D.)  Poem.  Speech and Action.  Harvard, July 11, 1849.  16°, pp. 15.  Cambridge, 1849.

ROBINSON, (J. H.)  Nick Whiffles.  A Drama.  12°, pp. 35.  Boston, 1858.

ROBINSON, (T. R.)  Poems.  12°, pp. 140.  Brooklyn, 1808.

RODMAN, (T. P.)  Poem before New Bedford Mechanics' Association, July 4, 1833.  8°, pp. 15.  New Bedford, 1833.

RODMAN, (W. M.)

Mr. Rodman was mayor of the city of Providence, R. I., two years, June, 1857–59.

— Poem.  July 4, 1856.  8°, pp. 18.  Providence, 1856.

RODNEY, (R. B., U. S. N.)  Alboin and Rosamond.  16°, pp. 100.  Philadelphia, 1870.

— Pay-Day at Babel, etc.  Sq. 18°, pp. 65.  New York, 1872.

ROGERS, (D.)  A Poem on Liberty.  8°, pp. 29.  Albany, 1804.

ROGERS, (G.)  George Washington.  Crowned by Equality, etc.  18°, pp. 36.  New York, 1848.

— My Adopted Country.  In Three Parts.  12°, pp. 74.  New York, 1851.

ROGERS, (H. G.)  The Surrender of Creuta.  A Tragedy.  12°, pp. (with Letters from Italy, etc.,) 70.  New York, 1857.

ROGERS, (J. W.)  "La fitte;" or, The Greek Slave.  In Four Cantos.  8°, pp. 61.  Boston, London and Montreal, 1870.

— Washington Pillory.  8°, pp. 8.  No place, no date.

ROGERS, (R.)

Robert Rogers was born at Dunbarton, N. H., not far from 1730, his father, James R., an Irishman, being an early settler of that town.  During the French war he entered the army, having command of what was known as "Rogers' Rangers."  In 1765, while in England, he received an appointment from the King as Governor of Michillmackinac. After various fortunes we find him, in the war of the Revolution, a Loyalist Colonel of the Queen's Rangers.  In 1778 he was proscribed and banished, and we have no information

ROGERS, (R.)—*Continued.*

with regard to his subsequent history. His "Journals" and "Concise Account of North America," have been highly commended.

— Ponteach ; or, The Savages of America. A Tragedy. 8°, pp. 110. London, 1766.

This volume was published anonymously, and is believed to be very rare. Parkman, in his "History of the Conspiracy of Pontiac," says: "I am not aware of the existence of any copy besides my own and that in the library of the British Museum."

ROMANCE AFTER MARRIAGE. A Comedy. (Anon.) 12°, pp. 28. New York, no date.

ROOT, (G. F.) The Flower Queen. 12°, pp. 93. New York, 1852.

ROSE, (E. M. P.) Poetry of Locofocoism. 18°, pp. 48. Wellsburg, Va., 1848.

ROSE, (R. H.) Sketches in Verse. Lg. 8°, pp. viii, 184. Philadelphia, 1810.

A fine, uncut, and very rare copy.

ROUQUETTE, (A. E.)

Adrian Emmanual Rouquette, of mingled European and American parentage, was born at New Orleans in 1813, and received his education at the Royal College in Nantes, France. It was his purpose to enter the profession of law, and he studied with that end in view, but subsequently decided to become a clergyman in the Roman Catholic Church. Besides performing the duties of his office, he gave instruction in the Seminary in New Orleans, spending a part of his time at his residence in Mandeville, in the parish of St. Tammany, La. Of his later history we have no information.

— Wild Flowers. 8°, pp. 72. New Orleans, 1848.

This volume "falls in the rank of occasional verses, within the range of topics growing out of the peculiar views of his church, and shows a delicate sensibility in the choice of subjects."

ROUX, (A. A.) Louise Neckar French. 12°, pp. 46. New York, 1850.

ROVER, (R.) The Early Settlers in the West. A Poem. 8°, pp. 32. Cleveland, Ohio, 1859.

ROWLEY, (A.) Ten Chapters of the Book of Job. Translated from the Common Version into Verse. 8°, pp. 24. Boston, 1825.

ROWSON, (MRS. S.)

Susanna Haswell was born at Portsmouth, Eng., in 1761, and settled, with her father, Lieutenant William Haswell, of the Royal Navy, on the Island of Nantucket. At the time of the Revolution she returned to England, and in 1786 married William Rowson. In 1793 she came with her husband to the United States, was an actress for a time, and then a teacher near Boston. She died in Boston, March 2, 1824.

— Slaves in Algiers. A Play. 12°, pp. 74. Philadelphia, 1794.

Rudd, (E. B.)  Poem.  8°, pp. 15.  New York, 1861.

Rude Veins of a Poetic Conformation.  12°, pp. 179.  New York,
1845.

> The author's name written in pencil, W. A. Spies.

Rufus, (W.)  Rufiana.  12°, pp. 144.  New York, 1826.

Runnell, (E. B.)  The Wreath of Love.  Vol. 1.  18°, pp. 164.  New
York, 1852.

Ruschenberger, (Mrs. ———.)  The Bold Scotch Dragon.  A Play.
18°, pp. 48.  Philadelphia, no date.

Rush, (J., M. D.)

> James Rush, son of Dr. Benjamin Rush, was born at Philadelphia, March 1, 1785, grad-
> uated at Princeton in 1805, studied medicine and practiced his profession several years.
> He died at Philadelphia, May 26, 1869.  He bequeathed over a million of dollars to the
> establishment and support of " The Ridgway Branch of the Philadelphia Library."

— Hamlet.  A Dramatic Prelude.  12, pp. 122.  Philadelphia, 1834.

Rushtabow.  By Sundown.  (Anon.)  8°, pp. 33.  New York, 1848.

Rusling, (J.)

> Joseph Rusling, an English Methodist minister, was born in Lincolnshire in 1788, and
> died in 1839.

— Devotional Exercises, etc.  18°, pp. 236.  Philadelphia, 1836.

Russell, (C. P.)  In Tenebris.  13th Annual Convention of the Delta
Psi Fraternity, Columbia, S. C., December 6, 1859.  8°, pp. 26.
Columbia, S. C., 1860.

Russell, (J. M.)  Fourth of July Poems.  8°, pp. 16.  Boston, 1798.

Russell, (S.)  Poems, edited by.  12°, pp. ix, 118.  Philadelphia,
1859.

Russian Ball, The; or, The Adventures of Miss Clementina
Shoddy.  12°, pp. 32.  New York, 1863.

Rustic Rhymes.  (Anon.)  16°, pp. 113.  Philadelphia, 1859.

Ryder, (G. M.)  Gillian, etc.  12°, pp. x, 106.  Philadelphia, 1658.


Sacred Melodies.  (Compiled.)  12°, pp. 111.  New York, 1841.

Saddle, In the.  (Anon.)  18°, pp. 185.  Boston, 1882.

St. George, (J.) Leisure Moments. Containing Corola, etc. 16°, pp. 152. Baltimore, 1840.

St. John, (T. P.) Annus Mirabilis. Delivered at the 46th Anniversary of the Philoxenian Society, Columbia College. 8°, pp. 15. Published for the Society. New York, 1848.

St. Jonathan. The Lay of a Scald. (Anon.) 12°, pp. 48. New York, 1838.

St. Katharine's Spire; or, The Devil at Work in the Church. A Ritualistic Melody in Four Parts. 18°, pp. 88. New York, 1872.

St. Nicholas, A Visit from. Darley's Illustrations. 4°. No date.

Saltus, (F. S.)

Frank S. Saltus, a journalist, who has written under the signature of "Cupid Jones."

— Honey and Gall. Poems. 12°, pp. 231. Philadelphia, 1873.

Sanborn, (R. S.) Theism. 16°, pp. 52. Rockford, Ill., 1873.

Sands, (G. W.) Mazelli, etc. 12°, pp. vi, 156. Philadelphia, 1849.

Sands, (R. C.)

Robert Charles Sands was born at Flatbush, L. I., May 11, 1799, graduated at Columbia College in 1815, was admitted to the New York bar in 1820, devoted himself to literary pursuits, and was assistant editor of the *New York Commercial Advertiser* five years. He died December 17, 1832. His Memoir was written by his friend, G. C. Verplanck. 2 vols. 8°. 2d Edition, 1835.

— The Bridal of Vaumond. 16°, pp. 186. New York, 1817.
— Writings. Prose and Verse. 2 vols. pp. 391, 408. New York, 1834.

Sandys, (G.)

George Sandys was born at York, England, in 1577, educated at Oxford, an extensive Oriental traveller, in 1621 went to Virginia as Colonial Treasurer, returned to England in 1624, and engaged in literary pursuits. He died at Bexley Abbey, Kent, in March, 1644.

— A Paraphrase, etc. 8°, pp. 240. London, 1676.

Sangster, (C.)

A journalist born in Kingston, Canada, in 1822.

— The St. Lawrence, etc. 12°, pp. 262. Kingston and New York, 1856.

32

SANGSTER, (MARGARET E.) · Poems of the Household.    °8, pp. 259.
   Boston, 1882.

   "Many of these bits of verse, now gathered into a volume, originally appeared in
   *Harper's Monthly and Bazar, Christian Intelligencer, Sunday School Times*, and else_
   where."

SANTA CLAUS AND JENNY LIND.    (Anon.)    Sq. 18°, not paged.    New
   York, 1850.

SARGENT, (E.)

   Epes Sargent was born at Gloucester, Mass, in 1814, was educated at the Boston Latin
   School, entered Harvard College, but did not complete the course, devoted himself as
   author and editor to literary pursuits.  Allibone classifies his works under forty distinct
   heads.  (See Allibone's Dictionary of Authors, pp. 1931–32.)

— Songs of the Sea.    12°, pp. 208.    Boston, 1847.
— Same.    2d Edition.    12°, pp. 208.    Boston, 1849.
— The Light of the Light-House, etc.    4°, pp. 16.    New York, 1844.
— The Woman who Dared.    12°, pp. vi, 270.    Boston, 1870.
— Velasco.    A Tragedy.    12°, pp. 115.    Boston, 1837.
— Same.    New York, 1839.

SARGENT, (H. J.) ·

   Henry Jackson Sargent, known as "Residuary Legatee of the late 'Walter Ano-
   nym,'" was born at Boston in 1809.  He entered Harvard College in 1828, but did not graduate.  The productions of his pen were published in several magazines and periodicals of
   the day.

— Feathers from a Moulting Muse.    12°, pp. 270.    Boston, 1854.

SARGENT, (J. O.)

   John Osborne Sargent was born at Gloucester, Mass., in 1810, graduated at Harvard
   in 1830, was admitted to the bar and practiced in Boston, New York and Washington.  He
   has been engaged in journalism, was an able political speaker, and has written a number
   of books for the press.

— The Last Night.    A Romance-Garland.    From the German of Anas-
   tasius Grün.    12°, pp. ix, 200.    New York, 1871.

SARGENT, (L. M.)

   Lucius Manlius Sargent was born at Boston, 1786, entered Harvard in 1804, did not
   graduate, but in 1842 received the degree of A. M., studied law, an earnest advocate of the
   temperance cause, and the writer of many temperance tales, etc.  He died at Roxbury,
   Mass., June 2, 1867.

— Cœlii Symposii Ænigmata.    12°, pp. iv, 35.    Bostoniæ, 1807.
— Hubert and Ellen, with other Poems.    4°, pp. 135.    Boston, 1812.
— Same.    24°, pp. 96.    Boston, 1815.

Sargent, (W.)

>Winthrop Sargent was born at Philadelphia, September 23, 1825, graduated at the University of Pennsylvania 1845, and at Cambridge Law School 1849, practiced in his native city and in New York. He was an able editor of American historical works, etc. He died at Paris, France, May 18, 1870.

— Selections of the Loyalist Poetry of the Revolution.  8°, pp. vii, 203. Philadelphia, 1857.

>The copy of Sargent's Loyalist Poetry in "The Harris Collection" is richly bound, with gilt upper edges, and the front and lower edges untrimmed. It is No. 37 of the edition of 99 that was originally published, and was subscribed for by Thomas F. Betton, of Philadelphia. The preface makes the statement that "from a large collection of the Loyalist Poetry of the American Revolution belonging to J. Francis Fisher and to Winthrop Sargent, of Philadelphia, this selection has been edited. Much of it has heretofore existed but in manuscript; and such pieces as are in print are now hardly to be found beyond the confines of two or three libraries. For this reason they are printed; and because they are the productions of a very important party, concerning whose conduct and motives very little is known save by the report of its foes and subjugators."

>The volume is one of exceeding great interest, and to those who would enter into the spirit of the Royalists of Revolutionary times it is of the highest value. Mr. Sargent says: "As these pieces were written in the days when a spade was called a spade, they may reasonably be expected to contain more than one ' strong, old-fashioned English word familiar to all who read their Bibles ! ' "

>The notes, pp. 151-203, are full of the sort of information one would like to have about the men and events of the stirring times of which they treat. The editor says: "There is now no probability that the whole record of the Revolution will ever be displayed. It is said that the English government once thought of setting forth its own story, and that Robert Southey was selected to prepare it for the public; but that, for one reason or another, the idea was dropped, never probably to be revived. The great change in International feeling since that day has made such a step no longer advisable; and the fact that the Tories, whose numbers and circumstances would have rendered their testimony indispensable, have died and made no sign, in itself offers an almost insuperable obstacle."

Satan Unbound.  A Dramatic Poem.  12°, pp. 19.  (Anon.  In pencil, "A Marylander.")  No place, no date.

Satires.  American, etc.  A 12° volume.  The following make up the contents of the volume:

1.  The Paradise of Fools.  By Nathan Nobody, with Critique by Simon Snappingturtle, Esq.

2.  The Quacks of Helicon.  By L. A. Wilmer.

3.  American Bards.  By Gorham H. Worth.

4.  The Dwarf.  By James Rees.

5.  The Hours of Childhood.  (Anon.)

6.  Cabiro.  By George H. Calvert.  Cantos I and II.

7.  Childe Martin.  (Anon.)

8.  The Loco's Lament.  (Anon.)

Satires. — *Continued.*

9.  The Wyoming Monument.  Title-page gone.
10.  No Slur, Else Slur.  A Dancing Poem.  By Nobody.
11.  Music of the Spheres.  By Henry Morford.
12.  Our City Clubs.  By a City Poet.
13.  The Battle of the Thames, October 5, 1813.  (Anon.)
14.  Humbugs of Speculation.

Sator, (H. H.)  Hercules.  8°, pp. 54.  Albany, 1856.

Saunders, (C. H.)  Rosina Meadows, the Village Maid.  A Drama.
12°, pp. 52.  Boston, no date.

— The Pirate's Legacy.  12°, pp. 26.  Boston, no date.

Saunders, (J. M.)  Miscellaneous Poems.  18°, pp. 144.  Philadelphia, 1834.

Savage, (J.)

John Savage was born at Dublin, Ireland, December 13, 1828.  He was an artist of
growing celebrity in his native land.  Having exposed himself to the displeasure of the
Government in 1848, he left his home and came to the United States, and has been engaged
in literary pursuits.  He took an active part in the civil war by raising Irish volunteers.
One of his war songs, "The Starry Flag," was very popular.

— Faith and Fancy.  12°, pp. 118.  New York, 1864.
— Lays of the Fatherland.  12°, pp. vi, 120.  New York, 1850.
— Poems.  Second Collected Edition.  12°, pp. 324.  New York, 1870.

Savage, (M. J.)

A Unitarian clergyman of Boston.

— Poems.  16°, pp. 247.  Boston, 1882.

Sawyer, (L.)

Lemuel Sawyer, of North Carolina, wrote the Memoirs of John Randolph.

— Blackbeard.  A Comedy.  16°, pp. 66.  Washington, 1824.
— The Wreck of Honor.  A Tragedy.  16°, pp. 86.  New York, date
torn from the title-page.

Sawyer, (Mrs. C. M.)

Caroline M. Fisher was born at Newton, Mass., in 1812, married, in 1832, Rev. Dr. T. J.
Sawyer, an eminent Universalist minister, resided in New York City and in Clinton,
N. Y.  She has been a frequent contributor to various periodicals.

— Poems of Mrs. Julia H. Scott, bound with Memoir.  12°, pp. 328.
Boston, 1853.

Saxe, (J. G.)

John Godfrey Saxe was born at Highgate, Vt., June 2, 1816, graduated at Middlebury College 1839, commenced the practice of law at St. Albans, Vt., in 1843, removed, 1850, to Burlington, Vt., and, for five years, edited *The Sentinel*. As a lecturer at lyceums, etc., he was very successful. For a time he edited the *Albany Evening Journal*, and subsequently resided in Brooklyn.

— Clever Stories, etc. Lg. 12°, pp. vi, 192. Boston, 1865.

— Leisure Day Rhymes. 8°, pp. 268. Boston, 1875.

— Poems. 12°, pp. viii, 128. Boston, 1850.

— Same. 2d Edition. 12°, pp. 140. Boston, 1850.

— Same. 3d Edition. 12°, pp. 152. Boston, 1851.

— Same. New Edition enlarged. 12°, pp. 182. Boston, 1852.

— Same. 5th Edition enlarged. 12°, pp. 192. Boston, 1854.

— Same. Complete Edition. 18°, pp. 308. Boston, 1861. Blue and Gold Series.

— Progress. 2d Edition. New York, 1847.

Several other poems, referred to in the Catalogue, bound up with " Progress."

— The Flying Dutchman. With 16 Comic Illustrations. 12°, not paged. New York, 1862.

— The Masquerade. 12°, pp. 237. Boston, 1866.

— The Money King, etc. 12°, pp. 180. Boston, 1850.

— Same. 1860.

— The Proud Miss Macbride. With Illustrations by A. Hoppin. 8°, pp. 38. Boston, 1874. .

Scales, (W.) The Quintessence of Universal History. 8°, pp. 22. No place, 1806.

Scanlan, (M.) Love and Land. 8°, pp. vii, 262. Chicago, 1866.

Allibone says " this volume is intended to fan the spirit of Irish animosity to England into a ' stronger and more concentrated flame.' "

Schadd, (J. C.) Nicholas of the Flue. 12°, pp. 144. Washington, 1866.

School, The, for Politicians; or, Non-Committal. A Comedy in Five Acts. 8°, pp. v, 179. New York, 1840.

Schoolcraft, (H. R.) (Colcraft, *pseud.*)

Henry Rowe Schoolcraft was born at Guilderland, near Albany, March 28, 1793, and was greatly distinguished as genealogist, mineralogist, antiquary and ethnologist. (See Johnson's Encyclopædia, vol. iv, pp. 128–29.) He died at Washington, December 10, 1864.

SCHOOLCRAFT, (H. R.) — *Continued.*

— Alhalla; or, The Land of Talladega. A Tale of the Creek War. 16°, pp. 116. New York and London, 1843.

— Helderbergia. 8°, pp. 54. Albany, 1855.

— Transallegania; or, The Groans of Missouri. 16°, pp. 24. New New York, 1820.

— The Rise of the West. 12°, pp. 20. New York, 1841.

SCIENCE, PROGRESS OF, THE. A Poem delivered at Harvard College, before a Committee of Overseers, April 21, 1780. By a Junior Sophister. 4°, pp. 10. No place, 1780.

SCIMITAR. By the Sharpe Family. Sm. 24°, pp. 32. Boston, 1840.

SCOTT, (J., D. D.)

James Scott was born at Langside, Scotland, in 1806, educated at Glasgow and Belfast, came to New York in 1832, and was pastor of churches at Fox Hill and German Valley, N. Y., and of the First Reformed Dutch Church, Newark, N. J. He furnished valuable contributions to the literature of his adopted country.

— The Guardian Angel. 12°, pp. 191. New York, 1859.

SCOTT, (J. M.)

A native of Connecticut.

— Blue Lights; or, The Convention. 16°, pp. 150. New York, 1817.

— The Sorceress; or, Salem. 16°, pp. xii, 120. Salem, Mass., 1817.

SCOTT, (MRS. JULIA H.)

Julia H. Kinney was born at Shesequin, Pa., in 1800, married, in 1835, Mr. David L. Scott, of Towanda, Pa., in 1842.

— Poems. 16°, pp. iv, 216. Boston, 1843.

SCOTT, (M. Y.) Fatal Jest. 16°, pp. 142. New York, 1819.

— The Deaf and Dumb. 8°, pp. 23. New York, 1819.

SCOTTISH FIDDLE, THE LAY OF. (Supposed to be written by Walter Scott, Esq.) 18°, pp. 262. New York, 1813.

SCOVELL, (T. P.) Poem delivered July 6, 1836, before the Senior Class of Yale. 8°, pp. 10. New Haven, 1836.

SCRIPTURES, SEARCH THE. (Anon.) 8°, pp. 148. San Francisco, 1881.

SEA CAPTAIN, THE. (By the author of "The Lady of Lyons.") 8°, pp. 88. New York, 1839.

Sea Serpent, The; or, Gloucester Hoax. 12°, pp. 34. Charleston, 1819.

Sealy, Celer, (*pseud.*) Echoes from the Garrett. 16°, pp. xii. 132. Rochester, N. Y., 1862.

Searles, (Mrs. R. A.) Scraps and Poems. 16°, pp. 82. Cincinnati, 1851.

Sears, (R.) Mineral Waters of Saratoga. 16°, pp. 108. Ballston Spa, 1819.

Searson, (J.)

John Searson was born in Ireland, not far from 1750, was educated by his uncle, a clergyman of the Church of England, came to this country and took up his residence in Philadelphia, where he engaged in mercantile pursuits. Before leaving Ireland he published two volumes. In the dedication of his "Mount Vernon" to George Washington, he says: "I did myself the honor to visit your Excellency 15th May last, so as to obtain an adequate idea of Mount Vernon; wishing to compose a poem on that beautiful seat, which I now most humbly dedicate to your Excellency." Mr. Searson seems to regard himself as competent to carry out the plan which he has proposed to himself. In the preface to the readers of "Mount Vernon," he alludes to the visit referred to, which, he says, he made "so as to enable me to make an exact poetical description of it. I am," he adds, "fond of rural, descriptive poetry, and have endeavored to make this as pleasing and exact as possible." And, lest some envious critical persons might call in question his claims to the regards of the American people, he gives an item of his personal experience. "I published," he says, "a rural, romantic and descriptive poem on Down-Hill, the seat of the Earl of Bristol, Bishop of Londonderry, in Ireland, for which the gentlemen of that country actually gave me a guinea a copy, and Sir George Hill, from Dublin, gave me five guineas in the city of Londonderry." Unfortunately for our estimate of the intrinsic value of this poem, judged by the generous sum paid for it, he tells us that Sir George gave him "more, I am assured, as feeling from my having seen better days than from the intrinsic value of it."

—. Poems. 8°, pp. 94. Philadelphia, 1797.

— Mount Vernon. A Poem, etc. 8°, pp. 85. Philadelphia, no date.

That the author had some reasonable ground for his suspicions about the real value of his poetical effusions, is judged by the perusal of the following lines on the first page of this poem:

> " 'Tis through romantic scenes we here may go
> Not scar'd with fear nor frighten'd with a foe;
> Mount Vernon, I have often heard of thee,
> And often wish'd thy beauties for to see.
> Pleas'd to the last, I view this pleasant seat,
> And found its views elegant and neat;
> The prospect from it must e'er please the mind,
> When elegant Potowmack here we find.
> From right to left, from left to right we see,
> Th' beauteous Potowmack, that arm of the sea.
> See ships and vessels passing by the door,

SEARSON, (J.) — *Continued.*

> Almost ev'ry day and every hour.
> Indeed, the prospect is so very fine,
> Such rural scenes must e'er the thoughts refine."

The other pieces in the volume, of which there are several, are of the same general style and merit with the above.

SEAWEEDS FROM THE SHORES OF NANTUCKET. 16°, pp. 135. Boston, 1853.

SECESSION. A Poem by an East Tennesseean. 12°, pp. 64. Philadelphia, 1864.

SEGA, (G.) Componimenti Poetici. 8°. Filadelfia, 1829.

SEISS, (J. A.)

Joseph Augustus Seiss, D. D., was born near Emmittsburg, Md., in 1823, and, for a time, was pastor of a Lutheran Church in Baltimore. Subsequently he became pastor of St. John's Church in Philadelphia, where he now (1880) resides. Dr. Seiss has been an able and voluminous writer. Allibone enumerates twenty distinct works as the productions of his pen. His review and editorial articles have been very numerous.

— Recreation Songs. Lg. 12°, pp. 37. Philadelphia, 1878.

SELBY, (C.)

Charles Selby was a popular actor and dramatist of London who died in 1863.

— Boots at the Swan. A Farce. 8°, pp. 29. New York and Baltimore, no date.

SELECTIONS FROM THE BEST SPANISH POETS. (F. J. Vingist.) 12°, pp. 192. New York, 1856.

SERPENT, THE, SATAN, AND FALSE PROPHET, THE TRINITY OF EVIL. (Anon.) 8°, pp. 20. No place, no date.

SERULAN, (*pseud.*, supposed to be transposition of the letters in Laurens.) Poems. 8°, pp. 134. Charleston, 1859.

SEWARD, (ANNA.)

Miss Seward was born at Egan, Derbyshire, England, in 1747. She resided at Litchfield, where she died, March 25, 1809. Sir Walter Scott became her literary executor, and published, 3 vols., 1810, her Poetical Works and Correspondence.

— Monody on Major André. Fourth American Edition. 16°, pp. 22. Boston, 1798.

SEWARD, (E. S.) Columbiad Poems. 18°, pp. 127. Baltimore, 1840.

Sewell, (J.)

Jotham Sewell, a Congregational minister of Maine.

— Mode of Baptism. 8°, pp. 7. Augusta, Me., no date.

Sewell, (J. M.)

Jonathan Mitchell Sewell was born, according to Allen (see Biographical Dictionary, p. 730), at York, Me., in 1740, and, according to Duyckinck, in Salem, Mass., in 1748. His parents dying when he was young, he was adopted by his uncle, Chief Justice Sewell, of Massachusetts. Duyckinck says he passed through Harvard, but his name does not appear in the General Catalogue. For a time he engaged in mercantile pursuits, and then studied law, and for a few years was Register of Probate for Grafton county, N. H. Subsequently he removed to Portsmouth, N. H., where he died March 29, 1808.

The poems referred to below were, for the most part, the productions of his youth. They are paraphrases of Ossian, patriotic odes, epilogues, and a few epigrams. One of his songs, " War and Washington," was composed at the beginning of the American Revolution, and was very popular. Two lines of his from the " Epilogue to Cato" are familiar. With a slight change they were the motto of Park Benjamin's *New World :*

> " No pent-up Utica contracts your powers,
> But the whole boundless continent is yours."

— Miscellaneous Poems. 16°, pp. 304. Portsmouth, N. H., 1801.

Very rare. Two copies.

— Verses, etc. 24°, pp. 5. Boston, 1797.

Sewell, (S.)

The name of the author of this little volume is given in pencil as Stephen Sewell. Of the four translations, one in Greek and three in Latin, we give a few lines of the Twenty-Third Psalm :

> " Est dominus pastor mihi ; nunquam rebus egebo :
> Me facit et viridi lentum procumbere in herba :
> Ad placidas deducit aquas cum frigore in umbris."

— Carmina Sacra. Sq. 12°, pp. 8. Wigorniæ, Mass., 1789.

Sexton, Song of. Addressed to his Shovel. (Anon.) pp. 4. No date.

Shad-Fishers. By the " Pleasant Bard." 12°, pp. 24. Greenfield, Mass., 1854.

Shadow of the Rock, The, etc. (Anon.) Sq. 18°, pp. 224. New York, 1867.

Shakers, Some Lines in Verse About. (Anon.) 8°, pp. 56. New York, 1846.

Shanly, (C. O.) The Monkey of Porto Bello. 8°, pp. 6. New York, 1867.

33

SHARSWOOD, (W.)   The Betrothed ; or, Love in Death.   A Play in Five
  Acts.   8°, pp. 79.   Philadelphia, 1865.

SHATZEL, (J.)   The Mexican, etc.   16°, pp. 124.   New York, 1841.

SHEA, (J. A.)

Born at Cork, Ireland, 1802, came to this country in 1827, was editor and contributor
of magazines, etc., until his death in New York, August 15, 1845. This volume is dedicated to W. C. Bryant.

— Adolph, etc.   8°, pp. viii, 168.   New York, 1831.
— Clontarf.   12°, pp. x, 138.   New York, 1843.
— Poem.   Delivered at Suffield, Conn., August 5, 1845.   12°, pp. 13.
  New York, 1845.
— Poems.   Collected by his Son.   12°, pp. 204.   New York, 1846.
— Wild Flowers.   Parnassian.   18°, pp. 72.   Washington, 1836.

SHELLY, (A. F.)   Ostrea.   12°, pp. 72.   New York, 1857.

SHELTON, (F. W.)

Frederic William Shelton was born at Jamaica, Long Island, not far from the year
1814. His father, Nathan Shelton, was a highly esteemed physician of Jamaica. The
subject of this sketch graduated at the College of New Jersey in 1834. Being inclined to
literary pursuits, rather than to the duties of professional life, he spent much of his time
for a few years in his home, in reading and writing for the periodicals of the day, especially the " Knickerbocker Magazine." In 1847 he was ordained as a minister of the Episcopal church, and after preaching to parishes on Long Island, in 1854, became Rector of a
church at Montpelier. His life as a clergyman of country parishes afforded him themes for
not a few humorous sketches which were the productions of his busy pen. Among his works
are " The Rector of St. Bardolph's; or, Superannuated;" " Peeps from a Belfry; or, The
Parish Sketch Book." His " Up the River," being a series of rural sketches, is referred
to as " an exceedingly pleasant book in its tasteful, truthful observations of nature and
animal life, and the incidents of the country, interspersed with occasional criticisms of
favorite books, and invigorated throughout by the individual humors of the narrator." Mr.
Shelton died in 1881.

— The Trollopiad ; or, Travelling Gentlemen in America.   A Satire.
  12°, pp. 151.   New York, 1837.

This volume was published anonymously by " Nil Admirari," and was dedicated to
Mrs. Trollope.   " It is in rhyming pentameter, shrewdly sarcastic, and liberally garnished
with notes preservative of the memory of the series of gentlemen whose hurried tours in
America and flippant descriptions were formerly so provocative of the ire of native writers."

SHEPARD, (I. F.)

Isaac Fitzgerald Shepard, a well-known poet, residing in Boston.

— Pebbles from Castalia.   8°, pp. x, 156.   Boston, 1840.

Mr. Shepard dedicates this volume " To the Rev. Hubbard Winslow," his pastor and
friend, and, at the time, minister of the Congregational Church in Bowdoin street, Boston.

SHEPARD, (I. F.) — *Continued.*

— Poetry of Feeling, etc.   Sm. 24°, pp. 128.   Boston, 1844.

> The author alludes gratefully to the reception that was given to his " Pebbles from Castalia." He says that " of more than fifty reviews and notices that came to his knowledge, one alone, and that in his own city, spoke in anything like discourteous terms; while many of them were filled with generous praise."

SHEPARD, (Mrs. D. ELLEN GOODMAN.)   Cut-Flowers.   Edited by J. G. Holland.   12°, pp. 168.   Springfield, Mass., 1854.

SHEELEIGH, (M.)

> Matthias Sheeleigh was born at Charlestown, Chester county, Pa., December 20, 1821. He is of German descent, of the fourth generation in America, the name originally having been Schillich. His studies were pursued at Gettysburg, where he graduated from the College and Theological Seminary, and was ordained to the ministry in the Evangelical Lutheran Church in 1852. His pastorates have been with five churches, the latter of which, in Fort Washington, Pa., is now (1886) under his charge. Dr. Sheeleigh has written much as an editor for the periodical press, and as a large contributor, in both prose and poetry, to magazines, etc. He has now (1880) a number of books nearly ready for the press, among which are a volume of his Sonnets, more than four hundred in number, a collection of translations of " Dies Iræ," and a similar work representing Luther's great hymn:
>
> " Ein feste Burg," etc.

— A Gettysburgiad : A Jubilee Poem.   Pronounced at the Semi-Centennial Celebration of the Lutheran Theological Seminary, Gettysburg, Pa.   Sm. 4°, pp. 32.   Philadelphia, 1876.

— Hymns (Original) for the Seventh Semi-Centennial Jubilee of the Reformation.   1517–1867.   16°, pp. 18.   Philadelphia, 1867.

— Luther : A Song-Tribute on the Four Hundredth Anniversary of his Birth.   Sm. 4°, pp. 104.   Illustrated.   Philadelphia, 1883.

— Poem for the Luther Statue Unveiling.   Read on the occasion, in the Memorial Lutheran Church, Washington, D. C., May 20, 1884.

SHILLABER, (B. P.)

> Benjamin Penhallow Shillaber was born at Portsmouth, N. H., in 1814, became a printer, was a compositor at Demara, Guiana, 1835–37, and in the office of the *Boston Post* 1840–47. His " sayings of Mrs. Partington " have given him a world-wide celebrity.

— Rhymes with Reason, etc.   8°, pp. x, 336.   Boston, 1853.

— Wide-Swath.   Embracing " Lines in Pleasant Places," etc.   (Mrs. Partington, *pseud.*)   Popular Edition.   12°, pp. 305.   Cambridge, 1882.

SHIPP, (B.)   Fame, and other Poems.   12°, pp. 212.   Philadelphia, 1848.

— The Progress of Freedom, etc.   12°, pp. 219.   New York, 1852.

Shippey, (J.)

> Josiah Shippey was born near New Brunswick, N. J., February 1, 1778. The first of his ancestors who came to America was from the city of London. His father, John Shippey, suffered much during the Revolutionary war, his house having been burned by the British and Hessians after they had used it for a barrack. The subject of this sketch was a graduate of Columbia College in 1796. He did not study a profession, but devoted himself, through life, chiefly to mercantile pursuits. The date of his death we have been unable to ascertain.

— Specimens.  8°, pp. 238.  New York, 1841.

Shiras, (C. P.)  The Redemption of Labor.  8°, pp, v, 120.  Pittsburg, Pa., 1852.

Shortfellow, Henry Wandsworth, (*pseud.*)  The  Song of Drop O'Wather.  16°, pp. 111.  London and New York, 1856.

> A parody on Longfellow's "Hiawatha."

Shrimpton, (Charles.)  The Inebriate.  16°, pp. 48.  Cincinnati, 1858.

Sigourney, (Mrs. L. H.)

> Lydia Howard Huntley was born at Norwich, Conn., September 1, 1791.  She showed, as a child, remarkable precocity, being able to read readily at the age of three years, and, when seven, writing simple verses.  Having completed her school education, she was engaged in teaching, first in Norwich, then in Hartford.  She published her first volume, "Moral Pieces in Prose and Verse," in 1815.  In 1819 she married Mr. Charles Sigourney, a merchant of Hartford, and resided in that city during the remainder of her life.  She died June 10, 1865.  (See Allibone, pp. 2100–01.)

— Pocahontas, etc.  12°, pp. 283.  New York, 1841.
— Same.  12°, pp. 308.  London, 1841.
— Poems.  12°, pp. 228.  Boston, 1827.
— Same.  12°, pp. xi, 288.  Philadelphia, 1834.
— Same.  18°, pp. xii, 256.  New York, 1841.
— Same.  Religious, etc.  12°, pp. 352.  London, 1841.
— Same.  Sm. 24°, pp. 255.  Philadelphia, 1846.
— Same.  Sq. 16°, pp. 254.  New York, 1853.
— Poems for the Sea.  12°, pp. 152.  Hartford, 1850.
— Poetical Works.  Edited by F. W. N. Bayley.  18°, pp. x, 236.  London, 1863.
— Poetry for Seamen.  12°, pp. 63.  Boston, 1845.
— Scenes in My Native Land.  12°, pp. 319.  Boston, 1845.
— Select Poems.  4th Edition.  12°, pp. 324.  1843.
— Same.  With Illustrations.  11th Edition.  8°, pp. 338.  Philadelphia, 1857.

SIGOURNEY, (MRS. L. H.) — *Continued.*
— The Daily Counsellor.  8°, pp. 402.  Hartford, 1859.
— The Weeping Willow.  Sm. 24°, pp. 128.  Hartford, 1852.
— Traits of the Aborigines.  12°, pp. 284.  Cambridge, 1822.
— Voices of Home.  12°, pp. 152.  Hartford, 1852.
— Whisper to a Bride.  2d Edition.  16°, pp. 80.  Hartford, 1850.

SILL, (E. R.)  The Hermitage, etc.  16°, pp. 152.  New York, 1868.

SILVER WEDDING SONG, THE.  Testimonial to Mr. and Mrs. A. A. Livermore, May 17, 1863.  (Anon.)  No place, no date.

SIMMONS, (J. F.)  The Welded Link, etc.  12°. pp. 264.  Philadelphia, 1881.

SIMMONS, (J. W.)
James Wright Simmons was born in South Carolina, pursued his studies at Harvard, but did not graduate.  He settled in one of the Western States.

— Blue Beard; or, The Marshal of France.  8°, pp. 110.  Philadelphia, 1822.
— The Exile's Return, etc.  12°, pp. xi, 117.  Philadelphia, 1822.
— The Greek Girl.  12°, pp. 142. ' Boston, 1852.
— The Maniac's Confession, etc.  12°, pp. 96.  Philadelphia, 1821.

SIMMS, (W. G.)
William Gilmore Simms was born at Charleston, S. C., April 17, 1806, and, at the age of twenty-one was admitted to the bar of his native State.  Abandoning the legal profession, he devoted his life to literary pursuits, and became one of the most popular and voluminous writers in the United States.  A very full account of the productions of his facile pen may be found in Allibone, pp. 2104–6.  He died in June, 1870.

— Areytos; or, Songs of the South.  12°, pp. vi, 108.  Charleston, S. C., 1846.
— Atalantis.  8°, pp. 80.  New York, 1832.
— Same.  8°, pp. 144.  New York, 1848.
— Donna Florida.  16°, pp. 97.  Charleston, 1843.
— Early Lays.  12°, pp. viii, 108.  Charleston, 1827.
— Egeria.  12°, pp. xii, 319.  Philadelphia, 1853.
— Grouped Thoughts.  12°, pp. 61.  Richmond, Va., 1845.
— Lyrical and other Poems.  16°, pp. 198.  Charleston, 1827.

In the volume is a newspaper cutting giving an extract from the *Richmond Whig,* March 23, 1865.  "The elegant country seat of Mr. Simms, 'Woodlawn,' near Midway, was burned, together with most of his valuable library.  Few men have suffered more than he

SIMMS, (W. G.) — *Continued.*

by the revolution. His stereotype plates in the hands of his publishers, confiscated; his plantation ruined; his stock driven off; his house burned — but still he is erect, undismayed, and confident of the successful issue of the cause."

A paragraph in the *Augusta Sentinel* says that when the Yankees were at Midway, Generals Howell, Smith and Blair placed a heavy guard over the residence of Mr. Simms and preserved it from pillage. The day after they left, a negro applied the torch and burned it and its valuable contents to the ground.

— Norman Maurice. An American Drama. Lg. 8°, pp. 31. Richmond, Va., 1851.

— Same. 8°, pp. 169. Richmond, 1853.

— Poems by a Collegian. 8°, pp. vi, 95. Charlottesville, Va., 1833.

The authorship of this volume is ascribed to Simms simply because on the title-page some one has written in pencil the name " Wm. G. Simms." The compiler is doubtful on the subject. No source of information to which he has access sets it down as the production of the pen of the distinguished poet of the South. In the collected Songs, Ballads, etc., found in the "Areytos" of Simms, none of the poems in this volume are reproduced. They are said to be "Poems by a Collegian," but we are not aware that Simms ever was in college as a student. The author, whoever he was, says "he has been desirous to leave among those who have taken an interest in his welfare, and with whom he has been in habits of daily intercourse, a slight memorial of himself, ere more important duties urge their claims to consideration." He adds: "Nearly all the present poems were written between the ages of sixteen and nineteen."

— Poems. 2 vols. 8°, pp. 348, 360. New York, 1853.

— Sabbath Lyrics; or, Songs from Scripture. A Christmas Gift of Love. 8°, pp. 72. Charleston, 1847.

— Southern Passages and Pictures. 12°, pp. 228. New York, 1839.

— The Cassique of Accabee. A Tale of Ashley River, etc. Sq. 18°, pp. 112. New York, 1849.

— The City of the Silent. A Poem delivered at the Consecration of Magnolia Cemetery, Charleston, S. C., November 19, 1850. 8°, pp. 54. Charleston, 1850.

— The Vision of Cortes. 16°, pp. 150. Charleston, 1829.

SIMON, (MRS.) Review of Modern Genius. 12°, pp. 116. New York, 1823.

SINCLAIR, (C. B.)

See Mary Forrest's " Women of the South Distinguished in Literature."

— Poems. 12°, pp. viii, 160. Augusta, Ga., 1860.

SISTERS, THE ORPHAN. (Anon. A Catholic Clergyman.) 12°, pp. 18. Baltimore, 1862.

SKETCHES FOR THE FAIR.  (Anon.)  8°, pp. 17.  No place, no date.

SKINNER, (G. W.)  Æræ.  A Poem.  12°, pp. 47.  Boston, 1852.

SKINNER, (J., M. D.)  The Revolutionary War in Verse.  8°, pp. 253. Binghampton, 1829.

SLAVERY, POEMS ON.  (Longfellow, Whittier, Southey, H. B. Stowe, etc.)  Dedicated to the Rt. Hon. the Earl of Shaftsbury.  16°, pp. 232.  London, 1853.

SLAVERY, THE GOSPEL OF.  A Primer of Freedom.  (By Iron Gray, *pseud.*)  18°, not paged.  New York, no date.

SLENDER, ROBERT.  (A *pseud.* for Philip Freneau.)  A Journey from Philadelphia to New York by way of Burlington and South Amboy. Extracted from the Author's Journal.  12°, pp. 28.  Philadelphia, 1787.

SMILES AND FROWNS, ETC.  (Anon.)  Sq. 16°, pp. 128.  Philadelphia, 1852.

SMILEY, (MISS ——.)  Poems.  (By Matilda, *pseud.*)  12°, pp. 311. Richmond, 1851.

SMITH, (A.)  Poems.  12°, pp. 190.  Boston, 1853.

SMITH, (A. L.)  The Romaunt of Lady Helen Clyde.  43 Stanzas.  Sq. 12°, not paged.  New York, 1882.

SMITH, (ANNIE R.)  Home Here, etc.  12°, pp. 112.  Rochester, 1855.

SMITH, (B.)  Poems.  12°, pp. 128.  Pittsburgh, 1842.

SMITH, (C.)

Charles Smith was born not far from 1768, and, for a time, was a bookseller in the city of New York.  Some of the plays of Kotzebue and Schiller were translated by him.  He was the editor of "The Monthly Military Repository," New York, 1796-97.  2 vols. 8°. Dr. J. W. Francis says that the Revolutionary descriptions "were supplied by Baron Steuben and General Gates."  Mr. Smith died in 1840.

— Abbe de L'Epee; or, The Orphan.  From the German of Kotzebue. 8°, pp. 42.  New York, 1801.

— Sparks from a Smith's Forge.  12°, pp. 71.  New York, 1852.

SMITH, (E. D.)  Destiny.  8°, pp. 27.  New York, 1846.

SMITH, (E. H.)  Black Hawk.  12°, pp. v, 299.  New York, 1848.

SMITH, (ELIHU H.)

Elihu Hubbard Smith was born at Litchfield, Conn., September 4, 1771, and graduated at Yale College in 1786. Being but fifteen years of age when he completed his academic studies, he was regarded by his father as being too young to enter upon a course of professional study, and by him was placed under the charge of Rev. Dr. Dwight, then pastor of the Congregational Church at Greenfield, Mass., with whom he remained for a time, and then, under the tuition of his father, who was a physician, he fitted himself for the practice of medicine, receiving his degree from the Medical School of Philadelphia. He took up his residence in New York in 1793, where he combined literary with professional pursuits. In connection with two other physicians he was a party to the establishment of the "New York Medical Repository."

To Dr. Smith is to be ascribed the honor of editing the first collection of American poetry ever made in this country, which was brought out in 1793. This collection contains poems by Hopkins, Humphrey, Dwight, Trumbull, Barlow, etc. His death came in the way of the discharge of his professional duties. New York, in 1798, was visited by the yellow fever. One of his patients, a young Italian, who had been attacked by the fever, was removed to the apartments of his physician, the latter, in a few days, succumbing to the infection, and both dying, the event in the case of Dr. Smith occurring September 21, 1798.

He is supposed to have been the author of "André, a Tragedy," which was performed in New York in 1798.

— Edwin and Angelina.   8°.   New York, 1797.

SMITH, (ELIZA W.)   Myths and Idyls.   8°.   Boston, 1881.

SMITH, (J.)   Divine Hymns.   12°, pp. 171.   Elizabeth-Town, 1810.

SMITH, (EMELINE SHERMAN.)

She was born at New Baltimore, near New York, in 1823, and married James M. Smith, a New York lawyer. "Her distinguishing characteristics are a religious delight in nature, and a contentment with home affections and pleasures, which, in one form or another, are the material of the finest poetry of women."

— Poems and Ballads.   8°, pp. 336.   New York, 1859.
— The Fairy's Search.   Sm. 24°, pp. 124.   New York, 1847.

SMITH, (MRS. E. O.)

Elizabeth Oakes Prince was born at North Yarmouth, Me., August 12, 1806, and from infancy resided in Portland, where, at an early age, she married Seba Smith, the famous "Jack Downing," whose letters, couched in Yankee phraseology, procured for him a world-wide renown. He also wrote "Powhatan, a Metrical Romance," in Seven Cantos, which was published in 1841. He wrote also other works, and was a generous contributor to the periodical literature of the day.

The earliest poems of Mrs. Smith were written anonymously. Her husband becoming involved in business troubles growing out of what is known as the "Eastern Land Speculations," Mrs. Smith resorted to her pen to procure the means of support for her family. In 1842 she took up her residence in New York, and entered at once upon what proved to be a career of literary success. Subsequently she removed to Hollywood, Carteret county, N. C.

— Old New York; or, Democracy in 1689.   12°, pp. 65.   New York, 1853.

Smith, (Mrs. E. O.) — *Continued.*

— Poetical Writings. 32°, pp. 204. Second Edition. New York, 1846.

— The Lover's Gift. Sm. 24°, pp. x, 128. Hartford, 1848.

— The Sinless Child, etc. 12°, pp. xxxiv, 177. New York and Boston, 1843.

> This poem was first published in the "Southern Literary Messenger," in 1842. In this edition is an address " To the Reader " by the editor, John Keese, pp. vii–xii, a characteristic sketch of Mrs. Smith by John Neal, pp. xv–xxxiv, and an analysis of Mrs. Smith's genius and character, by H. H. Tuckerman.

Smith, (J. H.) The Latter Day's Intelligencer. 16°, pp. vi, 144. St. Clairsville, Ohio, 1847.

Smith, (J. S., M. D.)

> Dr. James S. Smith, a brother of William Smith, author of " The History of the Province of New York from its first Discovery," etc., was born some time previous to 1760, graduated at Leyden, and died at an advanced age in New York in 1812.

— The Mirror of Merit and Beauty. Sm. 16°, pp. 79. New York, 1808.

Smith, (J. S.) The Siege of Algiers. A Tragi-Comedy. 8°, pp. 140. Philadelphia, 1823.

> The writer, Jonathan S. Smith, says : " In this drama will be strongly exemplified the great contrast between the government, customs and manners of unlettered despotism, and those of the more free and enlightened nations, and one scene herein will also enable the female part of the latter to form a just estimate between their own happy condition in life, and the truly miserable and circumscribed state of those unfortunate women of the former, doomed to drag out a debased existence under the jealous eye of a bearded tyrant ! "

Smith, (Mrs. Pogson.) The Arabians. 18°, pp. viii, 56. Philadelphia, 1844.

Smith, (R. P.)

> Richard Penn Smith was born at Philadelphia in 1799, was admitted to the bar in 1821, was editor of "The Aurora," 1822–27, and wrote " Forsaken," a novel, in two volumes. Fifteen of his plays were produced on the Philadelphia stage. One of these was Caius Marius, written for Edwin Forrest, and acted by him. He wrote several Comedies and Farces. His death occurred in 1854.

— Poems. Miscellaneous Works Collected by his son, H. W. Smith. 8°, pp. 137. Philadelphia, 1856.

— The Deformed. A Play. 12°, pp. 87. Philadelphia, 1830.

— The Disowned. A Play. 12°, pp. 67. Philadelphia, 1830.

— The Eighth of January. 16°, pp. iv, 54. Philadelphia, 1829.

34

Smith, (S.)

Seba Smith was born in 1792, at Buckfield, Me., the place of his birth being a log-house which had been erected by his father in the woods of that town. In 1802 his family removed to Bridgton, Me. The boy's life was one of constant activity, either on a farm, or in a grocery or brick yard or iron foundry. He fitted himself for college chiefly by his own endeavors, and graduated at Bowdoin with the highest honors of his class in 1818. Among his classmates were Rev. Dr. Rufus Anderson, for so many years the able Secretary of the American Board of Commissioners for Foreign Missions, Rev. Dr. Benjamin Hale, President of Geneva, or Hobart Free College, in Western New York, and Gideon Lane Sowle, LL. D., for several years Principal of Exeter Phillips Academy. After graduation Mr. Smith spent some time in teaching, travelling at home and abroad, and then for four years was connected, as assistant editor and joint proprietor, of the *Eastern Argus*, Portland. For seven years, 1830–37, he had the management of the *Portland Daily Courier*. "Much of its success was due to the "Downing" letters. The ability, the good sense, the gen-uine humor, and more than all the unmitigated Yankeeisms of the kind-hearted "Major" soon made him popular, and his effusions appeared in all the papers. These were sought with avidity and read by everybody. During a period of intense political strife the "Downing" letters, with their good-natured satire and admirable irony, furnished matter that both sides could laugh at, and this did much to allay the bitterness of party."

Allusion has been made in the sketch of Mrs. Elizabeth O. Smith to the pecuniary embarrassments of her husband. He became, on removing to New York, a large contrib-utor to various periodicals, etc., and in 1857 took the editorial charge of "Putnam's Monthly." After a life of great literary activity he died at Patchogue, L. I., July 28, 1868.

— Powhatan. A Metrical Romance in Seven Cantos. 12°, pp. 198. New York, 1841.

Poe, in his "Literati," speaks disparingly of this poem.

Smith, (S. F.)

Samuel Francis Smith was born at Boston, October 21, 1808, graduated at Harvard 1829, pursued his theological studies at Andover, and was the pastor of the Baptist Church in Waterville, Me., 1834–42, and in Newton, Mass., 1842–54. He was, for a time, editor of the "Baptist Missionary Magazine," and contributed to Dr. Lieber's "Encyclopædia Americana." As the author of the National Hymn, "My Country, 'tis of Thee," and the Missionary Hymn, "The Morning Light is Breaking," he has a world-wide reputation. His present (1886) residence is Newton, Mass.

— Juvenile Lyre. Hymns, etc., for Schools. 8°, pp. vi, 72. Boston, 1835.

Smith, (S. J.)

Samuel J. Smith, a grandson of Samuel Smith, the historian of New Jersey, was born in 1771. Most of his life was passed at the ancestral home near Burlington, N. J. He died in 1835.

— Miscellaneous Writings. Prose and Poetry. 8°, pp. 222. Phila-delphia and Boston, 1836.

Smith, (S. Louisa P.) Poems. 8°, pp. 250. Providence, 1829.

Smith, (W. M.)

William Moore Smith, the eldest son of Rev. Dr. Smith, first Provost of the Philadel-phia College, was born June 1, 1759, and was an eminent lawyer. He died March 12, 1821. (See Catalogue of Philadelphia Library, vol. 2, p. 479.)

Smith, (W. M.) — *Continued.*

— Poems.  Sm. 12°, pp. 141.  Philadelphia, 1786.

— Poems on Several Occasions.·  Written in Pennsylvania.  12°, pp. 16.  Boston, 1779.

Smith, (W. R.)

William Russell Smith was born in Alabama about the year 1813, was educated at the University of Alabama, practiced law at Greensboro, was an army officer in the Creeks' war, 1836, established the *Tuscaloosa Monitor* in 1838, held offices of civil trust, was opposed to secession, but was a member of the Confederate Congress 1861–65. Subsequently he became President of the State University.

— Diomede.  From the Iliad of Homer.  Lg. 8°, pp. v, 52.  New York and London, 1869.

— The Uses of Solitude.  4°, pp. 64.  Montgomery, Alabama, 1860.

Smucker, (S. S.)  The Spanish Wife.  8°, pp. 96.  New York, 1854.

Sneak, Ye, Yclepid Copperhead.  (Anon.)  18°, pp. 30.  Philadelphia, 1863.

Snelling, (W. J.)

William Joseph Snelling was born at Boston, December 26, 1804, was a Cadet at West Point, made his appearance as a writer about 1828, and contributed articles to the magazines, etc., of the day, and for a time was editor of the *Boston Herald*. He died at Chelsea, Mass., December 24, 1848.

— Truth.  18°, pp. vi, 52.  Boston, 1831.

— Same.  18°, pp. v, 72.  Boston, 1832.

Snider, (D. J.)  Clarence.  A Drama.  8°, pp. 45.  St. Louis, 1872.

Society Without Veil.  (Anon.)  12°, pp. 218.  New York, 1851.

Soldier's, The, Armor of Strength.  Devotional Exercises, etc., for Soldiers in the Civil War.  (Anon. · P. J. at the end of the Preface.)  12°, pp. 96.  Brooklyn, 1863.

Solitary Musings.  (Anon.)  8°, pp. 18.  No place, 1825.

Somerby, (W. F.)  Sabbath in the City.  12°, pp. 208.  Boston, 1854.

Sommershall, or Sommersall, (J.)  Poems.  12°, pp. 51.  Savannah, 1853.

Somerville, (J. S.)  Plume of the Classics, etc.  16°, pp. 60.  Washington, 1820.

SONG BOOKS.

The compiler cannot speak with absolute certainty on the subject, and will be glad to
be corrected if he is mistaken, but he thinks that in the number and the variety of Song
Books by American writers the "Harris Collection" is without a rival. Mr. Harris seems
to have had almost a passion for collecting books and pamphlets which may be classed
under this head.

The College Song Books all date back to a period comparatively recent, indicating
that this is a sort of literature that has sprung up in modern times. Outside of a certain
and quite limited range, these college songs will awaken but little interest. Within that
range, however, they will be associated in the memory of college graduates with some of
the most cheery and happy hours of their student life. Especially will this be true of the
Song Books of the Secret Societies. Many of them contain allusions, catch words, etc.,
profoundly mysterious to the uninitiated, but very suggestive to those who have sung
them in unison, with well-remembered voices, whose harmony still lingers in the ear. It
has been most truthfully said: "There is probably no more justly popular music than college songs when sung in chorus; not because of being artistic in composition or rendition,
but because of their cheer, and the fond recollections they awaken in so many a mind."
In the "Harris Collection," as will be noticed, there are some twenty volumes of these
College Song Books.

— American College Song Book, The.  Lg. 8°.  Chicago, 1882.

The origin of the American College Song Book is thus stated by the compiler:

"The songs sung by the boys of thirty years since are still familiar to the boys of
to-day; partly because of their real merit, and also because for some unknown reason, no
one has taken upon himself the task of producing something fresh and more properly char-
acteristic of the present." To supply what was supposed to be a want in the direction
alluded to, fifty of the leading colleges and universities of the United States were each
invited to contribute four of her best songs, original, as far as possible, for such purposes.
With very few exceptions, the invitation was responded to by the colleges, and the result
is the following compilation of nearly two hundred and fifty songs, "most of them entirely
new, yet including some of the old, old songs, which, having been sung by thousands of
college boys, belong among college traditions, and will probably remain favorites for years
to come." The compiler expresses his special thanks to Mr. Edgar O. Silver, of Brown
University, for the valuable assistance he has rendered him in his work.

— Biennial Songs of Sixty-Six.  Williams.  8°.  Troy, no date.
— Same.  Sixty-Seven.  Williams.  8°.  Troy, no date.
— Brown University, June 12th.  Ode for Class of 1856.  16°.  Prov-
idence, no date.
— Delta Kappa Epsilon Songs.  8°.  Providence, no date.
— [Jenckes, (T. A.)]  Song [sung in Commons Hall, Brown Univer-
sity.  8°.  Providence, 1842.]
— Sans Souci Songs.  12°.  New York, 1859.
— Songs and Toasts for the Hamilton Junior Exhibition Supper.  8°.
Utica, 1868.
— Songs for Sophomore Supper, Class of 1860, Dartmouth College,
July 23, 1858.  Lg. 8°.  No place, no date.

Song Books — *Continued.*

— Songs of Alpha Delta Phi.  12°.  New Haven, 1855.
— Same.  12°.  New York, 1859.
— Same.  12°.  Albany, 1864.
— Songs of the College of the City of New York.  12°.  New York, 1866.
— Songs of the Delta Kappa Epsilon.  12°.  New Haven, 1857.
— Songs of the Delta Kappa.  By the Class of '65.  12°.  New Haven, 1862.
— Songs of the Psi Upsilon.  12°.  New York, 1857.
— Songs of the Sigma Phi.  8°.  Boston, 1861. ·
— Songs (The) of Union.  8°.  Watertown, N. Y., 1865.
— Songs of Williams.  8°.  New York, 1859.
— Songs of Yale.  8°.  New Haven, 1853.
— Same.  8°.  New Haven, 1855.
— Waite, (H. R.)  Carmina Collegensia.  Lg.8°.  Boston, 1868.

Every college in the United States was solicited to contribute its songs to this collection, and nearly all having songs are represented in the above. Nearly one thousand songs were sent to the compiler from which to make his selection. The arrangement of the music was under the supervision of J. C. Johnson, of Boston. Much interesting and useful information concerning twenty-one of the universities and colleges where songs are here represented is found in an Appendix to the volume. The distinctive colors of fourteen of the colleges are as follows:

| | | | | |
|---|---|---|---|---|
| 1. Harvard | Red. | 9. Amherst | | Purple and White. |
| 2. Yale | Blue. | 10. Wesleyan | | Lavender. |
| 3. Brown | Brown. | 11. University of New | | |
| 4. Dartmouth | Green. | | York | Violet. |
| 5. Williams | Purple. | 12. Western Reserve | | Bismark and Purple. |
| 6. Bowdoin | White. | 13. Michigan | | Azure Blue and Maize. |
| 7. Union | Magenta. | 14. Rochester | | Magenta and White. |
| 8. Hamilton | Orange. | | | |

## SONG BOOKS, (MARTIAL, NAVAL AND PATRIOTIC.)

The great war crises in the history of the country have given occasion to the production of a large number of patriotic songs. These have done their part in awakening and intensifying the heroic spirit. They have been sung around camp fires, on the decks and in the forecastles of ships, in hospitals, and around the domestic hearth. Who can compute the influence of such songs as "Hail Columbia," "The Star Spangled Banner," and "My Country, 'tis of Thee"?  Edward Gillespy, in his preface to "The Columbian Naval Songster," justly remarks: "The achievements of ancient heroes owe their transmission to posterity more to the celebration of the poet than to the pen of the historian." He adds: "Feeling an ardent and patriotic desire that none of the elegant poetic compositions on the five glorious naval victories obtained by American valor over a portion of the boasted navy of Great Britain, hitherto considered invincible, the following collection was

SONG BOOKS, (MARTIAL, NAVAL AND PATRIOTIC.) — *Continued.*

commenced from the first that appeared after the destruction of the Guerriere, preserving none but such as possessed real merit either in the beauty of the composition or the pure patriotic sentiments which they express."

— American Muse, The.　18°.　New York, 1814.

— American Songster, The.　32°.　New York, no date.

— American Songster, The New.　18°.　Philadelphia, 1817.

— American Star, The.　2d Edition.　18°.　Richmond, 1817.

— American Naval and Patriotic Songster, The.　32°.　Baltimore, 1831.

— Same.　18°.　New York, 1840.

— American Song Book.　18°.　Philadelphia, 1813.

— Banner of Freedom, The.　(See Page, A.)

— Bird of Birds, The.　18°.　New York, 1818.

— Blackbird, The.　12°.　New York, 1823.

— Book, The, of American Songs.　(See Paul, H.)

— Canary Bird, The.　18°.　Philadelphia, 1830.

— Columbian Harmonist, The.　18°.　Albany, 1815.

— Columbia Naval Melody.　12°.　Boston, 1813.

— Columbian Naval Songster, The.　(See Gillespy, E.)

— Columbia's Naval Triumph.　18°.　New York, 1813.

— Columbian Songster, The.　12°.　Wrentham, Mass., 1799.

— Same.　18°.　Baltimore, 1812.

— Eagle and Harp, The.　12°.　Baltimore, 1812.

— Every-Day Song Book, The.　32°.　New York, no date.

— General Armstrong.　American Independence.　Royal Sport.　Sweet William.　16°.　No place, about 1812.

— Gillespy, (E.)　Columbian Naval Songster.　12°.　New York, 1813.

— Household Song Book, The.　32°.　New York, no date.

— Humming Bird, The.　18°.　Baltimore, 1809.

— Hymn Book.　32°.　New York, 1861.

— Hymns, Religious and Patriotic, for Sailors and Soldiers.　24°.　Boston, 1861.

— McCarty, (W.)　National Songs, etc., relating to the War of 1846.　18°.　Philadelphia, 1846.

— Same.　Songs, Odes, and Other Poems.　18°, 3 vols.　Philadelphia, 1842.

— Mocking-Bird, The.　18°.　Alexandria, 1814.

SONG BOOKS, (MARTIAL, NAVAL AND PATRIOTIC.) — *Continued.*

— Moore, (F.)   Songs and Ballads of the Revolution.   12°.   New . York, 1856.

> One of the choice volumes in the Martial, Naval and Patriotic Series of Song Books is Frank Moore's " Songs and Ballads of the Revolution."  Many of these, we are told, " are taken from the newspapers and periodical issues of the time; others from original ballad-sheets and broadsides; while some have been received from the recollections of a few surviving soldiers, who heard and sang them amid the trials of the camp and the field. Nearly every company had its ' smart one,' or poet, who beguiled the weariness of the march or the encampment by his minstrelsy, grave or gay; and the imperfect fragments which survive to us provoke our regret that so few of them have been preserved."

— Same.   Songs of the Soldiers.   24°.   New York, 1864.

— National . Songs, etc., relating to the War of 1846.   (See Mc-Carty, W.)

— Naval Songster, The.   16°.   Charlestown, 1815.

— Page, (A.)   Banner of Freedom, The.   12°.   Providence, 1841.

— Parlour Song Book, The.   32°.   New York, no date.

— Patriotic Songs.   Lg. 8°.   New York, 1844.

— Patriotic Songster.   18°.   New York, no date.

— Paul, (H.)   The Book of American Songs.   16°.   London, 1857.

— Rough and Ready Songster, The.   32°.   New York, no date.

— Soldier's Companion, The.   32°.   New York, no date.

— Songs, Naval, Patriotic, etc.   18°.   New York, 1818.

— Songs, Odes, and other Poems.   (See McCarty, W.)

— Songster's Museum, The.   18°.   Hartford, 1835.

— Star Spangled Banner, The.   2d Edition.   18°.   Wilmington, 1817.

— Uncle Sam's Naval and Patriotic Songster.   16°.   New York, no date.

— Virginia Warbler, The.   16°.   Richmond, 1845.

SONG BOOKS, ETC., (MASONIC.)

> Masonic Song Books are largely represented in " The Harris Collection."  In " The Constitutions of the Ancient and Honorable Fraternity of Free and Accepted Masons," prepared by Brother Thaddeus Mason Harris, and printed by Brother Isaiah Thomas, at Worcester, in 1792, a large octavo volume of 288 pages, pp. 216–286 are devoted to " Oratorio, Odes, Anthems, Prologues and Songs."  However true it may be of the Masonic Songs of more modern times, that they are the productions of true poetic genius, this can hardly be said of those which were written a century since.  We give the following:

> " When a Lodge of Free Masons are clothed in their aprons
> In order to make a new Brother,
> With firm hearts and clean hands they repair to their stands,
> And justly support one another."

SONG BOOKS, ETC., (MASONIC.) — *Continued.*

The writer of this song seems to be called on to vindicate "the Craft" in their decision not to receive women into their mystic ranks:

"The ladies claim right to come into our light,
    Since the Apron, they say, is their bearing;
Can they subject their will? Can they keep their tongues still,
    And let talking be changed into hearing?

"This difficult task is the least we can ask,
    To secure us on sundry occasions;
When with us they comply, our utmost we'll try
    To raise Lodges for Lady Free Masons.

"Till this can be done, must each Brother be mum,
    Tho' the fair one should wheedle or tease on;
Be just, true and kind, but still bear in mind
    At all times that you are a Free Mason."

— Alford, (L. A.)  Masonic Gem.  2d Edition.  12°.  New York, 1868.
— Chisel, (C.)  Lamentation of Free Masonry.  12°.  Norwich, 1829.
— Clark, (W. R.)  A Masonic Poem.  8°.  Trenton, 1860.
— Eastman, (L.)  Masonic Melodies.  8°.  Boston, 1818.
— Fraternal Tribute to Masonic Character of Washington.  8°. Charlestown, 1790.
— Hardcastle, (J.)  The Masonic Museum.  12°.  New York, 5816.
— Macoy, (R.)  The Masonic Vocal Manual.  18°.  New York, 1854.
— Masonic Choir.  Lg. 16°.  1864.
— Masonic Lyre, The.  Sm. 16°.  New York, 1854.
— Masonic Minstrel.  8°.  Dedham, 1816.
— Masonic Museum, The.  (See Hardcastle, J.)
— Masonic Odes, etc.  Lg. 8°.  Worcester, 1792.
— Masonic Vocal Manual, The.  (See Macoy, R.)
— Melodies for the Craft.  16°.  Cincinnati, 1852.

SONG BOOKS, (NEGRO MINSTREL.)

The negro minstrelsy literature (if so dignified a name can properly be given to this species of writing) of "The Collection" is remarkable both for quantity and quality. One is amazed to know that such a mass of what seems, for the most part, to be "puerile stuff," could have been produced at all, and still more amazed that there could have been such a demand for these songs as to warrant their production. One hundred volumes of negro song books indicates a popularity of a certain kind for this sort of literature that is simply marvellous.

— Arlington's Banjo Songster.  18°.  New York, no date.
— Billy Birch's Ethiopian Melodist.  18.  New York, 1862.

Song Books, (Negro Minstrel.) — *Continued.*

— Bob Hart's Plantation Songster. 18°. New York, 1862.
— Book, The, of Negro Songs. 32°. New York, no date.
— Brady's Ethiopian Drama. Nos. 1–8, 12–20. 12°. New York, no date.
— Brower's, (Frank.) (See Frank Brower's.)
— Bryant's Cane Brake Refrains. 18°. New York, 1863.
— Bryant's Essence of Old Virginny. 18°. New York, 1857.
— Bryants' New Songster. 18°. New York, 1864.
— Bryant's Power of Music. 18°. New York, 1859.
— Bryant's Songs from Dixie's Land. 18°. New York, 1861.
— Buckley's Ethiopian Melodies. 18°. New York, 1853.
— Same. No. 4. 18°. New York, 1857.
— Buckley's Melodies. 18°· New York, 1853.
— Buckley's Song Book. 12°. New York, 1855.
— Carncross & Sharpley's Minstrel. 18°. Philadelphia, 1860.
— Charley Fox's Bijou Songster. 18°. New York, 1858.
— Charley Fox's Minstrel Companion. 18°. Philadelphia, 1863.
— Charley Fox's Sable Songster. 18°. New York, 1859.
— Christy's (George) Essence of Old Kentucky. 18°. New York, 1862.
— Christy's Negro Serenaders. 32°. New York, 1848.
— Christy's Negro Songster. 32°. New York, 1860.
— Christy's New Songster and Black Joker. 18°. New York, 1863.
— Christy's Plantation Melodies. 18°. Philadelphia, 1851.
— Same. No. 2. 18°. Philadelphia, 1853.
— Same. No. 2. 18°. Philadelphia, 1854.
— Same. No. 3. 18°. Philadelphia, 1853.
— Same. No. 4. 18°. Philadelphia, 1854.
— Same. No. 5. 18°. Philadelphia, 1856.
— Christy's and White's Ethiopian Melodies. 18°. Philadelphia, no date.
— Christy (George) & Wood's Melodies. 18°. New York, 1854.
— Collins, (J. H.) (See Unsworth's.)
— Converse's, (Frank.) (See Frank Converse's.)
— Dandy Jim and Dan Tucker's Jaw Bone. 32°. New York, 1844.

SONG BOOKS, (NEGRO MINSTREL.) — *Continued.*

— Deacon Snowball's Negro Melodies.　32°.　Boston, 1843.
— Dime Negro Melodies.　No. 1.　(See Song Books.)　(Rebellion and Slavery.)
— Same.　No. 2.　18°.　Philadelphia, 1865.
— Same.　No. 3.　18°.　Philadelphia, 1865.
— Same.　No. 4.　18°.　Philadelphia, 1865.
— Same.　No. 5.　18°.　Philadelphia, 1865.
— Same.　No. 6.　18°.　Philadelphia, 1865.
— Dixey's Essence of Burnt Cork.　18°.　Philadelphia, 1859.
— Dixey's Songster.　18°.　Philadelphia, 1860.
— Eph Horn's Own Songster.　18°.　New York, 1864.
— Flat Nose, The, and Thick Lip, Melodist.　32°.　New York, no date.
— Fox, (C. H.)　(See Charley Fox's.)
— Fox's, (Charley.)　(See Charley Fox's.)
— Frank Brower's Black Diamond Songster.　18°.　New York, 1863.
— Frank Converse's "Old Cremona."　18°.　New York, 1863.
— George Christy's.　(See Christy's, George.)
— Harry Pell's Ebony Songster.　18°.　New York, 1864.
— Hart's, (Bob.)　(See Bob Hart's.)
— Hooley's Black Star Songster.　18°.　New York, 1865.
— Hooley's Opera House Songster.　18°.　New York, 1863.
— Horn's, (Eph.)　(See Eph Horn's.)
— Jasper Jack's Bran New Collection.　32°.　New York, [1843?]
— Jim Crow Song Book, The.　32°.　Ithica, 1847.
— Johnson's Original Comic Songs.　18°.　New York, 1855.
— Kentucky and Virginny Minstrel.　32°.　New York, no date.
— Lucy Neal's Nigga Warbler.　32°.　Philadelphia, [1843?]
— Mac Dill Darrel Dime Melodist, The.　18°.　New York, 1860.
— Same.　No. II.　18°.　New York, 1860.
— Matt Peel's Banjo.　18°.　New York, 1858.
— Morris', (Pete.)　(See Pete Morris'.)
— My Dearest May, and Rosa Lee's Song Book.　32°.　New York, [1843?]
— Negro, The, Forget-Me-Not Songster.　32°.　Philadelphia, 1844.
— Negro, The, Singer's Own Book.　32.　Philadelphia, no date.
— Negro's, De, Original Piano-Rama.　18°.　Philadelphia, 1850.

Song Books, (Negro Minstrel.) — *Continued.*

— Nelse Seymour's Big-Shoe Songster.  18°.  New York, 1863.
— New Popular, The, Forget-Me-Not Songster.  32°.  Cincinnati, no date.
— Nigger Melodies.  32°.  New York, no date.
— Peel's, (Matt.)  (See Matt Peel's.)
— Pete Morris' American Comic Melodist.  18°.  New York, 1857.
— Sam Sharpley's Iron-Clad Songster.  18°.  New York, 1864.
— Sanford's Ethiopian Melodies.  18°.  Philadelphia, 1855.
— Same.  18°.  Philadelphia, 1860.
— Seymour's, (Nelse.)  (See Nelse Seymour's.)
— Sharpley's, (Sam.)  (See Sam Sharpley's.)
— Shiney Eye, De, Crooked Shin, and Oh, Susannah Songster.  32°.  New York, no date.
— Southern Songster, and Mrs. Tucker's Delight.  32°.  [Philadelphia, 1843?]
— Tom Vance's Circus Songster.  18°.  New York, 1855.
— Tom Vance's Kom-e-kill Songster.  18°.  Philadelphia, 1866.
— Townsend, (B. O'N.)  Plantation Lays.  12°.  Columbia, 1884.
— United States Screamer, De.  32°.  Philadelphia, no date.
— Unsworth's Burnt Cork Lyrics.  Edited by J. H. Collins.  18°.  New York, 1859.
— Vance's, (Tom.)  (See Tom Vance's.)
— Vaughn and Fox's Banjo Songster.  18°.  New York, 1860.
— Virginia Serenaders, The, Illustrated Songster.  18°.  New York, no date.
— Same.  18°.  Philadelphia, no date.
— White's New Book of Plantation Melodies.  18°.  New York, 1848.
— Same.  18°.  New York, 1849.
— Same.  18°.  Philadelphia, no date.
— White's New Ethiopian.  18°.  New York, 1850.
— White's New Illustrated Melodeon.  18°.  New York, 1848.
— Same.  18°.  Philadelphia, no date.
— White's Serenaders.  18°.  New York, 1851.
— Wood's Minstrels' Songs.  18°.  New York, 1852.
— Same.  18°.  New York, 1853.
— Same.  18°.  New York, 1855.

SONG BOOKS, (NEGRO MINSTREL.) — *Continued.*

— Wood's New Plantation Melodies. 18°. New York, 1853.
— Ya-Hoo Roarer. 32°. New York, [1843?]

SONG BOOKS, (PRESIDENTIAL CAMPAIGN.)

### Campaign of 1840.

— Harrison and Log Cabin Song Book, The. 18°. Columbus, 1840.
— Harrison Medal Minstrel, The. 32°. Philadelphia, 1840.
— Harrison Melodies. 18°. Boston 1840.
— Log Cabin and Hard Cider Melodies, The. 18°. Boston, 1840.
— Log Cabin Song Book, The. 12°. New York, 1840.
— Tippecanoe Song Book. 18°. Philadelphia, 1840.

### Campaign of 1844.

— American Republican Songster, The. (See De Le Ree, P.)
— Clay Minstrel, The. 32°. New York, 1842.
— De Le Ree, (P.) The American Republican Songster. 2d Edition.
    12°. New York, 1844.
— Democratic Lute, The. (See Hickey, J.)
— Harry Clay Melodist, The. 18°. Boston, 1842.
— Harry Clay Songster, The. 32°. Boston, 1842.
— Hickey, (J.) The Democratic Lute. 18°. Philadelphia, 1844.
— National Clay Melodist, The. 2d Edition. 24°. Boston, 1844.
— National Clay Minstrel, The. 32°. Philadelphia, 1843.
— Same. New Edition. 32°. Boston, 1843.
— Patriotic Songs. 8°. New York, 1844.
— Song, A, etc. By T. Williams. 8°. Providence, 1844.
— That Same Old 'Koon's Roarer. 32°. New York, no date.
— Whig Songs for the Mendon Clay Club. 12°. Boston, 1844.

### Campaign of 1848.

— All the Letters and Songs of Old Zach's Campaigns, etc. Edited by
    S. Horn. 8°. New York, 1848.
— Cass & Butler Songster. 32°. Philadelphia, 1848.
— Free Soil Minstrel, The. 12°. New York, 1848.
— Rough and Ready Melodist, The. 18°. New York, 1848.

Song Books, (Presidential Campaign.) — *Continued.*
— Rough and Ready Songs. 8°. New York, 1848.
— Taylor and Fillmore Songster. 32°. New York, 1848.

*Campaign of 1852.*
— Scott Songster, The. 32°. Ciucinnati, 1852.

*Campaign of 1856.*
— Blodget, (W. P.) Rocky Mountain Song Book. 8°. Providence, 1856.
— Drew, (T.) Fremont Songs. 16°· Boston, 1856.
— Freeman's Glee Book, The. 18°. New York, 1856.
— Fillmore and Donelson Songs. 12°. New York, 1856.
— Fremont Songs. 24°. Boston, 1856.
— Republican Campaign Songster, The. 18°. New York, 1856.
— Rocky Mountain Song Book. (See Blodget, W. P.)

*Campaign of 1860.*
— Bungay, (G. W.) The Bobolink Minstrel. 18°. New York, 1860.
— Burleigh, (W. H.) Republican Campaign Songster. 18°. New York, 1860.
— Civis, (G. W.) Songs for the Great Campaign of 1860. 12°. New York, 1860.
— Democratic Campaign Songster, The. 18°. New York, 1860.
— Drew, (T.) Republican Songs for the People. Sm. 16°. Boston, 1860.
— Honest Abe of the West. Broadside.
— Hutchinson, (J. W.) Connecticut Wide-Awake Songster. 18°. New York, 1860.
— Same. Hutchinson's Republican Songster. 18°. New York, 1860.
— Lincoln and Hamlin. Campaign Song. Broadside.
— Republican Songs. 18°. Boston, 1860.
— Wide-Awake Vocalist, The. Ob. 16°. New York, 1860.

*Campaign of 1864.*
— Campaign Songs. (See Potts, W. D.)
— Herbert, (S.) McClellan Campaign Melodist. 8th Edition. 16°. New York, 1864.

Song Books, (Presidential Campaign.) — *Continued.*

— Little Mac's Campaign Songs.  12°.  New York, 1864.
— Little Mac's Campaign Songster, The.  18°.  New York, 1864.
— McClellan Campaign Melodist.  (See Herbert, S.)
— Pott's (W. D.) Campaign Songs.  12°.  New York, 1864.
— President Lincoln Campaign Songster, The.  18°.  New York, 1864.
— Republican Campaign Songster, The.  32°.  Cincinnati, 1864.
— Tremaine Brothers', The, Lincoln and Johnson Campaign Song Book.  18°.  New York, 1864–1865.

*Campaign of 1868.*

— "Brick" Pomeroy's.  (See G. E. L.)
— G. (E. L.)  "Brick" Pomeroy's Democratic Campaign Song Book.  16°.  New York, 1868.
— Seymour Campaign Songster.  32°.  New York, 1868.

*Campaign of 1872.*

— Cummings, (A. J.)  The Sun's Greeley Campaign Songster.  16°.  New York, 1872.
— "The Farmer of Chappaqua" Songster, The.  16°.  New York, 1872.
— Grant & Wilson Campaign Songster, The.  16°.  New York, 1872.
— Greeley & Brown Campaign Songster, The.  16°.  New York, 1872.

*Campaign of 1880.*

— Campaign Primer, The.  Sq. 18°.  New York, 1880.

Song Books, (Rebellion and Slavery.)

— American Union Songster, The.  16°.  Indianapolis, 1862.
— Anti-Slavery Harp, The.  Edited by W. W. Brown.  12°.  Boston, 1848.
— Anti-Slavery Hymns.  18°.  Hopedale, Mass., 1844.
— Anti-Slavery Poems.  Liberty Chimes.  18°.  Providence, 1845.
— Army Melodies.  (See Dadmun, J. W.)
— Army and Navy Melodies.  (See Dadmun, J. W.)
— Ballads of the South.  (Dawley's Ten-Penny Song Books.  No. 2.)  18°.  New York, 1864.

Song Books, (Rebellion and Slavery.) — *Continued.*

— Ballads of the War. (Dawley's Ten-Penny Songs Books. No. 1.) 18°. New York, 1864.
— Bang's Penny Songster. No. 1. 16°. Providence, no date.
—. Same. No. 2. 16°. Providence, no date.
— Banner Songster, The. 18°. New York, 1865.
— Beadle's Dime Knapsack. 18°. New York, 1862.
— Beadle's Dime Military. Edited by W. R. Wallace. 16°. New York, 1861.
— Beadle's Dime Songs for the War. 16°. New York, 1861.
— Beadle's Dime Union. No. 1. 16°. New York, 1861.
— Same. No. 2. 16°. New York, 1861.
— Same. No. 3. 16°. New York, 1862.
— Billy Holmes's Comic Local Lyrics. 12°. New York, 1866.
— Book of Words. (See Hutchinson Family.)
— Brown, (W. W.) (See the Anti-Slavery Harp.)
— Buckley's Dime Knapsack. 18°. New York, 1862.
— Buckley's Melodist. 18°. Boston, 1864.
— Burton, (E.) Events of 1875–76 Songster. 18°. New York, no date.
— Camp Songs. 32°. Boston, 1862.
— Chanticleer Songster, The. 18°. New York, 1866.
— Chimes of Freedom and Union. 18°. Boston, 1861.
— Clark, (G. W.) The Liberty Minstrel. 7th Edition. 12°. New York, 1844.
— Continental Songster, The. 18°. Philadelphia, 1863.
— Copperhead Minstrel, The. 12°. New York, 1863.
— Dadmun, (J. W.) Army Melodies. 16°. Boston, 1861.
— Same. Army and Navy Melodies. 16°. Boston, 1862.
— Same. Union League Melodies. 16°. Boston, 1864.
— Dawley's Ten-Penny Song Books. (See Ballads.)
— Dime Negro Melodies. No. 1. Happy Contraband. 18°. Philadelphia, 1864.
— Flag of Our Union Songster, The. 18°. New York, 1861.
— Free Soil Minstrel. 12°. New York, 1848.
— Furness, (W. H.) A Song for the Times. 8°. No place, no date.
— General Lee Songster, The. 18°. Macon, Ga., 1865.

Song Books, (Rebellion and Slavery.) — *Continued.*

— George Munroe's Ten Cent Song Book. 16°. New York, no date.
— Guiding Star Songster, The. 12°. New York, 1865.
— Holmes's, (Billy.) (See Billy Holmes's.)
— Hutchinson Family, Book of Words of the. 12°. New York, 1851.
— Same. 12°. New York, 1852.
— Same. 12°. New York, 1853.
— Same. 12°. Boston, 1855.
— Jack Morgan Songster, The. Sm. 16°. Raleigh, 1864.
— Lincoln, (J.) Anti-Slavery Melodies. 12°. Hingham, 1843.
— Little Mac Songster, The. 18°. New York, 1862.
— Lyrics for Freedom. 12°. New York. 1862.
— Moral Songster, The. 18°. Philadelphia, 1862.
— Munroe's, (George.) (See George Munroe's.)
— Naval Songster, The. 18°. Philadelphia, 1862.
— New and Enlarged Edition. (See Patriotic Song Book.)
— New and Popular Songs. 8°. Philadelphia, 1865.
— New Confederate Flag, The. No. 1. 4th Edition. 16°. Mobile, 1864.
— Patriotic Song Book, The. New and Enlarged Edition. Ob. 16°. New York, 1862.
— Poole, (J. F.) Fattie Stewart's Comic Songster. 18°. New York, 1863.
— Purdy, (S. S.) Purdy's Paul Pry Songster. 16°. New York, 1865.
— Rataplan, The; or, The "Red, White and Blue" Warbler. Ob. 16°. New York, 1861.
— Red, White and Blue. 16°. Indianapolis, 1861.
— Shilling Song Book, The. No. 1. (See Song Books, Various.)
— Same. No. 2. 16°. Boston, 1862.
— Same. No. 3. 16°. New York, 1864.
— Soldiers' and Sailors' Patriotic Songs. L. P. Society, No. 49. 8°. New York, 1864.
— Soldier's Companion, The. 2d Edition. 12°. Boston, 1861.
— Same. 5th Edition. 12°. Boston, 1862.
— Soldier's Hymn Book, The. 70th Thousand. 32°. New York, 1861.

SONG BOOKS, (REBELLION AND SLAVERY.) — *Continued.*

— Soldier's Hymn Book, The. 140th Thousand. 32°. New York, 1861.
— Song, A, for the Times. (See Furness, W. H.)
— Songs and Ballads of Freedom. 12°. New York, 1864.
— Songs and Choruses, The, in Uncle Tom's Cabin. No place, 1853.
— Songs for the Union. 8°. New York. no date.
— Same. 18°. Philadelphia, 1861.
— Same. 18°. Philadelphia, 1864.
— Songs for War Time. 16°. Boston, 1863.
— Songs of the Free. 12°. Boston, 1836.
— Songs of Love and Liberty. 18°. Raleigh, 1864.
— Songs of the Nation for 1861. 18°. New York, 1861.
— Songs of the War. 12°. Albany, 1863.
— Songster, Red, White and Blue. 18°. New York, no date.
— Songster, The Banner. 18°. New York, 1865.
— Songster, The Chanticleer. 18°. New York, 1866.
— Songster, The Repository. 18°. New York, 1811.
— Southern Soldier's Prize Songster, The. 16°. Mobile, 1864.
— Stars and Stripes Songster, The. 18°. New York, 1861.
— Same. No. 2. 18°. New York, 1864.
— Stockwell, (W. W.) New Songs and Poems. 16°. Cleveland, 1864.
— Tent and Forecastle Songster, The. 18°. New York, 1862.
— Tony Pastor's New Union Song Book. 18°. New York, 1862.
— Touch the Elbow Songster. 18°. New York, 1862.
— Trumpet of Freedom. Ob. 8°. Boston, 1864.       .
— Tucker, (H.) (See Rataplan, The.)
— Uncle Sam's Army Songster. 16°. Indianapolis, 1862.
— Union League Melodies. (See Dadmun, J. W.)
— United States of America. (See Songs of the Nation for 1861.)
— Wallace, (W. R.) (See Beadle's Dime Military.)
— War-Songs for Freemen. Sq. 16°. Boston, 1862.
— Same. 2d Edition. Sq. 16°. Boston, 1863.
— Same. 3d Edition. Sq. 16°. Boston, 1863.
— Same. 4th Edition. Sq. 16°. Boston, 1863.

36

Song Books, (Rebellion and Slavery.) — *Continued.*

— War-Songs for Freedom.  Sq. 16°.  New York, 1862.
— War Songs of the American Union.  12°.  Boston, 1861.
— War Songs of the South.  18°,  Richmond, 1862.
— Yankee Doodle Songster, The.  18°.  Philadelphia, 1861.
— Yankee Volunteer's Songster, The.  18°.  Philadelphia, 1862.

  For other Song Books relating to the Rebellion and Slavery, *See Supra* Presidential Campaign Song Books—Campaigns of '56, '00 and '64.

Song Books, (Temperance.)

— Anderson Temperance Minstrel.  32°.  New York, no date.
— Bonner, (T. D.)  The Mountain Minstrel.  32°.  Concord, 1847.
— Same.  The Temperance Harp.  32°.  Northampton, 1842.
— Crystal Fount.  32°.  New York, 1854.
— Cold Water Melodies, The.  3d Edition.  18°.  Boston, 1842.
— Hubbard, (S.)  The New Temperance Melodist.  12°.  Boston, 1859.
— Pearce, (B. W.)  The New England Temperance Songster.  Nos. 1 and 2.  18°.  Pawtucket, 1845.
— Same.  Nos. 3 and 4.  16°.  Pawtucket, 1845.
— Pic-Nic Songs.  12°.  Boston, no date.
— Pierpont, (J.)  Cold Water Melodies.  18°.  Boston, 1842.
— Same.  2d Edition.  18°.  Boston, 1843.
— Slocum, (S.)  The Cold Water Melodies.  32°.  Providence, 1831.
— Temperance Song Book.  Sq. 16°.  Boston, 1842.
— Temperance Songster, The.  32°.  New York, no date.
— Trowbridge, (A.)  Temperance Melodeon.  Lg. 8°.  Boston, 1844.
— Waugh, (T.)  The Temperance Muse.  24°.  Providence, 1842.

Song Books (Various.)

— Advent Hymn Book.  24°.  Concord, N. H., 1843.
— Same.  24°.  Nashville, 1843.
— Allen, (W.)  Sacred Songs.  18°.  Northampton, 1867.
— Alline, (H.)  Hymns and Spiritual Songs.  12°.  Stonington-Port Ct., 1802.
— American Songster.  18°.  Baltimore, 1799.
— American Republican Harmonist.  18°.  Philadelphia, 1803.
— American Union Songster.  18°.  Indianapolis, 1862.

Song Books (Various.) — *Continued.*

— American Comic Songster, The.  18°.  New York, 1834.
— American Musical Miscellany, The.  12°.  Northampton, 1798.
— American Songster, The.  16°.  New York, 1788.
— Same.  16°.  New York, 1803.
— Angelo's Original Comic Songs.  18°.  Philadelphia, 1862.
— Apollo, The.  12°.  Philadelphia, 1793.
— Arey, (Mrs. H. E. G.)  Household  Songs, etc.  12°.  New York, 1865.
— Arkansas Traveller's Songster, The.  18°.  New York, 1863.
— Ballou, (A.)  The Hopedale Collection of Hymns.  12°.  Hopedale, 1849.
— Baltimore  Musical  Miscellany, The.  2 vols.  12°.  Baltimore, 1804–1805.
— Beadle's Dime Songs of the Olden Time.  16°.  New York, 1863.
— Beadle (I. P.) & Company's Ten Cent Song Book.  No. 1.  16°.  New York, 1863.
— Beadle's (I. P.) Ten Cent Song Book.  No. 2.  16°.  New York, 1863.
— Same.  No. 3.  16°.  New York, 1863.
— Berry's (J. S.) Comic Song Book.  18°.  New York, 1863.
— Berry's Comic Songs.  18°.  Philadelphia, 1856.
— Billy Emerson's Nancy Fat Songster.  18°.  New York, 1866.
— Black Crook Songster, The.  18°.  New York, 1867.
— Bob Smith's Clown Song and Joke Book.  18°.  New York, 1863.
— Boys of New York.  A Song and Joke Book.  16°.  New York, no date.
— Broadside Songs and Ballads relating to Slavery and the Rebellion, about 500.
— Same.  Miscellaneous, about 1,600.
— Brooks, (C. T.)  Songs of Field and Flood.  18°.  Boston, 1853.
— Buckley's Song Book for the Parlor.  12°.  New York, 1855.
— Carleton's (Will.) "Dandy Pat" Songster.  18°.  New York, 1866.
— Carols Quoit Club; or, Noctes Gymnasii.  Published by order of the Washington Social Gymnasium.  Lg. 8°.  Boston, 1839.
— Cartee, (C. S.)  The Souvenir Minstrel.  18°.  Philadelphia, 1837.
— Charlie Melville's Ballad Songster.  18°.  New York, 1860.

Song Books (Various.) — *Continued.*

— Columbian Songster.  (See Baltimore Musical Miscellany.)
— Comic and Sentimental Song Book.   (See Offord, W.)
— Concert Room Comic Songster, The.  18°.  Philadelphia, 1860.
— Convivial Songster, The.  18°.  New York, 1862.
— Cottage Melodies.  18°.  New York, 1859.
— Crosby, (F. J.)  The Flower Queen.  Ob. 8°.  New York, 1852.
— Cullen, (C. C.)  American Melodies.  12°.  Trenton, 1864.
— Cummings, (J. W.)  Songs for Catholic Schools.  18°.  Boston, 1862.
— Curween, (H.)  French Love Songs.  Translations.  16°.  New York, 1861.
— Dan Kelly's Songster.  16°.  New York, 1869.
— Diamond Songster, The.  24°.  Baltimore, 1817.
— Donaldson, (P.)  The Odd-Fellows' Minstrel.  32°.  New York, 1848.
— Donnybrook Fair Comic Songster, The.  Edited by E. T. Johnson. 18°.  New. York, 1863.
— Dyer, (S.)  Songs and Ballads.  12°.  New York, 1857.
— Emerson's (Billy.)  (See Billy Emerson's.)
— English's (Joe) Irish Comic Songster.  18°.  New York, 1864.
— Fenian War Songs, The.  18°.  New York, 1866.
— Fireside Song Book, The.  32°.  New York, no date.
— Fitz, (A.)  The Dramatic Song Book.  18°.  Boston, 1868.
— Foster, (S. C.)  The American Dime Song Book.  18°.  Philadelphia, 1859.
— Same.  No. 2.  18°.  Philadelphia, 1860.
— Same.  The Love and Sentimental Songster.  18°.  New York, 1862.
— Fred May's Comic Irish Songster.  18°.  New York, 1862.
— Fred Shaw's.  (See Shaw's, Fred.)
— Fred Wilson's Book of Original Songs.  16°.  Boston, 1860.
— Free and Easy Comic Songster.  18°.  New York, 1864.
— Frisky Irish Songster, The.  18°.  New York, 1862.
— Gannon's (Phil. J.) Original Irish Songster.  12°.  Philadelphia, 1859.
— Gentle Annie Melodist.  No. 1.  18°.  New York, 1860.

Song Books (Various.) — *Continued.*

— Gentle Annie Melodist. No. 2. 18°. New York, 1859.
— Go it! while You're Young Songster. 32°. New York, no date.
— Goodwin, (E. C.) Wayside Songs. 12°. New York, 1856.
— Goose Hangs High Songster, The. 18°. New York, 1866.
— Grigg's Southern and Western Songster. 18°. Philadelphia, 1836.
— Gus Shaw's. (See Shaw's, Gus.)
— Hagen, (J. C.) Ballads of the Revolution. 16°. New York, 1866.
— Harmonica. The Collection of Popular Songs. 16°. New York,
    1840.
— Harrison's Comic Songster. 18°. New York, 1849.
— Hastings, (T.) The Mother's Nursery Songs. 12°. New York,
    1835.
— Heart and Home Songsters, The. 18°. New York, 1862.
— Heine, (H.) Book of Songs. Leland Translation. 3d Edition.
    New York, 1868.
— Hewitt, (M. E.) Songs of Our Land, etc. 12°. Boston, 1846.
— Hickok, (J.) (See Social Lyrist, The.)
— Hill, (T.) Songs and Poems. Vol. ii. 12°. Worcester, 1852.
— Hobbs, (G. W.) Songs and Stories. Sq. 18°. No date.
— Hooley's High Daddy Songster. 18°. New York, 1865.
— Hopkinson, (J.) Song Adapted to the President's March. 8°. Phila-
    delphia, no date.
— Hutchinson, (Ellen M.) Songs and Lyrics. 18°. Boston, 1881.
— Irwin P. Beadle's. (See Beadle's, I. P.)
— Irwin P. Beadle & Co's. (See Beadle, I. P. & Co's.)
— J. S. Berry's. (See Berry's, J. S.)
— Joe English's. (See English's, Joe.)
— Jovial Songster, The. 18°. New York, 1805.
— Lanigan's Ball Comic Songster, The. 18°. New York, 1863.
— Larkin, (S.) (See Nightingale, The.)
— League Meeting Songs. 18°. Philadelphia, 1866.
— Leon, De (T. C.) South Songs. 18°. New York, 1866.
— Lyte, (E. O.) School Room Songs. 8°. Philadelphia.
— Magazine of Songs. 18°. New York, no date.
— May's (Fred.) (See Fred May's.)
— Melville's (Charlie.) (See Charlie Melville's.)

SONG BOOKS (VARIOUS.) — *Continued.*

— Minstrel of Zim.  Religious Songs.  16°.  Philadelphia, 1845.
— Moore, (Julia A.)  The Sentimental Song Book.  Sq. 18°.  Cleveland, 1877.
— Same.  American Melodies.  18°.  New York, 1841.
— Morris, (G. P.)  Songs and Ballads.  8°.  New York, 1844.
— Same.  24°.  New York, 1846.
— Same.  24°.  New York, 1852.
— Morris' (Pete) American Comic Melodist.  18°.  New York, 1857.
— Mulchinock, (W. P.)  Ballads and Songs.  New York, 1851.
— Munroe's Song Book for the Million.  No. 5.  16°.  New York, 1864.
— Same.  No. 6.  16°.  New York, 1863.
— Munsell's Songs of the American Press.  18°.  Albany, no date.
— New England Pocket Songster, The.  32°.  Claremont, N. H., 1835.
— New Pocket Song Book, The.  32°.  New York, no date.
— Nightingale, The.  Edited by S. Larkin.  12°.  Portsmouth, 1804.
— Same ; or, Musical Companion.  New York, 1814.
— Odd Fellows' Minstrel, The.  (See Donaldson P.)
— O'Donnell, (K.)  The Song of Iron, etc.  18°.  Philadelphia, 1863.
— Offord, (W.)  Comic and Sentimental Song Book.  18°.  Brooklyn, 1865.
— O'Reilly, (J. B.)  Songs, Legends, etc.  12°.  Boston, 1878.
— Same.  Songs from the Southern Seas.  16°.  Boston, 1873.
— Same.  Songs of United Germany.  Lg. 8°.  New York, 1870.
— Parlor Songster.  24°.  New York, 1844.
— Pastor's (Tony.)  Book of Six Hundred Comic Songs and Speeches.  18°.  New York, 1867.
— Same.  Carte de Visite Album Songster.  18°.  New York, 1865.
— Same.  "444" Combination Songster.  18°.  New York, 1864.
— Same.  Comic and Eccentric Songster.  18°.  New York, 1862.
— Same.  Great Sensation Songster.  Edited by J. F. Poole.  18°.  New York, 1863.
— Same.  New Irish Comic Songster.  18°.  New York, 1863.
— Same.  "Own" Comic Vocalist.  Edited by J. F. Poole.  18°.  New York, 1863.
— Same.  Waterfall Songster.  18°.  New York, 1866.

Song Books (Various.) — *Continued.*

— Paul, (H.) The Book of American Songs. 18°. London, 1857.
— Pearl Songster, The. 32°. New York, 1846.
— People's New Songster, The. 32°. No place, 1862.
— Pete Morris'. (See Morris', Pete.)
— Phil. J. Gannon's. (See Gannon's, Phil. J.)
— Poole, (J. F.) The Double-Quick Comic Songster. 18°. New York, 1862.
— Same. Comic Songster. 18°. New York, 1863.
— Same. (See also Pastor's, Tony.) ·
— School Songs for the Million. 8°. Boston, 1850.
— Shaw's (Fred.) American Diadem. 32°. New York, 1860.
— Same. Champion Comic Melodist. 18°. New York, 1860.
— Same. Dime American Comic Songster. 18°. New York, 1860.
— Shaw's (Gus) Comic Song and Recitation Book. 18°. New York, 1860.
— Same. New Comic Songs. 18°. Philadelphia, 1860.
— Same. Original Comic Songs. 18°. New York, 1857.
— Shilling Song Book, The. 32°. New York, 1860.
— Same. No. 2. 32°. Boston, no date.
— Singer's Own Book, The. 32°. Philadelphia, 1839.
— Smith's (Bob.) (See Bob Smith's.)
— Social Lyrist, The. By J. H. Hickok. 18°. Harrisburg, Pa., 1840.
— Song Book, Public. 18°. Baltimore, no date.
— Song Book, Scotch. 24°. New York, 1822.
— Song, Whaling. 18°. New Bedford, 1831.
— Songs, A Book of, for Little Sisters. Sq. 16°. New York, 1854.
— Songs, A Choice Selection. 18°. Philadelphia, no date.
— Songs in the Night. 5th Edition. 16°. Boston, 1858.
— Songs of the Free. 12°. Boston, 1836.
— Songs of the Florences. 18°. New York, 1860.
— Songs of the League. 24°. Worcester, 1848.
— Songs of the Ocean. 32°. New York, no date.
— Songs of the Quilt. 8°. New London, 1845.
— Songs of the Woodlands, etc. 12°. New York, 1859.
— Songs of Zion, for Methodists. 24°. Baltimore, 1817.

SONG BOOKS (VARIOUS.) — *Continued.*

— Songs—Rote, of the Normal Music Course. Lg. 8°. New York, 1883.

— Songs, Sacred, for Family and Social Worship. 12°. New York, 1842.

— Songs, San Souci. 18°. New York, 1859.

— Songs. Single leaves bound in 4 volumes. Lg. 8°. New York, no date.

> Published by H. Marsan, as follows: Vol. i, called List No. 4, 100 Songs; Vol. ii, List No. 10, 100 Songs; Vol. iii, List No. 13, 102 Songs; Vol. iv, List No. 15, 102 Songs. The songs in the last three volumes are alphabetically arranged.

— Songs, Spiritual. Hastings and Mason. 18°. Utica, 1832.

— Songster, The Chanticleer. 18°. New York, 1866.

— Songster, The Western. 18°. Title-page gone.

— Songster, The Western Sisters. 18°. New York, no date.

— Songster, Our Girls. 18°. New York, no date.

— Songster's Miscellany, The. 18°. Philadelphia, 1817.

— Temple of Harmony, The. 16°. Baltimore, 1801.

— Tony Pastor's. (See Pastor's, Tony.)

— Variety Songster, The. 32°. New York, no date.

— Virginia Nightingale. 18°. Title-page gone.

— Vocal Lyre, The. 24°. Newark, N. J., 1852.

— Western Songster. 24°. Philadelphia, 1835.

— Will Carleton's. (See Carleton's, Will.)

— Wilson's (Fred). (See Fred Wilson's.)

— Zion's Songster, The Southern. 24°. Raleigh, 1864.

SOPHIA; OR, THE REIGN OF WOMAN. (Anon.) 8°, pp. 40. New York, 1864.

> Sold at the New York Metropolitan Fair for the benefit of the United States Sanitary Commission.

SORAN, (C.) The Petapsco, and Other Poems. 8°, pp. viii, 84. Baltimore, 1841.

— Same. 3d Edition. 12°, pp. 194. Baltimore, 1858.

> "Many of the articles," says the author, "in the volume were composed whilst in the actual performance of mechanical labor, and written out in moments of relaxation, and all of them are the fruits of time stolen from more important employments."

SOUDER, (MRS. E. A.) An Appeal for the Floating Church, etc. 8°, pp. 83. Philadelphia, 1851.

Soule, (B. L.)   A Poem delivered in Saco, Me., July 4, 1839.   8°, pp. 19.   Saco, 1839.

Soule, (R., Jr.)   Poems, bound in "Memorials of the Sprague Family."   8°.   Boston, 1847.

South, (C.)   Revenge.   12°, pp. 32.   New York, 1843.

Southern Chivalry.   (Anon.)   12°, pp. 78.   Philadelphia, 1861.

Southwick, (S.)

Solomon Southwick was born in Rhode Island about the year 1774, and died at Albany, N. Y., in 1839.   He was the editor of the *Albany Register*, and other papers, and published several pamphlets.

— The Pleasures of Poverty.   8°, pp. 80.   Albany, 1823.

Spaulding, (Mrs. A. M.)   Patriotic Poems.   16°, pp. 287.   New York, 1866.

Specimens of the American Poets.   8°, pp. xxiii, 263.   London, 1822.

Speech and Songs of a Greek Indian Against the Immoderate Use of Spirituous Liquors.   8°, pp. 68.   London, 1759.

Spencer, (H. L.)   Poems.   12°, pp. 95.   Boston, 1850.

Sperry, (H. T.)   Country Love vs. City Flirtation.   Illustrated by A. Hoppin.   Sq. 12°, pp. 90.   New York, 1865.

Spierin, (G. H.)

Born at Newburg, N. Y., December 26, 1787, of Irish descent, his father being an A. M. of Trinity College, Dublin.   He early in life developed poetical talent, and wrote many poems which he destroyed.   He died at the age of sixteen years and eight months.

— Poems.   8°, pp. xviii, 211.   Charleston, S. C., 1805.

Spinney, (S. R.)   Carmilhan: An Epic Poem.   8°, pp. 39.   Boston, 1870.

Spirit Congress, The.   A Poem from the MS. of a Maniac.   (Anon.)   12°, pp. 37.   New York, 1859.

Spirit of Seventy-Six.   (Anon.)   3d Edition.   12°, pp. 141.   Boston, 1868.

— Same.   6th Edition.

37

Spirit of the Fair. Nos. 1–17. From April 5th to April 23, 1864. Published in the interests of the New York Sanitary Fair. 4°, pp. 206. New York, 1864.

Several poems in the volume. Among the writers are Bryant, R. H. Stoddard, George W. Curtis, Gail Hamilton, George H. Boker, Lord Houghton, C. T. Brooks, Bayard Taylor, J. R. Lowell and Julia Ward Howe.

Spirit, The, of the Farmers' Museum. A Selection from the " Lady Preacher's Gazette." 12°, pp. 318. Walpole, N. H., 1801.

Spirit, The, of the Public Journals; or, Beauties of the American Newspapers. For 1805. 16°, pp. xii, 300. Baltimore, 1806.

Spofford, (Harriet P.) Poems. 12°, pp. 172. Boston, 1882.

Born at Calais, Me., in 1835, was married, in 1865, to R. S. Spofford, Jr., of Newburyport, Mass.

Spooner, (Mrs. Mary A.) Gathered Leaves. 8°, pp. 180. New York, 1848.

Sprague, (Achsa W.) The Poet, etc. 12°, pp. xxiii, 304. Boston, 1864.

Sprague, (A. W.)

Alfred White Sprague was born at Oahu, Sandwich Islands, and graduated at Amherst College in 1847. He wrote articles for educational journals, and published " Elements of Natural Philosophy," etc.

— " I Still Live." 12°, pp. 19. Oswego, N. Y., 1862.

Sprague, (C.)

Charles Sprague was born at Boston, October 20, 1701. His father was one of the patriots of Boston who took part in the famous act of throwing the tea into the harbor. The subject of this sketch was placed, a boy of only thirteen, in a dry goods mercantile house, and at the age of twenty-five years, became a partner in the house which he had served as an apprentice. When the Globe Bank was established, in 1825, he was chosen Cashier of the institution, a position which he held until his death, January 21, 1875. Sprague has been called " the American Pope for his terseness, his finished elegance, his regularity of metre, and his nervous point."

— Curiosity, a Phi Beta Kappa Poem, August 27, 1829. 8°, pp. 30. Boston, 1829.

— Ode. September 17, 1830. 8°, pp. 22. Boston, 1830.

— Poems. 12°, pp. 130. New York, 1850.

— Prize Ode. Recited at the Representation of the Shakspeare Jubilee, February 13, 1824. 8°, pp. 8. No place, no date.

— Prize Poems, etc. 8°, pp. 130. Boston, 1824.

— The Poetical and Prose Writings. 16°, pp. vii, 205. Boston, 1850.

Sprague, (C.) — *Continued.*

— Writings of, First Collected. Poems. 8°, pp. 1–124. New York, 1841.

> The volume contains thirty-one poems and two orations: the one, the Boston 4th of July, 1825, oration, and the other on Intemperance, 1827.

— Same. 2d Edition. 16°, pp. 58. New York, 1843.

Spring Blossoms. Poems written by a Child between Six and Fifteen Years. 16°, pp. vi, 94. Boston, 1854.

Sproat, (G. T.) The Pilgrim's Song. 18°, pp. 90. Taunton, 1830.

Sproat, (Mrs. N.) Village Poems. 18°, pp. 67. New York, no date.

Spunkiard. (By an American Youth.) 8°, pp. 23. Newburgh, 1798.

> "A Congressional Display of Spit and Cudgel."

Stagg, (E.) Poems. 12°, pp. 259. St. Louis, 1852.

> Under date of St. Louis, April, 1852, the author writes in his Preface: "Most of the 'Earlier Poems' were written from twelve to fifteen years ago, and appeared over the initial 'S.' In the *Commercial Bulletin*, a newspaper then published in this city; the others were composed at different times during the last five years."

— Thoughts and Feelings. 16°, pp. 105. New York, 1847.

Stampa, (Gaspara.)

> Gaspara Stampa, an Italian lady, was born of Milanese parentage, in Padua, in 1553, removed to Venice in early life, where, at the age of twenty-six, she became the affianced of the Count of Collato, who, at the end of three years, entered the service of Henry II., and fascinated by the charms of the famous Diane de Poitiers' abandoned the object of his early love. The sonnets translated by Fleming describe her affection for her lover and the profound grief into which she was plunged by his abandonment of her. "They reveal her impassioned nature, her anguish, and her despair; they render her name famous throughout Italy. It was even said that no verse more sweet and elegant and impassioned had ever been written. It is the record of a heart-breaking tragedy, but it celebrates hours of triumphant joy." Well has she been called "The Sappho of Venice."

— Memoir of Her Life, by Eugene Benson, and a Selection from Her Sonnets, translated by George Fleming. 16°, pp. 83. Boston, 1881.

Standfast, (R.) Dialogue between a Blind Man and Death. 12°, pp. 16. London and Boston, no date.

Standish, (M., Jr.) The Times. 8°, pp. 27. Plymouth, 1809.

Stanley, (E. S.) Life's Perilous Places. 18°, pp. 30. Hartford, 1865.

Stars of Columbia, etc. (Anon.) 8°, pp. 8. New York, 1813.

STARS, OUR. (Entered by E. N. Gunnison.) Several Poems in the volume. 12°, pp. 120. No place, 1863.

STARS, THE, FOR THE CROWN. (Anon.) 12°, pp. 24. Fall River, 1872.

STATE STREET. A Satire. (Anon.) 16°, pp. 29. Boston, 1874.

STAYMAN, (J. K.)

John K. Stayman, Professor of Ancient Languages and Classical Literature in Dickenson College.

— Flowers and Fossils. 16°, pp. 320. Philadelphia, 1870.

STEARNS, (C.)

Charles Stearns was born at Leominster, Mass., July 10, 1753, graduated at Harvard in 1773, studied Theology, was Tutor at Cambridge, 1780–81, was called, January 15, 1781, to the pastorate of the church in Lincoln, Mass., and ordained November 7, 1781.' In 1792 he became Principal of a school in the town where he was the minister, remaining in this position ten years. Harvard College, in 1810, conferred on him the degree of D. D. His ministry in Lincoln continued to the close of his life, July 26, 1826.

— Dramatic Dialogues. 12°, pp. 540. Leominster, Mass., 1798.

— The Ladies' Philosophy of Love. A Poem in Four Cantos. Written in 1774. 12°, pp. iv, 76. Leominster, 1797.

In the Preface, Dr. Stearns says : "When the Poem was written, the Author was in his 22d year, and under no obligation to any of the fair, but mere good will. Since that time he has been a lover, a husband, a father of a numerous family, a pastor, a preceptor for many years to youth of both sexes. His experience has not disproved, but confirmed his principles."

A fine copy, bound in elegant style by Bedford.

STEDMAN, (E. C.)

Edmund Clarence Stedman was born at Hartford, Conn., October, 8, 1833, and was a son of the poetess, Mrs. E. C. Kinney, by a former husband; graduated at Yale in 1853, removed to New York in 1855, and became poetical contributor to the *Tribune*, was war correspondent of the *World*, 1861–63, studied law, and since 1865 has been a banker in New York. He takes high rank among literary men of the country.

— Alice of Monmouth. 12°, pp. 151. New York, 1864.

— Rip Van Winkle. Illustrations by Sol. Eytinge, Jr. 4°, pp. 8. Boston, 1870.

— Poems. 12°, pp. viii, 196. New York, 1860.

" This volume is mostly composed of such productions as have stood the tests of time and the reviews, to which they have been subjected, by the author, in the earnest desire to prefer his art to himself."

— The Blameless Prince, etc. 16°, pp. viii, 192. Boston, 1869.

— The Prince's Ball. 12°, pp. 63. New York, 1860.

STEELE, (J. B.)  Poems.  12°, pp. 384.  New York, 1863.

STEELE, (S. S.)  Book of Plays.  12°, pp. 349.  Philadelphia, 1860.
 Designed for private theatricals.

— The Brazen Drum.  A National Anthem.  18°, pp. 42.  New York, no date.

STERNE, (S.)  Giorgio, etc.  16°, pp. 195.  Boston, 1881.
— Poems.  16°, pp. 244.  New York, 1875.

STERRY, (ABBY H.)  Effusions.  12°, pp. 150.  New London, 1818.

STEVENS, (G. L.)  The Patriot.  A Drama.  8°, pp. 86.  Boston, 1834.

STEVENSON, (D. C.)  The Centennial Poems.  18°, pp. 45.  Austin, 1876.

STEVENSON, (R.)  Liberal Odes, No. 1.  24°, pp. 18.  New York, 1813.

STEWART, (J. M.)  An Essay, etc.  16°, pp. vi, 62.  Norwich, Conn., 1852.

STILES, (H. R., M. D.)
 Henry Reed Stiles was born in the city of New York, March 10, 1832, was educated at the University of New York, and Williams College, and received the degree of M. D. from the New York Medical School in 1855, practiced in Galena, Ill., and Brooklyn, N. Y.  He has filled important offices connected with his profession in Brooklyn and New York.

— Bundling ; its Origin, Progress and Decline in America.  Sq. 16°, pp. 139.  Albany, 1869.

STILLMAN, (G. A.)  Life, Real.  12°, pp. 137.  New York, 1854.

STIRLING, (E.)  The Bloomer Costume.  12°, pp. 20.  New York, no date.

STOCKTON, (T. H.)
 Thomas Hewlings Stockton was born at Mount Holly, N. J., June 4, 1808.  For several years he was Chaplain in Congress and, as a Methodist clergyman, had charge of several churches.  Died October 9, 1868.

— Poems.  12°, pp. ix, 285.  Philadelphia, 1862.

STODDARD, (C. W.)  Poems.  8°, pp. 123.  San Francisco, 1867.

STODDARD, (R. H.)
 Richard Henry Stoddard was born at Hingham, Mass., in July, 1825, removed to New York, and was a workman in an iron foundry in that city.  He was in the New York Custom House, 1852-70.  Since 1870 he has devoted himself to literary pursuits.

STODDARD, (R. H.) — *Continued.*

— Poems. 12°, pp. 127. Boston, 1852.

— Songs of Summer. 12°, pp. vii, 192. Boston, 1857.

— Same. 12°, pp. 229. Boston, 1857.

— The Book of the East, etc. 12°, pp. v, 249. Boston, 1871.

— The King's Bell. 12°, pp. 72. New York, 1863.

— Same. Illustrated. 8°, pp. 60. New York, 1876.

— The Story of Putnam the Brave. 4°, pp. 8. Boston, 1869. Illustrations by Alfred Fredericks.

STOKES, (E. H.) Songs of the Sea. 8°, pp. 32. Ocean Grove, N. J., 1879.

STORIES FOR ALICE. (Anon.) Sq. 16°, pp. 128. Philadelphia, 1857.

STORM. A Poem. (By a Citizen of Philadelphia.) 18°, pp. 123. Philadelphia, 1788.

Very rare. The poem describes "the late tempest which raged with such destructive fury throughout the southern parts of North America in July, 1788."

STORY, (I.) (Peter Quince, *pseud.*)

Isaac Story was born at Marblehead, Mass., August 25, 1774, graduated at Harvard, 1793, was admitted to the bar and practiced in Castine, Me., and Rutland, Mass. He died at Marblehead July 19, 1803. Mr. S. was a cousin of the distinguished Judge Joseph Story.

— A Parnassian Shop. 8°, pp. vii, 155. Boston, 1801.

The following is given as the inscription on the sign-board of the "Parnassian Shop:"

"Peter's Shop contains the largest and most fashionable assortment of Apollo-Ware; beautiful and variegated Odes, by the yard or piece; Songs suitable for any and every occasion, single or by the set; one crate of broken Elegies, which can be so joined together as to suit the vilest and worthless characters; also a few Elastic Trusses — calculated with great care and ingenuity for loose Politicians; one Trepanning Instrument to be used on such persons, only, who have cracked their skulls in trying to pull down good government. A few bundles of Invitations, Addresses, Excuses, Conundrums, Whip-Syllabubs and Deifications, together with a new-invented Bib and Spatterdasher for the sole benefit and behoof of Slovenly *Critics.*

"Besides the above mentioned articles, Peter has a more pleasing and diversified assortment in his large Ware-House, which will be opened as soon as Apollo-Ware becomes more fashionable. Peter keeps constantly for sale, in the back part of his shop, *Parnassian-Trinkets, Heliconian-spouts* and *Pegassuses* on truckles, for the accommodation of young and lame Poetasters; also a very ingenious Spinning-Wheel, which will turn off Epic-Poems of any length and on any subject, with the utmost ease and dispatch; besides furnishing them with glossaries and obsolete quotations, all of which will be sold on the most reasonable terms for cash or short credit. Peddlars and Ballad-Singers may depend on making good bargains and receiving ample encouragement, at said back apartment, where they will find a number of heavy moulded geniusses eternally at pen nibbing. Peter has with much care and expense procured a curious and complicated Water-

S̲tory, (I.)   (Peter Quince, *pseud.*) — *Continued.*

> Machine for grinding with astonishing rapidity hard and cramp phrases into Epitaphs, Rebusses, Epigrams, Catches, Love-Pills, Dying Psalms and Wit-Crackers:—these are sold by the groce or box, to Country Traders at a reduced price."
> " N. B.  Cash and the highest price given for *new ideas.*"

S̲tory, (J.)

> Joseph Story was born at Marblehead, Mass., September 18, 1779, and was a graduate of Harvard, 1798, admitted to the bar 1801, appointed Associate Justice of the United States Supreme Court, November 18, 1811.  He was chosen Dane Professor of Law, Harvard Law School, June 11, 1829.  He died September 10, 1845.  (See Allibone, pp. 2273-75.)

— The Power of Solitude.  8°, pp. 100.  Boston, no date.  1802[?]

> In the " Proem " to this poem the author says : " In the following poem the pertinent division of Zimmerman is adopted as uniting elegance and method.  Wherever the author has been sensible of imitation he has given full credit.  Probably much has escaped his notice, as similarity of thought on a subject which has incidentally claimed attention from almost every poetic genius is as unavoidable as it is congenial.  Illustrations have sometimes been caught from other compositions, but only when their features admitted of enlargement, or required new colorings to mark the outlines of analogy.  Allusion is admitted in digression to give variety to a subject whose details are almost necessarily uniform.  In fine, it was the author's design to avoid equally sterility of incident and exuberance of ornament—whether this be accomplished, the reader must be determined."

— Same.  2d Edition.  With Fugitive Poems.  16°, pp. 260.  Salem, 1804.

S̲tory, T̲he, o̲f Æ̲neas a̲nd D̲ido B̲urlesqued.  From the Fourth Book of the Æneid of Virgil.  (Anon.)  18°, pp. 94.  Charlestown, 1784.

S̲tory, (W. W.)

> William Wetmore Story, son of Judge Joseph Story, was born at Salem, Mass., February 19, 1819, graduated at Harvard 1838, studied law and was admitted to the bar.  Preferring to be an artist, he abandoned his profession, went to Rome in 1848, and has made that city his permanent home.  He takes the highest rank among sculptors.

— A Roman Lawyer in Jerusalem.  First Century.  16°, pp. 32.  Boston, 1870.

— Graffiti d'Italia.  16°, pp. 412.  New York, 1868.

— Nature and Art.  Phi Beta Kappa Poem, Harvard, August 29, 1844.  Boston, 1844.

— Poems.  12°, pp. viii, 249.  Boston, 1847.

— Same.  12°, pp. 307.  Boston, 1856.

S̲towe, (H̲arriet B.)

> She was born at Litchfield, Conn., June 14, 1812, was associated for several years with her sister Catherine in teaching in Hartford, Conn., and was married, in 1832, to Professor C. E. Stowe, then of Lane Seminary, Cincinnati.  Her most successful work is " Uncle Tom's Cabin."  (See Allibone, pp. 2278-80.)

— Religious Poems.  12°, pp. 107.  Boston, 1867.

STRAY LEAVES.  (By S. B. P.  Anon.)  Sq. 18°, pp. xi, 85.  No place, no date.

STREET, (A. B.)

> Alfred Billings Street was born at Poughkeepsie, N. Y., in 1811.  In 1839 he removed to Albany, where he practiced law.  For many years he has held the post of State Librarian.

— A Poem Delivered at the Pittsfield Young Ladies' Institute.  8°, pp. 8.  Albany, 1852.
— Drawings and Tintings.  4°, pp. 48.  New York, 1844.
— Frontenac.  12°, pp. xiii, 327.  London, 1849.

> The "Eclectic Magazine," June, 1849, alludes to Frontenac as "a poem of singular power and beauty."

— Same.  12°, pp. 324.  New York, 1849.
— Poems.  Complete Edition.  8°, pp. 319.  New York, 1845.
— Same.  2 vols.  12°, pp. v, 302, 338.  New York, 1867.

STREETER, (R. M.)  Poem.  Class Day, Brown University, June 15, 1865.  Lg. 8°, pp. 15.  Providence, 1865.

STRIBLING, (B. F. W.)  Poems.  Sq. 16°, pp. 233.  Beardstown, Ill., 1857.

STRONG, (G. A.)  (Under the *pseud.*, Marc Anthony Henderson.)

> George A. Strong, a Professor in Kenyon College.

— The Song of Milkanwatha.  2d Edition.  12°, pp. viii, 144.  Cincinnati, 1856.

STRONG, (T.)  The Tears of Columbia.  8°, pp. 32.  Dedham, 1812.

STROTHER, (J. H.)  The Golden Calf; or, The Almighty Dollar.  12°, pp. 32.  New York, 1854.

> The author's presentation copy to R. W. Griswold.

STRUGGLE FOR EXISTENCE.  (By Gavilan Peak, Pope[?])  12°, pp. 72.  New York, 1872.

STUART, (C. D.)

> Carlos D. Stuart was born at Berlin, Vt., July 28, 1820, went to New York in 1840, and devoted himself to literary pursuits.  For a time he was a Universalist preacher.  He was co-editor of the *New York Sun*, 1843–53, and established the *New Yorker*, was for a time connected with the *New York Mirror*.  He died at Northampton, Mass., in February, 1862.

— Ianthe, etc.  12°, pp. 224.  New York, 1843.

STUDENTS, THE.  A Drama.  (Anon.)  8°, pp. 108.  New York, 1850.

Studies, Winter. (Anon.) 18°, pp. 43. Philadelphia, 1856.

Stump, (Judge.) The Battle of Cannae. 8°, pp. 54. Baltimore, 1856.

Suicide, The. A Dialogue at Yale, September 13, 1797. 12°, pp. 20. Litchfield, no date.

Summer Songs. (By H. M. M.) 12°, pp. 108. Philadelphia, 1865.

Sumner, (C. P.)

Charles Pinckney Sumner was born at Milton, Mass., January 20, 1776, graduated at Harvard 1796, studied law, appointed High Sheriff of the county of Suffold, in 1825, and held office nearly to the time of his death, April 24, 1839. He was the father of Charles Sumner.

— The Compass. A Poetical Performance at Harvard University, September, 1795. 12°, pp. 12. Boston, no date.

Superstition Detected. (Anon.) 12°, pp. 24. Philadelphia, 1831.

This play comprises "a comic narrative of his conviction and condemnation, together with his last will and confession. By a Connecticut Brickmaker." To which is added, "The Downfall of Despotism." A Poem. The work is designed to ridicule the orthodox doctrines of Satanic influence and future retribution. The "personæ dramatis" are "AROZAN, a young collegian just entered upon the ministry, emblematical of ecclesiastical tyranny. MATILDA, mother of the young clergyman, whose future prospects and support depended on his success. HONDORUS exposes their fallacy in lively colours and demonstratively shows that religious liberty is as necessary to our happiness in this world as civil liberty, and being deprived of either is an outrage on the human character."

Sutherland, (J. T.)

The author was imprisoned for an infraction of the neutrality law in the famous Navy Island expedition, in 1837, against the constituted authorities of the Canadas. He became a prisoner March 4, 1838, in the citadel. In the volume are two or three short poems.

— Loose Leaves from the Portfolio of a late Prisoner in Canada. 12°, pp. 36. New York, 1839.

Suttliffe, (A.) Poems. 12°, pp. 144. Boston, 1859.

Swan, (C.) The Petapsco. 2d Edition. 12°, pp. 144. Baltimore, 1842.

Swan, (J. R.) The Prophecy of the Santon, etc. 12°, pp. 116. Worcester, 1847.

"The Prophecy of the Santon" was suggested by reading the following from Irving's Conquest of Granada: "Wo! wo! wo! to Granada! exclaimed the voice; its hour of desolation approaches. The ruins of Zahara will fall upon our heads; my spirit tells me that the end of our empire is at hand. All shrunk back aghast and left the denouncer of woe standing alone in the centre of the hall. He was (says the Arabian historians) one of those holy men termed Santons, who pass their lives in hermitages, in fasting, meditation, and prayer, until they attain to the purity of saints and the foresight of prophets."

38

SWANWICK, (J.)

> John Swanwick was elected a Representative from Pennsylvania in the Fourth Congress, was re-elected to the Fifth Congress, serving from December 7, 1795, to 1798, when he died.
>
> The author of the volume referred to below says: "One part of life is usually passed in reviewing the other; the following poems were written in that early period of it, on which we are accustomed to look back with more than usual pleasure. They are collected in a volume as memorials of persons and of scenes that recall the most grateful sensations to the mind; they demand no praise, having never been professedly written to obtain it, and they hope to escape censure as trifles by which the cares of a busy life were diverted or assuaged."

— Poems.  Sm. 24°, pp. 174.  Philadelphia, 1797.

SWAYZE, (MRS. J. C.)  Ossawattomie Brown.  12°, pp. 27.  New York, 1859.

SWEENEY, (R.)  Odds and Ends.  12°, pp. 156.  New York, 1826.

SWEET, (J. P.)  Lake George.  12°, pp. 55.  New York, 1863.

SWEETSER, (H. P.)  Poem.  Annual Excursion of the Carpet (Boston) Dealers, June 26, 1869.  A leaflet of 4 pages.

SYBELLE, ETC.  By L.  (Anon.)  12°, pp. 192.  New York, 1862.

TABLE ROCK ALBUM, AND SKETCHES OF THE FALLS AND SCENERY ADJACENT.  3d Edition.  12°, pp. 108.  Buffalo, 1850.

TABLET, A FAMILY.  A Selection of Original Poetry.  (Anon.)  16°, pp. 81.  Boston, 1796.

TAGGART, (CYNTHIA.)

> She was born in Rhode Island in 1801, her father having been a Revolutionary soldier, who was reduced to poverty while the British troops were on the island.  Her life was one of protracted physical suffering, which she bore with remarkable fortitude and Christian resignation.  She died March 23, 1849.

— Poems.  12°, pp. xxii, 98.  Providence, 1834.

TAINTER, (E. C.)  The Battle of Freedom.  A Greek Poem delivered at Commencement, Union College, July 23, 1863.  8°, 65 lines.  Printed at Shanghai, China, 1874.

TAIT, (J. R.)

> John R. Tait was born at Cincinnati in 1834, and was a graduate of Bethany College, Va.  He was the editor of a magazine published at Bethany, entitled "The Stylus."  In 1860 he published "Life, Legend and Landscape."

— Dolce Far Niente, etc.  16°, pp. 75.  Philadelphia, 1859.

TALBOYS, (W. P.)  The Story of Don Sebastian.  8°, pp. 8.  No place, no date.

TALISMAN, THE.  18°, pp. x, 342.  New York, 1838.

"The Talisman" was continued three years, its contributors being G. C. Verplanck, W. C. Bryant. R. C. Sands, etc.  The "Dream of the Princess Papantzin," p. 291, was written by Sands.  One or two other poems are bound up in this volume.

TALLEY, (SUSAN A.)

A native of Virginia, who became deaf at the age of nine.  She was an artist as well as poet.

— Poems.  16°, pp. 183.  New York, 1859.

TANEY, (R. B.)

In "The Harris Collection" is a copy of the poems of Francis S. Key, the author of "The Star Spangled Banner."  The volume is the beautiful edition published in New York by Robert Carter & Brothers, 1857, and was among the books added by Senator Anthony to the "Collection."  In the introduction is a letter from Hon. Chief Justice Taney, narrating the incidents connected with the origin of the song.  It may not be out of place in these notes to relate these incidents by condensing the facts as they are given by Judge Taney.

A prominent gentleman, Dr. Beanes, residing in Upper Marlboro', Md., had been made a prisoner in 1814 by the British, and taken to Baltimore and placed on board one of the ships of the English fleet.  Mr. Key undertook to procure the release of his friend.  As preparations were now making to attack Fort McHenry, Key was sent on board the vessel in which he had come to Baltimore, accompanied by Dr. Beanes, whose release he had obtained.  They were not suffered, however, to sail away or to land, a guard of soldiers preventing them.  The vessel was anchored in a position which enabled them to see distinctly the flag of the fort from the deck.  They remained on deck during the whole night, watching every shell from the moment it was fired, until it fell.  With breathless interest they listened to hear if an explosion followed.  Suddenly, not long before daylight, while it was too dark to see distinctly, the firing ceased.  Whether the enemy had given up the attack, or had been successful and the fort had surrendered, they had no means of knowing.  Judge Taney says "they paced the deck for the residue of the night in painful suspense, watching with intense anxiety for the return of day, and looking every few minutes at their watches to see how long they must wait for it; and as soon as it dawned, and before it was light enough to see objects at a distance, their glasses were turned to the fort, uncertain whether they should see the stars and stripes, or the flag of the enemy.  At length the light came, and they saw that ' our flag was there.'  He proceeds to relate the story of Mr. Key as he told him personally of the circumstances under which 'The Star Spangled Banner' was written.  He said to the Judge that he had, under the excitement of the hour, written a song, and, remarked Mr. T., "he handed me a printed copy" of the same.  When I had read it and expressed my admiration, I asked him how he found time, in the scenes he had been passing through, to compose such a song?  He said he commenced it on the deck of their vessel, in the fervor of the moment, when he saw the enemy retreating to their ships, and looked at the flag he had watched for so anxiously as the morning opened; that he had written some lines, or brief notes, that would aid him in calling them to mind. upon the back of a letter which he happened to have in his pocket; and for some of the lines, as he proceeded, he was obliged to rely on his memory; and that he finished it in the boat on his way to the shore, and wrote it out as it now stands, at the hotel, on the night he reached Baltimore, and immediately after he arrived.  He

Taney, (R. B.) — *Continued.*

said that on the next morning he took it to Judge Nicholson to ask him what he thought of it; that he was so much pleased with it that he immediately sent it to a printer, and directed copies to be struck off in handbill form."

The music for this national hymn was arranged by A. W. Berg.

Tappan, (W. B.)

William Brigham Tappan was born at Beverly, Mass., October 29, 1794. For six years he was engaged in teaching. In 1826 he removed to Boston and became general agent of the American Sunday School Union for New England. He died of cholera at Grantville (Needham), Mass., June 20, 1849.

— Late and Early Poems. 32°, pp. 256. Worcester, 1849.
— Lyrics. 12°, pp. 252. Philadelphia and New York, 1822.
— Lyric Poems. 16°, pp. 140. Philadelphia, 1826.
— Missions. 32°, pp. 32. Boston, 1838.
— New England. 18°, pp. 108. Philadelphia, 1819.
— Poems. 12°, pp. x, 252. Philadelphia, 1822.
— Same. 18°, pp. xvi, 324. Philadelphia and Boston, 1836.
— Same. 2 vols. pp. 360, 324. Philadelphia and Boston, 1836.
— Poems and Lyrics. 16°, pp. 264. Boston, 1842.
— Poetry of Life. 16°, pp. 304. Boston, 1848.
— Poetry of the Heart. 32°, pp. 256. Troy, 1846.
— Sacred and Miscellaneous Poems. 8°, pp. 332. Boston, 1847.
— Songs of Judah, etc. 18°, pp. xi, 204. Philadelphia, 1820.
— The Daughter of the Isles. 32°, pp. 352. Boston, 1844.
— The Memento. 32°, pp. 128. Boston, 1849.
— The Poet's Tribute. 16°, pp. 324. Boston, 1840.
— The Sunday School, etc. 16°, pp. 251. Boston, 1848.

Tardy George. (Anon.) 4°, pp. 4. New York, 1865.

Privately printed. Sixty copies.

Taveau, (A. L.)

A poet of Charleston, S. C., who wrote under the signature of " Alton."

— Magic Word, The. (By Alton, *pseud.*) 16°, pp. iv, 188. Boston and Cambridge, 1855.

Tayleure, (C. W.) Horseshoe Robinson; or, The Battle of King's Mountain. A Legendary Patriotic Drama. 12°, pp. 40. New York, no date.

— The Boy Martyrs. 12°, pp. 30. Boston, 1859.

Taylor, (B.)

Bayard (named when an infant James Bayard Taylor) was the son of a Pennsylvania farmer, and was born January 11, 1825, in the village of Kenneth Square, Chester county, Penn. His early education was limited. He was indentured at the age of seventeen in a printing office at Westchester. Early in life he began to write poems which were published in the "New York Mirror" and "Graham's Magazine." When a young man the passion for foreign travel seized him, and having saved forty dollars from money paid for his poetical productions, and having received one hundred dollars in advance for letters to be written from abroad for the *United States Gazette* and the *Saturday Evening Post*, he commenced his tour in the old world. With some remittances from home added to the above, he was able to remain abroad for two years, making pedestrian tours through the prominent countries of Europe, mostly on foot, his expenses being but five hundred dollars. For several years after his return he was engaged in literary pursuits, and held for some time an important position on the editorial staff of the *New York Tribune*, and was the correspondent of that paper while making an extended tour in Europe and Asia and Africa of upwards of fifty thousand miles of travel, during an absence from the United States of two years and four months. He published his travels in several instructive and entertaining volumes. Subsequently he made other tours in the old world. In 1862 he was appointed Secretary to the American Legation at the Court of St. Petersburg, and in 1863 performed the duties of Chargé d'Affaires. In February, 1878, he was sent to Berlin as Minister to Germany, and died December 19th of that year.

— A Book of Romances, Lyrics and Songs. 12°, pp. 153. Boston, 1858.

— Home Pastorals, Ballads and Lyrics. 16°, pp. vi, 214. Boston, 1875.

— Lars : A Pastoral of Norway. 16°, pp. 144. Boston, 1873.

— National Ode. 4°, pp. 12. July 4, 1876.

Fac simile of the manuscript by heliotype process.

— Poems of the Orient. 5th Edition. 16°, pp. 203. Boston, 1855.

— The Ballad of Abraham Lincoln. Illustrations by Eytinge. 4°, pp. 8. Boston, 1870.

— The Picture of St. John. 16°, pp. vi, 220. Boston, 1866.

— The Poet's Journal. 12°, pp. iv, 204. Boston, 1863.

— Translation of Gœthe's Faust. The Second Part. Lg. 8°, pp. xvi, 556. Boston, 1871.

— Ximena ; or, The Battle of the Sierra Morena, and other Poems. 16°, pp. vi, 84. Philadelphia, 1844.

Taylor, (B. F., LL. D.)

Benjamin Franklin Taylor was born at Louisville, N. Y., in 1822, and graduated at Madison University. As a journalist he has been connected with the *New York Tribune* and the *Chicago Evening Journal*, and has acquired a high reputation at the West as a lecturer.

TAYLOR, (B. F., LL. D.) — *Continued.*

— Dulce Domum ; the Burden of the Song. 8°, pp. 159. Chicago, 1884.

— Old-Time Picture and Sheaves of Rhyme. 16°, pp. 194. Chicago, 1874.

> The following is the brief but graceful preface to this volume :
>
> "Set adrift in the newspapers like thistle-down in the fall wind, a few poems of mine have ‘lodged’ at last between the lids of a book.
>
> "Never thinking seriously about it until it was too late to think at all, I find myself fearing that their meaning to me is a sort of personal property I cannot make over to anybody, and that I should have slipped them in among the leaves of the Family Record, between the book of Malachi and the gospel according to St. Matthew, as being the very place in a world of sinners about the safest from perusal.
>
> "A friend once sent me some withered pansies, but he brightened and humanized the faded things by writing a single line: ‘From the grave of Hamlet, Prince of Denmark.’ Ah! how beautiful they turned, and what treasures they became!
>
> "Less fortunate than the pansies, this sheaf of rhymes has nobody to write the single line: ‘Only this.’ I suspect one or two of them of being better than I once thought, because several clever people have stolen them and never returned them."

TAYLOR, (MRS. J. M.) Mott's Party, etc. 12°, pp. 50. Holmesburg, 1872.

TAYLOR, (R. H.) A Remembrancer. 8°, pp. 30. New York, 1848.
— Poems. Sq. 8°, pp. 126. New York, 1848.

TAYLOR, (S. W.) The Storming of Quebec. 18°, pp. 126. Philadelphia, 1829.

> This little volume belonged to the department of American Poetry and Plays in the library of Judge Greene, and was purchased at the sale of the library of Rev. Dr. R. W. Griswold. We have been unable to obtain any information respecting the author, except that his name was Samuel W. Taylor.

TAYLOR, (V.) Things as They Will Be. 2d Edition. 18°, pp. 17. New York, 1819.

TEGNÉR, (E.)

> Esaias Tegnér, the son of a Swedish clergyman, was born in 1782, and graduated at the University of Lund in 1803, with the highest honors of his class. A few years later he was appointed Professor of Greek in his native University, and at the same time entered the Swedish Church. In 1824 he was elected Bishop of Wexiö, and expended his chiefest energies in the labors of his diocese. He had tendencies to mental aberration which finally resulted in temporary insanity. Recovering the use of his reason, he was able to attend to his Episcopal duties for a time. He resigned his office in 1845, and died the year following. Fridthjof, or Frithiof, was the son of Thorsten, King Bele's bravest and most trusty chieftain. In this volume we have the "Segn," that is, the say, or tale, of his romantic life.

Tegnér, (E.) — *Continued.*

— Fridthjof's Saga : a Norse Romance.   Translated from the Swedish by
T. A. E. and M. A. L. Holcomb.   12°, pp. xiii, 213.   Chicago, 1877.

A translation of the same, with illustrations, was made by L. A. Sherman, Ph. D., and
published in an elegant 4° volume, pp. xiii, 238, by James R. Osgood & Co., Boston, 1878
A copy of this beautiful edition is in "The Harris Collection."

Tellez, (Mrs. A.)   Reunedo.   3d Edition.   12°, pp. 234.   New York, 1864.

Temple, (C. C.)   Popular Delusions.   8°, pp. 36.   Boston, 1857.

Temple, (N.) and Trevor, (E.)   Tannhäuser ; or, The Battle of the
Bards.   8°, pp. xi, 125.   Mobile, 1865.

Terry, (J. O.)

John Orville Terry resided at Orient, Suffolk county, Long Island.

— Poems.   18°, pp. 292.   New York, 1850.

This volume consists of Songs, Satire and Pastoral Descriptions, chiefly depicting the
scenery and illustrating the manners and customs of the ancient and present inhabitants
of Long Island.   It is dedicated to Thaddeus B. Glover, Esq.

Terry, (Rose.)   (Mrs. Rollin Cooke.)

She was born at West Hartford, Conn., February 17, 1827, and married, 1873, Mr. R
H. Cooke, of Winsted, Conn.   "Most of her writings are short tales of great power and
literary merit."

— Poems.   16°, pp. 231.   Boston, 1861.   ·

Thacher, (W.)   A Battle between Truth and Error.   Sm. 12°, pp. vi,
48.   Middletown, Conn.

A poetical attack on what are regarded as "the fierce doctrines of Calvinism."

Thalatta.   (Names of Compilers not given.)   A Book for the Seaside.
12°, pp. 206.   Boston, 1853.

It is understood that the compilation was made by S. Longfellow and T. W. Higginson.

Thatcher, (B. B.)

Benjamin Bussey Thatcher was born at Warren, Me., in 1809, graduated at Bowdoin
College in 1826, studied law, but did not practice, preferring to devote himself to literary
pursuits.   He was, says Mr. Tuckerman, "an indefatigable writer, always engaged upon
a review, a lecture, a book, newspaper, magazine, or some other literary enterprise."
He was a frequent contributor to the "North American Review" when Alexander H.
Everett was its editor.   He was editor, for a time, of the "Colonizationist," wrote for
"Harper's Family Library," the "Lives of the Indians" and "Indian Traits" for their
"Juvenile Series."   He visited Europe 1836–38, and wrote for the papers in this country
interesting sketches of his travels and his intercourse with distinguished individuals
whom he met in the old world.   Not long after his return home he died, the event taking
place at Boston, July 14, 1840.   There is a fine engraving of him in the "History of Bowdoin College," p. 356.

THATCHER (R. B.) — *Continued.*

— The Boston Book.   12°, pp. 360.   Boston, 1837.

> Editions of the same, 1841 and 1850, the first of which, viz., 1641, was edited by George S. Hillard.   Mr. Thatcher edited the volume for 1837.

THAXTER, (A. W.)

> Adam Wallace Thaxter was born at Boston in 1832, graduated at Harvard in 1852, and from the Dane Law School in 1854.   He died in 1864.   He wrote several plays.   For several years he was co-editor of the *Boston Evening Gazette.*   For some time previous to his death he had been engaged upon two historical works, " Rebellions that were Failures," and " The Bastards of History."

— A Poem.   16°, pp. 38.   Cambridge, 1850.

THAXTER, (CELIA.)   Poems.   18°, pp. viii, 188.   New York, 1874.

— Poems for Children.   Illustrated.   Lg. 8°, pp. 153.   Boston, 1884.

THERESA, (a *pseud.*)

> The author, in her preface to the readers of her little volume, says : " It will be unnecessary to inform you that I wear the breeches, and that my husband wears petticoats; that I hold the purse-strings, and that he holds his tongue; that I say what I choose, and that he chooses what I say."   She dedicates her work to Dr. Timothy Syllogism, her husband :

> " TIMOTHEO SYLLOGISMO
> VIRO
> PETTICOATISSIMO.
> HOC POEMA
> AD VARIOS MODOS,
> IN DOMINANDO VIRO,
> NECESSARIOS.
> LEPIDE SPECTANS,
> SUO MARITO
> DICAT, DEDICATQUE
> UXOR BREECHISSIMA,
> THERESA."

— The Breechiad.   16°, pp. 22.   Boston, 1807.

THOMAS, (C.)   Soin de la Patrie.   8°, pp. 9.   San Francisco, 1869.

THOMAS, (D.)

> Daniel Thomas was born at Middleborough, Mass., graduated at Brown University in 1803, was ordained in 1808 minister of the church in South Abington, Mass., and was in office till his death in 1847.

— A Poem.   8°, pp. 12.   Wrentham, Mass., 1802.

THOMAS, (EDITH M.)   A New Year's Masque, etc.   12°, pp. 138.   Boston, 1885.

THOMAS, (F. W.)

> Frederic William Thomas was born at Charleston, S. C., in 1811, was educated at Baltimore, began to study law at seventeen, practiced for a time, then removed to Cincinnati and assisted his father in the editorial management of the *Commercial Advertiser,*

THOMAS, (F. W.) — *Continued.*

and was a frequent contributor to the local periodicals. Subsequently he was journalist, lecturer, author, for a short time a minister in the Methodist Episcopal Church, Professor of Rhetoric, etc., in the Alabama University, and again a practicing lawyer and editor. He died September 30, 1800.

— The Beechen Tree. 12°, pp. 95. New York, 1844.

— The Emigrant. 8°, pp. vi, 48. Cincinnati, 1833.

— Same. With a Memoir. Cincinnati, 1872.

THOMAS, (G. B.) A Sketch. 8°, pp. 4. No place, no date.

THOMAS, (J.) Origin and Course of Intemperance. 18°, pp. vii, 59. New York, 1832.

— The Pilgrim's Hymn Book. 24°, pp. 206. Winchester, Va., 1816.

— The Pilgrim's Muse. Sm. 24°, pp. vii, 219. Winchester, Va., 1816.

THOMAS, (L. B.) Verses. 8°, pp. 35. Baltimore, 1877.

Twenty copies printed.

THOMAS, (L. F.) Cortez, the Conqueror. 8°, pp. 73. Washington, 1857.

See "Southern Quarterly Review," III, p. 277.

THOMAS, (L. G.) Poems. 16°, pp. viii, 139. New York, 1871.

THOMAS, (W. G.) The Minor Poetry of Gœthe, etc. 8°, pp. xxxiv, 335. Philadelphia, 1859.

THOMPSON, (A. C., D. D.)

Augustus C. Thompson was born at Goshen, Litchfield county, Conn., in 1812, educated, in part, at Yale College, which conferred on him in 1841 A. M., studied theology at East Windsor, Conn., and at Berlin, Germany, and was installed pastor of the Eliot Church, Roxbury, now Boston, in 1842. He is the author of several devotional books.

— Lyra Cœlestis. Hymns on Heaven. 12°, pp. xxii, 382. Boston, 1863.

THOMPSON, (GEORGE.)

The author, who was confined four years and eleven months in a Missouri prison for attempting to aid some slaves to liberty, says: "These poems were composed at various times during a space of nearly five years, while pursuing my daily duties within the confines of a slaveholders' prison."

— The Prison Bard. 12°, pp. 215. Hartford, 1848.

THOMPSON, (MRS. A.) The Lyre of Troja. 18°, pp. 180. Geneva, N. Y., 1829.

39

THOMPSON, (J. R.)

John R. Thompson was born at Richmond, Va., October 23, 1823, pursued his academic studies at East Haven, Conn., was educated at the University of Virginia, and admitted to the bar in 1845. He became the editor of the " Southern Literary Messenger" in 1847, and made it a periodical of high character, taking rank with the best magazines of the country. " He is," says Griswold, " one of the most accomplished and most useful writers of the Southern States." One of his works, " Across the Atlantic; or, European Episodes," which was announced for publication in 1856, unfortunately was burnt. A distinguished literary gentleman who had read it, before it was destroyed by the flames, pronounced it " a fresh, graceful and brilliant book." One or two other important literary works were prepared by Mr. Thompson, but failed for some reason of publication. Duyckinck speaks of his poetical writings as having been " finished with care, and displaying a delicate sentiment."

— Poem.   University of Virginia, July 1, 1869.   8°, pp. 12.

— Poesy.   An Essay in Rhyme.   8°, pp. 16.   Washington, 1859.

THOMPSON, (M.)

Maurice Thompson was born at Fairfield, Ind., September 9, 1844. He was educated on his father's estates in Georgia, and subsequently returned to his native State and took up his residence in Crawfordsville. He was the author of several works. Those best known are " Hoosier Mosaics " (1875), " The Witchery of Archery" (1878), " A Tallahassee Girl " (1882), and " His Second Campaign " (a novel, 1883).

— Songs of Fair Weather.   12°, pp. iv, 99.   Boston, 1883.

A beautiful edition, printed by J. R. Osgood & Co.

THOMPSON, (M. M.)   (Q. K. Philander Doesticks, *pseud.*)

Mortimer M. Thompson was born at Riga, N. Y., in 1831, was educated in part at the Michigan University, was connected for a time with a theatrical company, moved to New York in 1852, and gained much reputation as a writer of humorous poetry. He died in New York, June 26, 1865.

— Nothing to Say.   16°, pp. xi, 60.   New York, 1857.

— Plu-ri-bus-tah.   12°, pp. 261.   New York, 1861.

THOMPSON, (P.)   Quoit Club Carols ; or, Noctes Gymnasii.   8°, pp. 39.   Washington, 1839.

THOMPSON, (W. T.)

William Theodore Thompson, a humorous writer and journalist at Baltimore, Augusta and Savannah, Ga.

— Major Jones' Courtship ; or, Adventures of a Christmas Eve.   A Domestic Comedy.   By Major Joseph Jones, (a *pseud.*)   12°, pp. 61.   Savannah, 1850.

THOMSON, (C. W.)

Charles West Thomson was born at Philadelphia in 1798, and became a clergyman in the Protestant Episcopal Church. He contributed to several annuals, to " Graham's Magazine," and to religious periodicals of the day.

— Elliner, etc.   12°, pp. 98.   Philadelphia, 1826.

THOMSON, (C. W.) — *Continued.*

— The Love of Home, etc. 12°, pp. x, 120. Philadelphia, 1845.

— The Sylph, etc. 18°, pp. 110. .Philadelphia, 1828.

— The Uncertainty of Literary Fame. 8°, pp. (with Brooks' Address, Pennsylvania College, Gettysburg, Pa., February 14, 1840,) 47. Baltimore.

THOMSON, (S.)

Samuel Thomson was born in 1769, and was the founder of the " Thomsonian System " of medicine. He says " the poem was written by me while in Newburyport jail, in 1809, on a charge for murder, for which I was honorably acquitted by a special session of the Supreme Court, without having an opportunity to make any defense. It was printed and circulated in a hand-bill, as a looking-glass in which the doctors might see their own con-duct and the effects of their medicine on patients in cases of pleurisy and fevers when treated according to art." He died at Boston in 1873.

— Learned Quackery Exposed. 12°, pp. 24. Boston, 1824.

— Same. 12°, pp. 43. Boston, 1836.

THORN COTTAGE ; OR, THE POET'S HOME. A Memorial of Frederic Knight, Esq., of Rowley, Mass. (Anon.) 18°, pp. 108. Boston, 1855.

THURBER, (C.)

Charles Thurber, son of Rev. Laban Thurber, was born at Brookfield, Mass., January 2, 1803, graduated at Brown University in 1827, Principal of Milford, Mass., Academy, four year*, and of Latin School, Worcester, eight years, was engaged in secular busi-ness eighteen years, and, for a number of years, travelled with his family and devoted himself to literary pursuits. Mr. Thurber has delivered many poems on commencement and other occasions, which have been well received. His present (1886) residence is Brooklyn, N. Y.

— A Poem at Commencement Dinner, Brown University, September 5, 1855. 8°, pp. 8.

THURID, ETC. (G. E. O. Anon.) 12°, pp. 123. Boston and New York, 1874.

THURSTON, (ELIZABETH A.) Mosaics of Life. 8°, pp. 305. Philadel-phia, 1881.

A book of poetical extracts.

TILTON, (T.)

Theodore Tilton was born in the city of New York, October 2, 1835, was educated at the New York Free Academy, and as a journalist was connected with the *Independent* and other papers. He acquired notoriety on account of his lawsuit against Henry Ward Beecher, in which the jury stood nine for the defendant and three for the plaintiff. He has been a popular lecturer.

TILTON, (T.) — *Continued.*

— The Fly.  Sq. 16°, not paged.  New York, no date.

— The Hungry Kittens.  8°, pp. 4.  New York, 1866.

— The True Church!  Illustrated by Granville Perkins.  Lg. 8°, not paged.  Philadelphia, 1867.

— The King's Ring.  Illustrated.  Lg. 8°, pp. 7.  New York, 1847.

— The Sexton's Tale.  16°, pp. 173.  New York, 1867.

TIMES, THE.  A Satire.  (Peter Pickle, *pseud.*)  12°, pp. 85.  New York, 1853.

TIMES, THE, AND THE MEN.  A Satire.  (Anon.)  12°, pp. 49.  Philadelphia, 1871.

TIPPERARY WARBLER.  (Anon.)  A Play in Three Acts.  12°, pp. 51.  Rochester, N. Y., 1865.

TOBACCO.  A Satire by a non-Sucker.  2d Edition.  8°, pp. 42.  No place, 1859.

TODD, (MRS. S. H.)  Occasional Poems.  16°, pp. vi, 215.  Boston, 1851.

TOKEN, A, OF ESTEEM.  (Anon.)  8°, pp. 53.  West Chester, Pa., 1853.

TOPLIFF, (N.)

The writer, Nathaniel Topliff, who calls himself "A Farmer of Dorchester," says: "As the following Poems originated in sincere and ardent love of my country, and a desire to aid the cause of truth, morality and religion, so I hope they will be read with candour even by numbers of good men whose religious tenets and political sentiments are different from my own.  If found to aid the cause of virtue or of our country's highest prosperity, my highest ambition will be gratified."

— Poems.  12°, pp. 169.  Boston, 1809.

TOUCH, A, AT THE TIMES.  (Anon.)  18°, pp. 45.  Portland, Me., 1840.

TOUCHSTONE, (GEOFFREY.)  (A *pseud.*)  He wou'd be a Poet.  8°, pp. 38.  Philadelphia, 1776.

— A House of Wisdom in a Bustle.  A Poem descriptive of the noted Battle lately fought in C-n-g-ss.  8°, pp. 28.  Philadelphia, 1798.

TOWNSEND, (ELIZA.)

She was born at Boston in June, 1789, and died January 12, 1854.  See an obituary notice by Rev. C. Francis in *Boston Advertiser* published soon after her death.

— Poems and Miscellanies.  8°, pp. 355.  Boston, 1856.

Townsend, (E. W.)

Elizabeth W. Haydock was born at Philadelphia.

— The White Dove, etc.  16°, pp. 128.  Philadelphia, 1858.

Townsend, (G. A.)

George Alfred Townsend was born at Georgetown, Del., in 1841, educated in the Philadelphia High school.  As a journalist he was connected with the *Philadelphia Inquirer*
and with *The Press*.  In 1862 he was the war correspondent of the *New York Herald*, and
correspondent of several journals in England and France, and of the *New York World*.
While in Europe, 1866–67, he wrote for American papers, and for several years he was on
the editorial staff of the *Chicago Tribune*.

— Poems.  12°, pp. 160.  Washington, 1870.
— The Bohemians ; or, Life in a Newspaper.  12°, pp. 52.  Philadelphia, 1861.

Townsend, (Mary A.)  Down the Bayou, etc.  12°, pp. 230.  Boston,
1882.
— The Captain's Story.  16°, pp. 41.  Philadelphia, 1874.

Townsend, (R. H.)  Rhymes.  18°, pp. 160.  Baltimore, 1836.

Townsend, (W.)  Fourth of July Ode, 1803.  8°, pp. 3.  No place, no
date.

Tracy, (C. M.)  Poem.  Dedication City Hall, Lynn, Mass.  8°, pp.
36.  November 30, 1867.

Tragedy, The Gospel.  (Anon.)  16°, pp. 119.  Worcester, Mass.,
1795.

Treasures of Darkness.  (By E. L., Authoress of " Night Watches.")
12°, pp. 248.  Philadelphia, 1854.

Tributes, Poetical, to the Memory of Abraham Lincoln.  8°, pp.
xii, 306.  Philadelphia, 1865.

Trinity, The Orthodox.  (Anon.)  24°, pp. 16.  No place, no date.

Triumph of Peace.  (Anon.)  12°, pp. 96.  New York, 1840.

Triumvirate, The State.  (Brevet Major Pindar Puff, *pseud.*)  12°,
pp. 212.  New York, 1819.

Trojan Sketch Book.  (Alba A. Goddard.)  12°, pp. 180.  Several
poems in the volume.  Troy, 1846.

TROLLOPE, (N.)  Scribes of Gotham.  12°, pp. viii, 36.  New York, 1833.

TROWBRIDGE, (J. T.)

 John Townsend Trowbridge was born at Ogden, Munroe county, N. Y., in 1827, and is well-known as an author and contributor to several magazines.

— A Home Idyl, etc.  16°, pp. 165.  Boston, 1881.
— Neighbor Jackwood.  A Domestic Drama.  12°, pp. 72.  Boston, 1857.
— The Vagabonds.  Darley's Illustrations.  8°, pp. iv, 15.  New York, 1864.
— The Story of Columbus.  4°.  Boston, 1870.

TRUE AND INFERNAL FRIENDSHIP ; OR, THE WISDOM OF EVE, AND THE CHARACTER OF THE SERPENT, WITH THE SITUATION, JOYS, AND LOSS OF PARADISE.  (Anon.)  12°, pp. 176.  Providence, 1813.

TRUESDELL, (MRS. H.)

 In 1853–54 she was a regular contributor to the " Parlor Magazine."  She wrote also for the " Ladies' Repository."  For a time she resided at Newport, Ky.  (See Coggeshall Poets and Poetry of the West, p. 544.)

— Poems.  11th Edition.  8°, pp. 212.  Cincinnati, Ohio, 1859.

TRUMBULL, (J.)

 John Trumbull was born at Waterbury, Conn., April 24, 1750, graduated at Yale, 1707, and was Tutor in that college, 1771–73.  He studied law under John Adams, practiced in New Haven, and in 1781 moved to Hartford.  McFingal, his most popular poem, passed through thirty editions.  He died at Detroit in May, 1831.

— Elegy on the Times.  12°, pp. 15.  New Haven, 1775.
— McFingal.  12°, pp. 44.  Philadelphia, 1776.
— Same.  London, 1776.
— Same.  16°, pp. 100.  Hartford, 1782.

 In its costly binding, one of the gems of the collection.  On a fly leaf is written in pencil 112.50.  Do these figures designate the sum paid for the volume?

— Same.  18°, pp. 110.  Boston, 1785.
— Same.  12°, pp. 95.  Philadelphia, 1791.
— Same.  12°, pp. 142.  London, 1791.
— Same.  12°, pp. 136.  New York, 1795.
— Same.  24°, pp. 112.  Albany, 1813.
— Same.  12°, pp. 120.  Philadelphia, 1839.
— Same.  8°.  Hartford, 1856.

Trumbull, (J.) — *Continued.*

— Same.  With B. J. Lossing's Notes.  12°, pp. 322.  New York, 1864.

— Same.  8°, and pp. 353–382 of some book or periodical, the poem being bound by itself.

— Poetical Works in 2 vols.  8°, pp. 176, 233.  Hartford, 1820.

— Progress of Dulness.  24°, pp. 72.  Wrentham, Mass., 1801.

Tucker, (M. E.[?])  Loew's Bridge.  A Broadway Idyl.  Sq. 16°, pp. 78.  New York, 1867.

Tucker, (Mary E.)  Poems.  12°, pp. 237.  New York, 1867.

Tucker, (St. G.)

St. George Tucker was born in Bermuda, June 29, 1752.  When his father was a young man he removed to Virginia, but much of his time was spent in England in the discharge of his duties as agent of the colony.  Of his four sons, two sided with the Loyalist and two with the American party in the war of the Revolution.  St. George graduated from William and Mary College in 1772, and studied law but did not practice, the war absorbing his time and interest.  A successful expedition to Bermuda is said to have been planned by him.  He was present at the battle of Yorktown where he held the rank of Lieutenant-Colonel, and where he was wounded from the explosion of a bomb.  He was appointed as Judge in the Virginia General Court, held also the position of Law Professor at William and Mary College, subsequently was advanced to the Court of Appeals, and afterwards to the District Court of the United States.  By his first wife, the widow of John Randolph, he had several children.  He died at Edgewood, Nelson county, Va., in November, 1827.

The following poem of Judge Tucker entitled, " Days of my Youth," has been much admired :

Days of my youth, ye have glided away :
Hairs of my youth, ye are frosted and gray :
Eyes of my youth, your keen sight is no more :
Cheeks of my youth, ye are furrowed all o'er :
Strength of my youth, all your vigor is gone :
Thoughts of my youth, your gay visions are flown :

Days of my youth, I wish not your recall :
Hairs of my youth, I'm content ye should fall :
Eyes of my youth, you much evil have seen :
Cheeks of my youth, bathed in tears you have been :
Thoughts of my youth, you have led me astray :
Strength of my youth, why lament your decay :

Days of my age, ye will shortly be past :
Pains of my age, yet awhile you can last :
Joys of my age, in true wisdom delight :
Eyes of my age, be religion your light :
Thoughts of my age, dread ye not the cold sod :
Hopes of my age, be ye fixed on your God.

— The Probationary Odes of Jonathan Pindar, Esq.  12°, pp. viii, 103.  Philadelphia, 1796.

TUCKER, (ST. G.) — *Continued.*

Dr. Griswold says: "When Dr. Wolcott's satires on George the Third, written under the name of "Peter Pindar," obtained, both in this country and in England, a popularity far beyond their merits, Judge Tucker, who admired them, was induced to publish in Freneau's *National Gazette,* a series of similar odes under the signature of "Jonathan Pindar," by which he at once gratified his political zeal and his political propensity. His object was to assail John Adams and other leading federalists for their supposed monarchical predilections. His pieces might well be compared with Wolcott's for poetical qualities, but were less playful and had far more accrbity."

"The Probationary Odes" are in two parts; part i, pp. 9–46; part ii. pp. 53–103. Pages 51–52 contains an amusing letter from a landlord signed "Timothy Touchpenny," in which he relates the circumstances under which part ii came into his possession.

TUCKERMAN, (F. G.)

Frederick G. Tuckerman was born at Boston in 1821, went through a part of the Harvard course, graduated at the Dane Law School in 1842, and was admitted to the Suffolk bar in 1845.

— Poems.  12°, pp. 235.  Boston, 1864.

TUCKERMAN, (H. T.)

Henry Theodore Tuckerman was born at Boston, April 20, 1813, and was educated in the public schools of his native city, spent several years, at different times, in Europe, devoted himself to literary pursuits, and was a frequent contributor to the periodicals of the day. As an art critic he took high rank. He died in 1871.

— A Sheaf of Verse Bound for the Fair, (*i. e.* the N. Y. San. Com. Fair.)  12°, pp. 48.  New York, 1864.
— Poems.  12°, pp. vii, 175.  Boston, 1851.

TUEL, (J. E.)  Putnam Portraits, Done in Ink.  (By Jet, *pseud.*)  12°, pp. 30.  New York, 1855.

TURNBULL, (J. D.)  Rudolph.  18°, pp. 141.  Boston, 1799.
— Same.  1807.
— Same.  1813.
— Same.  Hallowell, 1813.
— Same.  Boston, 1826.
— Wood Dæmon ; or, The Clock has Struck.  A Drama.  24°, pp. 34. Boston, 1808.

TURNER, (E. S.)  Out-of-Door Rhymes.  16°, pp. 187.  Boston, 1872.

TURNER, (JULIANA F.)  The Harp of the Beech Woods.  Original Poems. 12°, pp. 156.  Montrose, Penn., 1822.

TURNER, (J. W.)  The Minstrel's Gift.  12°, pp. 120.  Boston, 1852.

TURRELL, (MRS. JONES.)  Some of her poems in memoirs by her husband.  12°.  London, 1741.

TWEEDLE HALL ; OR, NEW YORK CITY POLITICS IN 1870. (Anon.) 12°,
pp. 11. No place, no date.

TYLER, (R.)
Robert Tyler was a son of President John Tyler.

— Ahasuerus. 12°, pp. 46. New York, 1842.
— Death ; or, Medorus's Dream. 12°, pp. 66. New York, 1843.
— Poems. 12°, pp. 101. Philadelphia, 1839.

TYLER, (T. P.) The Unseen Witnesses. Trinity College, Hartford,
August 5, 1846. 8°, pp. 11. Hartford, 1846.

TYNG, (D. A.)
Dudley Atkins Tyng was born in Prince George's county, Md., 1825, graduated at the
University of Pennsylvania, 1842, and was ordained 1846. He was his father's assistant at
St. George's Church, New York, and afterwards was Rector of several Episcopal churches,
and died near Philadelphia, April 19, 1858.

— Stand up for Jesus, etc. 12°, pp. 47. Philadelphia, 1858.


UMPHAVILLE, (A.) The Siege of Baltimore, etc. 12°, pp. 144. Baltimore, 1817.

UNDERWOOD, (T. H.) Our Flag. A Poem in Four Cantos. 12°, pp.
41. New York, 1862.

UNION, THE. (Anon.) 12°, pp. 48. Boston, 1860.

UNTAUGHT BARD, THE. (Anon.) 12°, pp. 260. New York, 1804.

UPHAM, (T. C.)
Thomas Cogswell Upham was born at Deerfield, N. H., January 30, 1799. The year
following his birth his father removed to Rochester, N. H., where for some years he occupied a conspicuous position in the community. The subject of this sketch graduated at
Dartmouth College in 1818, and at the Andover Theological Seminary in 1821. Among
his seminary classmates were Rev. Drs. Baxter Dickinson, George E. Pierce, and Alva
Woods. After graduation he became the assistant of Professor Moses Stuart in the
department of Hebrew. In 1823 he was ordained as a Congregational minister, and was,
for a little more than a year, colleague with Rev. Joseph Haven, in Rochester, N. H. In
the spring of 1825, he entered upon his duties as Professor of Mental and Moral Philosophy
in Bowdoin College, where he distinguished himself as an able instructor and the accomplished author of many valuable works in his special department, and several of a highly
devotional character. Of one of the productions of his pen, "Letters: Æsthetic, Social
and Moral, written from Europe, Egypt, and Palestine," a writer in the "North American
Review," No. lxxxi, speaks in commendation. " While as a book of travels, it is meagre
in its details in England, France, and Rome, it is profoundly interesting among the Wal-
denses, eminently suggestive and impressive in Egypt and in the desert of Sinai, rich

UPHAM, (T. C.) — *Continued.*

almost beyond comparison among the scenes hallowed by the presence of our Saviour. But it is inestimably precious as a record of the author's inward life and spiritual experience in communion with Nature in her solitudes, her grandeur and her beauty, with humanity under various phases of civilization and religion, and with the memorials of supernatural events, sacred history, religious heroism, and Christian martyrdom."

Professor Upham resigned his professorship in 1867, and took up his residence in Kennebunk, Me. His death took place in the city of New York in April, 1872.

— American Cottage Life. 2d Edition. 12°, pp. 212. Brunswick, Me., 1850.
— Same. 3d Edition. 12°, pp. x, 251. Portland, 1852.
— Same. 7th Edition. 12°, pp. 251. Boston, no date.
— Odes for Centennial Celebration, 1823. 8°, pp. 8.
— The Home in the West. 24°, pp. 19. Hanover, N. H., 1817.
— The Religious Offering. 12°, pp. 176. New York, 1835.

VAGARIES, THE POETICAL, OF A KNIGHT OF THE FOLDING-STICK ; OR, PASTE-CASTLE. To which is annexed the History of the Garret, etc., etc. Translated from the Hieroglyphics of the Society. (By a Member of the Order of Blue-String.) 18°, pp. 143. Gotham, 1815. •

VAIL, (J. C.)

The *nom de plume* of John Cooper Vail, a humorous writer of the day, was Zekel Allspice. Some of the poems in this volume appeared originally in the *Saturday Emporium*, the *New York Literary American* and the *Boston Museum*.

— Poems. 8°, pp. viii, 156. New York, 1851.

VAIL, (J.)

Rev. Joseph Vail was pastor of the Third church in East Haddam, Conn.

— Noah's Flood, etc. 8°, pp. 28. New London, 1796.

VALEDICTORY POEM BEFORE CLASS OF 1830, HARVARD. (Anon.) 8°, pp. 16. Cambridge, 1830.

VALENTINE WRITER. (Anon.) 18°, pp. 32. New York, 1848.

VALMORE, (MADAME DESBORDES.) Poems translated by Harriet W. Preston. 12°, pp. 227. Boston, 1873.

VANDENHOFF, (G.)

A celebrated elocutionist of the day. He was born in England about 1820, came to New York in 1847, and was an actor until 1856. He studied law and was admitted to the bar in 1858.

Vandenhoff, (G.) — *Continued.*

— Common Sense, etc.   12°, pp. 48.   Boston, 1858.

— Life ; or, Men, Manners, Modes and Measures.   A Poem for Union.
12°, pp. 41.   New York, 1861.

Van Wart, (Irving.)   The Golden Cross, etc.   Sm. 4°, pp. 180.   New
York, 1870.

Vaso Waters, (G.)   Political Geography.   8°, pp. 80.   Cincinnati, no
date.

Vaux, (R.)   The Habeas Corpus.   4°, pp. 8.   Philadelphia, 1862.

Verdi, (J.)

Guisepe Verdi was born near Parma, Italy, October 9, 1814.   He was chosen a member of the Senate in 1874, and Commander of the Legion of Honor in 1875.

— The Two Foscari.   A Tragedy.   Translations from the Italian.   12°,
pp. 23.   Boston, 1847.

Verity, J. (*pseud*[?])   The Twins.   8°, pp. 56.   No place, 1856.

Vermont, Poets and Poetry of.   Edited by Abby Maria Hemmenway.
12°, pp. 400.   Rutland, Vt., 1858.

Vermont Wool-Dealer.   A Farce.   (Anon.)   12°, pp. 18.   New
York, no date.

Very, (J.)

Jones Very was born at Salem, Mass., August 28, 1813, graduated at Harvard 1836,
and for a time was Greek Tutor in the University, studied theology and was licensed, but
never took charge of a church.   He died May 8, 1880.

— Poems.   Introductory Memoir by W. P. Andrews.   12°, pp. 160.
Boston, 1883.

Vicksburgh, A Walk About, etc.   (Anon.)   12°, pp. 204.   Boston,
1844.

Vinton, (J. D., M. D.)

Jonathan Dwight Vinton was born at Chesterfield, Mass., August 21, 1831, spent his
early life on a farm, teaching in the winter.   He received the degree of M. D. from the
Philadelphia University of Medicine and Surgery in 1864, practiced his profession in Phœ-
nixville, Pa., until 1869, when he removed to Philadelphia, were he now (1886) resides.

— Poems.   18°, pp. 56.   Philadelphia, 1884.
— Same.   Translations.   Miscellaneous, Sacred, and Humorous.
Illustrated.   12°, pp. 240.   Philadelphia, 1886.

VIRGINIA ; OR, THE FATAL PATENT.  (Anon.)  12°, pp. 63.  Washington, 1825.

VISION OF DON CROCKER.  (Supposed to have been written by Chancellor Kilty, of Maryland.)  12°, pp. vii, 71.  Baltimore, 1814.

VISION, A, OF FAITH.  12°, pp. 24.  New York, privately printed, 1817.

VOCALISTS, PENNSYLVANIA.  Book of Words.  18°, pp. 12.  Bradford, no date.


WA-WA-WANDA.  A Legend of Old Orange.  (Anon.)  12°, pp. viii, 180.  New York, 1860.

WADDELL, (F. L.)  An Autumn Dream.  12°, pp. 31.  New York, 1857.
— The Drift Wood Spar.  12°, pp. 12.  No place, 1853.

WADDELL, (J. H.)  Facts and Fancy.  12°, pp. 8.  New York, 1819.

WADE, (R. A.)  Poem on Niagara Falls.  12°, pp. 23.  Louisville, Ky., 1874.

WAINWRIGHT, (D. W., M. D.)  Wheat and Chaff.  A Comedy.  12°, pp. 84.  New York, 1858.

WAINWRIGHT, (H.).  Rhymings.  12°, pp. 90.  New York, 1860.

WALCOT, (C. M.)  "A Good Fellow."  A Comedy.  12°, pp. 14.  New York, 1856.

WALDEN, (I.)  Miscellaneous Poems.  18°, pp. 50.  Washington, 1872.
— Same.  2d Edition.  18°, pp. 96.  Washington, 1873.

WALDREN, (W. W.)  Last Lays of My Harp.  Sm. 4°.  A MS. volume of 111 pages.
— Pocahontas.  12°, pp. 108.  New York, 1841.

WALKER, (J.)

> Jesse Walker was born at Whiting, Addison county, Vt., and graduated at Middlebury College, 1833.  He commenced the practice of law in Buffalo in 1836, and was Judge of Erie county.  He died in 1854[?]

— Poems.  12°, pp. vii, 196.  Buffalo, 1854.

WALLACE, (MRS. E. D.)  England's Last Queen.  16°, pp. 11.  New York, 1871.

WALLACE, (W. R.)

William Ross Wallace was born at Lexington, Ky., in 1819, was educated at the Bloomington and South Hanover Colleges, Indiana, was admitted to the bar, and began practice, but soon relinquished it to devote himself to literary pursuits. He removed to New York and became a contributor to "Harper's Magazine," the "Knickerbocker," etc. He died in 1881.

— Alban, the Pirate. 12°, pp. 65. New York, 1848.

— Meditations in America. 12°, pp. 143. New York, 1851.

— The Battle of Tippecanoe, etc. 12°, pp. 105. Cincinnati, 1837.

— The Liberty Bell. How's Illustrations. 4°, pp. 4. New York, 1862.

— Wordsworth. 12°, pp. 8. New York, 1846.

WALLACK, (J. L.) Veteran, The; or, France and Algeria. 12°, pp. 63. New York, no date.

WALN, (R., JR.)

Robert, son of Robert Waln, a distinguished citizen of Philadelphia, was born in 1797, and died in 1824. Among his works were a History of China in 4° numbers. (See Kettell's Specimens," etc., vol. iii, p. 213.)

— American Bards. A Satire. 8°, pp. 80. Philadelphia, 1820.

In "American Bards," a poem of more than nine hundred lines, the author praises a few of the American poets, to whom he refers, and severely satirizes others. The "Sisyphi Opus," alluded to in the next title, is a "continuation of his previous work, but mostly occupied with a caveat against the introduction of foreign vices into the United States. He makes up a formidable list of wives sold at Smithfield, betting noblemen and bruised prize-fighters, as an offset to the stories by English travellers of society in our frontier settlements."

— Sisyphi Opus; or, Touches at the Times. 8°, pp. 62. Philadelphia, 1820.

WALTER, (W. B.)

William Bicker Walter, the son of a Boston merchant, was born in that city April 10, 1796. He was the grandson of Rev. William Walter, D. D., an eminent clergyman of the Protestant Episcopal Church, who was installed, July 22, 1764, Rector of Trinity Church, Boston, and continued in office until March 17, 1776, when, on the evacuation of Boston, he went, with many others, with General Howe, to Halifax. He returned to Boston and became Rector of Christ Church, May 28, 1792. He died in office December 5, 1800. (See "Sprague's Annals," vol. v, pp. 226-33.)

The subject of this sketch graduated at Bowdoin College in 1818. In a sketch of him in the "History of Bowdoin College," we are told that "his college life could hardly be called happy. He seemed always to feel that his superior refinement was not appreciated by those around him. He wore, for the most part, an air of Byronic gloom, and generally kept himself secluded. His style of speaking was highly theatrical. When in the heat and torrent of his passion he endeavored to harrow up the feelings of his auditors, his attitudes and contortions often became irresistibly ludicrous. He possessed considerable imaginative power, and wrote verses readily and in great abundance. Odes, sonnets and

WALTER, (W. B.) — *Continued.*

translations from his pen made their appearance in newspapers and magazines. On taking the master's degree in 1821, he entertained the audience with a poem styled the "Dream of a Sepulchre." From some impressions, probably of a hereditary calling, he began to prepare himself for taking orders in the Episcopal Church. This he soon gave up. In 1822 he went into the Southern States with the view of giving lectures on poetry, etc. The attempt was unsuccessful. "He was discouraged, became the prey of a morbid melancholy, and died suddenly in Charleston, S. C., April 23, 1822." (See "History of Bowdoin College," pp. 210–11.)

— Poems. 8°, pp. 71. Boston, 1821.
— Sukey. 8°, pp. 88. Boston, 1821.
— Same. Baltimore, 1821.

This poem was evidently suggested by Fitz-Greene Halleck's "Fanny." "The story is little more than a thread connecting various passages of description and reflection. The poem extends to one hundred and seventy-one six-line stanzas, and contains several melodious passages, many of which, however, are close imitations of Byron and Montgomery."

WALTER, (W. H.) Chorals and Hymns, Ancient and Modern, chiefly from the German. First Part. Lg. 8°, pp. 52. New York, 1862.

WANDERER, THE. A Rambling Poem. By a Clerk in Market Street. (Anon.) 18°, pp. xiii, 107. Philadelphia, 1836.

The author says: "Should any one's curiosity be excited to know who the author is (we merely suppose a case for argument's sake), it cannot be gratified, unless those who may be so inquisitive purchase a sufficient number of copies to line his pockets so effectually that he may abandon his subordinate, though respectable employment, which at present fills his mouth; yea, unless it is insured, as the author has no relish whatever for a garret and a lean appearance, the wise Shakespeare, Dryden, Goldsmith, Savage, Burns, and a host of others to the contrary notwithstanding."

— or, Horatio and Letitia, and Vales of Peace. (Anon.) 12°, pp. 133. Utica, 1811.

— The Poetical, etc. (Anon.) 18°, pp. 112. New York, 1796.

WALTON, (J. F.) The River of Life. 8°, pp. 8. New York, 1856.

This poem, by J. Francis Walton, was pronounced at the one hundred and second Commencement of Columbia College, and printed by request.

WAR. The Sorehead. (Anon.) A Campaign Satire for 1872. 8°, pp. 44. New York, no date.

WARBLER. In Four Numbers. 24°, pp. 217. Hallowell, 1805.

WARD, (J. W.)

James Warren Ward was born at Newark, N. J., in 1818. He pursued his studies in the Boston Latin School, of which he was a medal scholar. His tastes leading him to the study of the natural sciences, he became a pupil of John Locke, Professor of Chemistry in the Ohio Medical College. Some of his early productions in prose and verse were pub-

Ward, (J. W.) — *Continued.*

lished in the *Cincinnati Mirror,* etc.  In the science of botany he became a proficient, and, in 1855, was co-editor with J. W. Warder in the management of the "Western Horticultural Review."  A volume entitled "Yorick and Other Poems," published in Cleveland, Ohio, in 1838, was incorrectly ascribed to him.  Mr. Ward is now (1886) the Secretary and Librarian of the Grosvenor Library, Buffalo, N. Y.

— The Song of Higher Water.    8°, pp. iv, 30.    New York and Cincinnati, 1868.

— Woman.    12°, pp. 41.    Cincinnati and New York, 1852.

Ward, (M.)  Poems.    18°, pp. 108.    Plymouth, N. H., 1826.

Most of the poems of Milton Ward were composed at the age of fifteen.  One of the most beautiful of these was "The Lyre," quoted in "Kettell's Specimens of American Poetry," vol. iii, pp. 340–41.

Ward, (N.)

Nathaniel Ward was born at Haverhill, Suffolk, England, in 1570, graduated at Emmanuel College, England, in 1603, studied law and practiced seven years.  After a few years' travel on the Continent he returned to England, took orders in the Established Church, and, for a time, was Rector of Stondon Massey, Essex, but was finally silenced by Archbishop Laud in 1633, and came to America in 1634.  "Perhaps," says Prof. M. C. Tyler, "no other Englishman who came to America in those days brought with him more of the ripeness that is born, not only of time and study, but of distinguished early associations, extensive travel in foreign lands, and varied professional experience at home." Not long after his arrival in Massachusetts, he was invited to become the minister to the church in Ipswich, in a section of the State which bore the Indian name of Agawam. Here he remained two or three years and then resigned on account of failing health.  For a few years more he made himself useful to the infant colony in various ways, his legal education fitting him to render good service in preparing a code of laws.  (See "Massachusetts Historical Society Collection," Third Series, viii, 191.)  In 1647 he returned to England, and in 1648 became Rector of a parish at Shenfield, Essex, retaining this position till his death in 1653.

— *Mercurius Anti-mechanicus* | Or The | Simple Coblers | Body | With his Lap-full of *Caveats* (or *Take* | *heeds*), Documents, *Advertisements* and *Præ* | *monitions* to all his *honest fellow-trades* | *men*-Preachers | but more especially a dozen of them, in or about | the City of *London.*

But if these things continue so,
Poore Scholler whither will thou go?
Thy Sciences are children's knacks,
*Logical Arts* a Nose of Wax.
The Russet Coats do now defie thee,
Alas, the buckram Swaines out vie thee.
To Preach, lo they have Toleration,
And they do scorne thine Ordination;
O learned Slug, take notice of thy guides,
They work six days and yet they Preach beside.

WARD, (N.) — *Continued.*

> —— *Hæ nugæ in seria ducunt.* Hor.
> —— *Fuma proxima flamma.* ——

By *Theodore de la Guarden.*

*London*, Printed for *John Walker*, at the sign of the Starre in
Popes-head alley.  1648.

Nathaniel is a Hebrew word, the Greek translation of which is Theodorus, or, in English, Theodore.  The French of Ward is de la Guarden.  Hence the *nom de plume*, Theodore de la Guarden, or Nathaniel Ward.

We have included this small 4° volume of 52 pages in the "Collection," because its author lived long enough in America to be regarded as a citizen of Massachusetts.  While most of the volume is prose, there are a few poetical productions in it.  The volume when it came into the hands of some previous owner wanted pp. 33–36.  These four pages have been supplied, by copy, the work having 'been executed on thin glazed cloth, and so well done that it is not easy to tell whether it is printed or written, probably the latter.  The work is rare, and in its way exceedingly quaint and curious.  Believing in the necessity of regular ordination to qualify a man to become a preacher, it vexed the pious soul of worthy Mr. Ward that all sorts of persons took it upon themselves to be expounders of the Word, and preachers of the gospel.  He proposes, therefore, to take to task sundry tradesmen and craftsmen who set themselves up as evangelists, and gives his ghostly exhortations to the "Handicraft *Preachers*, especially these 12 that follow, who are, or have been in and about the City of London," viz.: The Confectioner; The Smith; The Right and Left Shoe-Maker; The Needless Tailor from his working im(posture); The Saddler; The Porter; The Labyrinthian Box-maker; The All-be-Smearing Soap-boiler, or the Sleepy Sopor; The Both-handed Glover; The White-handed Mealman; The Chicken-man; and, The Button-maker.

Our limits forbid our giving but a single extract from this singular and most witty production of Nathaniel Ward.  We select from the exhortation to the "The Studding Saddler."

"*Saddle me this Querie.*"

When was the *tayle* mistaken for the reines, the *saddle* thrust under the *belly*, and the *rider's head* shut up in a *sachel-bag* (by *Hada-I-wist* and *Shall-I-wink*) to travell to *Horse-head-down?*

*The Horse-taile or conclusion.*

> Who puts a doublet on an Horse,
>   Or on a man a saddle,
> Or claps a stockin on his head,
>   Sure that mans braine is addle.
> Then let not men ungilted padle
>   In Streames of Sanctuary,
> Above horse backs to fidle fadle
>   With what their heads cann't carry.
> Then either leave thy trade or cease to Teach
>   abandon all thy drifts
> Unless thy Gyant *Grace* so high can reach,
>   as to make void all *Gifts.*
> O meddle not above the *Pileon,*
> Thou knowst thy self it is a silly one.
> The Kingdome will be ne're the worse
> By putting *th' Sadle* o' th' right *Horse.*"

Ward, (N.) — *Continued.*

— The | Simple Cobler | of | Agawam | in America. | Willing | To help Mend his Native Country, lamen | tably tattered, both in the upper | Leather | and sole, with all the honest stitches he | can take. | And as willing never to be paid for his work | by Old English wonted pay. | *It is his Trade to patch all the year long, gratis.* | Therefore | I Pray Gentlemen keep your Purses. | By Theodore de le Guard. | The Fifth Edition, with some Amendments. | *In rebus arduis ac tenui spe, fortissima | quæque consilia tutissima sunt.* Cic. | In English, |

> When boots and shoes are torn up to the lefts, |
> Cobblers must thrust their awles up to the hefts. |
>
> This is no time to fear *Appelles gramm :* |
> *Ne sutor quidem ultra crepidam.* |

London : Printed by *J. D. & R. I.* for *Stephen Bowtell,* at | the sign of the Bible, in Pope's Head Alley, 1647. Re | printed at *Boston in N. England,* for *Daniel Henchman,* | at his Shop in King's Street, 1713.

The above is the title of a remarkable book; a small 4°. "To the Reader," one leaf. Text, pp. 5–59, largely prose. A few poetical productions in the volume.

Professor Tyler, in his "History of American Literature," vol. 1, pp. 220–40, has given an admirable notice of this work, with copious extracts from the same. In the "Monthly Anthology" for May, 1809, there is an article on Ward written by Dr. J. G. Cogswell, who says : "For some time after its publication it was so much read and admired that four editions of it were printed in London within a few years. But when its style became obsolete, its allusions unknown, and the subjects of which it treats less interesting, it laid neglected on the shelves, the dust was suffered to gather upon its leaves, and it has now long been noticed only by those whose reverence for every American relict may have led them to examine its contents." That Dr. Cogswell did not speak amiss when he referred to the style as being in some parts, at least, of the volume "obsolete," is evident from the following with regard to which Professor Tyler says : "He will be a bold man who can affirm at sight in what language this sentence is written, or what it means": "If the whole conclave of hell can so compromise exadvarse and diametrical contradictions as to compolitize such a multimonstrous manfrey of heteroclites and quicquilibets quality, I trust I may say with all humble reverence, they can do more than the Senate of heaven." The address to King Charles I., whom he arraigns as the cause of the fearful state of affairs in England, is bitter to the verge of absolute ferocity. It is too long to quote.

As if writing from his Agawam home in the new world, the Cobbler says :

> "So farewell England old,
>   If evil times ensue,
>   Let good men come to us,
>   Wee'l welcome them to New.

41

WARD, (N.) — *Continued.*

> "And farewell Honor'd Friends,
>     If happy days ensue,
> You'l have some Guests from hence.
>     Pray Welcome us to you.
>
> "And farewell simple World,
>     If thou'lt thy Cranium mend,
> There is my Last and All.
>     And a Shoem-Akers
>                 End."

It has sometimes been claimed that the oft-quoted words, *Fiat justitia ruat cœlum*, "let justice be done though the heavens fall," originated with Lord Mansfield, who used them in the celebrated case of The King vs. Wilkes, 1768. The expression, however, is found on p. 13 of this volume, thus antedating, by twenty-one years, Lord Mansfield's use of it.

## WARD, (S).

Samuel Ward, a son of Samuel W., an eminent merchant of New York, and descended from a distinguished Rhode Island ancestry, at the head of which was Roger Williams, was born at New York in January, 1813. His grandfather, Lieutenant Colonel Ward, of Revolutionary fame, having, in 1816, removed to Long Island, the subject of this sketch was an inmate of his family while pursuing his studies preparatory to entering college. Subsequently he became a pupil of Dr. Cogswell and George Bancroft at the Round Hill School at Northampton, Mass., and graduated at Columbia College, New York, in 1831. Several of his classmates became eminent in their professions. Among them were Rev. Dr. W. E. Eigenbrodt, of the General Theological Seminary, N. Y.; President Robert Emory, D. D., of Dickinson College, 1842–48; Hon. J. L. O'Sullivan, United States Minister to Portugal; Rev. Dr. R. G. Vermilye, of the Theological Institute, Conn., and Professor Robert Watts, Professor of Anatomy, College of Physicians and Surgery, New York. After graduating, Mr. Ward went abroad to complete his studies, and spent several years in Germany. He was a man of most versatile powers and talents, speaking several languages so correctly as to be mistaken for a native of other countries than his own. In subsequent years, as a man of letters, and as the friend of literary men, statesmen and artists, he had a warm place in the hearts of a large circle of acquaintances. His death, the result of a severe attack of malarial disease contracted during a short stay in Naples, occurred at Pegli, Italy, May 19, 1884. Mr. Ward was a brother of Mrs. Julia Ward Howe.

— LYRICAL RECREATIONS.  16°, pp. xvi, 271.  New York, 1865.

The Introduction is in the form of a letter to Samuel L. M. Barlow. The writer says: "When a bachelor overripe takes to himself a wife in the bud, he is apt to imagine that he owes his friends some explanations. It is the privilege of youth to woo Euterpe, and my hair is gray. *Qui s'excuse s'accuse,* I know, but when the accusation is sure to come, the excuse may as well get the start of it; and turning rhymster as I do on the wrong side of half a century, I venture to entreat you, who bear all burdens lightly, to circulate my *apologia* among those who may care to hear it."

— Same.  16°, pp. xii, 247.  London, 1883.

Some of the poems in the first series are not reprinted in this, and there are numerous additions in the second series, some of them in French. Special interest is attached to this volume, it being a presentation copy from the author to Senator Anthony, and it is said to have been the last book whose pages were turned over by him prior to his decease.

WARD, (T.)

Thomas Ward was born at Newark, N. J., June 8, 1807, studied at Princeton, but his name does not appear as a graduate. He received the degree of M. D. from Rutgers College, N. Y. His *nom de plume* was "Flaccus." He died in 1873.

— A Month of Freedom. 12°, pp. 90. New York, 1837.

— Passaic. A Group of Poems touching that River, etc. 12°. New York, 1842.

WARDWELL, (S. S.)

Mr. Wardwell was a native of Rhode Island.

— Sabbath-school Melodies. 12°, pp. 43. Boston, no date.

— The Village of Hermonia. A Temperance Poem, etc. 12°, pp. 32. Providence, 1839.

WARE, (CATHERINE AND ELEANOR.) The Wife of Leon, etc. 12°, pp. viii, 256. New York, 1844.

WARE, (H., JR.)

Henry Ware, Jr., was born at Hingham, Mass., April 21, 1794, graduated at Harvard in 1812, was pastor of the Second Congregational (Unitarian) church, Boston, 1817–30, Parkman Professor of Divinity, Cambridge, 1830–42. He died September 22, 1843.

— Poem pronounced at Cambridge, Mass., February 23, 1815, at the Celebration of Peace between the United States and Great Britain. 8°, pp. 11. Cambridge, 1815.

— The Feast of Tabernacles. 12°, pp. x, 38. Cambridge, 1837.

— The Vision of Liberty. Harvard Phi Beta Kappa Poem, August 27, 1824. 8°, pp. 12. Boston, 1824.

WARFIELD, (MRS. C. A.) AND LEE, (MRS. E. P.)

The writers were sisters, Catherine Ann and Eleanor Percy Ware. They were born at Washington, Miss., the former, June 14, 1815, the latter in 1820. Catherine married Elisha Warfield, Jr., of Lexington, Ky., and resided in that city for many years, and then removed to a country residence about sixteen miles from Lexington. She died May 23, 1878. Eleanor married H. W. Lee, of Vicksburg. She died October 14, 1840. They were the authors of "The Wife of Leon," etc. See above.

— The Indian Chamber, etc. 12°, pp. 264. New York, 1846.

WARRDENEAU, (D. DE.) The Gift. A Tale of the Washington Soldiers' and Sailors' Orphans' Fair. 8°, pp. 10. Washington, 1866.

WARREN, (MRS. MERCY.)

Mercy Otis was born at Barnstable, Mass., September 25, 1728, married James Warren, a merchant of Plymouth, in 1754, and distinguished herself for the part she took as writer, counsellor, etc., in the Revolution. She died in 1814. (See Duyckinck, vol. 1, pp. 163–64.)

WARREN, (MRS. MERCY.)—*Continued.*

Griswold says: "her History of the 'Rise, Progress and Termination of the American War' will always be consulted as one of the most interesting original authorities upon the Revolution."

— Adulateur, The. A Tragedy. 12°, pp. 32. Boston, 1773.

— Poems. 12°, pp. 252. Boston, 1790.

WARREN, (O. G.) Dream of the Highlands. 12°, pp. 76. New York, 1840.

A spiritualistic writer.

WARWICK, ALABAMA; OR, HERE WE REST. Sq. 8°, not paged. Cleveland, Ohio, no date.

WASHBURN, (H. S.)

Henry Stevenson Washburn was born at Providence, R. I., in 1813, studied at the Worcester Academy and at Brown University, but did not graduate on account of ill health; for seven years was depositarian of the New England Sunday-school Union, and subsequently was in secular business in Worcester and Boston, three years was in the Massachusetts Legislature. He established the "Young Reaper," one of the periodicals of the American Baptist Publication Society, Philadelphia.

— From January to May. Delivered to the Massachusetts House of Representatives, May 7, 1872. 18°, pp. 29. Boston, 1872.

— Visions of the State House. The Dream of a Night. 18°, pp. 21. Boston, 1871.

WASHBURN, (J. B.) Yo Semite. 8°, pp. 15. San Francisco, 1871.

WASHINGTON'S BIRTH-DAY. (Anon.) Lg. 12°, pp. viii, 55. Albany, 1812.

WASHINGTON, (E. K.) Poems. 18°, pp. iv, 92. Philadelphia, 1867.

WASHINGTON, GEORGE, HYMNS AND ODES COMPOSED ON THE DEATH OF. (Compiler Anon.) 12°, pp. 12. Portsmouth, 1800.

WATERBURY, (J. B.)

Jared Bell Waterbury was born at New York in 1799, and graduated at Yale in 1822. He wrote a large number of religious books. Allibone mentions thirty-two. He was pastor of churches in Northampton, Mass., Hudson, N. Y., Bowdoin street, Boston, Stamford, Conn., was Secretary of the Brooklyn Branch of the Christian Commission in the civil war. He died December 31, 1876.

— The Brighter Age. 12°. Boston, 1830.

WATERSTON, (R. C.)

Robert Cassie Waterston was born at Kennebunk, Me., in 1812. He pursued his theological studies at the Harvard Divinity School, and for five years had charge of a sailors'

Waterston, (R. C.) — *Continued.*

Sunday-school. He was minister at large for six years in Boston under the auspices of the fraternity of (Unitarian) churches, and then became pastor of the church of the Saviour in that city, which position he held for seven years. He has taken a deep interest in questions of reform, education, etc., and wrote much on these subjects. Harvard College, in 1844, conferred on him the degree of A. M.

— The Widow's Son. 8°, pp. 14. Boston, 1843.

Watkins, (Frances E.) Poems. 18°, pp. 40. Boston, 1854.

Watts, (I., D. D.) The Psalms of David. 24°, pp. 274. New York, 1792.

— Same. 24°, pp. 316. New York, 1795.

— Same. With Hymns. 24°. Psalms, pp. 312. Hymns, pp. 272. Boston, 1801.

— Same. With additions by Dr. T. 'Dwight. 32°, pp. 498. New York, 1803.

— Same. Corrected by J. Barlow. 4th Edition. 18°, pp. 332. Hartford, no date.

— Same. 1822.

Watterston, (G.) 'The Child of Feeling. A Comedy. 18°, pp. 113. Georgetown, 1809.

Weal-Reaf. Record of Essex Institute held at Salem, Mass., in September, 1860. Sq. 8°, pp. 56. Salem, 1860.

Several short poems in the volume.

Weaver, (W. L.) Battle of the Frogs at Windham, Conn., in July, 1758. 8°, pp. 31. Willimantic, 1857.

This poem is founded upon what is known as "the old story of the frogs of Windham, Conn." The frogs referred to had a pitched battle for the possession of the water remaining in a ditch, which, in a time of drought, had become nearly dry. The event occurred on a dark night in July, 1758, and the people were greatly alarmed by the hideous outcries of the belligerents.

The account given by the Rev. Samuel Peters, in his "General History of Connecticut," is a fine illustration of the Munchausen style of writing:

"One night in July, 1758, the frogs of an artificial pond three miles square " (really never a fourth of a mile in extent), " and about five miles from Windham " (about one mile), finding the water dried up left the place in a body and marched or rather hopped towards Winnomantic river. They were under the necessity of taking the road and going through the town, which they entered about midnight. The bull-frogs were the leaders and the pipers followed without number. *They filled a road forty yards wide for four miles in length, and were for several hours in passing through the town unusually clamorous.* The inhabitants were equally perplexed and frightened; some expected to find an army of French and Indians; others feared an earthquake and dissolution of nature. The

WEAVER, (W. L.) — *Continued.*

consternation was universal. Old and young, male and female, fled naked from their beds with more shrieking than those of the frogs. The event was fatal to several women. The men, after a flight of half a mile, in which they met with many broken shins, finding no enemies in pursuit of them made a halt and summoned resolution enough to venture back to their wives and children, when they distinctly heard from the enemy's camp these words, *Wight, Hilderken, Dier Teté.* This last they thought meant treaty, and plucking up courage they sent a triumvirate to capitulate with the supposed French and Indians. These three men approached in their shirts and begged to speak with the General, but it being dark and no answer given they were sorely agitated for some time betwixt hope and fear; at length, however, they discovered that the dreaded inimical army was an army of thirsty frogs going to the river for a little water."

This volume contains three poems.

1. *The Frogs of Windham, an old Colony tale founded on facts.* This ballad, founded on Peters' account of the affair, appeared originally in the *Providence Gazette.*

2. *Bull Frog Song, originally entitled " Lawyers and Bull Frogs."* A more ancient copy of this ballad had the following title: *"A true relation of a strange battle between some Lawyers and Bull Frogs, set forth in a new song, written by a jolly farmer of New England."*

3. *The Bull-Frog Fight; a Ballad of the old time.* The end of the fight is thus described:

> "The courage of the Windham men
> Now rose exceeding high;
> And so they blazed away till dawn
> Lit up the eastern sky.

> "'Pe-ung,' 'pe-ung,' 'go-row,' 'go-row,'
> 'Chug,' 'chug,' 'peep,' 'peep,' and '*tee-te;*'
> 'Cease firing, boys,' the Captain said,
> 'The dogs desire a treaty.

> "Our heroes rested on their arms
> Till morning's light revealed
> The bodies of the prostrated frogs,
> Stretched out upon the field."

WEAVER, (LIEUTENANT.)　Journals of the Ocean, etc.　12°, pp. 228. New York, 1826.

WEBB, (F. J.)　Uncle Tom Dramatized.　12°, pp. 63.　London, 1856.

WEBB, (MRS. M. E.)　The Christian Slave.　8°, pp. iv, 67.　Boston, 1855.

WEBBER, (S.)

Samuel Webber, M. D., was born at Cambridge, Mass., not far from 1795, graduated at Harvard 1815, pursued his profession in Charlestown, and in 1822 removed to New York, where he died in 1880.

— Logan.　An Indian Tale, etc.　18°, pp. 54.　Cambridge, 1821.

— War.　18°, pp. vi, 48.　Cambridge, 1823.

WEBSTER, (MRS. M. M.)　Pocahontas.　A Legend.　12°, pp. 220. Philadelphia, 1840.

WEEKES, (R.)  Poems.  12°, pp. 368.  New York, 1820.

— Same.  2d Edition.  12°, pp. 418.  New York, 1823.

— The Advantages and Disadvantages of the Marriage State, as entered into with Religious or Irreligious Persons.  18°, pp. 48.  Stanford, 1805.

WEEKS, (R.)  The Life of William Penn, etc.  12°, pp. 186.  New York, 1822.

WEEKS, (R. K.)  Episodes and Lyric Pieces.  12°, pp. v, 164.  New York, 1870.     -

— Poems.  12°, pp. 142.  New York, 1866.

WEEMS, (M. L.)

Mason L. Weems, an Episcopal clergyman, who sometimes performed service at Pohick Church, near Mt. Vernon, where Washington attended.  His most celebrated work was "The Life of George Washington," which reached more than forty editions.  He died at Beaufort, S. C., May 23, 1825.

— Hymen's Recruiting Sergeant; or, The Matrimonial Tat-Too for the Old Bachelors.  4°, pp. 19.  Philadelphia, 1805.

— Same.  18°, pp. 52.  Hartford.

WEHNER, (J. H., M. D.)  Principles Form Character.  A Comedy.  12°, pp. 23.  New York, 1859.

WEISS, (P.)

Paul Weiss was born at Bethlehem, Pa., June 22, 1763, and died October 31, 1840.  The translation of John Gilpin was made while he was pastor at Emmaus, Pa., about 1813.

— John Gilpin, translated into German.  12°, pp. 25.  Philadelphia, 1869.

WELBY, (MRS. A. B.)  (Amelia, *pseud.*)

Amelia B. Coppuck was born at St. Michaels, Md., February 3, 1819.  When a child she removed with her parents to Kentucky, and resided in Lexington and Louisville.  In 1838 she married Mr. George B. Welby.  She began to write over the signature of "Amelia" in the *Louisville Journal* in 1837.  Her collected poems have passed through several editions.  She died at Louisville, Ky., May 3, 1852..

— Poems.  2d Edition.  12°, pp. vii, 200.  New York, 1846.

— Same.  A new Enlarged Edition.  Illustrated.  Lg. 8°, pp. 264.  New York and Philadelphia, 1850.

WELCH, (J. W.)  The Crowning Gift of Heaven.  8°, pp. 48.  Huntington, Pa., 1873.

WELLER, (CATHERINE.)  The Medley.  12°, pp. 192.  New York, 1810.

WELLMAN, (MRS. MARY W.)  Poem, etc., suggested by the ·Death of Hon. Daniel Webster.  12°.  Boston, 1854.

WELLS, (ANNA M.)

Anna Marla Wells was a sister of Mrs. F. S. Osgood, and was born in Gloucester, Mass., in 1797.  In 1829 she married Thomas Wells, United States Revenue Service, and took up her residence in Boston.

— Poems.  12°.  Boston, 1830.

Bound up in this volume are poems by Mrs. Sarah J. Hale and Mrs. Littlefield.

— Same.  Poems and Juvenile Sketches.  12°, pp. 99.  Boston, 1830.

WEPT-OF-THE-WISH-TON-WISH.  A Drama.  (Anon.)  12°, pp. 26. New York, 1856.

WESLEYAN CHECKS; OR, HINTS IN SATIRE.  Occasioned by reading Bishop Musgrave's Book on the Polity of the Methodist Episcopal Church.  (By Fletcheran, *pseud.*)  12°, pp. 21.  Baltimore, 1843.

WEST POINT LIFE.  (Anon.)  A Poem read before a Public Meeting of the Dialectic Society, United States Military Academy, March 5, 1859.  8°, pp. 16.  No place, no date.

WESTERN COUSIN, LETTERS TO.  (Anon.  Entered by Ruth N. Cromwell.)  8°, pp. 36.  New York, 1868.

WESTLAKE, (J. W.)  Anastasis.  8°, pp. 19.  New York, 1854.

WESTON, (E. P.)

Edward Payson Weston was born at Boothbay, Me., January 19, 1819.  (His father, a Congregational minister, subsequently became pastor of a church in Cumberland, Me.) He graduated at Bowdoin College in 1839.  For seven years, 1840–47, he was the Principal of Lewiston Falls, Me., Academy, and then, for thirteen years, 1847–60, he had charge of the Maine Female Seminary at Gorham, Me.  In 1860 he was appointed State Superintendent of Schools, and, while in office, was instrumental in establishing the Normal-School system, himself opening the first institution in Farmington.  For four years, 1865–69, he had charge of the Abbott Family School for boys at Farmington.  In 1869 he removed to Lake Forest, Ill., where for seven years, 1869–76, he conducted a seminary for young ladies. In 1876 he opened a similar institution at Highland Park, chartered under the name of "The Highland College for Women."

— The Bowdoin Poets.  12°, pp. ix, 188.  Brunswick, 1840.

WESTON, (J. M.)  Lucretia Borgia.  A Drama.  12°, pp. 60.  Boston, no date.

WETMORE, (P. M.)

Prosper Montgomery Wetmore was born at Stratford, Conn., February 14, 1798, and in early life removed to New York and entered upon a successful mercantile career.  He was the patron of art and good learning, and a distinguished and most useful member of the New York Historical Society.  He died at Great Neck, L. I., March 16, 1876.

Wetmore, (P. M.) — *Continued.*

— Lexington, etc. 8°, pp. 87. New York, 1830.

Wharton, (J., M. D.) The Virginia Wreath. 16°, pp. 105. Winchester, 1814.

What I Think. A Satire. (Anon.) 12°, pp. v, 45. No place, 1859.

Wheat-Sheaf, The. A Collection of Prose and Poetical Extracts. 12°, pp. xi, 416. Philadelphia, 1857.

Wheatley, (Phillis.)

A slave, born in Africa about 1754, came into possession of John Wheatly, of Boston, and became a prodigy of intellectual ability, writing, before she was seventeen, letters and poems which attracted the attention of scholars. Her married life with one John Peters, a colored man, was very unhappy. She died December 5, 1784.

— Elegaic Poem on the Death of George Whitefield. 12°, pp. 3. Boston and London, 1771.
— Poems. Sm. 8°, pp. 124. London, 1773.
— Same. 16°, pp. 89. Albany, 1793.

Elegantly bound by Bedford.

— Same. Bound in Vol. II, Negro Equalled, etc. 12°. Philadelphia, 1801.
— Same. 12°. Walpole, N. H., 1802.
— Same. With Memoir. Sm. 8°, pp. 103. Boston, 1834.
— Same. 2d Edition. 18°, pp. 110. Boston, 1835.
— Same. 3d Edition. 18°, pp. 135. Boston, 1838.

Wheeler, (A.) Immortality; or, The Pilgrim's Dream. 8°, pp. 88. New York, 1844.
— The Age. 8°, pp. vi, 24. New York, 1845.

Wheeler, (Ella.) Poems of Passion. 12°, pp. 100. Chicago, 1883.

Wheelock, (O.) Original Poems. 18°, pp. 32. No title-page.

Wheler, (C. S.)

Charles S. Wheler, editor of *Pontiac Jacksonian*, has written for several periodicals under the *nom de plume* of " Stern Wheeler."

— The Winnowing. 12°, pp. 57. Boston, 1851.

Whigs and Democrats. A Comedy. (Anon.) 12°, pp. vi, 80. Richmond, 1839.

42

WHIPPLE, (FRANCES H.)

A native of Rhode Island.

— The Original. 12°, pp. 108. Providence, 1829.

— The Envoy from Free Hearts to the Free. 18°, pp. 112. Pawtucket, R. I., 1840.

WHIPPLE, (O.) The Historic Progress of Civil and Rational Liberty, etc. 12°, pp. 54. Portsmouth, N. H., 1802.

WHIPPOORWILL. (Byron, a *pseud.* for Peleg Sturtevant.) Orandalie. 8°, pp. 56. Hudson, 1825.

WHITAKER, (H. C.)

Henry Clay Whitaker was born at Providence, R. I., May 25, 1818, and graduated at Brown University in the class of 1838. As a graceful writer of poetry, the productions of his pen have always been welcomed in his native city.

— Old-Fashioned Sounds. 12°, pp. 4. No place, no date.

— Poem before the Rhode Island Historical Society, July 19, 1872. 8°, pp. 7. Providence, 1873.

— Same. Opening of the new rooms of the Franklin Lyceum, Providence, November 19, 1858. 8°, pp. 14. Providence, 1859.

— Same. July 5, 1875. 8°, pp. 8. Providence, 1875.

WHITAKER, (MARY S.) Poems. 12°, pp. iv, 300. Charleston, 1850.

WHITE, (C. W.) Comfort to Mourners. 18°, pp. 36. Lowell, no date.

WHITE, (J. B.)

John Blake White, a Southern poet, was the author of "Mysteries of the Castle," "Modern Honour," etc.

— Foscari; or, The Venetian Exile. A Tragedy. 12°, pp. 52. Charleston, 1805.

WHITE, (J. J.)

He is the author of "Exposition of the Church of Christ and its Doctrines," forming a Supplement to "The End of Controversy Controverted." 12°, pp. 233. Philadelphia, 1855.

— Peace and other Poems. 12°, pp. 126. Philadelphia, 1867.

WHITE, ROSE AND RED. A Love Story. By the author of "St. Abe." 12°, pp. xii, 242. Boston, 1873.

WHITE, (R. G.)

Richard Grant White was born at New York in 1821, graduated at the University of New York 1839, and was admitted to the bar 1845. His life was devoted chiefly to literary pursuits, and especially to "Shakspeariana." He died April 8, 1885.

WHITE, (R. G.) — *Continued.*

— National Hymns. 8°, pp. x, 152. New York, 1861.
— Poetry, Lyrical, etc., of the Civil War. Selected and edited by. 8°, pp. xxii, 329. New York, 1866.

WHITE, (W. A.) Bethel. Twenty-fifth Anniversary of St. James' Church, Dunnington, Pa. 8°, pp. 10. Philadelphia, 1868.

— Poems by a Priest. 12°, pp. 35. Salisbury, Md., 1851.
— Following Jesus, etc. 12°, pp. 84. Philadelphia, 1845.

WHITE, (W. C.) The Clergyman's Daughter. A Tragedy. 18°, pp. 96. Boston, 1810.
— Orlando ; or, Parental Persecution. A Tragedy. 18°, pp. 64. Boston, 1797.

WHITED SEPULCHRE, THE. By Sophia. 8°, pp. 48. Nashua, 1869.

WHITEFIELD, (J. M.) America, etc. 18°, pp. viii, 85. Buffalo, 1852.

WHITEHEAD, (L., SR.) New House that Jack Built. 18°, pp. 29. New York, 1865.

WHITEMAN, (W. A.) Who Killed the Writ? 4°, pp. 4. Philadelphia, 1862.

On large paper. Only twenty copies printed. No. 13.

WHITING, (H.)

Henry Whiting was born at Lancaster, Mass., about 1700. and was in the United States Army and brevetted Brigadier-General for services at Buena Vista, February 23, 1847. He died at St. Louis, Mo., September 16, 1851.

— Sannillac. 12°, pp. 112. Boston, 1831.

WHITMAN, (B., JR.) The Heroes of the North ; or, The Battles of Lake Erie and Champlain. 8°, pp. 24. Boston, 1816.

WHITMAN, (S. H.)

Mrs. Sarah Helen (Power) Whitman was born at Providence, R. I., in 1803, and married, in 1828, John W. Whitman, a lawyer, of Boston. She died June 27, 1878.

— Edgar Poe and His Critics. 12°, pp. 81. New York, 1860.

Not a poem, but a prose vindication by Mrs. Whitman of the poet to whom she was betrothed. In the volume has been left by some one a number of newspaper notices, in a small envelope, which refer to the work.

**WHITMAN, (W.)**

Walter, or Walt Whitman, was born at West Hills, N. Y., in 1819, and has occupied various positions,—printer, school teacher, editor, a clerk in the Department of the Interior at Washington, etc. The most opposite opinions prevail with regard to the poems of Whitman. W. D. O'Connor, of New York, "boldly pits Walt Whitman not only against all the poets of the day, but demands for him place and rank beside the great masters, Æschylus, Homer, Dante and Shakspeare. He proclaims him the inspired bard and prophet of his era and land." On the other hand, Allibone says: "Public opinion says that any man in England who might issue such senseless trash as Walt Whitman's poems, would be considered a proper inmate for an asylum."

— After All, not to Create Only. Recited on opening Fortieth Annual Exhibition of American Institute, New York, September 7, 1871. 12°, pp. vii, 24. Boston, 1871.

— Drum Taps. 12°, pp. 24. New York, 1865.

— Leaves of Grass. 8°, pp. xii, 382. Brooklyn, 1855.

— Same. 4°, pp. 95. Brooklyn, 1855.

— Same. 8°, pp. 456. Philadelphia, 1882.

**WHITNEY, (ANNE.)** Poems. 12°, pp. 191. New York, 1859.

**WHITNEY, (H.)** Ontova, the Son of the Forest. 8°, pp. v, 128. New York.

**WHITNEY, (MRS. A. D. T.)** Mother Goose for Grown Folks. 12°, pp. 111. New York, 1860.

**WHITNEY, (T. R.)**

Thomas R. Whitney was born in the city of New York in 1804. He was a member of Congress, 1855–57. He died in 1858.

— Evening Hours. 12°, pp. iv, 118. New York, 1844.

— The Ambuscade. 12°, pp. 83. New York, 1845.

The scene is laid in Florida, near the Lake O-kee-cho-be. The time of action is one day.

**WHITTAKER, (C.)** Poems. 18°, pp. 58, Philadelphia, 1863.

**WHITTIER, (J. G.)**

John Greenleaf Whittier was born at Haverhill, Mass., December 17, 1807, and spent the earlier part of his life on his father's farm. He removed to Boston in 1829, and was engaged as a journalist in that city, and subsequently in Hartford. In 1831 he returned to Haverhill, and was occupied with agricultural pursuits for several years. For a brief period he was a resident of Philadelphia, where he edited *The Pennsylvania Freeman*, a strong anti-slavery paper. In 1840 he removed to Amesbury, Mass., where he has since resided. (For a sketch of Whittier, and a classification of his works, see Allibone, pp. 2704–5.)

— Among the Hills, etc. 16°, pp. 100. Boston, 1869.

— A Sabbath Scene. 12°, pp. 29. Boston, 1854.

— Hazel Blossoms. 16, pp. 133. Boston, 1875.

— In War Time, etc. 12°, pp. vii, 152. Boston, 1864.

Whittier, (J. G.) — *Continued.*

— Lays of My Home. 16°, pp. 122. Boston, 1843.
— Legends of New England. 12°, pp. 142. Hartford, 1831.
— Maud. With Illustrations. 8°, not paged. Boston, 1867.
— Miriam, etc. 16°, pp. 106. Boston, 1871.
— Mogg Megone. 32°, pp. 69. Boston, 1836.
— Moll Pitcher, etc. 18°, pp. 44. Philadelphia, 1840.
— National Lyrics. Sq. 16°, pp. 104. Boston, 1865.
— Poems. 12°, pp. 180. Philadelphia, 1838.
— Same. Illustrated by H. Billings. 8°, pp. viii, 384. Boston, 1849.
— Same. 2 vols. 18°, pp. 320, 303. Boston, 1857. Blue and Gold Series.
— Same. Written during the progress of the Abolition Question, between the years 1830 and 1838. 16°, pp. x, 103. Boston, 1837.
— Snow-Bound. 16°, pp. 52. Boston, 1866.
— Same. With Illustrations. 8°, pp. 65. Boston, 1868.
— Songs of Labor, etc. 16°, pp. x, 127. Boston, 1850.
— The Bay of Seven Islands, etc. 12°, pp. 85. Boston, 1883.
— The Chapel of the Hermits, etc. 16°, pp. vi, 118. Boston, 1853.
— The Literary Remains of John G. C. Brainard. 8°, pp. 228. Hartford, 1832.

Whittier prepared the biographical sketch of Brainard, who was born at New London, Conn., in October, 1796, graduated at Yale in 1815, and practiced law at Middletown, Conn. He died September 26, 1828. In the sketch of his life, his biographer places a very high estimate on the character and writings of his fellow-poet.

— The Panorama, etc. 16°, pp. vi, 141. Boston, 1856.
— The Pennsylvania Pilgrim, etc. 16°, pp. xiii, 129. Boston, 1872.
— The Prayer of Agassiz. 12°, pp. 6. Cambridge, 1874.
— The Tent on the Beach, etc. 16°, pp. vi, 172. Boston, 1867.

Whittlesey, (S. C.) Heart-Drops. 8°, pp. 341. New York, 1852.

Whitwell, (B.) Phi Beta Kappa. Harvard, April 28, 1806. 8°, pp. 23. Boston, 1806.

Wigglesworth, (M.)

Michael Wigglesworth was born October 28, 1631, probably in Yorkshire, Eng., came to this country in 1638, graduated at Harvard in 1651, was tutor in the college for several years, was ordained pastor of the church in Malden in 1656, and, with some interruptions of his work on account of ill health, occupied this position till his death, June 10, 1705.

Wigglesworth, (M.) — *Continued.*

— Meat out of the Eater; or, Meditations concerning the Necessity, End and Usefulness of Afflictions unto God's Children. All tending to Prepare them *For,* and Comfort them *Under,* the Cross. Corrected and Amended by the Author in the year 1703. The Fifth Edition. Sm. 12°, pp. 143. 1717.

In beautiful binding, by Bedford. Of this volume Professor Tyler says: "Here we have simply the Christian doctrine of comfort in sorrow, translated into metrical jingles. With nearly all sensitiveness to literary form torpid in New England, and with devout feeling warm and alert, it is not strange that this clumsy but sympathetic poem should have found there a multitude of admirers. It was first published probably in 1669; ten years afterwards it had passed through at least four editions; and during the entire Colonial age it was a much-read manual of solace in affliction. And, indeed, it is such poetry as might still serve that purpose, at least by plucking from the memory a rooted sorrow, and substituting a literary anguish in place of it."

— The Day of Doom. 6th Edition. 18°, pp. 82. Boston, 1715.

For an account of this "blazing and sulphurous" poem, as Professor Tyler calls it, see "History of American Literature," vol. ii, pp. 27–35.

— Same. 7th Edition. 18°, pp. 104. Boston, 1751.
— Same. From the 6th London Edition. 18°, pp. 90. Newburyport, 1811.

In a note on a fly-leaf, John Ward Dean writes: "At the great fire in Newburyport, May 31, 1811, the year this volume was printed, the printing office and bookstore of E. Little & Co., the publishers, were burnt. Probably the greater portion of this edition was destroyed. I have not been able to hear of more than two copies in existence, namely, the present copy, and one belonging to James Lenox, Esq., of New York City."

— Same. From the 6th London Edition. 24°, pp. 95. Boston, 1828.

The above five volumes were elegantly bound by Francis Bedford, London, and are beautiful specimens of that accomplished binder's art.

— The Church Moves. A Curiosity of Literature and Theology. Extracts from "The Day of Doom." 12°, pp. 16. Boston, no date.

Wilcox, (C.)

Carlos Wilcox was born at Newport, N. H., October 22, 1794, graduated at Middlebury College in 1813, and at Andover in 1817. He was settled as a Congregational minister in Pittstown, N. J., and in Huntington, Newton and Norwalk, Conn. For about two years, 1824–26, he was pastor of the North Congregational Church, Hartford. He died May 29, 1827.

— The Age of Benevolence. Book I. 18°, pp. 72. New Haven, 1822.

Wilde, (R. S.) Summer Rose. 8°, pp. 70. Savannah, 1870.

A vindication of the author against the charge of plagiarism.

WILDER, (A. C.)  Poem.  Dedication of the new Town Hall, Leominster, Mass.  8°, pp. 2.  Fitchburg, Mass., 1852.

WILDMAN, (H. B.)  Beaver Brook Mountain, etc.  8°, pp. 24.  New York, 1847.

This is No. 1 of Landscape Views of New England.

— Lays from the Glen.  12°, pp. viii, 144.  New York, 1855.

WILKINS, (G. P.)  My Wife's Mirror.  A Comedy.  12°, pp. 16.  New York, 1856.

WILKINSON, (W. C.)

William Cleaver Wilkinson was born at Westford, Vt., October 10, 1833, graduated at Rochester University in 1857, and the Theological Seminary in 1859.  He was pastor of the Wooster Place Baptist Church, New Haven, resigning on account of ill health.  Subsequently he was settled in Cincinnati, then for a few years had charge of a private school in Tarrytown, N. Y.  In 1872 he was elected Professor in the Rochester Theological Seminary.  Professor Wilkinson has contributed many able articles to the popular periodicals of the day.

— Webster.  An Ode.  4°, pp. 122.  New York, 1822.

In the notes Mr. Wilkinson makes an elaborate defence against charges brought against the moral and religious character of Mr. Webster.

WILLARD, (MRS. E.)

Emma Hart, a descendant of Thomas Hooker, was born at Berlin, Conn., February 23, 1787.  She was a successful teacher, being for seventeen years Principal of a Ladies' Seminary at Troy, N. Y.  She was the compiler of school books which had a large circulation, and was distinguished as an author.  She died at Troy, April 15, 1870.

— The Fulfillment of a Promise.  Sm. 16°, pp. 124.  1861.

WILLARD, (J.)  A Poem Sacred to the Memory of.  (Anon.)  12°, pp. 16.  Boston, 1757.

WILLARD, (S.)  Hymns.  18°, pp. xvii, 128.  Greenfield, Mass., 1824.

WILLIAM AND ELLEN.  A Poem in Three Cantos.  (Anon.)  18°, pp. 158.  New York, 1811.

WILLIAMS, (MRS. CATHARINE R.)

Mrs. Williams was born at Providence, R. I., in 1790, and was the author of several works in prose and poetry.

— Original Poems.  16°, pp. vii, 107.  Providence, 1828.

WILLIAMS, (J.)

The alias of Williams was Anthony Pasquin.  He was born in England and made himself notorious on account of his scurrilous attacks on men and things.  Lord Kenyon, in 1797, adjudged him " a common libeller," and Lord Macaulay speaks of him as " a malig-

314        HARRIS COLLECTION.

WILLIAMS, (J.) — *Continued.*

nant and filthy baboon " and " a polecat." He emigrated to this country, where he
became editor of a Democratic paper. He died in 1818. Allibone mentions thirteen distinct productions of his pen.

— The Hamiltoniad. 8°, pp. 104. Boston, no date.

WILLIAMS, (JENNY P.) Scattered Verses and Letters, etc. 8°, pp. 64.
New York, 1869.

WILLIAMS, (MRS. H. DWIGHT.) Voices from the Silent Land. Lg. 8°,
pp. 274. Boston, etc., 1854.

WILLIAMSON, (A. J.) Poems in Three Parts. 18°, pp. 151. Toronto,
1836.

WILLIAMSON, (J. B.) Preservation; or, The Hovel of the Rocks. A
Play. 8°, pp. vii, 75. Charleston, S. C., 1800.

WILLIAMSON, (W. C.) Poem before Alpha Delta Phi, 25th Anniversary,
New York, 24th and 25th June, 1857. Lg. 8°, pp. 15. New
York, 1858.

WILLIS, (ANNA.) Memoir, in which are several of her Poems. 12°.
New York, 1854.

WILLIS, (N. P.)

Nathaniel Parker Willis was born at Portland, Me., January 20, 1806, according to
some authorities, 1807 according to others, graduated at Yale College in 1827, and spent
his life in literary pursuits as editor, author, etc. He died at his beautiful residence,
" Idlewild," near Newburgh, on the Hudson, January 20, 1867. (See Allibone, pp. 2756–57.)

— Bianca Visconti. 12°, pp. 108. New York, 1839.
— Melanie, the Usurer. 12°, pp. 149. New York, 1839.
— Poem. Delivered before the Society of United Brothers, Brown
University, September 6, 1831, etc. 8°, pp. 76. New York,
1831.
— Poems. Complete Edition. 8°, pp. 352. New York, 1850.
— Same. 18°, pp. ix, 370. New York, 1861.
— Sacred Poems. New Mirror Extra. 4°, pp. 48. New York, 1843.
— Same. 32°, pp. 126. New York, 1863.
— The Lady Jane. New Mirror Extra. No. 3. 4°. New York,
1844.

WILLIS, (N. P.) — *Continued.*

— Editor. The Legendary. Vol. I. 12°, pp. 286. Boston, 1828.
> In this volume are poems by Willis, Pierpont, Mellen, and others.

— Tortesa, the Usurer. 12°, pp. 149. New York, 1839.

— Two Ways of Dying for a Husband. 8°, pp. 245. London, 1839.

WILMER, (L. A.)
> Lambert A. Wilmer was born in 1805, and was for a time editor of *The Baltimore Saturday Visitor*, and afterwards was connected with *The Pennsylvanian*. He died at Brooklyn, N. Y., December 21, 1863.

— Liberty Triumphant. 12°, pp. vi, 34. Philadelphia, 1853.

— Somnia. 12°, pp. 23. Philadelphia, 1848.

— The Quacks of Helicon. A Satire. 18°, pp. 54. Philadelphia, 1841.

WILMSHURST, (Z.) Liberty's Centennial. A Poem for 1876. 12°, pp. 22. New York, 1876.

WILSON, (A.)
> Alexander Wilson was born at Paisley, Scotland, July 6, 1766, and worked as a weaver for several years. He came to Philadelphia in 1794, and after a few years entered upon his great work as the American Ornithologist, to which he devoted the remaining years of his life. He died at Philadelphia, August 23, 1813.

— The Foresters. 12°, pp. 100. Philadelphia, 1804.
> A poem descriptive of a pedestrian journey to the Falls of Niagara in the autumn of 1804.

— Same. 18°, pp. 104. West Chester, Pa., 1838.

WINCHELL, (J. F.) The Village Poet; or, Dreams of the Pound Master. 12°, pp. 12. No place, no date.

WINCHESTER, (E.)
> Elhanan Winchester was born at Brookline, Mass., 1751, was the first minister of the Baptist church in Newton, Mass., subsequently became a preacher of Universal Restoration. Died at Hartford, Conn., April, 1797.

— Poems. 8°, pp. 72. Boston, 1773.

— The Progress and Empire of Christ. 12°, pp. 352. Brattleboro, 1805.

WINSLOW, (B. D.)
> Benjamin Davis Winslow was born at Boston in 1815, graduated at Harvard in 1835, and at the Episcopal General Theological Seminary, N. Y., in 1838. For a short time he was the assistant of Dr. afterwards Bishop Doane, at St. Mary's church, Burlington, N. J. He died November 21, 1839, at the early age of twenty-four.

43

WINSLOW, (B. D.) — *Continued.*
— Class Poem, Harvard, 1835. 8°, pp. 28. Cambridge, 1835.
— Sermons and Poetical Remains. 8°, pp. 317. New York, 1841.

WINTER STUDIES IN THE COUNTRY. (Anon.) 18°, pp. 43. Philadelphia, 1856.

WISDOM. (Anon.) 18°, pp. 16. Philadelphia, 1787.
— Same. 18°, pp. 22. Newport, 1804.

WINTER, (W.)

William Winter was born at Gloucester, Mass., July 15, 1836, graduated at the Harvard Law School, and was admitted to the Suffolk bar. He has devoted himself to literary pursuits, as poet, literary and dramatic critic, lecturer, etc. His poems are highly commended by Rev. Dr. A. P. Peabody.

— Poems. 12°, pp. 143. Boston, 1855.

The author's gift to W. C. Bryant, January 1, 1855.

WOLCOTT (SISTERS. ELIZA AND SARAH G.) Poems. 18°, pp. 174. New Haven, 1830.

WOLCOTT, (R.)

Roger Wolcott was born at Windsor, Conn., January 4, 1679. He had very few opportunities for acquiring an education in that early period in the colonial history of Connecticut. As soon as he became of age he engaged in what proved to be successful business, and rose to positions of military and civil trust in his native State. He was Governor, 1751–54. He died May 17, 1767. A descriptive poem of his, of fifteen hundred lines, has the title, *A Brief Account of the Agency of the Honorable John Winthrop, Esq., in the Court of King Charles the Second, Anno Dom. 1662, where he obtained a Charter for the Colony of Connecticut.*

In the annotated catalogue of the John Carter Brown Library, vol. iii, p. 101, the Hon. John R. Bartlett has the following note: "It is stated by Mr. Stevens, in his 'Nuggets,' that Mr. Dewey, a maker of woolen cloth in Colchester, Connecticut, was at the expense of printing this book on the condition of inserting his advertisement at the end. Indeed, the worthy clothier intimates as much in his advertisement: 'Having been something at charge in promoting the Publishing of the fore-going Meditations, do here take the liberty to Advertise my Country People of some Rules which ought to be observed in doing their part, that so the Clothiers might be assisted in the better performance of what may be expected of them, that the cloth which is made amongst us may both Wear and Last better than it can possibly do, except these following Directions are observed by us.'" Then follow his seven rules.

The interest in the book centres in the historical poem upon Winthrop's obtaining of Charles II. the Charter of Connecticut. After the Restoration the "Sages of Connecticut" sent Winthrop, their Governor, to England to present an address and to "ask the King for charter liberties." Not long after his arrival in London it was announced to Charles, who "was in his council sat," that

> "An Agent from Connecticut doth wait,
> With an Address before your Palace gate.
> *Let him come in, says Charles, and let us Hear
> What has been done, and what's a doing there.*"

Wolcott, (R.) — *Continued.*

> Winthrop admitted, discharges himself in homespun numbers, redolent rather of truth than poetry, filling some sixty pages, in which he recounts the national, civil, political and military history of the colony from the earliest time till "Great Sassacus and his Kingdom fell."
>
> The copy in "The Harris Collection" is in a somewhat dilapidated condition. It was originally bound in boards covered with calf-skin. A quarter of the second cover is gone, and a small piece of the leather on the upper right corner of the first cover has been torn off. It looks as though it had been "through fire and through water." There is no title-page, and the first pages eight of the Preface are wanting. At the top of page 1 is written "Henry Barnard, Hartford, Conn., January 1, 1841."

— Some Improvement of Vacant Hours. 18°, pp. vi, 78. Title-page gone. The volume published in New London, 1725.

Woman's Wish! Against Man's Will. (By a Buckeye. Anon.) 12°, pp. 51. New York, 1859.

Women, The Two. By Delta. (Anon.) 12°, pp. 23. Milwaukee, 1868.

Wonderful W. P. ! !, The. (Anon.) 18°, pp. 8. No place, no date.
> Preface dated Concord, N. H., February, 1868.

Wood, (M. Elva.) Songs of the Noon and Night. 16°, pp. 251. New York, 1866.

Woodmansee, (J.) The Closing Scene. A Vision. 16°, pp. 296. Cincinnati, 1857.

Woodward, (B. W.) A Washington's Birth-day Poem. Our Country. February 22, 1862. 8°, pp. 14. Geneva, N. Y., 1862.

Woodward, (D.) Slavery. 16°, pp. 92. Boston, 1856.

Woodworth, (D.) The Pilgrim Fathers. Sq, 18°, pp. 15. Albany, 1843.

Woodworth, (S.)
> Samuel Woodworth was born at Scituate, Mass., January 13, 1785. By trade he was a printer. In 1812 he removed to New York, where for several years he was editor and publisher. He died December 9, 1842. His beautiful poem "The Bucket," has given him a reputation similar in character to that of John Howard Payne, the author of "Home, Sweet Home."

— Beasts at Law. 12°, pp. 104. New York, 1811.
— Bubble and Squeak, etc. 12°, pp. 104. New York, 1814.
— La Fayette. 18°, pp. 42. Imperfect copy.
— Melodies. 2d Edition. 18°, pp. 288. New York, 1826.

WOODWORTH, (S.) — *Continued.*

— New Haven.   A Poem, Satirical and Sentimental, etc.   12°, pp. 34.
   New York, 1809.

— Poems, Odes. Songs, etc.   12°, pp. xii, 288.   New York, 1818.

— Same.   2 vols.   18°, pp. 238, 288.   New York, 1861.

— Quarter-Day ; or, The Horrors of the First of May.   12°, pp. 35.
   New York, 1812.

— The Complete Coiffeur.   2 Parts.   12°, pp. 108–98.   New York,
   1817.

— The Deed of Gift.   A Comic Opera.   18°, pp. 72.   New York, 1822.

— The Forest Rose.   A Pastoral Opera.   18°, pp. 42.   New York, 1825.

WOOLF, (B. E.)   Don't Forget Your Opera Glasses.   A Farce.   12°, pp.
   15.   Boston, no date.

WORSTER, (C. II.)   A Poetical Epistle to His Excellency George Washington, Esq.   4°, pp. 11.   London, 1780.   Springfield, reprinted
   1782.

> The writer says that " the sole purpose of publishing this Poem is for the charitable
> purpose of raising a few guineas to relieve in a small measure the distresses of some hun-
> dreds of American prisoners now suffering confinement in the gaols of England." A note
> signed J—— T—— informs the reader that " 15,000 copies of this Poem were sold in the
> city of London, in about three weeks, at Two Shillings and Sixpence, Sterling, each, and
> the money appropriated to the Benefit of the Americans."

WORTHINGTON, (G. F.)   Sacred Poems.   3d Edition.   18°, pp. 170.
   Baltimore, 1868.

> This volume of poems by the Rev. George F. Worthington is composed of selections
> from volumes which the author had previously published and of pieces furnished to differ-
> ent periodicals.

— Same.   4th Edition.   18°, pp. 197.   Baltimore, 1871.

WORK, (H. C.)   The Upshot Family.   A Sero-Comic Poem.   12°, pp.
   64.   Philadelphia, 1868.

WREATH, A, FOR HOME.   (Anon.)   18°, pp. 86.   New York, 1837.

WREATH, THE.   A Selection of Elegant Poems.   12°, pp. 168.   New
   York, 1813.

WREATH, THE GRECIAN, OF VICTORY.   16°, pp. 119.   New York, 1824.
   One or two poems in the volume.

WRIGHT, (ELIZABETH C.)   Lichen Tufts.   12°, pp. 228.  New York, 1860.

WRIGHT, (FRANCES.)   Altorf.   A Tragedy.   12°, pp. 83.   Philadelphia, 1819.

WRIGHT, (J.)  Poems.  12°, pp. 48.  Boston, 1812.

WRIGHT, (N. H.)

> Nathaniel H. Wright was born at Concord, Mass., in 1787, and was a printer by trade.
> The "Kaleidoscope" was edited by him.  He died in 1824.

— The Fall of Palmyra.  Sm. 24°, pp. xviii, 143.  Middlebury, Vt..
  1817.⸱

WRIGHT, (W. B.)  The Brook, etc.  12°, pp. 167.  New York, 1873.

WYNKOOP, (M. B.)

> Matthew Bennett Wynkoop, a printer in New York.

— Song Leaves.  12°, pp. vii, 113.  New York, 1852.

WYTHES, (J. H.)  The Spirit World.  16°, pp. 106.  Philadelphia,
  1849.

XARIFFA'S POEMS.  (Anon.)  8°, pp. 262.  Philadelphia, 1870.

> There are in the volume about one hundred and fifty poems and sonnets.

XLANTIES, THE ; OR, FORTY THIEVES.  A Burlesque.  8°, pp. 41.  Philadelphia, 1857.

YAHOO ; A SATIRICAL RHAPSODY.  8°, pp. xiv, 98.  New York, 1833.

YANKEE DOODLE.  Darley's Illustrations.  4°, not paged.  New York,
  no date.

YATES, (JENNIE.)  Fragments.  18°, pp. 132.  Baltimore, no date.

YELLOTT, (C.)  Professor of Insanity, The ; or, A New Way to Make a
  Fortune.  A Drama.  12°.  Baltimore, 1856.

YELLOTT, (G.)  The Thompsonian Quack.  8°, pp. vi, 70.  Baltimore,
  1848.

YONKERS, CHRONICLES OF.  (Anon.)  8°, pp. 23.  Yonkers, 1864.

YOUNG, (J. A.)

> Rev. James Alexander Young, M. D., of Laurell, Md., wrote under the signature of
> "Nobody, Nothing of Nowheres."

— Age of Brass ; or, The Fum Dynasty."  A Satire.  12°, pp. 48.
  Baltimore, 1844.

YOUNG LIFE.  (Anon.)  18°, pp. 64.  Albany, 1838.

Young, (C. W.)   Greatness Reviewed; or, The Rise of the South, etc.
8°, pp. vi, 72.   Savannah, 1851.

Young, (E. R.)   Address before the Brothers' Charitable Society, Providence, November 21, 1827.   8°, pp. 18.   Providence, 1827.

Young, (E. R.)   One Year in Savannah.   8°, pp. 16.   Providence, 1820.

Yang-Pii-We-Wing-Tzonga-Foii; or, Musings Over a Cup of Tea. 4°, pp. li.   New York, 1868.

The dedication is "To the Honorable Anson Burlingame, Envoy Extraordinary to the Western Nations and High Minister Plenipotentiary of the First Chinese Rank, and to the Most Mighty Mandarin, Chih-Kang and Sun-Chiakee, of the Second Chinese Rank, and to the Associated High Envoy and Ministers, and to all the Representatives of the Ancient and Central Flowery Kingdom who compose the Chinese Embassy, in fraternal good feeling this volume is dedicated by an American Chinaman."

Young Lady's Book.   Selections from British and American Poets. 24°, pp. 320.   Philadelphia, 1835.

Young, (W.)

Pierre Jean de Béranger was born of humble parentage in Paris, August 19, 1780.   He removed to Péronne in boyhood, and lived until he was seventeen with an aunt who kept a small inn in that place.   Here he learned the printer's trade.   In 1797 he returned to Paris, where, for many years, he had a hard struggle with poverty,   In 1803 he was kindly aided by Lucien Bonaparte, and, after various fortunes, obtained a clerkship in the University of Paris.   He now devoted himself much to literary pursuits, especially to the writing of songs.   His political sentiments, boldly published in his poems, brought him into collision with the government, and more than once he was fined and imprisoned. This treatment made him the idol of the people, and his works were exceedingly popular. His election to the National Assembly, by the electors of the Department of the Seine, was an evidence of the high esteem in which he was held.   In the later years of his life he resided in Passy.   His death occurred in July, 1857.

— Two Hundred of the Lyrical Poems of Béranger done into English Verse.   12°, pp. 400.   New York, 1850.

Zappone, (A.)   Latin Poems.   2d Edition.   8°, pp. 15.   Washington, 1849.

Zieber, (J. L.)   Original Firemen's Songs, etc.   18°, pp. 72.   Philadelphia, etc., 1868.

Zilia.   In Three Cantos.   (Anon.)   8°, pp. 54.   New York, 1830.

Zorilla, (J.)   Poesias.   3 vols.   8°.   Valparaiso, 1845.